Also by Sue Grafton

A is for Alibi

&

B is for Burglar

Two Novels in One

Sue Grafton

St. Martin's Paperbacks

Published in the United States by St. Martin's Paperbacks, an imprint of St. Martin's Publishing Group

A IS FOR ALIBI & B IS FOR BURGLAR: A IS FOR ALIBI copyright © 1982 by Sue Grafton and B IS FOR BURGLAR copyright © 1985 by Sue Grafton.

For information, address St. Martin's Publishing Group, 120 Broadway, New York, NY 10271.

www.stmartins.com

ISBN: 978-1-250-80095-4

Our books may be purchased in bulk for promotional, educational, or business use. Please contact your local bookseller or the Macmillan Corporate and Premium Sales Department at 1-800-221-7945, ext. 5442, or by email at MacmillanSpecialMarkets@macmillan.com.

Printed in the United States of America

St. Martin's Paperbacks edition / December 2021

10 9 8 7 6 5 4 3 2 1

A is for Alibi

For my father,
Chip Grafton,
who set me on this path

The author wishes to acknowledge the invaluable assistance of the following people: Steven Humphrey, Roger Long, Alan Tivoli, Barbara Stephans, Marlin D. Ketter of Investigations Unlimited and Joe Driscoll of Driscoll and Associates Investigations, both of Columbus, Ohio, and William Christensen, Police Captain, City of Santa Barbara.

1

My name is Kinsey Millhone. I'm a private investigator, licensed by the state of California. I'm thirty-two years old, twice divorced, no kids. The day before yesterday I killed someone and the fact weighs heavily on my mind. I'm a nice person and I have a lot of friends. My apartment is small but I like living in a cramped space. I've lived in trailers most of my life, but lately they've been getting too elaborate for my taste, so now I live in one room, a "bachelorette." I don't have pets. I don't have houseplants. I spend a lot of time on the road and I don't like leaving things behind. Aside from the hazards of my profession, my life has always been ordinary, uneventful, and good. Killing someone feels odd to me and I haven't quite sorted it through. I've already given a statement to the police, which I initialed page by page and then signed. I filled out a similar report for the office files. The language in both documents is neutral, the terminology oblique, and neither says quite enough.

Nikki Fife first came to my office three weeks ago. I occupy one small corner of a large suite of offices that house the California Fidelity Insurance Company, for whom I once worked. Our connection now is rather loose. I do a certain number of investigations for them in exchange for two rooms with a separate entrance and a small balcony overlooking the main street of Santa Teresa. I have an answering service to pick up calls when I'm out and I keep my own books. I don't earn a lot of money but I make ends meet.

I'd been out for most of the morning, only stopping by the office to pick up my camera. Nikki Fife was standing in the corridor outside my office door. I'd never really met her but I'd been present at her trial eight years before when she was convicted of murdering her husband, Laurence, a prominent divorce attorney here in town. Nikki was in her late twenties then, with striking white-blonde hair, dark eyes, and flawless skin. Her lean face had filled out some, probably the result of prison food with its high starch content, but she still had the ethereal look that had made the accusation of murder seem so incongruous at the time. Her hair had grown out now to its natural shade, a brown so pale that it appeared nearly colorless. She was maybe thirty-five, thirty-six, and the years at the California Institute for Women had left no visible lines.

I didn't say anything at first; just opened the door and let her in.

"You know who I am," she said.

"I worked for your husband a couple of times."

She studied me carefully. "Was that the extent of it?"

I knew what she meant. "I was also there in court when you were being tried," I said. "But if you're asking if I was involved with him personally, the answer is no. He wasn't my type. No offense. Would you like coffee?"

She nodded, relaxing almost imperceptibly. I pulled the coffeepot from the bottom of the file cabinet and filled it from the Sparkletts water bottle behind the door. I liked it that she didn't protest the trouble I was going to. I put in a filter paper and ground coffee and plugged in the pot. The gurgling sound was comforting, like the pump in an aquarium.

Nikki sat very still, almost as though her emotional gears had been disengaged. She had no nervous mannerisms, didn't smoke or twist her hair. I sat down in my swivel chair.

"When were you released?"

"A week ago."

"What's freedom feel like?"

She shrugged. "It feels good, I guess, but I can survive the other way too. Better than you'd think."

I took a small carton of half-and-half out of the little refrigerator to my right. I keep clean mugs on top and I turned one over for each of us, filling them when the coffee was done. Nikki took hers with a murmured thanks.

"Maybe you've heard this one before," she went on, "but I didn't kill Laurence and I want you to find out who did."

"Why wait this long? You could have initiated an investigation from prison and maybe saved yourself some time."

She smiled faintly. "I've been claiming I was innocent for years. Who'd believe me? The minute I was indicted, I lost my credibility. I want that back. And I want to know who did me in."

I had thought her eyes were dark but I could see now that they were a metallic gray. Her look was level, flattened-out, as though some interior light were growing dim. She seemed to be a lady without much hope. I had never believed she was guilty myself but I couldn't remember what had made me so sure. She seemed passionless and I couldn't imagine her caring enough about anything to kill.

"You want to fill me in?"

She took a sip of coffee and then set the mug on the edge of my desk.

"I was married to Laurence for four years, a little more than that. He was unfaithful after the first six months. I don't know why it came as such a shock. Actually, that's how I got involved with him . . . when he was with his first wife, being unfaithful to her with me. There's a sort of egotism attached to being a mistress, I suppose. Anyway, I never expected to be in her shoes and I didn't like it much."

"According to the prosecutor, that's why you killed him."

"Look, they needed a conviction. I was it," she said with the first sign of energy. "I've just spent the last eight years with killers of one kind or another and believe me, the motive isn't apathy. You kill people you hate or you kill in rage or you kill to get even, but you don't kill someone you're indifferent to. By the time

Laurence died, I didn't give a damn about him. I fell out of love with him the first time I found out about the other women. It took me a while to get it all out of my system . . ."

"And that's what the diary was all about?" I asked.

"Sure I kept track at first. I detailed every infidelity. I listened in on phone calls. I followed him around town. Then he started being more cautious about the whole thing and I started losing interest. I just didn't give a shit."

A flush had crept up to her cheeks and I gave her a moment to compose herself. "I know it looked like I killed him out of jealousy or rage, but I didn't care about that stuff. By the time he died, I just wanted to get on with my own life. I was going back to school, minding my own business. He went his way and I went mine . . ." Her voice trailed off.

"Who do you think killed him?"

"I think a lot of people wanted to. Whether they did or not is another matter. I mean, I could make a couple of educated guesses but I don't have proof of anything. Which is why I'm here."

"Why come to me?"

She flushed again slightly. "I tried the two big agencies in town and they turned me down. I came across your name in Laurence's old Rolodex. I thought there was a certain kind of irony hiring someone he had once hired himself. I did check you out. With Con Dolan down at Homicide."

I frowned. "It was his case, wasn't it?"

Nikki nodded. "Yes it was. He said you had a good

memory. I don't like having to explain everything from scratch."

"What about Dolan? Does he think you're innocent?"

"I doubt it, but then again, I did my time so what's it to him?"

I studied her for a moment. She was forthright and what she said made sense. Laurence Fife had been a difficult man. I hadn't been all that fond of him myself. If she was guilty, I couldn't see why she would stir it all up again. Her ordeal was over now and her so-called debt to society had been taken off the books except for whatever remaining parole she had to serve.

"Let me think about it some," I said. "I can get in touch with you later today and let you know."

"I'd appreciate that. I do have money. Whatever it takes."

"I don't want to be paid to rehash old business, Mrs. Fife. Even if we find out who did it, we have to make it stick and that could be tough after all this time. I'd like to check back through the files and see how it looks."

She took a manila folder out of her big leather bag. "I have some newspaper clippings. I can leave those with you if you like. That's the number where I can be reached."

We shook hands. Hers was cool and slight but her grip was strong. "Call me Nikki. Please."

"I'll be in touch," I said.

I had to go take some photographs of a crack in a side-walk for an insurance claim and I left the office shortly after she did, taking my VW out the freeway. I like my cars cramped and this one was filled with files and law books, a briefcase where I keep my little automatic, cardboard boxes, and a case of motor oil given to me by a client. He'd been cheated by two con artists who had "allowed" him to invest two grand in their oil company. The motor oil was real enough but it wasn't theirs; just some Sears thirty-weight with new labels pasted on. It had taken me a day and a half to track them down. In addition to the junk, I keep a packed overnight case back there, too, for God knows what emergency. I wouldn't work for anyone who wanted me *that* fast. It just makes me feel secure to have a nightgown, toothbrush, and fresh underwear at hand. I have my little quirks I guess. The VW's a '68, one of those vague beige models with assorted dents. It needs a tune-up but I never have time.

I thought about Nikki as I drove. I had tossed the manila folder full of clippings on the passenger seat but I really didn't need to look at them. Laurence Fife had done a lot of divorce work and he had a reputation as a killer in court. He was cold, methodical, and un-scrupulous, taking any advantage he could. In Califor-nia, as in many states, the only grounds for divorce are irreconcilable differences or incurable insanity, which eliminates the trumped-up adultery charges that were the mainstay of divorce attorneys and private eyes in the old days. There is still the question of property settlements and custody—money and children—and

Laurence Fife could get his clients anything. Most of them were women. Out of court, he had a reputation as a killer of another kind and the rumor was that he had mended many a broken heart in that difficult period between interlocutory and final decrees.

I had found him shrewd, nearly humorless, but exact; an easy man to work for because his instructions were clear and he paid in advance. A lot of people apparently hated him: men for the price he extracted, women for the betrayal of their trust. He was thirty-nine years old when he died. That Nikki was accused, tried, and convicted was just a piece of bad luck. Except for cases that clearly involve a homicidal maniac, the police like to believe murders are committed by those we know and love, and most of the time they're right—a chilling thought when you sit down to dinner with a family of five. All those potential killers passing their plates.

As nearly as I could remember, Laurence Fife had been having drinks with his law partner, Charlie Scorsoni, the night of his murder. Nikki was at a meeting of the Junior League. She got home before Laurence, who arrived about midnight. He was taking medication for numerous allergies and before he went to bed, he downed his usual capsule. Within two hours, he was awake—nauseated, vomiting, doubled over with violent stomach cramps. By morning, he was dead. An autopsy and lab tests showed that he'd died as a result of ingesting oleander, ground to a fine powder and substituted for the medication in the capsule he took: not a masterly plot, but one employed to good effect. Oleander is a common California shrub. There was one in the Fife's backyard as a matter of fact. Nikki's fingerprints were found on the vial along with his. A diary was discovered among her possessions, certain entries detailing the fact that she'd found out about his adulteries and was bitterly angry and hurt, contemplating divorce. The District Attorney established quite nicely that no one divorced Laurence Fife without penalty. He'd been married and divorced once before and though another attorney had handled his case, his impact was evident. He obtained custody of his children and he managed to come out ahead financially. The state of California is scrupulous in its division of assets, but Laurence Fife had a way of maneuvering monies so that even a fifty-fifty split gave him the lion's share. It looked as if Nikki Fife knew better than to try disentangling herself from him legally and had sought other means.

She had motive. She had access. The grand jury heard the evidence and returned an indictment. Once she got into court, it was simply a question of who could persuade twelve citizens of what. Apparently the D.A. had done his homework. Nikki hired Wilfred Brentnell from Los Angeles: a legal whiz with a reputation as the patron saint of lost causes. In some sense, it was almost like admitting her guilt. The whole trial had a sensational air. Nikki was young. She was pretty. She was born with money. The public was curious and the town was small. It was all too good to miss.

2

Santa Teresa is a Southern California town of eighty thousand, artfully arranged between the Sierra Madres and the Pacific Ocean—a haven for the abject rich. The public buildings look like old Spanish missions, the private homes look like magazine illustrations, the palm trees are trimmed of unsightly brown fronds, and the marina is as perfect as a picture postcard with the blue-gray hills forming a backdrop and white boats bobbing in the sunlight. Most of the downtown area consists of two- and three-story structures of white stucco and red tile, with wide soft curves and trellises wound with gaudy maroon bougainvillea. Even the frame bungalows of the poor could hardly be called squalid.

The police department is located near the heart of town on a side street lined with cottages painted mint green with low stone walls and jacaranda trees dripping lavender blossoms. Winter in Southern California consists of an overcast and is heralded not by autumn but by fire. After the fire season come the mud slides. And then the status quo is restored and everything goes on as before. This was May.

After I dropped the roll of film off to be developed, I went into the Homicide Department to see Lieutenant Dolan. Con is in his late fifties with the aura of the unkempt: bags under his eyes, gray stubble or its illusion, a pouchy face, and hair that's been coated with some kind of men's product and combed across a shiny place on top. He looks like he would smell of Thunderbird and hang out under bridges throwing up on his own shoes. Which is not to say he isn't very sharp. Con Dolan is a lot smarter than the average thief. He and killers run about neck and neck. He catches them most of the time and only occasionally guesses wrong. Few people can outthink him and I'm not sure why this is true, except that his powers of concentration are profound and his memory clear and pitiless. He knew why I was there and he motioned me back to his office without a word.

What Con Dolan calls an office would do for a secretary anywhere else. He doesn't like being shut away and he doesn't much care for privacy. He likes to conduct his business tipped back in his chair with his attention half-turned to what's going on around him. He picks up a lot of information like that and it saves him needless talk with his men. He knows when his detectives come and go and he knows who's been brought in for questioning and he knows when reports aren't being done on time and why.

"What can I do for you?" he said, but his tone didn't indicate any particular desire to help.

"I'd like to look at the files on Laurence Fife."

He arched an eyebrow at me ever so slightly. "It's against department policy. We're not running a public library here."

"I didn't ask to take them out. I just want to look. You've let me do that before."

"Once."

"I've given you information more times than that and you know it," I said. "Why hesitate on this?"

"That case is closed."

"Then you shouldn't have any objections. It's hardly an invasion of anyone's privacy."

His smile then was slow and humorless and he tapped a pencil idly, loving, I imagined, the power to turn me down cold. "She killed him, Kinsey. That's all there is to it."

"You told her to get in touch with me. Why bother with it if you don't have a doubt yourself?"

"My doubts have nothing to do with Laurence Fife," he said.

"What then?"

"There's more to this one than meets the eye," he said evasively. "Maybe we'd like to protect what we've got."

"Are 'we' keeping secrets?"

"Oh I got more secrets than you ever dreamed about," he said.

"Me too," I said. "Now why are we playing games?"

He gave me a look that might have been annoyance and might have been something else. He's a hard man to read. "You know how I feel about people like you."

"Look, as far as I'm concerned, we're in the same business," I said. "I'm straight with you. I don't know what kind of gripes you have with the other private investigators in town, but I stay out of your way and I've got nothing but respect for the job you do. I don't understand why we can't cooperate with one another."

He stared at me for a moment, his mouth turning down with resignation. "You'd get more out of me if you'd learn to flirt," he said grudgingly.

"No I wouldn't. You think women are a pain in the ass. If I flirted, you'd pat me on the head and make me go away."

He wouldn't take the bait on that one but he did reach over and pick up the phone, dialing Identification and Records.

"This is Dolan. Have Emerald bring me the files on Laurence Fife." He hung up and leaned back again, looking at me with a mixture of speculation and distaste.

"I better not hear any complaints about the way you handle this. If I get one call from anyone—and I'm talking about a witness who feels harassed or anyone else, including my men or anybody else's men—you're up shit creek. You got that?"

I held up three fingers beside my temple dutifully. "Scout's honor."

"When were you ever a Scout?"

"Well, I was a Brownie once for almost a week," I said sweetly. "We had to paint a rose on a hanky for Mother's Day and I thought it was dumb so I quit."

He didn't smile. "You can use Lieutenant Becker's office," he said when the files arrived. "And stay out of trouble."

I went into Becker's office.

It took me two hours to sort through the mass of paperwork but I began to see why Con had been reluctant to let me look because just about the first thing that came to light was a series of Telexes from the West Los Angeles Police Department about a second homicide. At first, I thought it was a mistake—that communiqués from another case had been inadvertently sandwiched into the wrong file. But the details nearly leapt off the page and the implications made my heart go pitty-pat. An accountant named Libby Glass, Caucasian, female, age twenty-four, had died from ingesting ground oleander four days after Laurence Fife died. She had worked for Haycraft and McNiece, a business-management firm representing the interests of Laurence Fife's law firm. Now what the hell was that about?

I flipped through copies of investigators' reports, trying to piece together the story from terse departmental memorandums and penciled summations of telephone calls flying back and forth between the Santa Teresa and West Los Angeles police departments. One memo noted that the key to her apartment had been found on the key ring in Laurence Fife's office desk drawer. A lengthy interview with her parents didn't add anything. There was an interview with a surly sounding ex-boyfriend named Lyle Abernathy, who seemed convinced that she was romantically involved with a "certain unnamed Santa Teresa attorney," but no one had pinned it down much beyond that. Still, the connection was ominous enough and it looked like Nikki Fife's alleged jealous rage might have included the object of her husband's philanderings as well as the man himself. Except that there wasn't any proof.

I made notes, jotting down last-known addresses and telephone numbers for whatever good that might do after all these years, and then I pushed my chair back and went to the door. Con was talking to Lieutenant Becker but he must have known what I wanted because he excused himself, apparently satisfied that I hadn't missed the point. I leaned on the doorframe, waiting. He took his sweet time ambling over.

"You want to tell me what that was about?"

His expression was bemused but there was an air of bitterness about it. "We couldn't make it stick," he said flatly.

"You think Nikki killed her too?"

"I'd be willing to bet on it," he snapped.

"I take it the D.A. didn't see it that way."

He shrugged, shoving his hands in his pockets. "I can read the California Evidence Code as well as the next man. They called off my dogs."

"The stuff in the file was all circumstantial," I said.

"That's right."

I shut my mouth, staring off at a row of windows

that badly needed to be cleaned. I didn't like this little turn of events at all and he seemed to know that. He shifted his weight.

"I think I could have nailed her but the D.A. was in a big hurry and he didn't want to jeopardize his case. Bad politics. That's why you didn't like being a cop yourself, Kinsey. Working with a leash around your neck."

"I still don't like that," I said.

"Maybe that's why I'm helping you," he said and the look in his eyes was shrewd.

"What about follow-up?"

"Oh we did that. We worked on the Libby Glass angle for months, off and on. So did the West LAPD. We never turned up anything. No witnesses. No informants. No fingerprints that could have placed Nikki Fife at the scene. We couldn't even prove that Nikki *knew* Libby Glass."

"You think I'm going to help you make your case?"

"Well, I don't know about that," he said. "You might. Believe it or not, I don't think you're a bad investigator. Young yet, and sometimes off the wall, but basically honest at any rate. If you turn up evidence that points to Nikki, I don't think you'd hold that back now, would you?"

"*If* she did it."

"If she didn't, then you don't have anything to worry about."

"Con, if Nikki Fife has something to hide, why would she open this whole thing up again? She couldn't be that kind of fool. What could she possibly gain?"

"You tell me."

"Listen," I said, "I don't believe she killed Laurence in the first place so you're going to have a hell of a time persuading me she killed someone else as well."

The phone rang two desks over and Lieutenant Becker held up a finger, looking over at Con. He gave me a fleeting smile as he moved away.

"Have a good time," he said.

I scanned the file again quickly to make sure I hadn't overlooked anything and then I closed it up and left it on the desk. He was deep in conversation with Becker again when I passed the two of them and neither looked up at me. I was troubled by the idea of Libby Glass but I was also intrigued. Maybe this was going to be more than a rehash of old business, maybe there was more to be turned up than a trail that was eight years cold.

By the time I got back to the office, it was 4:15 and I needed a drink. I got a bottle of chablis out of my little refrigerator and applied the corkscrew. The two coffee mugs were still sitting on my desk. I rinsed out both and filled mine with wine tart enough to make me shudder ever so slightly. I went out onto the second-floor balcony and looked down at State Street, which runs right up the middle of downtown Santa Teresa, eventually making a big curve to the left and turning into a street with another name. Even where I stood, there were Spanish tile and stucco arches and bougainvillea growing everywhere. Santa Teresa is the only town I ever heard of that made the main street narrower, planted trees instead of pulling them up, and constructed cunning telephone booths that look like small confessionals. I propped myself up on the waist-high ledge and sipped my wine. I could smell the ocean and I let my mind go blank, watching the pedestrians down below. I already knew that I would go to work for Nikki but I needed just these few moments for myself before I turned my attention to the job to be done.

At 5:00 I went home, calling the service before I left.

Of all the places I've lived in Santa Teresa, my current cubbyhole is the best. It's located on an unpretentious street that parallels the wide boulevard running along the beach. Most of the homes in the neighborhood are owned by retired folk whose memories of the town go back to the days when it was all citrus groves and resort hotels. My landlord, Henry Pitts, is a former commercial baker who makes a living now, at the age of eighty-one, by devising obnoxiously difficult crossword puzzles, which he likes to try out on me. He is usually also in the process of making mammoth batches of bread, which he leaves to rise in an old Shaker cradle on the sunporch near my room. Henry trades bread and other baked goods to a nearby restaurant for his meals and he has also, of late, become quite crafty about clipping coupons, declaring that on a good day he can buy $50.00 worth of groceries for $6.98. Somehow these shopping expeditions seem to net him pairs of panty hose, which he gives to me. I am halfway in love with Henry Pitts.

The room itself is fifteen feet square, outfitted as

living room, bedroom, kitchen, bathroom, closet, and laundry facility. Originally this was Henry's garage and I'm happy to say that it sports no stucco, red Spanish tile, or vines of any kind. It is made of aluminum siding and other wholly artificial products that are weather-resistant and never need paint. The architecture is completely nondescript. It is to this cozy den that I escape most days after work and it was from here that I called Nikki and asked her to meet me for a drink.

3

I do most of my hanging out in a neighborhood bar called Rosie's. It's the sort of place where you look to see if the chair needs brushing off before you sit down. The plastic seats have little rips in them that leave curls of nylon on the underside of your stockings and the tables have black Formica tops hand-etched with words like *hi*. To the left above the bar, there's a dusty marlin, and when people get drunk, Rosie lets them shoot rubber-tipped arrows at it with a toy gun, thus averting aggressions that might otherwise erupt into vicious barroom snits.

The place appeals to me for a couple of reasons. Not only is it close to my home but it is never attractive to tourists, which means that most of the time it's half-empty and perfect for private conversations. Then, too, Rosie's cooking is inventive, a sort of devil-may-care cuisine with a Hungarian twist. It is with Rosie that Henry Pitts barters baked goods, so I get to eat his breads and pies as a dividend. Rosie is in her sixties with a nose that almost meets her upper lip, a low forehead, and hair dyed a remarkable shade of rust, rather like the color of cheap redwood furniture. She also does tricky things with an eyebrow pencil that makes her eyes look small and suspect.

When Nikki walked in that night, she hesitated, scanning the place. Then she spotted me and moved through the empty tables to the booth where I usually sit. She slid in across from me and eased out of her jacket. Rosie ambled over, eyeing Nikki with uneasiness. Rosie is convinced that I do business with Mafia types and drug crazies and she was probably trying to determine the category into which Nikki Fife might fit.

"So are you eating something or what?" Rosie said, getting straight to the point.

I glanced at Nikki. "Have you had dinner?"

She shook her head. Rosie's eyes moved from Nikki to me as though I might be translating for a deaf-mute.

"What have you got tonight?"

"It's veal porkolt. Veal cubes, lotta onion, paprika, and tomato paste. You'll love it. You'll go nuts. It's the best kinda stew I make. Henry's rolls and everything, and on a plate I'm gonna put some good soft cheese and a coupla gherkins."

She was already writing the order down as she spoke, so it didn't require much from us in the way of consent. "You gonna have wine too. I'll pick the kind."

When Rosie had left, I related the information I'd picked up in the files about the murder of Libby Glass, including the telephone calls that had been traced to Laurence's home phone.

"Did you know about her?"

Nikki shook her head. "I heard the name but it was through my attorney, sometime during the trial, I think. I can't even remember now what was said."

"You never heard Laurence mention her? Never saw her name written down anyplace?"

"No little love notes if that's what you mean. He was meticulous about that sort of thing. He was once named as corespondent in a divorce action because of some letters he wrote and after that, he seldom put anything personal in writing. I usually knew when he was involved with someone but never because he left cryptic notes or telephone numbers on matchbook covers or anything like that."

I thought about that one for a minute. "What about phone bills though? Why leave those around?"

"He didn't," Nikki said. "All the bills were sent to the business-management firm in Los Angeles."

"And Libby Glass handled the account?"

"Apparently she did."

"So maybe he called her on business matters."

Nikki shrugged. She was a little less remote than she had been but I still had the feeling that she was one step removed from what was happening. "He was having an affair with *someone*."

"How do you know?"

"The hours he kept. The look on his face." She paused, apparently thinking back. "Sometimes he would smell of someone else's soap. I finally accused him of that and afterwards he had a shower installed at the office and used the same kind of soap there that we used at home."

"Did he see women down at the office?"

"Ask his partner," she said with the faintest tinge of bitterness. "Maybe he even screwed 'em on the office couch, I don't know. Anyway it was little things. It sounds stupid now, but once he came home and the edge of his sock was turned down. It was summer and he said he'd been out playing tennis. He had on tennis shorts and he'd worked up a sweat all right, but not out on a public court. I really zapped him that time."

"But what would he say when you confronted him?"

"He'd admit it sometimes. Why not? I didn't have any proof and adultery isn't grounds for divorce in this state anyway."

Rosie arrived with the wine and two paper napkins wrapped around some silverware. Nikki and I were both silent until she'd departed again.

"Why did you stay married to him if he was such a jerk?"

"Cowardice I guess," she said. "I would have divorced him eventually, but I had a lot at stake."

"Your son?"

"Yes." Her chin came up slightly, whether from pride or defensiveness I wasn't sure. "His name is Colin," she said. "He's twelve. I have him in a boarding school up near Monterey."

"You also had Laurence's kids living with you at the time, didn't you?"

"Yes, that's right. A boy and a girl, both in school."

"Where are they now?"

"I have no idea. His ex-wife is here in town. You

might check with her if you're curious. I don't hear from them."

"Did they blame you for his death?"

She leaned forward, her manner intense. "Everyone blamed me. Everyone believed I was guilty. And now I take it Con Dolan thinks I killed Libby Glass too. Isn't that what you were getting at?"

"Who cares what Dolan thinks? I don't think you did it and I'm the one going to work on this thing. Which reminds me. We ought to get the financial end of it clarified. I charge thirty bucks an hour plus mileage. I'd like to have at least a grand up front. I'll send you an itemized accounting from week to week indicating what time I've put in doing what. Also, you have to understand that my services are not exclusive. I sometimes handle more than one case at a time."

Nikki was already reaching into her purse. She took out a checkbook and a pen. Even looking at it upside down, I could see that the check was for five thousand dollars. I admired the carelessness with which she dashed it off. She didn't even have to check her bank balance first. She pushed it across the table to me and I tucked it into my purse as though I disposed of such matters as casually as she.

Rosie appeared again, this time with our dinner. She put a plate down in front of each of us and then stood there until we began to eat. "Mmm, Rosie it's wonderful," I said.

She wiggled slightly in place, not yielding her ground.

"Maybe it don't suit your friend," she said, looking at me instead of Nikki.

"Marvelous," Nikki murmured. "Really it is."

"She loves it," I said. Rosie's gaze slid across to Nikki's face and she finally seemed satisfied that Nikki's appreciation of the dish was equaled only by my own.

I let the conversation wander while we ate. Between the good food and the wine, Nikki seemed to be letting down her guard. Under that cool, unruffled surface, signs of life were beginning to show, as though she were just wakening from a curse that had rendered her immobile for years.

"Where do you think I should start?" I asked.

"Well I don't know. I've always been curious about his secretary back then. Her name was Sharon Napier. She was already working for him when he and I met, but there was something not right about her, something in her attitude."

"Was she involved with him?"

"I don't think so. I really don't know what it was. I could just about guarantee they didn't have any sexual ties, but something had gone on. She was sometimes sarcastic with him, which Laurence never tolerated from anyone. The first time I heard her do it, I thought he'd cut her down, but he never batted an eye. She never took any guff from him at all, wouldn't stay late, wouldn't come in on weekends when he had a big case coming up. He never complained about her either, just went out and hired temporary help when he needed it. It wasn't like him, but when I asked him about it, he acted as if I were crazy, reading significance into the situation when there wasn't any. She was gorgeous, too, hardly the run-of-the-mill office type."

"Do you have any idea where she is now?"

Nikki shook her head. "She used to live up on Rivera but she's not there now. At least, she's not listed in the telephone book."

I made a note of her last-known address. "I take it you never knew her well."

Nikki shrugged. "We had the customary exchanges when I called the office but it was just routine stuff."

"What about friends of hers or places she might hang out?"

"I don't know. My guess is she lived way beyond her means. She traveled every chance she could and she dressed a lot better than I did back then."

"She testified at the trial, didn't she?"

"Yes, unfortunately. She'd been a witness to a couple of nasty quarrels I had with him and that didn't help."

"Well, it's worth looking into," I said. "I'll see if I can get a line on her. Is there anything else about him? Was he in the middle of any hassles when he died? Any kind of personal dispute or a big legal case?"

"Not that I knew. He was always in the middle of something big."

"Well, I think the first move is to talk to Charlie Scorsoni and see what he has to say. Then we'll figure it out from there."

I left money on the table for the dinner check and we walked out together. Nikki's car was parked close by, a dark green Oldsmobile ten years out of date. I waited until she'd pulled away and then I walked the half block to my place.

When I got in, I poured myself a glass of wine and sat down to organize the information I'd collected so far. I have a system of consigning data to three-by-five index cards. Most of my notes have to do with witnesses: who they are, how they're related to the investigation, dates of interviews, follow-up. Some cards are background information I need to check out and some are notes about legal technicalities. The cards are an efficient way of storing facts for my written reports. I tack them up on a large bulletin board above my desk and stare at them, telling myself the story as I perceive it. Amazing contradictions will come to light, sudden gaps, questions I've overlooked.

I didn't have many cards for Nikki Fife and I made no attempt to assess the information I had. I didn't want to form a hypothesis too early for fear it would color the entire course of the investigation. It did seem clear that this was a murder where an alibi meant little or nothing. If you go to the trouble to substitute poison for the medication in someone's antihistamine capsules, all you have to do afterward is sit back and wait. Unless you want to risk killing off others in the household, you have to be sure that only your intended victim takes that particular prescription, but there are plenty of pills that would satisfy that requirement: blood-pressure medication, antibiotics, maybe even sleeping pills. It doesn't matter much as long as you have access to the supply. It might take your victim two days or two weeks but eventually he'd dose himself properly and you could probably even manufacture a reasonable facsimile of surprise and grief. The plan has a further advantage in that you don't actually have to be there to shoot, bludgeon, hack up, or manually strangle your intended. Even where the motivation to kill is overpowering, it'd be pretty distasteful (one would think) to watch somone's eyes bug out and listen to his or her last burbling cries. Also, when done in person there's always that unsettling chance that the tables might be turned and you'd wind up on a slab in the morgue yourself.

As methods go, this little oleander number was not half bad. In Santa Teresa, the shrub grows everywhere, sometimes ten feet tall with pink or white blossoms and handsome narrow leaves. You wouldn't need to bother with anything so blatant as buying rat poison in a town where there are clearly no rats, and you wouldn't have to sport a false mustache when you went into your local hardware store to ask for a garden pest control with no bitter aftertaste. In short, the method for killing Laurence Fife, and apparently Libby Glass as well, was inexpensive, accessible, and easy to use. I did have a couple of questions and I made notes of those before I turned out the light. It was well after midnight when I fell asleep.

4

I went into the office early to type up my initial notes for Nikki's file, indicating briefly what I'd been hired to do and the fact that a check for five thousand dollars had been paid on account. Then I called Charlie Scorsoni's office. His secretary said he had some time free midafternoon, so I set up an appointment for 3:15 and then used the rest of the morning to do a background check. When interviewing someone for the first time, it's always nice to have a little information up your sleeve. A visit to the county clerk's office, the credit bureau, and the newspaper morgue gave me sufficient facts to dash off a quick sketch of Laurence Fife's former law partner. Charlie Scorsoni was apparently single, owned his own home, paid his bills on time, did occasional public-speaking stints for worthy causes, had never been arrested or sued—in short, was a rather conservative, middle-aged man who didn't gamble, speculate on the stock market, or jeopardize himself in any way. I had caught glimpses of him at the trial and I remembered him as slightly overweight. His current office was within walking distance of mine.

The building itself looked like a Moorish castle: two stories of white adobe with windowsills two feet deep, inset with wrought-iron bars, and a corner tower that probably housed the rest rooms and floor mops. Scorsoni and Powers, Attorneys-at-Law, were on the second floor. I pushed through a massive carved wooden door and found myself in a small reception area with carpeting as soft underfoot as moss and about the same shade. The walls were white, hung with watercolors in various pastels, all abstract, and there were plants here and there; two plump sofas of asparagus green widewale corduroy sat at right angles under a row of narrow windows.

The firm's secretary looked to be in her early seventies, and I thought at first she might be out on loan from some geriatric agency. She was thin and energetic, with bobbed hair straight out of the twenties and "mod" glasses replete with a rhinestone butterfly on the lower portion of one lens. She was wearing a wool skirt and a pale mauve sweater, which she must have knit herself, as it was a masterpiece of cable stitches, wheat ears, twisted ribs, popcorn stitches, and picot appliqué. She and I became instant friends when I recognized the aforementioned—my aunt having raised me on a regimen of such accomplishments—and we were soon on a first-name basis. Hers was Ruth; nice biblical stuff.

She was a chatty little thing, full of pep, and I wondered if she wasn't about perfect for Henry Pitts. Since Charlie Scorsoni was keeping me waiting, I took my revenge by eliciting as much information from Ruth as I could manage without appearing too rude. She told me she had worked for Scorsoni and Powers since the formation of their partnership seven years ago. Her husband had left her for a younger woman (fifty-five) and Ruth, on her own for the first time in years, had despaired of ever finding a job, as she was then sixty-two years old, "though in perfect health," she said. She was quick, capable, and of course was being aced out at every turn by women one-third her age who were cute instead of competent.

"The only cleavage I got left, I sit on," she said and then hooted at herself. I gave Scorsoni and Powers several points for their perceptiveness. Ruth had nothing but raves for them both. Still her rhapsodizing hardly prepared me for the man who shook my hand across the desk when I was finally ushered into his office forty-five minutes late.

Charlie Scorsoni was big, but any excess weight I remembered was gone. He had thick, sandy hair, receding at the temples, a solid jaw, cleft chin, his blue eyes magnified by big rimless glasses. His collar was open, his tie askew, sleeves rolled up as far as his muscular forearms would permit. He was tilted back in his swivel chair with his feet propped up against the edge of the desk, and his smile was slow to form and smoldered with suppressed sexuality. His air was watchful, bemused, and he took in the sight of me with almost embarrassing attention to detail. He laced his hands across the top of his head. "Ruth tells me you have a few questions about Laurence Fife. What gives?"

"I don't know yet. I'm looking into his death and this seemed like the logical place to start. Mind if I sit down?"

He gestured with one hand almost carelessly, but his expression had changed. I sat down and Scorsoni eased himself into an upright position.

"I heard Nikki was out on parole," he said. "If she claims she didn't kill him, she's nuts."

"I didn't say I was working for her."

"Well it's for damn sure nobody else would bother."

"Maybe not. You don't sound too happy about the idea."

"Hey listen. Laurence was my best friend. I would have walked on nails for him." His gaze was direct and there was something bristly under the surface—grief, misdirected rage. It was hard to tell what.

"Did you know Nikki well?" I asked.

"Well enough I guess." The sense of sexuality that had seemed so apparent at first was seeping away and I wondered if he could turn it off and on like a heater. Certainly his manner was wary now.

"How did you meet Laurence?"

"We went to the University of Denver together. Same fraternity. Laurence was a playboy. Everything came easily to him. Law school, he went to Harvard, I went to Arizona State. His family had money. Mine had none. I lost track of him for a few years and then I heard he'd opened his own law firm here in town. So I came out and talked to him about going to work for him and he said fine. He made me a partner two years later."

"Was he married to his first wife then?"

"Yeah, Gwen. She's still around town someplace but I'd be a little careful with her. She ended up bitter as hell and I've heard she's got surly things to say about him. She has a dog-grooming place up on State Street somewhere if that's any help. I try to avoid running into her myself."

He was watching me steadily and I got the impression that he knew exactly how much he would tell me and exactly how much he would not.

"What about Sharon Napier? Did she work for him long?"

"She was here when I hired on, though she did precious little. I finally ended up hiring a girl of my own."

"She and Laurence got along okay?"

"As far as I know. She hung around until the trial was over and then she took off. She stiffed me for some money I'd advanced against her salary. If you run into her, I'd love to hear about it. Send her a bill or something just to let her know I haven't forgotten old times."

"Does the name Libby Glass mean anything to you?"

"Who?"

"She was the accountant who handled your business down in L.A. She worked for Haycraft and McNiece."

Scorsoni continued to look blank for a moment and then shook his head. "What's she got to do with it?"

"She was also killed with oleander right about the time Laurence died," I said. He didn't seem to react with any particular shock or dismay. He made a skeptical pull at his lower lip and then shrugged.

"It's a new one on me but I'll take your word for it," he said.

"You never met her yourself?"

"I must have. Laurence and I shared the paperwork but he had most of the actual contact with the business managers. I pitched in occasionally though, so I probably ran into her at some point."

"I've heard he was having an affair with her," I said.

"I don't like to gossip about the dead," Scorsoni said.

"Me neither, but he did play around," I said carefully. "I don't mean to push the point, but there were plenty of women who testified to that at the trial."

Scorsoni smiled at the box he was drawing on his legal pad. The look he gave me then was shrewd.

"Well, I'll say this. One, the guy never forced himself on anyone. And two, I don't believe he would get himself involved with a business associate. That was not his style."

"What about his clients? Didn't he get involved with them?"

"No comment."

"Would *you* get in bed with a female client?" I asked.

"Mine are all eighty years old so the answer is no. I do estate planning. He did divorce." He glanced at his watch and then pushed his chair back. "I hate to cut this short but it's four-fifteen now and I have a brief to prepare."

"Sorry. I didn't mean to take up your time. It was nice of you to see me on such short notice."

Scorsoni walked me out toward the front, his big body exuding heat. He held the door open for me, his left arm extending up along the doorframe. Again, that barely suppressed male animal seemed to peer out through his eyes. "Good luck," he said. "I suspect you won't turn up much."

I picked up the eight-by-ten glossies of the sidewalk crack I'd photographed for California Fidelity. The six shots of the broken concrete were clear enough. The claimant, Marcia Threadgill, had filed for disability, asserting that she'd stumbled on the jutting slab of sidewalk that had been forced upward by a combination of tree roots and shifting soil. She was suing the owner of the craft shop whose property encompassed the errant walkway. The claim, a "slip and fall" case, wasn't a large one—maybe forty-eight hundred dollars, which included her medical bills and damages, along with compensation for the time she'd been off work. It looked like the insurance company would pay, but I had been instructed to give a cursory look on the off chance that the claim was trumped-up.

Ms. Threadgill's apartment was in a terraced building set into a hill overlooking the beach, not that far from my place. I parked my car about six doors down and got my binoculars out of the glove compartment. By slouching down on my spine, I could just bring her patio into focus, the view clear enough to disclose that she wasn't watering her ferns the way she ought. I don't know a lot about houseplants, but when all the green things turn brown, I'd take it as a hint. One of the ferns was that nasty kind that grow little gray hairy paws that begin, little by little, to creep right out of the pot. Anyone who'd own a thing like that probably had an inclination to defraud and I could just picture her hefting a twenty-five-pound sack of fern mulch with her alleged sprained back. I watched her place for an hour and a half but she didn't show. One of my old cohorts used to claim that men are the only suitable candidates for surveillance work because they can sit in a parked car and pee discreetly into a tennis-ball can, thus avoiding unnecessary absences. I was losing interest in Marcia Threadgill and in truth, I had to pee like crazy, so I put the binoculars away and found the nearest service station on my way back into town.

I stopped in at the credit bureau again and talked to my buddy who lets me peek into files not ordinarily made public. I asked him to see what he could find out about Sharon Napier and he said he'd get back to me. I did a couple of personal errands and then went home. It had not been a very satisfying day but then most of my days are the same: checking and cross-checking, filling in blanks, detail work that was absolutely essential to the job but scarcely dramatic stuff. The basic characteristics of any good investigator are a plodding nature and infinite patience. Society has inadvertently been grooming women to this end for years. I sat down at my desk and consigned Charlie Scorsoni to several index cards. It had been an unsettling interview and I had a feeling that I wasn't done with him.

5

Living with the climate in Santa Teresa is rather like functioning in a room with an overhead light fixture. The illumination is uniform—clear and bright enough—but the shadows are gone and there is a disturbing lack of dimension. The days are blanketed with sunlight. Often it is sixty-seven degrees and fair. The nights are consistently cool. Seasonally it does rain but the rest of the time, one day looks very much like the next and the constant, cloudless blue sky has a peculiar, disorienting effect, making it impossible to remember where one is in the year. Being in a building with no exterior windows gives the same impression: a subliminal suffocation, as though some, but not all, of the oxygen has been removed from the air.

I left my apartment at 9:00, heading north on Chapel. I stopped for gasoline, using the self-service pump and thinking, as I always do, what a simple but absurd pleasure it is to be able to do that sort of thing myself. By the time I found K-9 Korners, it was 9:15. The discreet sign in the window indicated that the place opened for business at eight. The grooming establishment was attached to a veterinarian's office on State Street just where it made the big bend. The building was painted flamingo pink, one wing of it housing a wilderness supply store with a mummy bag hanging in the window and a dummy, in a camping outfit, staring blankly at a tent pole.

I pushed my way into K-9 Korners to the accompaniment of many barking dogs. Dogs and I do not get along. They inevitably stick their snouts right in my crotch, sometimes clamping themselves around my leg as though to do some kind of two-legged dance. On certain occasions, I have limped gamely along, dog affixed, their masters swatting at them ineffectually, saying "Hamlet, get down! What's the matter with you!?" It is hard to look such a dog in the face, and I prefer to keep my distance from the lot of them.

There was a glass showcase full of dog-care products, and many photographs of dogs and cats affixed to the wall. To my right was a half door, the upper portion opening into a small office with several grooming rooms adjoining. By peering around the doorjamb, I could spot several dogs in various stages of being done up. Most were shivering, their eyes rolling piteously. One was having a little red bow put in its topknot, right between its ears. On a worktable were some little brown lumps I thought I could recognize. The groomer, a woman, looked up at me.

"Can I help you?"

"The dog just stepped on that brown lump," I said.

She looked down at the table. "Oh Dashiell, not

again. Excuse me a minute," she said. Dashiell remained on the table, trembling, while she grabbed for some paper towels, deftly scooping up Dashiell's little accident. She seemed pretty good-natured about it. She was in her mid-forties with large brown eyes and shoulder-length gray hair, which was pulled back and secured with a scarf. She wore a dark wine-colored smock and I could see that she was tall and slim.

"Are you Gwen?"

She glanced up with a quick smile. "Yes, that's right."

"I'm Kinsey Millhone. I'm a private investigator."

Gwen laughed. "Oh Lord, what's this all about?" She disposed of the paper towel and moved over to the half door and opened it. "Come on in. I'll be right back."

She lifted Dashiell from the table and carried him into a back room just off to the left. More dogs began to bark and I could hear a blower being turned off. The air in the place was dense with heat, scented with the smell of damp hair, and the odd combination of flea syrup and dog perfume. The brown linoleum tile floor was covered with assorted clippings, like a barber shop. In the adjoining room, I could see a dog being bathed by a young girl who worked over an elevated bathtub. To my left several dogs, beribboned, were waiting in cages to be picked up. Another young woman was clipping a poodle on a second grooming table. She glanced at me with interest. Gwen returned with a little gray dog under her arm.

"This is Wuffles," she said, half clamping the dog's mouth shut. Wuffles gave her a few licks in the mouth. She pulled her head back, laughing, and made a face.

"I hope you don't mind if I finish this up. Have a seat," she said affably, indicating a metal stool nearby. I perched, wishing I didn't have to mention Laurence Fife's name. From what Charlie Scorsoni had told me, it would rather spoil her good humor.

Gwen began to clip Wuffles's toenails, tucking the dog against her body to prevent sudden moves. "You're local, I assume," she said.

"Yes, I have an office downtown here," I said, pulling out my I.D. automatically. I held it toward her so she could read it. She gave it a glance, apparently accepting it without much suspicion or concern. It always amazes me when people take me on faith.

"I understand you used to be married to Laurence Fife," I ventured.

"Yes, that's right. Is this about him? He's been dead for years."

"I know. His case is being opened up again."

"Oh, *that's* interesting. By whom?"

"Nikki. Who else?" I said. "The Homicide Department knows I'm looking into it and I have their cooperation, if that helps you any. Could you answer some questions for me?"

"All right," she said. Her tone was cautious but there was also a note of interest, as though she considered it a curious inquiry but not necessarily bad.

"You don't sound that surprised," I said.

"Actually I am. I thought that was finished business."

"Well, I'm just starting to look into it and I may come up with a blank. We don't have to talk here if it's inconvenient. I don't like to interrupt your work."

"This is fine with me, as long as you don't mind watching me clip a few dogs. I really can't afford a time-out right now. We're loaded today. Hold on," she said. "Kathy, could you hand me that flea spray? I think we missed a few here."

The dark-haired groomer left the poodle long enough to reach up for the flea spray, which was passed over to Gwen. "That's Kathy, as you might have gathered," Gwen said. "The one up to her elbows in soapsuds is Jan."

Gwen began to spray Wuffles, turning her face away to avoid the fumes. "Sorry. Go ahead."

"How long were you married to Fife?"

"Thirteen years. We met in college, his third year, my first. I'd known him about six months I guess."

"Good years? Bad years?"

"Well I'm mellowing some on that," she said. "I used to think it was all a big waste but now I don't know. Did you know Laurence yourself?"

"I met him a couple of times," I said, "just superficially."

Gwen's look was wry. "He could be very charming if he wanted to, but at heart he was a real son of a bitch."

Kathy glanced over at Gwen and smiled. Gwen laughed. "These two have heard my version about a hundred times," she said by way of explanation. "Neither has ever been married so I tend to play devil's advocate. Anyway, in those days I was the dutiful wife, and I mean I played the part with a dedication few could match. I cooked elegant meals. I made lists. I cleaned the house. I raised the kids. I'm not saying I'm anything unique for that, except that I took it awfully to heart. I wore my hair up in this French roll, not a pin out of place, and I had these outfits to put on and take off, kind of like a Barbie doll." She stopped and laughed at the image of herself, pretending to pull a string from her neck. "Hello, I'm Gwen. I'm a good wife," she burbled in a kind of nasal parrot tone. Her manner was rather affectionate as though she, instead of Laurence, had died but was remembered fondly by dear friends. Part of the time she was looking at me, and part of the time she combed and clipped the dog on the table in front of her, but in any event her manner was friendly—hardly the bitter, withdrawn account I'd expected.

"When it was over, I was pretty angry—not so much at him as at myself for buying into the whole gig. I mean, don't get me wrong. I liked it at the time and it suited me fine, but there was also a form of sensory deprivation going on so that when the marriage blew up, I was totally unequipped to deal with the real world. He managed the money. He pulled the strings. He made the major decisions, especially where the kids were concerned. I bathed and dressed and fed them and he shaped their lives. I didn't realize it at the time because I was just running around anxious to please him, which was no easy task, but now that I look back on it, it was really fucked."

She glanced up at me to see if I'd react to the language, but I just smiled back.

"So now I sound like all the other women who came out of marriages in that era. You know, we're all faintly grumpy about it because we think we've been had."

"You said you'd mellowed some," I said. "How did that come about?"

"Six thousand dollars' worth of therapy," she said flatly.

I smiled. "What made the marriage blow?"

Her cheeks tinted slightly at that but her gaze remained just as frank. "I'd rather save that for later if you're really interested."

"Sure, fine," I said. "I didn't mean to interrupt anyway."

"Well. It wasn't all his fault," she said. "But it wasn't all mine either and he hosed me with that divorce. I'm telling you, I got beat up."

"How?"

"How many ways are there? I was scared and I was also naïve. I wanted Laurence out of my life and I didn't care much what it cost. Except the kids. I fought him tooth and nail over them, but what can I tell you? I lost. I've never quite recovered from that."

I wanted to ask her about the grounds for the custody battle but I had the feeling it was touchy stuff. Better to let that slide for the moment and come back to it later if I could. "The kids must have come back to you after he died, though. Especially with his second wife going to prison."

Gwen pushed at a strand of gray hair with a capable-looking hand. "They were almost college age by then. In fact, Gregory had left that fall and Diane left the year after. But they were very messed-up kids. Laurence was a strict disciplinarian. Not that I have any quarrel with that—I think kids need structure—but he was a very controlling person, really out of touch with anything emotional, rather aggressive in his manner of dealing with anyone, the kids in particular. So the two of them, after five years of that regime, were both withdrawn and shut-down. Defensive, uncommunicative. From what I could tell, his relation to them was based on attack, being held accountable, much like what he had done with me. Of course, I'd been seeing them alternate weekends and that sort of thing, and I had the usual summer visitation. I just didn't have any idea how far it had gone. And his death was a kick in the head to them on top of that. I'm sure they both had a lot of feelings that were never resolved. Diane went straight into therapy. And Gregory's seen someone since, though not regularly." She paused a moment. "I feel like I'm giving you case histories here."

"Oh no, I appreciate your candor," I said. "Are the kids here in town too?"

"Greg's living south of Palm Springs. Salton Sea. He has a boat down there."

"What sort of work does he do?"

"Well, he doesn't have to do anything. Laurence did provide for them financially. I don't know if you've checked on the insurance yet, but his estate was divided equally between the three kids—Greg, Diane, and Nikki's son, Colin."

"What about Diane? Where is she?"

"She's in Claremont, going to school. Working on

another degree. She's interested in teaching deaf children and she seems to do very well. It worried me some at first because I suspect, in her mind, it was all tied up—my divorce, Nikki, Colin, and her responsibility—even though it had nothing to do with her."

"Wait a minute. I don't understand what you mean," I said.

Gwen glanced up at me with surprise. "I thought you'd already talked to Nikki."

"Well, I talked to her once," I said.

"Didn't she tell you Colin was deaf? He was deaf from birth. I don't really remember what caused it, but there was nothing they could do about it apparently. Diane was very upset. She was thirteen, I think, when the baby was born and maybe she resented the intrusion. I don't mean to be so analytical at every turn but some of this came out with her psychiatrist and it seems pertinent. I think now she can articulate most of it herself—in fact she does—so I don't think I'm violating any confidence."

She selected a couple of strands of ribbon from about twenty spools hung on pegboard on the wall above the grooming table. She laid a blue and an orange on Wuffles's head. "What do you think, Wuf? Blue or orange?"

Wuffles raised her (I assumed) eyes and panted happily, and Gwen chose the orange, which I must admit made a certain jaunty sense against Wuffles's silver-gray mop of hair. The dog was docile, full of trust, loving every move even though half of Gwen's attention was turned to me.

"Gregory was into drugs for a while," Gwen said conversationally. "That's what his generation seemed to do while mine was playing house. But he's a good kid and I think he's okay now. Or as okay as he'll ever be. He's happy, which is a lot more than most of us can say—I mean, *I'm* happy but I know a lot of people who aren't."

"Won't he get tired of boating?"

"I hope so," Gwen said lightly. "He can afford to do anything he wants, so if the leisure begins to pall, he'll find something useful to do. He's very smart and he's a very capable kid, in spite of the fact that he's idle right now. Sometimes I envy him that."

"Do you think it would distress the kids if I talked to them?"

Gwen was startled at that, the first time she'd seemed disconcerted by anything. "About their father?"

"I may have to at some point," I said. "I wouldn't like to do it without your knowledge, but it might really help."

"I suppose it would be all right," she said, but her tone was full of misgivings.

"We can talk about it later. It may not be necessary at all."

"Oh. Well. I don't see how it could hurt. I must say, I don't really understand why you're into this business again."

"To see if justice was done, I guess," I said. "It sounds melodramatic, but that's what it amounts to."

"Justice to whom. Laurence or Nikki?"

"Maybe you should tell me what you think. I'm assuming there was no love lost between you and them, but do you think he got his 'just desserts'?"

"Sure, why not? I don't know about her. I figure she had a fair trial and if that's the way it came out, well she must have done it. But there were times I'd have done it myself if I had thought of some way."

"So if she killed him, you wouldn't blame her?"

"Me and half a dozen others. Laurence alienated a lot of people," she said carelessly. "We could have formed a club and sent out a monthly newsletter. I still run into people who sidle up to me and say 'Thank God he's dead.' Literally. Out of the corner of their mouths." Gwen laughed again. "I'm sorry if that sounds irreverent but he was not a nice man."

"But who in particular?"

She put her hand on her hip and gave me a jaded look. "If you got an hour, I'll give you a list," she said.

I laughed then. Her humor seemed irrepressible or maybe she was only feeling ill at ease. Talking to a private eye is often unnerving to people.

Gwen put Wuffles in an empty cage and then went into the other room and led out a big English sheepdog. She lifted its front feet first, placing them on the table, and then she heaved its hind legs up while the dog whined uneasily.

"Oh come on, Duke," she snapped. "This one is such a sissy."

"Do you think we could talk again soon?" I asked.

"Sure, I'd like that. I close up here at six. If you're free then, we can have a drink. By the end of the day, I'm ready for one."

"Me too. I'll see you then," I said.

I hopped down off my stool and let myself out. When the door closed, she was already chatting with the dog. I wondered what else she knew and how much of it she was willing to share. I also hoped to hell I could look that good in another ten years.

6

I stopped off at a pay phone and gave Nikki a call. She picked up on the third ring.

"Nikki? This is Kinsey. I have a request. Is there any way I can get into the house where you and Laurence lived?"

"Sure. I still own it. I'm just leaving to drive up to Monterey to bring Colin back but it's en route. I can meet you there if you like."

She gave me the address and said she'd be there in fifteen minutes or so. I hung up and headed for my car. I wasn't sure what I was after but I wanted to walk through the place, to get a feel for what it was like, living as they lived. The house was in Montebello, a section of town where there are rumored to be more millionaires per square mile than in any other part of the country. Most of the houses are not even visible from the road. Occasionally you can catch a glimpse of a tiled roof hidden away in tangles of olive trees and live oak. Many parcels of land are bordered by winding walls of hand-hewn stone overgrown with wild roses and nasturtiums. Towering eucalyptus trees line the roads, with intermittent palms looking like Spanish exclamation points.

The Fifes' house was on the corner of two lanes, shielded from view by ten-foot hedges that parted at one point to admit a narrow brick driveway. The house was substantial: two stories of putty-colored stucco with white trim. The facade was plain and there was a portico to one side. The surrounding land was equally plain except for patches of California poppies in shades of peach and rich yellow, gold, and pink. Beyond the house, I could see a double garage with what I guessed was a caretaker's quarters above. The lawns were well tended and the house, while it had an unoccupied look, didn't seem neglected. I parked my car on the portion of the drive that circled back on itself to permit easy exit. In spite of the red-tiled roof, the house looked more French than Spanish: windows without cornices, the front door flush with the drive.

I got out of my car and walked around to the right, my footsteps making no sound on the pale rosy bricks. In the rear, I could see the outline of a swimming pool and for the first time, I felt something chill and out of place. The pool had been filled to the brim with dirt and trash. An aluminum lawn chair was half-sunk in the sod, weeds growing through the rungs. The diving board extended now over an irregular surface of grass clippings and dead leaves, as though the water had thickened and congealed. A set of steps with handholds disappeared into the depths and the surrounding concrete apron was riddled with dark splotches.

I found myself approaching with uneasiness and I was startled out of my concentration by the sound of malicious hissing. Waddling toward me with remarkable speed were two huge white geese, their heads thrust forward, mouths open like snakes with their tongues protruding, emitting a terrifying sound. I gave a low involuntary cry and began to backtrack toward my car, afraid to take my eyes off them. They covered the ground between us at a pace that forced me into a run. I barely reached my car before they caught up with me. I wrenched the door open and slammed it again with a panic I hadn't felt in years. I locked both doors, half expecting the viperous birds to batter at my windows until they gave way. For a moment they balanced, half lifted, wings flapping, black eyes bright with ill-will, their hissing faces even with mine. And then they lost interest and waddled off, honking and hissing, pecking savagely at the grass. Until that moment, it had never even occurred to me to include crazed geese among my fears, but they had suddenly shot straight to the top of the list along with worms and water bugs.

Nikki's car pulled in behind mine. She got out with perfect composure and approached as I rolled my window down. The two geese appeared again around the corner of the house, making their flat-footed beeline for the flesh of her calves. She gave them an idle glance and then laughed. Both raised up again, short wings flopping ineffectually, their manner suddenly benign. Nikki had a bread bag in her hand and she tossed them some crumbs.

"What the hell *are* those things?" I eased out of the

car cautiously but neither paid the slightest attention to me.

"That's Hansel and Gretel," she said amicably. "They're Embden geese."

"The geese part I could tell. What happened? Did somebody train them to kill?"

"It keeps little kids off the property," she said. "Come on in." She inserted a key in the lock and the front door swung open. Nikki stooped to pick up some junk mail that had been pushed through the slot. "The mailman gives them saltines," she said as an afterthought. "They'll eat anything."

"Who else had keys to this place?" I asked. I noticed an alarm-system panel, which was apparently turned off.

She shrugged. "Laurence and me. Greg and Diane. I can't think of anyone else."

"Gardener? Maid?"

"Both have keys now but I don't think they did at the time. We did have a housekeeper. Mrs. Voss. She probably had one."

"Did you have a security system then?"

"We do now but that's only been in the last four years. I should have sold the place years ago but I didn't want to make decisions like that when I was in prison."

"It must be worth a lot."

"Oh sure. Real-estate values have tripled and we paid seven hundred and fifty thousand at the time. He picked it out. Put it in my name for business reasons, but it never did appeal to me much."

"Who did the decorating?" I asked.

Nikki smiled sheepishly. "I did. I don't think Laurence knew any better, but I took a subtle revenge. He insisted that we buy the place so I left all the color out."

The rooms were large, ceilings high, and plenty of light came in. The floors were dark-stained tongue and groove. The layout was very conventional: living room to the right, dining room to the left, with the kitchen behind. There was a sitting room beyond the living room and a long glassed-in porch along that side, running the length of the house. There was a curious air to the house, which I assumed was because no one had lived there for years, like a department-store display of especially elegant appointments. The furniture was still in place and there was no sign of dust. There were no plants and no magazines, no evidence of ongoing activity. Even the silence had a hollow tone, barren and lifeless.

The whole interior was done in neutral tones: grays and oyster whites, hazel and cinnamon. The couches and chairs were soft upholstered pieces with rounded arms and thick cushions, a sort of art deco look without any attempt at flash. There was a nice blend of modern and antique and it was clear that Nikki knew what she was doing even when she didn't care.

Upstairs, there were five bedrooms, all with fireplaces, all with bathrooms of remarkable size, deep closets, dressing rooms, the whole of it carpeted in thick fawn-colored wall-to-wall wool shag.

"This is the master suite?"

Nikki nodded. I followed her into the bathroom. Fat chocolate towels were stacked near the sink. There was a sunken tub, the surrounding ceramic tile a pale tobacco shade. There was a separate glassed-in shower that had been outfitted as a steam room. Soap, toilet paper, Kleenex.

"Do you stay here?" I asked as we came down the stairs.

"I haven't as yet, but I may. I have someone come in every two weeks to clean and of course there's a gardener on the premises all the time. I've been staying at the beach."

"You have another house out there?"

"Yes. Laurence's mother left it to me."

"Why you and not him?"

She smiled slightly. "Laurence and his mother didn't get along. Would you like some tea?"

"I thought you had to hit the road."

"I have time."

I followed her out to the kitchen. There was a cooking island in the center of the room with a big copper hood above the burners, a wide expanse of chopping block counter, and all manner of pans, baskets, and kitchen implements hanging on a circular metal rack that extended from the ceiling. All of the other counters were white ceramic tile; a double stainless-steel sink was sunk into one. There was a regular oven, a convection oven, a microwave, a refrigerator, two freezers, and impressive storage space.

Nikki put some water on to boil and perched herself on a wooden stool. I took up a stool across from her, the two of us sitting in the center of the room, which looked as much like a chem lab as a cook's dream.

"Who have you talked to so far?" she asked.

I told her about my conversation with Charlie Scorsoni.

"They seem like an odd pair of friends to me," I said. "My recollection of Laurence is a little hazy, but he always struck me as very elegant and cerebral. Scorsoni's very physical. He reminds me of a guy in an ad for chain saws."

"Oh Charlie's a real scrapper. From what I hear, he came up the hard way, bulldozing his way past all obstacles. Kind of like the blurb on a paperback: 'stepping over the bodies of those he loved . . .' Maybe Laurence liked that. He always talked about Charlie with grudging respect. Laurence had everything handed to him. Of course Charlie thought Laurence could do no wrong."

"That seemed clear enough," I said. "I don't suppose he had any motive for murder. Did you ever think he might have had a hand in it?"

Nikki smiled, getting up to take out cups, saucers, and tea bags. "At one time or another, I've considered everyone, but Charlie seems unlikely to me. He certainly didn't benefit financially or professionally . . ." She poured boiling water into both cups.

"As far as the eye can see," I said, dunking my tea bag.

"Well yes, that's true. I suppose there might have

been some kind of hidden dividend, but surely that would have come to light at some point in the last eight years."

"One would think." I went on to tell her about my interview with Gwen. Nikki's cheeks went ever so faintly pink.

"I feel bad about her," she said. "By the time they divorced, Laurence really hated her and I tended to fan the flames a bit. He never could take any responsibility for the failure of that marriage and as a result, he had to blame her and punish her. I didn't help. At first I really believed what he was saying about her. I mean, I personally thought she seemed like a capable person and I knew Laurence had been very dependent on her but it was safer to wean him away by feeding his bad feelings. You know what I mean? In some ways, his hating her so strongly was no different from his loving her, but it made me feel more secure to widen the breach. I'm ashamed of that now. When I fell out of love with him myself and he began to turn on me, I suddenly recognized the process."

"But I thought you were the downfall of that relationship," I said, looking at her carefully through the steam rising from my teacup.

Nikki ran both hands into her hair, lifting it away from her head and letting it fall again, giving her head a slight toss. "Oh no," she said, "I was his revenge. Never mind the fact that he'd been screwing around on her for years. He found out she was having an affair so he had me. Nice, huh? I didn't realize all this until much later, but that's how it was."

"Wait a minute. Let me see if I got this straight," I said. "He found out *she* was involved with someone, so he gets involved with you and then divorces her. From what I understand she got reamed."

"Oh yes. That's exactly what he did. The affair with me was his way of proving he didn't care. Taking the kids and the money was her punishment. He was very vindictive. It was one reason he made such a good attorney. He identified passionately with anyone who'd been wronged. He'd whip himself into a frenzy over the least little thing and then he'd use that as a driving force until he'd ground the opposition down. He was merciless. Absolutely merciless."

"Who did Gwen have the affair with?"

"You'd have to ask her that. I'm not sure I ever knew. It was certainly something he never talked about."

I asked her about the night Laurence died and she filled me in on those details.

"What was he allergic to?"

"Animal hair. Mostly dogs but cat dander too. For a long time he wouldn't tolerate pets in the house but then when Colin was two, someone suggested that we get him a dog."

"I understand Colin's deaf."

"He was born deaf. They test newborns' hearing so we knew right away, but nothing could be done for him. Apparently I had a mild case of German measles before I even realized I was pregnant. Fortunately that was the only damage he seemed to suffer. We were lucky to that extent."

"And the dog was for him? Like a guard dog or something?"

"Something like that. You can't watch a kid night and day. That's why we had the pool filled in. Bruno was a big help too."

"A German shepherd."

"Yes," Nikki said and then hesitated slightly. "He's dead now. He got hit by a car right out there on the road, but he was a great dog. Very smart, very loving, very protective of Colin. Anyway, Laurence could see what it did for him, having a dog like Bruno, so he went back on the allergy medication. He really did love Colin. Whatever his faults, and he had lots of them, believe me, he did love that little boy."

Her smile faded and her face went through an odd alteration. She was suddenly gone, disengaged. Her eyes were blank and the look she gave me was empty of emotion.

"I'm sorry, Nikki. I wish we didn't have to go into all of this."

We finished our tea and then got up. She removed the cups and saucers, tucking them into the dishwasher. When she looked back at me, her eyes were that flat gun-metal gray again. "I hope you find out who killed him. I'll never be happy until I know."

The tone of her voice made my hands numb. There was a flash in her eyes like the one I'd seen in the eyes of the geese: malevolent, unreasoning. It was just a flicker and it quickly disappeared.

"You wouldn't try to get even, would you?" I asked.

She glanced away from me. "No. I used to think about that in prison a lot but now that I'm out, it doesn't seem that important to me. Right now, all I want is to have my son back. And I want to lie on the beach and drink Perrier and wear my own clothes. And eat in restaurants and when I'm not doing that, I want to cook. And sleep late and take bubble baths . . ." She stopped and laughed at herself and then took a deep breath. "So. No, I don't want to risk my freedom."

Her eyes met mine and I smiled in response. "You better hit the road," I said.

7

I stopped off at the Montebello Pharmacy while I was in the neighborhood. The pharmacist, whose name tag said "Carroll Sims," was in his fifties, medium height, with mild brown eyes behind mild tortoise-shell frames. He was in the midst of explaining to quite an old woman exactly what her medication was and how it should be taken. She was both puzzled and exasperated by the explanation but Sims was tactful, answering her flustered inquiries with a benign good-will. I could imagine people showing him their warts and cat bites, describing chest pains and urinary symptoms across the counter. When it was my turn, I wished I had some little ill I could tell him about. Instead, I showed him my I.D.

"What can I do for you?"

"Did you happen to work here eight years ago when Laurence Fife was murdered?"

"Well I sure did. I own the place. Are you a friend of his?"

"No," I said, "I've been hired to look into the whole case again. I thought this was a logical place to start."

"I don't think I can be much help. I can tell you the medication he was taking, dosage, number of refills, the doctor who prescribed it, but I can't tell you how the switch was made. Well, I can tell you that. I just can't tell you who did it."

Most of the information Sims gave me I already knew. Laurence was taking an antihistamine called HistaDril, which he'd been on for years. He consulted an allergist about once a year and the rest of the time the refill on the medication was automatically okayed. The only thing Sims told me that I hadn't known was that HistaDril had recently been taken off the market because of possible carcinogenic side-effects.

"In other words, if Fife had just taken the medication for a few more years, he might have gotten cancer and died anyway."

"Maybe," the pharmacist said. We stared at one another for a moment.

"I don't suppose you have any idea who killed him," I said.

"Nope."

"Well, I guess that's that. Did you see any of the trial?"

"Just when I testified. I identified the pill bottle as one of ours. It had been pretty recently refilled but Fife himself had done that and we'd chitchatted at the time. He'd been taking HistaDril for so long we hardly needed to talk about that."

"Do you remember what you did talk about?"

"Oh, the usual thing. I think there was a fire burning across the backside of the city about that time and we talked about that. A lot of people with allergies were bothered by the increase in air pollution."

"Was it bothering him?"

"It bothered everyone a little bit but I don't remember him being any worse off than anyone else."

"Well," I said, "I thank you for your time. If you think of anything else, will you give me a buzz? I'm in the book."

"Sure, if I think of anything," he said.

It was midafternoon and I wasn't meeting Gwen again until 6:00. I felt restless and out of sorts. Bit by bit, I was putting together background information, but nothing was really happening yet, and as far as I knew nothing might ever come of it. As far as the state of California was concerned, justice had been served and only Nikki Fife stood in contradiction of this. Nikki and the nameless, faceless killer of Laurence Fife who had enjoyed eight years of immunity from prosecution, eight years of freedom that I was now being hired to violate. At some point, I was bound to tread on someone's toes and that someone was not going to be happy with me.

I decided to go spy on Marcia Threadgill. At the time she tripped on that crack in the sidewalk, she had just come from the craft shop, having purchased items necessary to make one of those wooden purses covered with assorted shells. I imagined her decoupaging orange crates, making clever hanging ornaments out of egg cartons festooned with plastic sprigs of lily of the valley. Marcia Threadgill was twenty-six years old and she suffered from bad taste. The owner of the craft shop had filled me in on the projects she had done and every bit of it reminded me of my aunt. Marcia Threadgill was cheap at heart. She turned common trash into Christmas gifts. This is the mentality, in my opinion, that leads to cheating insurance companies and other sly ruses. This is the kind of person who would write to the Pepsi-Cola bottling plant claiming to have found a mouse hair in her drink, trying to net herself a free case of soda.

I parked a few doors down from her apartment and got out my binoculars. I slouched, focusing on her patio, and then sat up. "Well I'll be damned," I breathed.

In place of the nasty brown withered fern was a hanging plant of mammoth proportions, which must have weighed twenty pounds. Now how had she lifted that up to attach to a hook high above her head? A neighbor? A boyfriend? Had she done it herself perchance? I could even see the price tag stuck to one side of the pot. She'd bought it at a Gateway supermarket for $29.95, which was quite a price considering that it was probably full of fruit flies.

"Shit," I said. Where was I when she hoisted that mama up? Twenty pounds of glossy plant and moist soil on a chain at shoulder height. Had she stood on a chair? I drove straight over to the nearby Gateway supermarket and headed back to the produce department. There were five or six such plants—Dumbo ears or elephant tongues, whatever the damn things are called. I lifted one. Oh my God. It was worse than I had thought. Awkward and heavy, impossible to manage without help. I picked up some film in the Ten Items or Less, No Checks line and loaded my camera. "Marcia, you little sweetheart," I cooed, "I'm gonna nail your ass."

I drove back to her apartment and got out my binoculars again. I'd no more than settled down on my spine, glasses trained on her patio, than Ms. Threadgill herself appeared, trailing one of those long plastic hoses, which must have been attached to her faucet inside. She misted and sprayed and watered and carried on, poking a finger down into the dirt, plucking a yellowing leaf from another potted plant on the patio rail. A real obsessive type by the look of it, inspecting the underside of leaves for God knows what pests. I studied her face. She looked like she'd spent about forty-five dollars having a free makeup demonstration in some department store. Mocha and caramel on her eyelids. Raspberry on her cheekbones. Lipstick the color of chocolate. Her fingernails were long and painted the approximate shade of cherry syrup in the sort of boxed candies you wish you hadn't bitten into so eagerly.

An old woman in a nylon jersey dress came out onto the patio above Marcia's and the two had a conversation. I guessed that it was some kind of complaint because neither looked happy and Marcia eventually flounced away. The old lady yelled something after her that looked dirty even in pantomime. I got out of the car and locked it, taking a clipboard and legal pad.

Marcia's apartment was listed on the register as 2-C.

The apartment above hers was listed under the name Augusta White. I bypassed the elevator and took the stairs, pausing first outside Marcia's door. She was playing a Barry Manilow album full-blast, and even as I listened she cranked up the volume a notch or two. I went up another flight and tapped on Augusta's door. She was there in a flash, her face thrust forward through the crack like a Pekingese, complete with bulging eyes, pug nose, and chin whiskers. "Yes?" she snapped. She was eighty years old if a day.

"I'm in the building next door," I said. "We've had some complaints about the noise and the manager asked me to look into it. Could I talk to you?" I held up my official-looking clipboard.

"Hold on."

She moved away from the door and stomped back into her kitchen to get her broom. I heard her bang on the kitchen floor a few times. From below, there was a mighty thump, as though Marcia Threadgill had whacked on the ceiling with a combat boot.

Augusta White stomped back, squinting at me through the crack. "You look like a real-estate agent to me," she said suspiciously.

"Well, I'm not. Honest."

"You look like one anyway so just go on off with your papers. I know all the people next door and you aren't one." She slammed the door shut and shot the bolt into place.

So much for that. I shrugged and made my way back down the stairs. Outside again, I made an eyeball assessment of the terraces. The patios were staggered in a pyramid effect and I had a quick flash of myself climbing up the outside of the building like a second-story man to spy on Marcia Threadgill at close range. I had really hoped I could enlist someone's aid in getting a firsthand report of Ms. Threadgill, but I was going to have to let it slide for a moment. I took some pictures of the hanging plant from the vantage point of my car, hoping it would soon wither and perish from a bad case of root rot. I wanted to be there when she hung a new one into place.

I went back to my apartment and jotted down some notes. It was 4:45 and I changed into my jogging clothes: a pair of shorts and an old cotton turtleneck. I'm really not a physical fitness advocate. I've been in shape maybe once in my life, when I qualified for the police academy, but there's something about running that satisfies a masochistic streak. It hurts and I'm slow but I have good shoes and I like the smell of my own sweat. I run on the mile and a half of sidewalk that tracks the beach, and the air is usually slightly damp and very clean. Palm trees line the wide grassy area between the sidewalk and the sand and there are always other joggers, most of them looking lots better than I.

I did two miles and then called it quits. My calves hurt. My chest was burning. I huffed and puffed, bending from the waist, imagining all kinds of toxic wastes pumping out through my pores and lungs, a regular purge. I walked for half a block and then I heard a car horn toot. I glanced over. Charlie Scorsoni had pulled in at the curb in a pale blue 450 SL that looked very good on him. I wiped the sweat trickling down my face on an upraised shirt sleeve and crossed to his car.

"Your cheeks are bright pink," he said.

"I always look like I'm having an attack. You should see the looks I get. What are you doing down here?"

"I felt guilty. Because I cut you short yesterday. Hop in."

"Oh no." I laughed, still trying to catch my breath. "I don't want to get sweat all over your seats."

"Can I follow you back to your place?"

"Are you serious?"

"Sure," he said. "I thought I'd be especially winsome so you wouldn't put me on your 'possibly guilty' list."

"Won't help. I'm suspicious of everyone."

When I came out of the shower and stuck my head around the bathroom door, Scorsoni was looking at the books stacked up on my desk. "Did you have time to search through the drawers?" I asked.

He smiled benignly. "They were locked."

I smiled and closed the bathroom door again, getting dressed. I noticed that I was pleased to see him and that didn't sit well with me. I'm a real hard-ass when it comes to men. I don't often think of a forty-eight-year-old man as "cute" but that's how he struck me. He was big and his hair had a nice curl to it, his rimless glasses making his blue eyes look almost luminous. The dimple in his chin didn't hurt either.

I left the bathroom, moving toward the kitchenette in my bare feet. "Want a beer?"

He was sitting on the couch by then, leafing through a book about auto theft. "Very literate taste," he said. "Why don't you let me buy you a drink?"

"I have to be somewhere at six," I said.

"Beer's fine then."

I uncapped it and handed it to him, sitting down at the other end of the couch with my feet tucked up under me. "You must have left the office early. I'm flattered."

"I'll go back tonight. I have to go out of town for a couple of days and I'll have to get my briefcase packed, tidy up some loose ends for Ruth."

"Why take time out for me?"

Scorsoni gave me a quizzical smile with the barest hint of irritation. "God, so defensive. Why not take time out for you? If Nikki didn't kill Laurence, I'm as interested as anyone in finding out who did it, that's all."

"You don't believe she's innocent for a minute," I said.

"I believe you believe it," he said.

I looked at him carefully. "I can't give you information. I hope you understand that. I could use any help you've got and if you have a brainstorm, I'd love to hear it, but it can't be a two-way street."

"You want to lecture an attorney about client privilege, is that it? Jesus Christ, Millhone. Give me a break."

"Okay, okay. I'm sorry," I said. I looked down at his big hands and then up at his face again. "I just didn't want my brain picked, that's all."

His expression relaxed and his smile was lazy. "You said you didn't know anything anyway," he pointed out, "so what's to pick? You're such a goddamn *grouch*."

I smiled then. "Listen, I don't know what my chances are on this thing. I don't have a feel for it yet and it's making me nervous."

"Yeah and you've been working on it—what—two days?"

"About that."

"Then give yourself a break while you're at it." He took a sip of beer and then with a small tap set the bottle on the coffee table. "I wasn't very honest with you yesterday," he said.

"About what?"

"Libby Glass. I did know who she was and I suspected that he was into some kind of relationship with her. I just didn't think it was any of your business."

"I don't see how it could make any difference at this point," I said.

"That's what I decided. And maybe it's important to your case—who knows? I think since he died, I've tended to invest him with a purity he never really had. He played around a lot. But his taste usually ran to the moneyed class. Older women. Those slim elegant ones who marry aristocracy."

"What was Libby like?"

"I don't really know. I ran into her a couple of times when she was setting up our tax account. She seemed nice enough. Young. She couldn't have been more than twenty-five or twenty-six."

"Did he tell you he was having an affair with her?"

"Oh no, not him. I never knew him to kiss and tell."

"A real gentleman," I said.

Scorsoni shot me a warning look.

"I'm not being facetious," I said hastily. "I've heard he kept his mouth shut about the women in his life. That's all I meant."

"Yeah, he did. He played everything close to his chest. That's what made him a good attorney too. He never tipped his hand, never telegraphed. The last six months before he died, he was odd though, protective. There were times when I almost thought he wasn't well, but it wasn't physical. It was some kind of psychic pain, if you'll excuse the phrase."

"You had drinks with him that night, didn't you?"

"We had dinner. Down at the Bistro. Nikki was off someplace and we played racquetball and then had a bite to eat. He was fine as far as I could tell."

"Did he have the allergy medication with him then?"

Scorsoni shook his head. "He wasn't much for pills anyway. Tylenol if he had a headache, but that was rare. Even Nikki admitted that he took the allergy cap after he got home. It had to be someone who had access to that."

"Had Libby Glass been up here?"

"Not for business as far as I know. She might have come up to see him but he never said anything to me. Why?"

"I don't know. I was just thinking that somebody might have dosed them both somehow at the same time. She didn't die until four days later but that's not hard to explain if the caps were self-administered."

"I never heard much about her death. I don't even think it hit the papers here. He was down in Los Angeles though, I do know that. About a week and a half before he died."

"That's interesting. I'm going down there anyway. Maybe I can check that out."

He glanced at his watch. "I better let you go," he said, getting up. I got up and ambled to the door with him, oddly reluctant to see him go.

"How'd you lose the weight?" I said.

"What, this?" he asked, slapping his midsection. He leaned toward me slightly as though he meant to confide some incredible regimen of denial and self-abuse.

"I gave up candy bars. I used to keep 'em in my desk drawer," he murmured conspiratorially. "Snickers and Three Musketeers, Hershey's Kisses, with the silver wrappers and the little paper wick at the top? A hundred a day . . ."

I could feel a laugh bubble up because his tone was caressing and he sounded like he was confessing to a secret addiction to wearing panty hose. Also because I knew if I turned my face, I'd be closer to him than I thought I could cope with at that point.

"Mars Bars? Baby Ruths?" I said.

"All the time," he said. I could almost feel the heat of his face and I slid a look up at him sideways. He laughed at himself then, breaking the spell, and his eyes held mine only a little longer than they should. "I'll see you," he said.

We shook hands as he left. I didn't know why—maybe just an excuse to touch. Even a contact that casual made the hairs stand up along my arm. My early-warning system was clanging away like crazy and I wasn't sure how to interpret it. It's the same sensation I have sometimes on the twenty-first floor when I open a window—a terrible attraction to the notion of tumbling out. I go a long time between men and maybe it was time again. Not good, I thought, not good.

8

When I pulled up in front of K-9 Korners at 6:00, Gwen was just locking up. I rolled down my car window and leaned across the seat. "You want to go in my car?"

"I better follow you," she said. "Do you know where the Palm Garden is? Is that all right with you?"

"Sure, that's fine."

She moved off toward the parking lot and a minute later she pulled out of the driveway in a bright yellow Saab. The restaurant was only a few blocks away and we pulled into the parking lot side by side. She had stripped off her smock and was brushing haphazardly at the lap of her skirt.

"Pardon the dog hair," she said. "Usually I head straight for a bath."

The Palm Garden is located in the heart of Santa Teresa, tucked back into a shopping complex, with tables outside and the requisite palms in big wooden tubs. We found a small table off to one side and I ordered white wine while she ordered Perrier.

"You don't drink?"

"Not much. I gave that up when I got divorced. Before that I was knocking back a *lot* of Scotch. How's your case?"

"It's hard to tell at this point," I said. "How long have you been in the dog-grooming business?"

"Longer than I'd like," she said and laughed.

We talked for a while about nothing in particular. I wanted time to study her, hoping to figure out what she and Nikki Fife had in common that both of them had ended up married to him. It was she who brought the conversation back around to the subject at hand. "So fire away," she said.

I curtsied mentally. She was very deft, making my job much easier than I'd thought she would. "I didn't think you'd be so cooperative."

"You've been talking to Charlie Scorsoni," she said.

"It seemed like a logical place to start," I said with a shrug. "Is he on your list?"

"Of people who might have killed Laurence? No. I don't think so. Am I on his?"

I shook my head.

"That's odd," she said.

"How so?"

She tilted her head, her expression composed. "He thinks I'm bitter. I've heard it from a lot of different sources. Small town. If you wait long enough, anyone's opinion about you will be reported back."

"It sounds like you'd be entitled to a little bitterness."

"I worked that through a long time ago. By the way,

this is where you can reach Greg and Diane if you're interested." She pulled an index card out of her purse with the two names, addresses, and telephone numbers.

"Thanks. I appreciate that. Any advice about how they should be approached? I was serious when I said I didn't want to upset them."

"No, no. They're straight shooters, both of them. If anything, you might find them a little *too* up front."

"I understand they haven't kept in touch with Nikki."

"Probably not, but that's too bad. Old business. I'd much rather see them let that go. She was very good to them." She reached back then and pulled the scarf out of her hair, shaking her hair slightly so that it would fall loose. It was shoulder-length, an interesting shade of gray that I didn't imagine had been tampered with. The contrast was nice . . . gray hair, brown eyes. She had strong cheekbones, nice lines around her mouth, good teeth, a tan that suggested health without vanity.

"What did you think of Nikki?" I asked, now that the subject had been broached.

"I'm not really sure. I mean, I resented the hell out of her back then but I'd like to talk to her sometime. I feel like we might understand each other a lot better. You want to know why I married him?"

"I'd be interested in that."

"He had a big cock," she said impishly and then laughed. "Sorry. I couldn't resist that. Actually he was awful in the sack. A regular screwing machine. Terrific if you like your sex depersonalized."

"I'm not crazy about that kind myself," I said dryly.

"Neither was I when I figured it out. I was a virgin when I married him."

"Jesus," I said. "That's a bore."

"It was an even bigger bore back then but it was all part of the message I was raised on. I always thought the failure was mine in terms of our sex life . . ." She trailed off and the faintest tint came to her cheeks.

"Until what," I ventured.

"Maybe I should have wine too," she said and signaled to the waitress. I ordered a second glass. Gwen turned to me.

"I had an affair when I turned thirty."

"Shows you had *some* sense."

"Well yes and no. It only lasted about six weeks but it was the best six weeks of my life. In a way, I was glad to see it end. It was powerful stuff and it would have turned my life around. I wasn't ready for that." She paused and I could see her reviewing the information in her head. "Laurence was always very critical of me and I believed I deserved it. Then I ran into a man who thought I could do no wrong. At first I resisted. I knew what I was feeling for this man but it went against the grain. Finally I just gave in. For a while I told myself it was good for my relationship with Laurence. I was suddenly getting something I'd needed for a long time and it made me feel very giving with him. And then the double life began to take its toll. I deceived Laurence for as long as I could but he began to suspect something was going on. I got so I couldn't tolerate his touch—too much tension, too much deceit. Too much good stuff somewhere else. He must have felt the change come over me because he began to probe and question, wanted to know where I was every minute of the day. Called at odd hours in the afternoon and of course I was out. Even when I was with Laurence, I was somewhere else. He threatened me with divorce and I got scared so I 'fessed up. That was the biggest mistake of my life because he divorced me anyway."

"As punishment."

"As only Laurence Fife knew how. In spades."

"Where is he now?"

"My lover? Why do you ask?"

Her tone was instantly guarded, her expression wary.

"Laurence must have known who he was. If he was punishing you, why not punish the other guy too?"

"I don't want to cast suspicion on him," she said. "That would be a lousy thing to do. He had nothing to do with Laurence's death. I'll give you a written guarantee."

"What makes you so sure? A lot of people were mistaken about a lot of things back then and Nikki paid a price for it."

"Hey," she said sharply, "Nikki was represented by the best lawyer in the state. Maybe she got a few bad breaks and maybe not, but there's no point in trying to lay the blame on someone who had nothing to do with it."

"I'm not trying to blame anyone. I'm just trying to come up with a direction on this thing. I can't force you to tell me who he is . . ."

"That's right and I think you'd have a hell of a time finding out from anyone else."

"Look, I'm not here to pick a fight. I'm sorry. Skip that for now."

Two patches of red appeared on her neck. She was fighting back anger, trying to get control of herself again. I thought, for a moment, she would bolt.

"I'm not going to press the point," I said. "That's a whole separate issue and I came here to talk to you. You don't want to talk about that then it's fine with me."

She still seemed poised for flight so I shut my mouth and let her work it out for herself. Finally I could see her relax a little and I realized then that I was as tense as she. This was too valuable a contact for me to blow.

"Let's go back to Laurence. Tell me about him," I said. "What were all the infidelities about?"

She laughed self-consciously then and took a sip of wine, shaking her head. "Sorry. I didn't mean to get upset but you took me by surprise."

"Yeah, well that happens now and then. Sometimes I surprise myself."

"I don't think he liked women. He was always expecting to be betrayed. Women were the people who did you in. He liked to get there first, or at least that's my guess. I suspect an affair for him was always a power relationship and he was top dog."

" 'Do unto others before they do unto you.' "

"Right."

"But who had an ax to grind with him? Who could have hated him that much?"

She shrugged and her composure seemed restored. "I've thought about that all afternoon and what's odd is that when it comes right down to it, I'm not sure. He had awful relationships with a lot of people. Divorce attorneys are never very popular, but most of them don't get murdered."

"Maybe it wasn't related to business," I suggested. "Maybe it wasn't an irate husband pissed off about alimony and child support. Maybe it was something else—'a woman scorned.'"

"Well there were a lot of those. But I think he was probably very slick about breaking things off. Or the women themselves were sufficiently recovered to recognize the limits of the relationship and move on. He did have an awful affair with the wife of a local judge, a woman named Charlotte Mercer. She'd have run him down in the street given half a chance. Or that's what I've heard since. She wasn't the type to let go gracefully."

"How'd you find out about it?"

"She called me up after he broke off with her."

"Before your divorce or afterwards?"

"Oh afterwards, because I remember thinking at the time that I wished she'd called sooner. I went into court with nothing."

"I don't understand," I said. "What good would it have done? You couldn't have gotten him on adultery even back then."

"He didn't get *me* on that either but it sure would have given me a psychological edge. I felt so guilty about what I'd done that I hardly put up a fight except when it came to the kids, and even then he beat me down. If she'd wanted to cause trouble, she could have been a big help. He still had his reputation to protect. Anyway, maybe Charlotte Mercer can fill you in."

"Wonderful. I'll tell her she's my number-one suspect."

Gwen laughed. "Feel free to mention my name if she wants to know who sent you. It's the least I can do."

After Gwen left, I looked up Charlotte Mercer's address in the telephone book by the pay phone in the rear. She and the judge lived up in the foothills above Santa Teresa in what turned out to be a sprawling one-story house with stables off to the right, the land all dust and scrub brush. The sun was just beginning to go down and the view was spectacular. The ocean looked like a wide lavender ribbon stitched up against a pink-and-blue sky.

A housekeeper in a black uniform answered the bell and I was left in a wide cool hallway while "the missus" was fetched. Light footsteps approached from the rear of the house and I thought at first the Mercers' teenage daughter (if there was one) had appeared in Charlotte's place.

"Yes, what is it?"

The voice was low and husky and rude and the initial impression of adolescence gave way rapidly.

"Charlotte Mercer?"

"Yes, that's right."

She was petite, probably five-four, maybe a hundred

pounds if that. Sandals, tank top, white shorts, her legs tawny and shapely. Not a line on her face. Her hair was a dusty blond, cut short, her makeup subdued. She had to be fifty-five years old and there was no way she could have looked that good without a team of experts. There was an artificial firmness to her jaw and her cheeks had that sleek tucked-up look that only a face-lift can provide at that late date. Her neck was lined and the backs of her hands were knotted with veins but those were the only contradictions to the appearance of slim, cool youth. Her eyes were a pale blue, made vivid by the skillful application of mascara and an eye shadow in two shades of gray. Gold bracelets jangled on one arm.

"I'm Kinsey Millhone," I said. "I'm a private investigator."

"Goody for you. What brings you here?"

"I'm looking into Laurence Fife's death."

Her smile faltered, sinking from minimal good manners into something cruel. She gave me a cursory inspection, dismissing me in the same glance. "I hope it won't take long," she said, and looked back. "Come out to the patio. I've left my drink there."

I followed her toward the back of the house. The rooms we passed looked spacious and elegant and un-used: windows sparkling, the thick powder-blue carpeting still furrowed with vacuum-cleaner tracks, fresh-cut flowers in professional arrangements on glossy tabletops. The wallpaper and drapes were end-less repetitions of the same blue floral print and every-thing smelled of Lemon Pledge. I wondered if she used it to disguise the mild scent of bourbon on the rocks that wafted after her. As we passed the kitchen, I could smell roast lamb laced with garlic.

The patio was shaded by latticework. The furniture was white wicker with bright green canvas cushions. She took up her drink from a coffee table of glass and wrought iron, plunking herself down on a padded chaise. She reached automatically for her cigarettes and a slim gold Dunhill. She seemed amused, as though I'd arrived solely to entertain her during the cocktail hour.

"Who sent you up here? Nikki or little Gwen?" Her eyes slid away from mine and she seemed to require no response. She lit her cigarette, pulling the half-filled ashtray closer. She waved a hand at me. "Have a seat."

I chose a padded chair not far from hers. An egg-shaped swimming pool was visible beyond the shrubs surrounding the patio. Charlotte caught my look.

"You want to stop and have a swim or what?"

I decided not to take offense. I had the feeling that sarcasm came easily to her, an automatic reaction, like someone with a smoker's cough.

"So who sent you up here?" she said, repeating herself. It was the second hint I had that she wasn't as sober as she should have been, even at that hour of the day.

"Word gets around."

"Oh, I'll bet it does," she said with a snort of smoke. "Well, I'll tell you this, sweetie pie. I was more than a piece of ass to that man. I wasn't the first and I wasn't the last but I was the fucking *best*."

"Is that why he broke it off?"

"Don't be a bitch," she said with a quick sharp look, but she laughed at the same time, low in her throat, and I suspected I might have gone up in her estimation. She apparently played fast and loose and didn't object to a cut now and then in the interest of a fair game. "Sure he broke it off. Why should I have secrets these days? I had a little wingding with him before he divorced Gwen and then he came back around a few months before he died. He was like some old tomcat, always sniffin' around the same back porch."

"What happened this last time?"

She gave me a jaded look as if none of it seemed to matter much. "He got involved with somebody else. Very hush-hush. Very hot. Screw him. He discarded me like yesterday's underpants."

"I'm surprised you weren't a suspect," I said.

Her brows shot up. "Me?" She hooted. "The wife of a prominent judge? I never even testified and they knew damn well that I was involved with him. The cops tiptoed around me like I was a fussy baby taking an unexpected nap. And who asked 'em to? I would have told 'em anything. Hell, I didn't give a shit. Besides, they already had their suspect."

"Nikki?"

"Sure, Nikki," she said expansively. Her gestures were relaxed, the hand with the cigarette waving languidly as she spoke. "You ask me, she was way too prissy to kill anyone. Not that anyone cared much what I thought. I'm just your Mrs. Loud-Mouth Drunk. What does she know? Who's going to listen to her? I could tell you things about anybody in this town and who'd pay attention to me? And you know how I find out? I'll tell you this. You'll be interested in this because that's what you do, too, find out about people, right?"

"More or less," I murmured, trying not to interrupt the flow. Charlotte Mercer was the type who'd barge right on if she didn't get sidetracked. She took a long drag on her cigarette, blowing smoke through her nose in two fierce streams. She coughed, shaking her head.

"Pardon me while I choke to death," she said, pausing to cough again. "You tell secrets," she went on, taking up from where she left off. "You tell the dirtiest damn thing you know and nine times out of ten, you'll net yourself something worse. You can try it yourself. I say anything. I tell stories on myself just to see what I get back. You want gossip, honey, you came to the right place."

"What's the word out on Gwen?" I asked, testing the waters.

Charlotte laughed. "You don't trade," she said. "You got nothing to swap."

"Well no, that's true. I wouldn't be in business long if I didn't keep my mouth shut."

She laughed again. She seemed to like that. My guess about her was that it made her feel important to know what she knew. I was hoping she liked to show off a little bit too. She might well have heard about Gwen's affair but I couldn't ask without tipping my hand so I just waited her out, hoping to pick up what I could.

"Gwen was the biggest chump who ever lived," she

said without much interest. "I don't like the type myself and I don't know how she held on to him as long as she did. Laurence Fife was one cold cookie, which was why I was so crazy about him if you haven't guessed. I can't stand a man who *fawns*, you know what I mean? I can't stand a man sucking up to me, but he was the kind who took you right on the floor and he didn't even look at you afterwards when he zipped up his pants."

"That sounds crude enough," I said.

"*Sex* is crude, which is why we all run around doing it, which is why I was such a good match for him. He was crude as he was mean and that's the truth about him. Nikki was too refined, too lah-de-dah. So was Gwen."

"So maybe he liked both extremes," I suggested.

"Well now, I don't doubt that. Probably so. Maybe he married the snooty ones and fooled around with flash."

"What about Libby Glass? Did you ever hear about her?"

"Nope. No dice. Who else?"

God, this woman made me wish I had a list. I thought fast, trying to milk her while she was in the mood. I had the feeling the moment would pass and she'd turn sullen again.

"Sharon Napier," I said, as though it were a parlor game.

"Oh yeah. I checked that one out myself. The first time I ever laid eyes on that little snake, I knew something was off."

"You think he was involved with her?"

"Oh no, it's better yet. Not her. Her *mother*. I hired a private dick to look that up. Ruined her life and Sharon knew about it, too, so up she pops years later and sticks it to him. Her parents broke up over him and Mommy had a nervous breakdown or turned to drink, some damn thing. I don't know all the details except he fucked everyone over but good and Sharon collected on that for *years*."

"Was she *blackmailing* him?"

"Not for bucks. For her livelihood. She couldn't *type*. She barely knew how to spell her own name. She just wanted revenge, so she shows up every day for work and she does what she feels like doing and thumbs her nose at him. He took anything she dished out."

"Could she have killed him?"

"Sure, why not? Maybe the gig wore thin or maybe just taking his pay from week to week wasn't good enough." She paused, pushing the ember out on her cigarette with a number of ineffectual stabs. She smiled over at me with cunning.

"I hope you don't think I'm rude," she said with a glance at the door. "But school's out. My esteemed husband, the good judge, is due home any second now and I don't want to sit and explain what you're doing in my house."

"Fair enough," I said. "I'll let myself out. You've been a big help."

"I'll bet." She got to her feet, setting her drink down on the glass-topped table with a resounding crack. There was no harm done and she recovered herself with a long slow look of relief.

She studied my face briefly. "You're gonna have to get your eyes done in a couple of years. Right now, you're okay," she pronounced.

I laughed. "I like lines," I said. "I earn mine. But thanks anyway."

I left her on the patio and went around the side of the house to where my car was parked. The conversation wasn't sitting that well with me and I was glad to be on my way. Charlotte Mercer was shrewd and perhaps not above using her drunkenness for its effect. Maybe she'd been telling the truth and maybe not. Somehow the revelation about Sharon Napier seemed too pat. As a solution, it seemed too obvious. On the other hand, the cops are sometimes right. Homicide usually isn't subtle and most of the time, you don't have that far to look.

9

It took me a day and a half to come up with an address on Sharon Napier. By means I'd just as soon not spell out, I tapped into the Department of Motor Vehicles computer and discovered that her driver's license had expired some six years back. I checked with the Auto Title Department, making a quick trip downtown, and found that a dark green Karmann Ghia was registered in her name with an address that matched the last-known address I had for her locally, but a side note indicated that the title had been transferred to Nevada, which probably meant that she'd left the state.

I placed a call to Bob Dietz, a Nevada investigator whose name I looked up in the National Directory. I told him what information I needed, and he said he'd call me back, which he did that afternoon. Sharon Napier had applied for and had been issued a Nevada driver's license; it showed a Reno address. His Reno sources, however, reported that she'd skipped out on a big string of creditors the previous March, which meant that she'd been gone for approximately fourteen months. He'd guessed that she was probably still in the state so he'd done some further nosing around. A small Reno credit company showed requests for information on her from Carson City and again from Las Vegas, which he thought was my best bet. I thanked him profusely for his efficiency and told him to bill me for his time but he said he'd just as soon trade tit for tat at some point, so I made sure he had my address and home phone if he needed it. I tried Information in Las Vegas, but there was no listing for her so I called a friend of mine down there and he said he'd check around. I told him I'd be driving to Los Angeles early in the week and gave him the number so he could reach me there in case it took him a while to pick up a lead on her.

The next day was Sunday and I devoted that to myself: laundry, housecleaning, grocery shopping. I even shaved my legs just to show I still had some class. Monday morning I did clerical work. I typed up a report for Nikki and put in another call to the local credit bureau just to double-check. Sharon Napier had apparently left town with a lot of money owed and a lot of people mad. They had no forwarding address so I gave them the information I had. Then I had a long talk with California Fidelity on the subject of Marcia Threadgill. For forty-eight hundred dollars, the insurance company was almost ready to settle with her and move on, and I had to argue with as much cunning as I could muster. My services on that one weren't costing them anything out of pocket and it pissed me off that they were halfway inclined to look the other way. I even had to stoop so low as to mention principles, which never sits that well with the claims manager. "She's cheating your *ass*," I kept saying, but he just shook his head as though there were forces at work that I was too dim to grasp. I told him to check with his boss and I'd get back to him.

By 2:00, I was on the road to Los Angeles. The other piece of the puzzle was Libby Glass and I needed to know how she fit into all of this. When I reached L.A., I checked into the Hacienda Motor Lodge on Wilshire, near Bundy. The Hacienda is not even re-motely hacienda-like—an L-shaped, two-story struc-ture with a cramped parking lot and a swimming pool surrounded by a chain-link fence with a padlock. A very fat woman named Arlette doubles as manager and switchboard operator. I could see straight into her apartment from the desk. It's furnished, I'm told, from her profits as a Tupperware lady, a little hustling she does on the side. She leans toward Mediterranean-style furniture upholstered in red plush.

"Fat is beautiful, Kinsey," she said to me confiden-tially as I filled out the registration card. "Looka here."

I looked. She was holding out her arm so that I could admire the hefty downhang of excess flesh.

"I don't know, Arlette," I said dubiously. "I keep try-ing to avoid it myself."

"And look at all the time and energy it takes," she said. "The problem is that our society shuns tubbos. Fat people are heavily discriminated against. Worse than the handicapped. Why, they got it easy compared to us. Everywhere you go now, there are signs out for them. Handicapped parking. Handicapped johns. You've seen those little stick figures in wheelchairs. Show me the international sign for the grossly over-weight. We got rights."

Her face was moon-shaped, surrounded by a girlish cap of wispy blonde hair. Her cheeks were perma-nently flushed as though vital supply lines were being dangerously squeezed.

"But it's so unhealthy, Arlette," I said. "I mean, don't you have to worry about high blood pressure, heart attacks . . ."

"Well there's hazards to everything. All the more reason we should be treated decently."

I gave her my credit card and after she made the im-print she handed me the key to room #2. "That's right up here close," she said. "I know how you hate being stuck out back."

"Thanks."

I've been in room #2 about twenty times and it is al-ways dreary in a comforting sort of way. A double bed. Threadbare wall-to-wall carpeting in a squirrel gray. A chair upholstered in orange plastic with one gimpy leg. On the desk, there is a lamp shaped like a football hel-met with "UCLA" printed on the side. The bathroom is small and the shower mat is paper. It is the sort of place where you are likely to find someone else's underpanties beneath the bed. It costs me $11.95 plus room tax in the off-season and includes a "Continental" breakfast—instant coffee and jelly doughnuts, most of which Arlette eats herself. Once, at midnight, a drunk sat on my front step and yelled for an hour and a half until the cops came and took him away. I stay there because I'm cheap.

I set my suitcase on the bed and took out my jogging clothes. I did a fast walk from Wilshire to San Vicente and then headed west at a trot as far as Twenty-sixth Street, where I tagged a stop sign and turned around, jogging back up to Westgate and across to Wilshire again. The first mile is the one that hurts. I was panting hard when I got back. Given the exhaust fumes I'd taken in from passing motorists on San Vicente, I figured I was about neck-and-neck with toxic wastes. Back in room #2 again, I showered and dressed and then checked back through my notes. Then I made some phone calls. The first was to Lyle Abernathy's last-known work address, the Wonder Bread Company, down on Santa Monica. Not surprisingly, he had left and the personnel office had no idea where he was. A quick check in the phone book showed no listing for him locally, but a Raymond Glass still lived in Sherman Oaks and I verified the street number I had noted from the police files up in Santa Teresa. I placed another call to my friend in Vegas. He had a lead on Sharon Napier but said it would take him probably half a day to pin it down. I alerted Arlette that he might be calling and cautioned her to make sure the information, if she took it, was exact. She acted a little injured that I didn't trust her to take phone messages for me, but she'd been negligent before and it had cost me plenty last time around.

I called Nikki in Santa Teresa and told her where I was and what I was up to. Then I checked my answering service. Charlie Scorsoni had called but left no number. I figured if it was important he'd call back. I gave my service the number where I could be reached. Having tagged all those bases, I went next door to a restaurant that seems to change nationalities every time I'm there. Last time I was in town, it was Mexican fare, which is to say very hot plates of pale brown goo. This time it was Greek: turdlike lumps wrapped in leaves. I'd seen things in roadside parks that looked about that good but I washed them down with a glass of wine that tasted like lighter fluid and who knew the difference? It was now 7:15 and I didn't have anything to do. The television set in my room was on the fritz so I wandered down to the office and watched TV with Arlette while she ate a box of caramel Ayds.

In the morning, I drove over the mountain into the San Fernando Valley. At the crest of the hill, where the San Diego Freeway tips over into Sherman Oaks, I could see a layer of smog spread out like a mirage, a shimmering mist of pale yellow smoke through which a few tall buildings yearned as though for fresh air. Libby's parents lived in a four-unit apartment building set into the crook of the San Diego and Ventura freeways, a cumbersome structure of stucco and frame with bay windows bulging out along the front. There was an open corridor dividing the building in half, with the front doors to the two downstairs apartments opening up just inside. On the right, a stairway led to the second-floor landing. The building itself affected no particular style and I guessed that it had gone up in the thirties before anybody figured out that California architecture should imitate southern mansions and Italian villas. There was a pale lawn of crab and Bermuda grasses intermixed. A short driveway along the left extended back to a row of frame garages, with four green plastic garbage cans chained to a wooden fence. The juniper bushes growing along the front of the building were tall enough to obscure the ground-floor windows and seemed to be suffering from some peculiar molting process that made some of the branches turn brown and the rest go bald. They looked like cut-rate Christmas trees with the bad side facing out. The season to be jolly, in this neighborhood, was long past.

Apartment #1 was on my left. When I rang the bell, it sounded like the br-r-r-r of an alarm clock running down. The door was opened by a woman with a row of pins in her mouth that bobbed up and down when she spoke. I worried she would swallow one.

"Yes?"

"Mrs. Glass?"

"That's right."

"My name is Kinsey Millhone. I'm a private investigator. I work up in Santa Teresa. Could I talk to you?"

She took the pins out of her mouth one by one and

stuck them into a pin cushion that she wore on her wrist like a bristling corsage. I handed her my identification and she studied it with care, turning it over as though there might be tricky messages written in fine print on the back. While she did that, I studied her. She was in her early fifties. Her silky brown hair was cut short, a careless style with strands anchored behind her ears. Brown eyes, no makeup, bare-legged. She wore a wraparound denim skirt, a washed-out Madras blouse in bleeding shades of blue, and the kind of cotton slippers I've seen in cellophane packs in grocery stores.

"It's about Elizabeth," she said, finally returning my I.D.

"Yes. It is."

She hesitated and then moved back into the living room, making way for me. I picked my way across the living-room floor and took the one chair that wasn't covered with lengths of fabric or patterns. The ironing board was set up near the bay window, the iron plugged in and ticking as it heated. There were finished garments hanging on a rack near the sewing machine on the far wall. The air smelled of fabric sizing and hot metal.

In the archway to the dining room, a heavyset man in his sixties sat in a wheelchair, his expression blank, his pants undone in front, heavy paunch protruding. She crossed the room and turned his chair around so that it faced the television set. She put headphones on him and then plugged the jack into the TV, which she flipped on. He watched a game show whether he liked it or not. A couple were dressed up like a boy and girl chicken but I couldn't tell if they were winning anything.

"I'm Grace," she said. "That's her father. He was in an automobile accident three years ago last spring. He doesn't talk but he can hear and any mention of Elizabeth upsets him. Help yourself to coffee if you like."

There was a ceramic percolator on the coffee table, plugged into an extension cord that ran back under the couch. It looked as if all the other appliances in the room were radiating from the same power source. Grace eased down onto her knees. She had about four yards of dark green silk spread out on the hardwood floor and she was pinning a handmade pattern into place. She held a magazine out to me, opened to a page that showed a designer dress with a deep slit up one side and narrow sleeves. I poured myself a cup of coffee and watched her work.

"I'm running this up for a woman married to a television star," she said mildly. "Somebody's sidekick. He got famous overnight and she says he's recognized even in the car wash now. People asking for his autograph. Has facials. Him, not her. He was poor, I hear, for the last fifteen years and now they go to all these parties in Bel Air. I do her clothes. He buys his on Rodeo Drive. She could, too, on the money he makes but it makes her feel insecure, she says. She's much nicer than he is. I already read in the *Hollywood Reporter*, 'New Two You,' him and somebody else 'pulling up steaks at

Stellini's.' She'd be smart to put an expensive wardrobe together before he leaves her if you ask me."

Grace seemed to be talking to herself, her tone distracted, a smile warming her face now and then. She picked up a pair of pinking shears and began to cut along the straight edge, the scissors making a crunching sound against the wood floor. For a while I didn't say anything. There was something hypnotic about the work and there seemed to be no compulsion to converse. The television flickered, and from an angle I could see the girl chicken jumping up and down, hands to her face. I knew the audience was urging her to do something—choose, pass, change boxes, take what was behind the curtain, give back the envelope, all of it taking place in silence while Libby's father looked on from his wheelchair incuriously. I thought she should consult her boy-chicken mate but he just stood there self-consciously like a kid who knew he was too old to be out in costume on Halloween. The tissue-paper pattern rustled as Grace removed it, folding it carefully before she laid it aside.

"I sewed for Elizabeth when she was young," she said. "Once she left home, of course, she only wanted store-bought. Sixty dollars for a skirt that only had twelve dollars' worth of wool at most, but she did have a good eye for color and she could afford to do as she pleased. Would you like to see a picture of her?" Grace's eyes strayed up to mine and her smile was wistful.

"Yes. I'd appreciate that."

She took the silk first and placed it on the ironing

board, testing the iron with a wet index finger as she passed. The iron spat back and she turned the lever down to "wool." There were two snapshots of Libby in a double frame on the windowsill and she studied them herself before she handed them to me. In one, Libby was facing the camera but her head was bent, her right hand upraised as though she were hiding her face. Her blonde hair was sun-streaked, cut short like her mother's but feathered back across her ears. Her blue eyes were amused, her grin wide, embarrassed to be caught, I couldn't think why. I'd never seen a twenty-four-year-old look quite so young or quite so fresh. In the second snapshot, the smile was only partially formed, lips parted over a flash of white teeth, a dimple showing near the corner of her mouth. Her complexion was clear, tinted with gold, lashes dark so that her eyes were delicately outlined.

"She's lovely," I said. "Really."

Grace was standing at the ironing board, touching up folds of silk with the tip of the iron, which sailed across the asbestos board like a boat on a flat sea of dark green. She turned the iron off and wiped her hands briefly down along her skirt, then took the pieces of silk and began to pin them together.

"I named her after Queen Elizabeth," she said and then she laughed shyly. "She was born on November 14, the same day Prince Charles was born. I'd have named her Charles if she'd been a boy. Raymond thought it was silly but I didn't care."

"You never called her Libby?"

"Oh no. She did that herself in grade school. She always had such a sense of who she was and how her life should be. Even as a child. She was very tidy—not prissy, but neat. She would line her dresser drawers with pretty floral wrapping papers and everything would be arranged just so. She liked accounting for the same reason. Mathematics was orderly and it made sense. The answers were always there if you worked carefully enough, or that's what she said." Grace moved over to the rocking chair and sat down, laying the silk across her lap. She began to baste darts.

"I understand she worked as an accountant for Haycraft and McNiece. How long was she there?"

"About a year and a half. She had done the accounts for her father's company—he did small-appliance repair—but it really didn't interest her, working for him. She was ambitious. She passed her CPA exam when she was twenty-two. She took a couple of computer courses, too, in night school, after that. She made very good grades. She had two junior accountants working under her, you know."

"Was she happy there?"

"I'm sure she was," Grace said. "She spoke of going to law school at one point. She enjoyed business management and finance. She liked working with figures and I know she was impressed because that company represented very wealthy people. She said you could learn a lot about someone's character by the way they spent money, what they bought and where—whether they lived within their means, that kind of thing. She said it was a study of human nature." Grace's voice was tinged with pride. It was hard for me to reconcile the idea of this prim-sounding CPA with the girl in the photographs who looked pretty, animated, bashful, and rather sweet, hardly a woman with a hard-driving purpose in life.

"What about her old boyfriend? Do you have any idea where he is now?"

"Who, Lyle? Oh, he'll be around in a bit."

"Here?"

"Oh my, yes. He stops by every day at noon to help me with Raymond. He's a lovely boy but of course you probably knew she broke off her engagement with him a few months before . . . she passed on. She went with Lyle all through high school and they both attended Santa Monica City College together until he dropped out."

"Is that when he went to work for Wonder Bread?"

"Oh no, Lyle's had many jobs. At the time Lyle left school, Elizabeth was in her own apartment and she didn't confide much in me but I feel she was disappointed in him. He was going to be a lawyer and then he simply changed his mind. He said law was too dull and he didn't like details."

"Did they live together?"

Grace's cheeks tinted slightly. "No, they didn't. It may sound odd and Raymond thought it was very wrong of me, but I encouraged them to move in together. I sensed that they were drifting apart and I thought it would help. Raymond was like Elizabeth, disenchanted with Lyle for quitting school. He told her she could do much better for herself. But Lyle adored her. I thought that should count for something.

He would have found himself. He had a restless nature, like many boys that age. He would have come to his senses and I told her so. He needed responsibility. She could have been a very good influence because she was so responsible herself. But Elizabeth said she didn't want to live with him and that was that. She was strong-willed when she wanted to be. And I don't mean that as criticism. She was as nearly perfect as a daughter could be. Naturally I wanted whatever she wanted but I couldn't bear to see Lyle hurt. He's very dear. You'll see when you meet him."

"And you have no idea what actually caused the breakup between them? I mean, could she possibly have been involved with someone else?"

"You're talking about that attorney up in Santa Teresa," she said.

"It's his death I'm looking into," I said. "Did she ever talk to you about him?"

"I never knew anything about him until the police came down from Santa Teresa to talk to us. Elizabeth didn't like to confide her personal affairs, but I don't believe Elizabeth would fall in love with a married man," Grace said. She began to fuss with the silk, her manner agitated. She closed her eyes and then pressed a hand to her forehead as though checking to see if she'd contracted a sudden fever. "I'm sorry. Sometimes I forget. Sometimes I pretend she got sick. The other makes me cringe, that someone might have done that to her, that someone could have hated her that much. The police here don't do anything. It isn't solved but no one cares anymore so I just . . . I simply tell myself she got sick and was taken. How could someone have done that to her?" Her eyes welled with tears. Her grief rolled across the space between us like a wash of salt water and I could feel tears form in my own eyes in response. I reached out and took her hand. For a moment, she clutched my fingers hard and then she seemed to catch herself, pulling back.

"It's been like a weight pressing on my heart. I will never recover from it. Never."

I phrased my next question with care. "Could it have been an accident?" I said. "The other man—Laurence Fife—died from oleander, which someone put in an allergy capsule. Suppose they'd been doing business together, going over accounts or something. Maybe she was sneezing or complaining about a stuffy nose and he just volunteered his own medication. People do that all the time."

She considered that for a moment uneasily. "I thought the police said the attorney died before she did. Days before."

"Maybe she didn't take the pill right away," I said, shrugging. "With something like that, you never know when someone will take a doctored capsule. Maybe she put it in her purse and swallowed it later without even realizing there was any jeopardy. Did she have allergies? Could she have been coming down with a cold?"

Grace began to weep, a small mewing sound. "I don't remember. I don't think so. She didn't have hay fever or anything like that. I don't even know who'd remember after all these years."

Grace looked at me then with those large, dark eyes.

She had a good face, almost childlike, with a small nose, a sweet mouth. She took out a Kleenex and wiped her cheeks. "I don't think I can talk about it anymore. Stay for lunch. Meet Lyle. Maybe he can tell you something that would help."

10

I sat on a stool in the kitchen and watched Grace make tuna fish salad for lunch. She had seemed to shake herself, as though wakening from a brief but vital nap and then she had put on her apron and cleared the dining-room table of the rest of her sewing paraphernalia. She was a woman who worked with care, her movements restful as she assembled placemats and napkins. I set the table for her, feeling like a well-behaved kid again while she rinsed lettuce and patted it dry, placing a layer on each plate like a doilie. She neatly pared thin ribbons of skin from several tomatoes and coiled them like roses. She fluted a mushroom for each plate, added two thin spikes of asparagus so that the whole of it looked like a flower arrangement. She smiled at me timidly, taking pleasure in the picture she had created. "Do you cook?"

I shook my head.

"I don't have much occasion to myself except when Lyle's here. Raymond wouldn't notice and I probably wouldn't bother at all if it were just for me." She lifted her head. "There."

I hadn't heard the truck pull into the driveway but she must have been tuned to Lyle's arrival. Her hand strayed unconsciously to a strand of hair, which she tucked back. He came in through a utility room off to the left, pausing around the corner, apparently to take off his boots. I heard two thunks. "Hey, babe. What's for lunch?"

He came around into the dining room with a grin, giving her cheek a noisy buss before he caught sight of me. He halted, the animation flickering off and on, then draining out of his face. He looked at her hesitantly.

"This is Miss Millhone," she said to him.

"Kinsey," I filled in, holding out my hand. He reached out and shook my hand automatically, but the central question still hadn't been answered. I suspected that I was intruding on an occasion that ordinarily admitted no variation. "I'm a private investigator from Santa Teresa," I said.

Lyle moved over to Raymond without another glance at me.

"Hey, Pops. How's it going today? You feeling okay?"

The old man's face registered nothing, but his eyes came into focus. Lyle took the headphones off, turning the set off too. The change in Lyle had been immediate and I felt as if I'd just seen snapshots of two different personalities in the same body, one joyful, the other keeping watch. He was not much taller than me and his body was trim, his shoulders wide. He had his shirt pulled out, unbuttoned down the front. His chest muscles were spare but well formed like those of a man who's been lifting weights. I guessed him to be about my own age. His hair was blond, worn long and faintly tinted with the green of a chlorinated swimming pool and hot sun. His eyes were a washed-out blue, too pale for his tan, his lashes bleached, his chin too narrow for the breadth of his cheeks. The overall effect was of a face oddly off—good looks gone slightly askew, as though under the surface there were a hairline crack. Some subterranean tremor had caused the bones to shift minutely and the two halves of his face seemed not quite to match. He wore faded jeans slung low on his hips and I could see the silky line of darkish hair pointing like an arrow toward his crotch.

He went about his business, ignoring me completely, talking to Grace while he worked. She handed him a towel, which he tucked under Raymond's chin, and then he proceeded to lather and shave him with a safety razor, which he rinsed in a stainless-steel bowl. Grace was taking out bottles of beer, removing the caps, pouring liquid into tulip glasses which she set at each place. There was no plate prepared for Raymond at all. When the shaving process had been completed, Lyle brushed Raymond's thinning white hair and then fed him a jar of baby food. Grace shot me a satisfied look. See what a dear he is? Lyle reminded me of an older brother caring for a toddler so that Mom would approve. She did. She looked on affectionately while Lyle scraped Raymond's chin with the bowl of the spoon, easing the drooling vegetable puree back into Raymond's slack mouth. Even as I watched, a stain began to spread across the front of Raymond's pants.

"Hey, don't worry about it, Pops," Lyle crooned, "we'll get you cleaned up after lunch. How's that?"

I could feel the muscles in my face setting with distaste.

During lunch, Lyle ate quickly, saying nothing to me and very little to Grace.

"What sort of work do you do, Lyle?" I said.

"Lay brick."

I looked at his hands. His fingers were long and dusted with mortar gray that had seeped down into the crevices of his skin. At this range, I could smell sweat, overlaid with the delicate scent of dope. I wondered if Grace noticed at all or if, perhaps, she thought it might be some exotic aftershave.

"I've got to make a run up to Vegas," I said to Grace, "but I'd like to stop back on my way up to Santa Teresa. Do you have any of Libby's belongings?" I was relatively certain she did.

Grace consulted Lyle with a quick look but his eyes were lowered to his plate. "I believe so. There are some boxes in the basement, aren't there, Lyle? Elizabeth's books and papers?"

The old man made a sound at the mention of her name and Lyle wiped his mouth, tossing the napkin down as he got up. He wheeled Raymond down the hallway.

"I'm sorry. I shouldn't have mentioned Libby," I said.

"Well that's all right," she said. "If you'll call or come by when you get back to Los Angeles, I'm sure it'd be all right if you looked at Elizabeth's belongings. There isn't much."

"Lyle doesn't seem to be in a very good mood," I remarked. "I hope he doesn't think I'm intruding."

"Oh no. He's quiet around people he doesn't know," she said. "I don't know what I'd do without him. Raymond is too heavy for me to lift. I have a neighbor who stops by twice a day to help me get him in and out of his chair. His spine was crushed in the accident."

Her conversational tone gave me the willies. "Do you mind if I use the bathroom?" I said.

"It's down the hall. The second door on the right."

As I passed the bedroom, I could see that Lyle had already lifted Raymond into bed. There were two straight-backed wooden chairs pushed up against the side of the double bed to keep him from falling out. Lyle was standing between the two chairs, cleaning Raymond's bare ass. I went into the bathroom and closed the door.

I helped Grace clear the table and then I left, waiting in my car across the street. I made no attempt to conceal myself and no pretense at driving away. I could see Lyle's pickup truck still parked in the driveway. I checked my watch. It was ten minutes to one and I figured he must be on a limited lunch hour. Sure enough, the side door opened and Lyle stepped out onto the narrow porch, pausing to lace his boots. He glanced over at the street, spotting my car, and seemed to smile to himself. Ass, I thought. He got into his truck and backed out of the driveway rapidly. I wondered for a moment if he intended to back straight across the street and into the side of my car, crushing me. He wheeled at the last minute, though, and flung the truck into gear, taking off with a chirp of rubber. I thought maybe we were going to have a little impromptu car chase but it turned out he didn't have that far to go. He drove eight blocks and then pulled into the driveway of a modest-sized Sherman Oaks house that was being refaced with red brick. I guessed it was a status symbol of some sort because brick is very expensive on the West Coast. There probably aren't six brick houses in the whole city of L.A.

He got out of his truck and ambled around to the back, tucking in his shirt, his manner insolent. I parked on the street and locked my car, following him. I wondered idly if he intended to smash my head in with a brick and then mortar me into a wall. He was not pleased with my arrival on the scene and he made no bones about that. As I rounded the corner, I could see that the owner of the house was disguising his little cottage with a whole new facade. Instead of looking like a modest California bungalow, it would look like certain pet hospitals in the Midwest, real high-rent stuff. Lyle was already mixing up mortar in a wheelbarrow in the back. I picked my way across some two-by-fours with crooked rusty nails protruding. A little kid would have to have a lot of tetanus shots after falling on those.

"Why don't we start all over again, Lyle," I said conversationally.

He snorted, taking out a cigarette, which he tucked into the corner of his mouth. He lit it, cupping crusty hands around the match, and then blew out the first mouthful of smoke. His eyes were small and one of them squinted now as the smoke curled up across his face. He reminded me of early photographs of James Dean—that defensive hunched stance, the crooked smile, the pointed chin. I wondered if he was a secret admirer of *East of Eden* reruns, staying up late at night to watch on obscure channels piped in from Bakersfield.

"Hey, come on. Why don't you talk to me," I said.

"I don't have nothin' to say to you. Why stir up all that shit again?"

"Aren't you interested in who killed Libby?"

He took his time about answering. He picked up a brick, holding it upright while he applied a thick layer of mortar to one end with a trowel, beveling the soft cement as if it were a gritty gray cheese. He laid the brick on the chest-high line of bricks where he'd been working and gave it a few taps with a hammer, bending down then to pick up the next brick.

I cupped my right hand to my ear. "Hello?" I said, as if I might have gone temporarily deaf.

He smirked, cigarette bobbing in his mouth. "You think you're real hot shit, don't you?"

I smiled. "Listen, Lyle. There's no point in this. You don't have to tell me anything and you know what I can do? Spend about an hour and a half this afternoon finding out anything I want to know about you. I can do it in six phone calls from a motel room in West Los

Angeles and I've even got someone paying me for my time, so it's nothing to me. It's fun, if you really want to know the truth. I can get your service records, credit rating. I can find out if you've ever been arrested for anything, job history, library books overdue . . ."

"Go right ahead. I got nothin' to hide."

"Why put us through all that stuff?" I said. "I mean, I can go check you out but I'll just come back around here tomorrow and if you don't like me now, you ain't gonna like me any better then. I might be in a bad mood. Why don't you just loosen up?"

"Aw, I'm real loose," he said.

"What happened to your plans to go to law school?"

"I dropped out," he said sullenly.

"Maybe the dope smoking got to you," I suggested mildly.

"Maybe you can go get fucked," he snapped. "Do I look like a lawyer to you? I lost interest, okay? That's no fuckin' crime."

"I'm not accusing you of anything. I just want to figure out what happened to Libby."

He flipped the ash off the cigarette and dropped it, chunking it into the dirt with the toe of his boot. I sat down on a pile of bricks that had been covered with a tarp. Lyle glanced over at me through lowered lids.

"What makes you think I smoke dope anyway?" he asked abruptly.

I tapped my nose, letting him know I'd smelled it on him. "Also laying brick doesn't seem that interesting," I said. "I figure if you're smart, you gotta do something to keep from going nuts."

He looked at me, his body relaxing just a little bit. "What makes you think I'm smart?"

I shrugged. "You went with Libby Glass for ten years."

He thought about that for a while.

"I don't know anything," he said, almost gruffly.

"You know more than I do at this point."

He was beginning to relent, though his shoulders were still tense. He shook his head, going back to his work. He took the trowel and moved the damp mass of mortar around like cake icing that has gone all granular. "She dumped me after she met that guy from up north. That attorney . . ."

"Laurence Fife?"

"Yeah, I guess it was. She wouldn't tell me anything about him. At first, it was business—something about some accounts. His law firm had just hooked up with the place she worked and she had to get all this stuff on the computer, you know? Set up to run smoothly from month to month. It was all real complicated, calls goin' back and forth, things like that. He came down a few times and she'd have drinks when they finished up, sometimes dinner. She fell in love. That's all I know."

He took out a small metal brace at right angles and hammered it into the wooden siding on the house, placing a mortar-laden brick on top.

"What's that do?" I asked out of curiosity.

"What? Oh. That keeps the brick wall from falling away from the rest," he said.

I nodded, halfway tempted to try laying brick myself. "And she broke up with you after that?" I asked, getting back to the point.

"Pretty much. I'd see her now and again, but it was over and I knew it."

He was beginning to drop the tension in his tone and he sounded more resigned than angry. Lyle buttered another brick with soft mortar and set it in place. The sun felt good on my back and I settled on my elbows, leaning back on the tarp.

"What's your theory?" I asked.

He looked at me slyly. "Maybe she killed herself."

"Suicide?" The thought hadn't even crossed my mind.

"You asked. I'm just tellin' you what I thought at the time. She sure was hung up on him."

"Yeah, but enough to kill herself when he died?"

"Who knows?" He lifted one shoulder and let it drop.

"How did she find out about his death?"

"Someone called her and told her about it."

"How do you know that?"

"Because she called me up. At first she didn't know what to make of it."

"She was grieving for him? Tears? Shock?"

He seemed to think back. "She was just real confused and upset. I went over there. She asked me to come and then she changed her mind and said she didn't want to talk about it. She was shaky, couldn't concentrate. It kind of made me mad that she was jerking me around, so I left. Next thing I knew, she was dead."

"Who found her?"

"The apartment manager where she lived. She didn't show up for work for two days and didn't call in, so her boss got worried and went over to her place. The manager tried peeping in the windows but the drapes were shut. They knocked some, front and back, and finally got in with a passkey. She was lying on the bathroom floor in her robe. She'd been dead for three days."

"What about her bed? Had it been slept in?"

"I don't know. The police didn't give that out."

I thought about that for a minute. It sounded like she might have taken a capsule at night, just as Laurence Fife had. It still seemed to me it might have been the same medication—some kind of antihistamine capsule in which someone had substituted oleander.

"Did she have allergies, Lyle? Was she complaining of a head cold or anything like that when you saw her last?"

He shrugged. "She might have, I guess. I don't remember anything like that. I saw her Thursday night. Wednesday or Thursday of that week when she heard that attorney was dead. She died on Saturday night late, they said. That much they put in the paper when it happened."

"What about this attorney she was involved with? Do you know if he kept anything at her place? Tooth brush? Razor? Things like that? Maybe she took medication that was meant for him."

"How do I know?" he said testily. "I don't stick my nose where it doesn't belong."

"Did she have a girl friend? Someone she might have confided in?"

"Maybe from work. I don't remember anyone in particular. She didn't have 'girl friends.'"

I took out my notebook and jotted down the telephone number at my motel. "This is where I can be reached. Will you give me a call if you think of anything else?"

He took the slip of paper and tucked it carelessly into the back pocket of his jeans. "What's in Las Vegas?" he asked. "How does that tie in?"

"I don't know yet. There may be a woman down there who can fill in some blanks. I'll be back through Los Angeles toward the end of the week. Maybe I'll look you up again."

Lyle had already tuned me out, tapping the next brick into place, troweling away the excess mortar that had drooled out between the cracks. I glanced at my watch. I still had time to check out the place where Libby Glass had worked. I didn't think Lyle was telling the whole truth, but I had no way to be sure. So I let it slide—for the time being anyway.

11

Haycraft and McNiece was located in the Avco Embassy building in Westwood, not far from my motel. I parked in an expensive lot adjacent to the Westwood Village Mortuary and went into the entranceway near the Wells Fargo Bank, taking the elevator up. The office itself was just to the right as I got off. I pushed through a solid teak door, lettered in brass. The interior was done with polished uneven red-tile flooring, mirrors floor to ceiling, and panels of raw gray wood, hung here and there with clusters of dried corn. A receptionist sat behind a corral to my left. A placard reading "Allison, Receptionist" sat on the corral post, the letters burned into the wood as though by some charred stick. I gave her my card.

"I wonder if I might talk to a senior accountant," I said. "I'm looking into the murder of a CPA who used to work here."

"Oh yeah. I heard about her," Allison said. "Hang on."

She was in her twenties with long dark hair. She

wore jeans and a string tie, her western-cut shirt looking like it had been stuffed with many handfuls of hay.
Her belt buckle was shaped like a bucking mustang.

"What is this? A theme park or something?" I asked.

"Huh?"

I shook my head, not willing to pursue the point, and
she clopped away in her high-heeled boots through
some swinging doors. After a moment, she returned.

"Mr. McNiece isn't in but the man you probably
want to talk to is Garry Steinberg with two r's."

"B-e-r-r-g?"

"No, G-a-r-r-y."

"Oh, I see. Excuse me."

"That's okay," she said. "Everybody makes that mistake."

"Would it be possible to see Mr. Steinberg? Just
briefly."

"He's in New York this week," she said.

"What about Mr. Haycraft?"

"He's dead. I mean, you know, he's been dead for
years," she said. "So actually now it's McNiece and
McNiece but nobody wants to have all the stationery
changed. The other McNiece is in a meeting."

"Is there anybody else who might remember her?"

"I don't think so. I'm sorry."

She handed me my card. I turned it over and jotted
down my motel number and my answering service up
in Santa Teresa.

"Could you give this to Garry Steinberg when he
gets back? I'd really appreciate a call. He can make it
collect if I'm not at the motel here."

"Sure," she said. She sat down and I could have sworn she eased the card straight into the trash. I watched her for a moment and she smiled at me sheepishly.

"Maybe you could just leave that on his desk with a note," I suggested.

She leaned over slightly and came up again, card in hand. She speared it on a vicious-looking metal spike near the phone.

I looked at her some more. She took the card off the spike and got up.

"I'll just put this on his desk," she said and clopped off again.

"Good plan," I said.

I went back to the motel and made some phone calls. Ruth, in Charlie Scorsoni's office, said that he was still out of town but she gave me the number of his hotel in Denver. I called but he wasn't in, so I left my number at the message desk. I called Nikki and brought her up to date and then I checked with my answering service. There were no messages. I put on my jogging clothes and drove down to the beach to run. Things did not seem to be falling into place very fast. So far, I felt like I had a lapful of confetti and the notion of piecing it all together to make a picture seemed very remote indeed. Time had shredded the facts like a big machine, leaving only slender paper threads with which to reconstruct reality. I felt clumsy and irritable and I needed to blow off steam.

I parked near the Santa Monica pier and jogged south along the promenade, a stretch of asphalt walk that parallels the beach. I trotted past the old men bent over their chess games, past thin black boys roller-skating with incredible grace, boogeying to the secret music of their padded headphones, past guitar players, dopers, and loiterers whose eyes followed me with scorn. This stretch of pavement is the last remnant of the sixties' drug culture—the barefoot, sag-eyed, and scruffy young, some looking thirty-seven now instead of seventeen, still mystical and remote. A dog took up company with me, running along beside me, his tongue hanging out, eyes rolling up at me now and then happily. His coat was thick and bristly, the color of caramel corn, and his tail curled up like a party favor. He was one of those mutant breeds with a large head, short body, and little bitty short legs, but he seemed quite self-possessed. Together, we trotted beyond the promenade, past Ozone, Dudley, Paloma, Sunset, Thornton, and Park; by the time we reached Wave Crest, he'd lost interest, veering off to participate in a game of Frisbee out on the beach. The last I saw of him, he had made an incredible leap, catching a Frisbee midflight, mouth turned up in a grin. I smiled back. He was one of the few dogs I'd met in years that I really liked.

At Venice Boulevard I turned back, running most of the way and then slowing to a walk as I reached the pier again. The ocean breeze served as a damper to my body heat. I found myself winded but not sweating much. My mouth felt dry and my cheeks were aflame. It hadn't been a long run but I'd pushed myself a little harder than I normally did and my lungs were burning: liquid combustion in my chest. I run for the same reasons I learned to drive a car with a stick shift and drink my coffee black, imagining that a day might come when some amazing emergency would require such a test. This run was for "good measure," too, since I'd already decided to take a day off for good behavior. Too much virtue has a corrupting effect. I got back in my car when I'd cooled down and I drove east on Wilshire, back to my motel.

As I unlocked the door to my room, the phone began to ring. It was my Las Vegas buddy with Sharon Napier's address.

"Fantastic," I said. "I really appreciate this. Let me know how to get in touch when I get down there and I'll pay you for your time."

"General delivery is fine. I never know where I'll be."

"You got it. How much?"

"Fifty bucks. A discount. For you. She's strictly unlisted and it wasn't easy."

"Let me know when I can return the service," I said, knowing full well that he would.

"Oh, and Kinsey," he said, "she's dealing blackjack at the Fremont but she's also hustling some on the side, so I hear. I watched her operate last night. She's very sharp but she's not fooling anyone."

"Is she stepping on someone's toes?"

"Not quite, but she's comin' close. You know, in this town no one cares what you do as long as you don't cheat. She shouldn't call attention to herself."

"Thanks for the information," I said.

"For sure," he said and hung up.

I showered and put on a pair of slacks and a shirt, then went across the street and ate fried clams drowned in ketchup with an order of french fries on the side. I got two cups of coffee to go and went back to my room. As soon as the door shut behind me, the phone began to ring. This time it was Charlie Scorsoni.

"How's Denver?" I asked as soon as he identified himself.

"Not bad. How's L.A.?"

"Fair. I'm driving up to Las Vegas tonight."

"Gambling fever?"

"Not a bit. I got a line on Sharon."

"Terrific. Tell her to pay me back my six hundred bucks."

"Yeah. Right. With interest. I'm trying to find out what she knows about a murder and you want me to hassle her about a bad debt."

"*I'll* never have occasion to, that's for sure. When will you be back in Santa Teresa?"

"Maybe Saturday. When I come back through L.A. on Friday, I want to see some boxes that belong to Libby Glass. But I don't think it will take long. What makes you ask?"

"I want to buy you a drink," he said. "I'm leaving Denver day after tomorrow, so I'll be in town before you. Will you call me when you get back?"

I hesitated ever so slightly. "Okay."

"I mean, don't put yourself out, Millhone," he said wryly.

I laughed. "I'll call. I swear."

"Great. See you then."

After I hung up, I could feel a silly smile linger on my face long after it should have. What was it about that man?

Las Vegas is about six hours from L.A. and I decided I might as well hit the road. It was just after 7:00 and not dark yet, so I threw my things in the backseat of my car and told Arlette I'd be gone for a couple of days.

"You want me to refer calls or what?" she said.

"I'll call you when I get there and let you know how I can be reached," I said.

I headed north on the San Diego Freeway, picking up the Ventura, which I followed east until it turned into the Colorado Freeway, one of the few benign roads in the whole of the L.A. freeway system. The Colorado is broad and sparsely traveled, cutting across the northern boundary of metropolitan Los Angeles. It is possible to change lanes on the Colorado without having an anxiety attack and the sturdy concrete divider that separates east- and westbound traffic is a comforting assurance that cars will not wantonly drift over and crash into your vehicle head-on. From the Colorado, I doglegged south, picking up the San Bernardino Freeway, taking 15 northeast on a long irregular diagonal toward Las Vegas. With any luck, I could talk to Sharon Napier and then head south to the Salton Sea, where Greg Fife was living. I could complete the circuit with a swing up to Claremont on my way back for a brief chat with his sister, Diane. At this point, I wasn't sure what the journey would net me but I needed to complete the basics of my investigation. And Sharon Napier was bound to prove interesting.

I like driving at night. I'm not a sightseer at heart and in travels across the country, I'm never tempted by detours to scenic wonders. I'm not interested in hundred-foot rocks shaped like crookneck squash. I'm not keen on staring down into gullies formed by rivers now defunct and I do not marvel at great holes in the ground where meteors once fell to earth. Driving anywhere looks much the same to me. I stare at the concrete roadway. I watch the yellow line. I keep track of large trucks and passenger vehicles with little children asleep in the backseat and I keep my foot pressed flat to the floor until I reach my destination.

12

By the time Las Vegas loomed up, twinkling on the horizon, it was well after midnight and I felt stiff. I was anxious to avoid the Strip. I would have avoided the whole town if I could. I don't gamble, having no instincts for the sport and even less curiosity. Life in Las Vegas exactly suits my notion of some eventual life in cities under the sea. Day and night mean nothing. People ebb and surge aimlessly as though pulled by invisible thermal currents that are swift and disagreeably close. Everything is made of plaster of paris, imitative, larger than life, profoundly impersonal. The whole town smells of $1.89 fried shrimp dinners.

I found a motel near the airport, on the outskirts of town. The Bagdad looked like a foreign legion post made of marzipan. The night manager was dressed in a gold satin vest and an orange satin shirt with full puffed sleeves. He wore a fez with a tassel. His breathing had a raspy quality that made me want to clear my throat.

"Are you an out-of-state married couple?" he asked, not looking up.

"No."

"There's fifty dollars' worth of coupons with a double if you're an out-of-state married couple. I'll put it down. Nobody checks."

I gave him my credit card, which he ran off while I filled out the registration form. He gave me my key and a small paper cup full of nickels for the slot machines near the door. I left them on the counter.

I parked in the space outside my door and left the car, taking a cab into town through the artificial daylight of Glitter Gulch. I paid the cabbie and took a moment to orient myself. There was a constant stream of traffic on East Fremont, the sidewalks crowded with tourists, hot yellow signs, and flashing lights—THE MINT, THE FOUR QUEENS—illuminating a complete catalogue of hustlers: pimps and prostitutes, pickpockets, corn-fed con artists from the Midwest who flock to Vegas with the conviction that the system can be beaten with sufficient cunning and industry. I went into the Fremont.

I could smell the Chinese food from the coffee shop and the odor of chicken chow mein mingled oddly with the perfumed jet trail left by a woman who passed me in a royal blue polyester print pantsuit that made her look like a piece of walking wallpaper. I watched idly as she began to feed quarters into a slot machine in the lobby. The blackjack tables were off to my left. I asked one of the pit bosses about Sharon Napier and was told she'd be in at 11:00 in the morning. I hadn't really expected to run into her that night, but I wanted to get a feel for the place.

The casino hummed, the croupiers at the craps tables shoveling chips back and forth with a stick like some kind of tabletop shuffleboard with rules of its own. I once made a tour of the Nevada Dice Company, watching with something close to reverence as the sixty-pound cellulose nitrate slabs, an inch thick, were cured and cut into cubes, slightly bigger than the finished size, hardened, buffed and drilled on all sides, a white resinous compound applied to the sunken dots with special brushes. The dice, in process, looked like tiny squares of cherry Jell-O that might have been served up like some sort of low-cal dessert. I watched people place their bets. The Pass line, the Don't Pass line, Come, Don't Come, the Field, the Big 6 and the Big 8 were mysteries of another kind and I couldn't, for the life of me, penetrate the catechism of wins, losses, numbers being rattled out in a low chant of intense concentration and surprise. Over it all there hung a pale cloud of cigarette smoke, infused with the smell of spilled Scotch. The darkened mirrors above the tables must have been scanned by countless pairs of eyes, restlessly raking the patrons below for telltale signs of chicanery. Nothing could escape notice. The atmosphere was that of a crowded Woolworth's at Christmas, where the throngs of frantic shoppers couldn't be trusted not to lift an item now and then. Even the employees might lie, cheat, and steal, and nothing could be left to chance. I felt a fleeting respect for the whole system of checks and balances that keeps so much money flowing freely and allows so little to slip back into the individual pockets from which it has been coaxed. A sudden feeling of exhaustion came over me. I walked back out to the street again and found a cab.

The "Middle Eastern" decor of the Bagdad halted abruptly at the door to my room. The carpet was dark green cotton shag, the wallpaper lime-green foil in a pattern of overlapping palms, flocked with small clumps that might have been dates or clusters of fruit bats. I locked the door, kicked off my shoes, and pulled down the chenille spread, crawling under the covers with relief. I put a quick call through to my answering service and another to a groggy Arlette, leaving my latest location with the number where I could be reached.

I woke up at 10:00 A.M., feeling the first faint stages of a headache—as though I had a hangover in the making before I'd even had a drink. Vegas tends to affect me that way, some combination of tension and dread to which my body responds with all the symptoms of incipient flu. I took two Tylenols and showered for a long time, trying to wash away the roiling whisper of nausea. I felt like I'd eaten a pound of cold buttered popcorn and washed it down with bulk saccharin.

I stepped out of my motel room, the light causing me to squint. The air, at least, was fresh and there was, by day, the sense of a town subdued and shrunken, flattened out again to its true proportions. The desert stretched away behind the motel in a haze of pale gray, fading to mauve at the horizon. The wind was mild and dry, the promise of summer heat only hinted at in the distant shimmering sunlight that sat on the desert floor in flat pools, evaporating on approach. Occasional patches of sagebrush, nearly silver with dust, broke up the long low lines of treeless wasteland fenced in by distant hills.

I stopped off at the post office and left a fifty-dollar money order for my friend and then I checked out the address he had given me. Sharon Napier lived in a two-story apartment complex on the far side of town, salmon-pink stucco eroding around the edges as though animals had crept up in the night to gnaw the corners away. The roof was nearly flat, peppered with rocks, the iron railings sending streaks of rust down the sides of the building. The landscaping was rock and yucca and cactus plants. There were only twenty units, arranged around a kidney-shaped pool that was separated from the parking area by a dun-colored cinder-block wall. A couple of young kids were splashing about in the pool and a middle-aged woman was standing in front of her apartment up on the landing, a grocery bag wedged between her hip and the door as she let herself in. A Chicano boy hosed down the walks. The buildings on either side of the complex were single-family dwellings. There was a vacant lot across the street in back.

Sharon's apartment was on the ground floor, her name was neatly embossed on the mailbox on a white plastic strip. Her drapes were drawn, but some of the hooks had come loose at the top, causing the lined fabric to bow inward and sag, forming a gap through which I could see a beige Formica table and two beige upholstered plastic kitchen chairs. The telephone sat on one corner of the table, resting on a pile of papers. Beside it was a coffee cup with a waxy crescent of hot-pink lipstick on the rim. A cigarette, also rimmed with pink, had been extinguished in the saucer. I glanced around. No one seemed to be paying any particular attention to me. I walked quickly through a passageway that connected the courtyard to the rear of the apartment building.

Sharon's apartment number was marked on the rear door, too, and there were four other back doors at intervals, the rear entrances emptying into little rectangles surrounded by shoulder-high cinder-block walls designed, I suspected, to create the illusion of small patios. The trash containers were lined up on the walkway outside the wall. Her kitchen curtains were drawn. I eased onto her little patio. She had arranged six geraniums in pots along the back step. There were two aluminum folding chairs stacked against the wall, a pile of old newspapers by the back door. There was a small window up on the right and a larger window beyond that. I couldn't judge whether it might be her bedroom or her neighbor's. I looked out across the vacant lot and then eased out of the patio, turning left along the walk, which opened out onto the street again. I got back in my car and headed for the Fremont.

I felt as if I'd never left. The lady in royal blue was still pasted to the quarter slot machine, her hair sculpted into a glossy mahogany scrollwork on top of her head. The same crowd seemed to be pressed to the craps table as though by magnetic force, the croupier pushing chips back and forth with his little stick as if it were a flat-bottomed broom and someone had made an expensive mess. Waitresses circulated with drinks and a heavyset man, whom I guessed to be plainclothes security, wandered about trying to look like a tourist whose luck had gone bad. I could hear the sounds of a female vocalist in the Carnival Lounge, singing a slightly flat but lusty medley of Broadway show tunes. I caught a glimpse of her, emoting to a half-deserted room, her face a bright powder pink under the spotlight.

Sharon Napier was not hard to find. She was tall, maybe five ten or better in her high-heeled shoes. She was the sort of woman you noticed from the ground up: long shapely legs looking slender in black mesh hose, a short black skirt flaring slightly at the tops of her thighs. She had narrow hips, a flat stomach, and her breasts were pushed together to form pronounced mounds. The bodice of her black outfit was tight and low-cut, her name stitched above her left breast. Her hair was an ashen blonde, pallid under the houselights; her eyes an eerie green, a luminous shade I guessed to be from tinted contact lenses. Her skin was pale and unblemished, the oval of her face as white as eggshell and as finely textured. Her lips were full and wide, the bright pink lipstick emphasizing their generous proportions. It was a mouth built for unnatural acts. Something about her demeanor promised cool improvisational sex for the right price and it would not be cheap.

She dealt cards mechanically, with remarkable speed. Three men were perched on stools ranged around the table where she worked. No one said a word. The communication was by the slightest lift of a hand, cards turned over or placed under substantial bets, a shoulder shrugged as the up card showed. Two down, one up. Flick, flick. One man scraped the edge of his up card against the surface of the table, asking for a hit. On the second round, one man turned up a blackjack and she paid off—two hundred and fifty dollars' worth of chips. I could see his eyes take her in as she flicked the cards back, shuffling quickly, dealing out cards again. He was thin, with a narrow balding head and a dark mustache, shirt sleeves rolled up, underarms stained with sweat. His gaze drifted down across her body and back up again to the immaculate face, cold and clean, the green eyes blazing. She paid no particular attention to him, but I had the feeling the two of them might do some private business later on. I retreated to another table, watching her from an easy distance. At 1:30, she took a break. Another dealer took her place and she crossed the casino, heading toward the Fiesta Room, where she ordered a Coke and lit up a cigarette. I followed.

"Are you Sharon Napier?" I asked.

She looked up. Her eyes were rimmed with dark lashes, the green taking on an almost turquoise hue in the fluorescent light overhead.

"I don't think we've met," she said.

"I'm Kinsey Millhone," I said. "May I sit down?"

She shrugged by way of consent. She took a compact out of her pocket and checked her eye makeup, removing a slight smudge of shadow from her upper lid. Her lashes were clearly false, but the effect was flashy, giving her eyes an exotic slant. She applied fresh lip gloss, using her little finger, which she dipped into a tiny pot of pink. "What can I do for you?" she asked, glancing up briefly from her compact mirror.

"I'm looking into the death of Laurence Fife."

That stopped her. She paused, her whole body going still. If I'd been taking a picture, it would have been the perfect pose. A second passed and she was in motion again. She snapped the compact shut and tucked it away, taking up her cigarette. She took a long drag, watching me all the while. She flicked an ash. "He was a real shitheel," she said brusquely, smoke wafting out with each word.

"So I've heard," I said. "Did you work for him long?"

She smiled. "Well, you've done your homework at any rate. I bet you even know the answer to that."

"More or less," I said. "But there's lots I don't know. Want to fill me in?"

"On what?"

I shrugged. "What it was like to work for him? How you felt about his death . . ."

"He was a prick to work for. I felt terrific about his death," she said. "I hated secretarial work in case you haven't guessed."

"This must suit you better," I said.

"Look, I got nothing to discuss with you," she said flatly. "Who sent you up here anyway?"

I took a flyer on that one. "Nikki."

She seemed startled. "She's still in prison. Isn't she?"

I shook my head. "She's out."

She took a moment to calculate and then her manner became somewhat more gracious. "She's got bucks, right?"

"She's not hurting, if that's what you mean."

She stubbed out her cigarette, bending the live ember under and mashing it flat. "I'm off at seven. Why don't you come out to my place and we can chat."

"Anything you'd care to mention now?"

"Not here," she said.

She rattled out her address and I dutifully jotted it down in my notebook. She glanced off to the left and I thought at first she was lifting a hand to greet a friend. Her smile flashed and then faltered and she glanced back at me with uncertainty, turning slightly so that my line of sight was blocked. I peered back over her shoulder automatically but she distracted my attention, touching the back of my hand with a fingernail. I looked at her. She towered over me, her expression remote.

"That was the pit boss. End of my break."

She told lies the way I do, with a certain breezy insolence that dares the listener to refute or contradict.

"I'll see you at seven then," I said.

"Make it seven forty-five," she said easily. "I need time to unwind from work."

I wrote out my name and the name of my motel, tearing a sheet from my notebook. She made a sharp crease and tucked the slip into her cigarette pack under the cellophane wrapper. She walked away without a backward glance, hips swaying gracefully.

The mashed butt of her cigarette was still sending up a drift of smoke and my stomach emitted a little message of protest. I was tempted to hang around, just to keep an eye on her, but my hands were feeling clammy and I longed to lie down. I didn't feel good at all and I was beginning to think that my flu symptoms might be more real than reactionary. The headache was creeping up again from the back of my neck. I walked out through the lobby. Fresh air helped me some but only momentarily.

I drove back to the Bagdad and bought a 7Up from the vending machine. I needed to eat but I wasn't sure anything would stay down. It was early afternoon and I didn't have to be anywhere until well after suppertime. I put the Do Not Disturb sign on my door and crawled back into my unmade bed, pulling the covers around me tightly. My bones had begun to ache. It was a long time before I got warm.

13

The telephone rang with startling shrillness and I awoke with a jolt. The room was dark. I had no idea what time it was, no idea what bed I was in. I groped for the phone, feeling flushed and hot, shoving the covers away from me as I propped myself up on one elbow. I flicked on the light, shading my eyes from the sudden harsh glare.

"Hello?"

"Kinsey, this is Sharon. Did you forget about me?"

I looked at my watch. It was 8:30. Shit. "God, I'm sorry," I said. "I fell asleep. Will you be there for a while? I can be right over."

"All right," she said coolly, as though she had better plans. "Oh, hang on. There's someone at my door."

She put the phone down with a clack and I pictured it resting on the hard Formica surface of the tabletop. I listened idly, waiting for her to come back. I couldn't believe I'd overslept and I was kicking myself for my stupidity. I heard the door open and her muffled exclamation of surprise. And then I heard a brief, nearly hollow report.

I squinted, sitting up abruptly. I pressed my ear to the phone, pressing my hand over the receiver. What was going on? The receiver was picked up on her end. I expected to hear her voice and I nearly spoke her name but some impulse made me clamp my mouth shut. There was the sound of breathing in my ear, the sexless hushed tones of someone slightly winded. There was a whispered "hello" that chilled me. I closed my eyes, willing myself to silence; an alarm had spread through my body in a rush that made my heart pound in my ears. There was a small breathy chuckle and then the line went dead. I slammed the phone down and reached for my shoes, grabbing my jacket as I left the room.

The jolt of adrenaline had washed my body clean of pain. My hands were shaking but at least I was in motion. I locked the door and went out to the car, my keys jingling as I tried to hit the ignition switch. I started the car and backed out rapidly, heading toward Sharon's apartment. I reached for the flashlight in my glove compartment, checking it. The light was strong. I drove, anxiety mounting. She was either playing games or dead, and I suspected I knew which.

I pulled up across the street. The building showed no particular signs of activity. No one was moving about. There were no crowds gathered, no police cars parked at the street, no sirens wailing an approach. There were numerous cars parked in the slots, and the lights in the building had been turned on in almost every apartment that I could see. I reached around in the backseat, removing a pair of rubber gloves from my locked briefcase. My hand touched the short barrel of my little automatic and I desperately longed to tuck that in my windbreaker pocket. I wasn't sure what I'd find in her apartment, wasn't sure who might be waiting for me, but the notion of being discovered there in possession of a loaded gun wouldn't do at all if she was dead. I left the gun where it was and got out, locking my car, tucking the keys into my jeans.

I moved into the front courtyard. It was dark, but several outdoor spots were placed strategically along the walk, six more green and yellow spots shooting upward along the cactus plants. The effect was more gaudy than illuminating. Sharon's apartment was dark and the gap in the drapes had been pulled tight. I tapped at the door. "Sharon?" I kept my voice low, scanning the front of the place for any signs of lights coming on. I pulled on the rubber gloves and tried the knob. Locked. I tapped again, repeating her name. There was no sound from inside. What was I going to do if someone was in there?

I moved along the short stretch of walk that led around the building to the rear. I could hear a stereo playing somewhere in one of the upstairs apartments. The small of my back ached and my cheeks felt as hot as if I'd just gotten back from a run, though whether it was from flu or fear I couldn't say. I moved quickly and silently along the rear walkway. Sharon's kitchen was the only one of the five that was dark. There was an outside bulb burning above each back door, casting a shallow but clear light onto each small patio. I tried the back door. Locked. I tapped on the glass.

"Sharon?" I strained for sounds inside the apartment. All was quiet. I scanned the rear entrance. If she had an extra set of keys outside, they would be hidden someplace close. I glanced back at the small panes of glass in her back door. If all else failed, I could always break one out. I slid my fingers along the top of the doorframe. Too narrow for keys. All the flowerpots seemed straight and a quick search revealed nothing tucked down in the dirt. There was no doormat. I lifted the pile of old newspapers, giving them a little riff, but no keys clattered out. The surrounding cinder-block patio wall was made of one-foot-square decorative "bricks," each design of sufficient intricacy to provide an ample, if not original, hiding place for a key. I hoped I wasn't going to have to check every single one. I glanced back at the small panes of glass, wondering if it might not be more to the point to pop one out with a padded fist. I looked down. There was a green plastic watering can and a trowel in one corner right up against the wall. I crouched, sliding my right hand into each of the decorative whorls of concrete. There was a key in one.

I reached up and gave the bulb above her back door a quick twist to the left. The patio was immersed in shadow. I fitted the key into the knob lock and opened the door a crack. "Sharon!" I whispered hoarsely. I was tempted to leave the apartment in darkness but I had to know if I was alone. I held the flashlight like a club, groping to my right until I found a switch. The recessed light above the sink went on. I saw the switch to the overhead kitchen light on the opposite wall. I crossed the room and flipped it on, ducking down and out of sight. I hunkered, holding my breath, my back against the refrigerator. I listened intently. Nothing. I hoped like hell I wasn't making a colossal fool of myself. For all I knew, the noise I'd heard was the popping of a champagne cork and Sharon was in the darkened bedroom performing illicit sexual acts with a little show dog and a whip.

I peered into the living room. Sharon was sprawled out on the living-room floor in a kelly green velour robe. She was either dead or sound asleep and I still didn't know who else might be in that apartment with me. I crossed to the living room in two steps and pressed myself up against the wall, waiting a moment before I peered back out into the darkened hallway. I couldn't see shit. I found a light switch just to my left and flipped it on. The hall was ablaze with light and the portion of the bedroom I could see seemed unoccupied. I felt for the bedroom switch and flipped it on, peering around quickly. I guessed the open doorway off to my right was the bathroom. There was no indication that the place had been ransacked. The sliding closet doors were shut and I didn't like that. From the bathroom, there was a faint metallic sound. I froze. My heart gave a thud and a half and I crouched. Me and my flashlight. I wished like hell I'd brought the gun. The little metallic squeak picked up again, assuming a rhythm that suddenly took on a familiar tone. I crept over to the door and flashed the light in. There was a goddamn little mouse going round and round in an exercise wheel. The cage sat on the bathroom counter. I flipped the light on. The bathroom was empty.

I crossed to the closet doors and slid one open, half waiting to get my head bashed in. Both sides of the closet were empty of anything but clothing. I let out the long breath I'd been holding and then did a second quick search of the place. I made sure the back door was locked, pulling the kitchen curtains across the window above the sink. And then I went back to Sharon. I flipped on the lamp in the living room and knelt down beside her. She had a bullet hole at the base of her throat, looking like a little locket filled with raw flesh instead of a photograph. Blood had soaked into the carpet under her head and it had darkened now to the color of uncooked chicken liver. There were small slivers of bone in her hair. I guessed that her spine had been shattered by the bullet on impact. Nice for her. No pain. She seemed to have been knocked straight back, arms flung out on either side of her body, her hips turned slightly. Her eyes were half open, the luminous green color looking sour now. Her blonde hair looked gray in death. If I'd gotten there when I was supposed to, she might not be dead, and I wanted to apologize for my bad manners, for the delay, for being sick, for being too late. I wanted to hold her hand and coax her back to life again but there was no way and I knew, in a quick flash, that if I'd been there on time, I might be dead myself.

I ran my gaze around the room with care. The carpeting was a high-low, matted with wear, so there were no shoe prints. I crossed to the front window and readjusted the drapes, making sure no crack appeared to afford a view from outside now that the lights were turned on. I made a brief tour again, taking in details this time. The bed was unmade. The bathroom was littered with damp towels. Dirty clothing bulged out of the hamper. An ashtray sat on the rim of the tub with several cigarette butts stubbed out, folded over and mashed flat in the manner I'd seen her use. The apartment was basically only those three rooms—living room with the dining table near the front windows, kitchen, and bedroom. The furniture looked as if it had been ordered by the boxcarload, and I assumed that little of it was actually hers. Whatever the disorder on the premises, it seemed to be of her own making—dishes in the sink, trash unemptied. I glanced down at the papers under the phone, a collection of past-due notices and bills. Apparently her penchant for financial chaos hadn't changed since her days in Santa Teresa. I picked up the whole batch and shoved them into my jacket pocket.

I could hear the little metallic squeak again and I went back to the bathroom, staring down at that foolish little creature. He was small and brown, with bright red eyes, patiently making his way around and around, going nowhere. "I'm sorry," I whispered, and tears stung my lips briefly. I shook my head. It was misplaced sentiment and I knew it. His water bottle was full but the plastic food dish was empty. I filled it with little green pellets and then I went back to the phone and dialed the operator, asking for the Las Vegas police. Con Dolan's warning sounded dully in my memory. All I needed was the LVPD holding me for questioning. One of those gravelly officious voices came on the line after two rings.

"Oh hello," I said. My voice had a tremor in it and I had to clear my throat quickly. "I, uh, heard some noise in my neighbor's apartment a little while ago and now I can't seem to get her to answer my knock. I'm worried that she's hurt herself. Is there any way you could check that out?"

He sounded irritated and bored, but he took down Sharon's address and said he'd send someone.

I checked my watch. I'd been in the apartment less than thirty minutes, but it was time to get out of there. I didn't want the phone to ring. I didn't want somebody knocking at the door unexpectedly. I moved toward the back, turning out lights as I went, unconsciously listening for sounds of someone approaching. I didn't have a lot of time to spare.

I glanced back at Sharon. I didn't like to leave her that way but I couldn't see the point in waiting it out. I didn't want to be linked to her death and I didn't want to hang around Las Vegas waiting for the coroner's inquest. And I certainly didn't want Con Dolan to find out I'd been here. Maybe the Mafia had killed her, or maybe some pimp, or maybe the man at the casino who'd looked at her with such hunger when she counted out his two hundred and fifty bucks. Or maybe she knew something about Laurence Fife that she wasn't supposed to tell.

I moved past her. Her fingers were relaxed in death, looking graceful, each tipped with a long rose-polished nail. I caught my breath. She had taken the slip with my name and motel jotted on it and had tucked it into her cigarette pack. But where was it? I looked around quickly, heart racing. I didn't see it on the Formica tabletop, though there was a cigarette that had apparently burned down to nothing, leaving only a perfect column of ash. There was no cigarette pack on the arm of the couch, none on the counter. I checked the bathroom again, listening acutely for sounds of the police. I could have sworn I heard a siren some distance off and I felt a ripple of alarm. Shit. I had to find that note. The bathroom trash was full of Kleenex and a soap wrapper, old cigarette butts. No cigarette pack on the bed table. None on the dresser top. I went back to the living room and looked down at her with distaste. There were two generous side pockets in the green velour robe. I gritted my teeth, feeling gingerly. The pack was on the right-hand side, with maybe six cigarettes left, the sharply creased slip of paper bearing my name still visible under the cellophane. I tucked it hastily into my jacket.

I turned out the remaining lights and slipped to the back door, opening it a crack. I could hear voices remarkably close. A garbage can lid clattered near the apartment to my right.

"You better tell the manager her light's burned out," a woman commented. She sounded as if she was standing right next to me.

"Why don't you tell *her*?" came the slightly annoyed reply.

"I don't think she's home. Her lights are off."

"Yes she is. I just saw the lights on a minute ago."

"Sherman, they're off. The whole place is dark. She must have gone out the front," the woman said. The wailing siren was very loud, its tone winding down like a phonograph.

My heart was pounding so hard it was making my chest burn. I eased out onto the darkened patio, pausing to tuck the keys back into the little crevice behind the plastic watering can. I hoped like hell it wasn't my car keys I was hiding there. I slipped out of the patio, turning left, moving toward the street again. I had to force myself to walk casually past the patrol car that was now parked out front. I unlocked my car and got in, pushing the lock down hastily as though someone were in pursuit. I stripped off the rubber gloves. My head was aching fiercely and I felt a flash of clammy sweat, bile rising up in my throat. I had to get out of there. I swallowed convulsively. The nausea welled up and I fought an almost irresistible urge to heave. My hands were shaking so badly I could hardly get my car started but I managed, finally, and pulled away from the curb with care.

As I drove past the entranceway, I could see a uniformed patrolman move around to the back of Sharon's apartment, hand on the gun at his hip. It seemed somewhat theatrical for a simple domestic complaint and I wondered, with a chill, if someone else had placed a call with a message more explicit than mine. Half a minute more and I'd have been trapped in that apartment with a lot of explaining to do. I didn't like that idea at all.

I went back to the Bagdad and packed, cleaning the place of fingerprints. I felt as if I were running a low-grade fever. All I really wanted to do was roll up in a blanket and go back to sleep. Head throbbing, I went into the office. The manager's wife was there this time, looking like a Turkish harem girl—if the word "girl" applied. She was probably sixty-five, with a finely wrinkled face, like something that had been left in the dryer too long. She wore a pale satin pillbox perched on her gray hair, veils draped provocatively over her ears.

"I'll be on the road at five in the morning and I thought I'd get my bill squared away tonight," I said.

I gave her my room number and she sorted through the upright file, coming up with my ledger card. I was feeling restless, anxious, and sick, and I wanted to be out on the road. Instead, I had to force myself, brightly, casually, to deal with this woman who moved in slow motion.

"Where you headed?" she asked idly, toting up the charges on the adding machine. She made a mistake and had to do it all over again.

"Reno," I said, lying automatically.

"Any luck?"

"What?"

"You win much?"

"Oh yeah, I'm doing pretty good," I said. "I really surprised myself."

"Better than most folk," she remarked. "You won't

be making any long-distance calls before you leave?" She gave me a sharp look.

I shook my head. "I'm going to hit the sack."

"You look like you could use some sleep," she said. She filled out the credit-card charge slip, which I signed, taking my copy.

"I didn't use the fifty dollars' worth of coupons," I said. "You might as well have those back."

She put the unused coupons in the drawer without a word.

Within minutes, miraculously, I was out on Highway 93, heading southeast toward Boulder City, where I took 95 south. I got as far as Needles and then I had to have relief. I found a cheap motel and checked in, crawled under the covers again, and slept for ten hours straight. Even that far down in oblivion, I felt an awesome dread of what had been set in motion and a pointless, aching sense of apology to Sharon Napier for whatever part I'd played in her death.

14

In the morning, I felt whole again. I ate a big breakfast in a little diner across the road from the motel, washing down bacon, scrambled eggs, and rye toast with fresh orange juice and three cups of coffee. I had the car filled up with gas, the oil checked, and then hit the road again. After Las Vegas, the desert drive was a pleasure. The land was spare, the colors subdued: a mild very pale lavender overlaid with fine dust. The sky was a stark, cloudless blue, the mountain ridges like crushed velvet, wrinkled dark gray along the face. There was something appealing about all that country unconquered yet, miles and miles of terrain without neon signs. The population was reduced to races of kangaroo rat and ground squirrel, the rocky canyons inhabited by kit fox and desert lynx. At fifty-five miles an hour, no wildlife was visible but I had heard the cries of tree frogs even in my sleep and I pictured now, from my speeding car, the clay and gravel washes filled with buff-colored lizards and millipedes, creatures whose adaption to their environment include the husbanding of moisture and an aversion to hot sun. There are parasol ants in the desert that cut off leaves and carry them as sunshades over their backs, storing them later like beach umbrellas in the subterranean chambers where they live. The idea made me smile, and I kept my mind resolutely from the recollection of Sharon Napier's death.

I found Greg Fife in a little gray humpbacked camper outside Durmid on the eastern shore of the Salton Sea. It had taken me a while to track him down. Gwen had said that he lived on his boat but the boat had been pulled out of the water for paint and repair and Greg was temporarily lodged in an aluminum trailer that looked like a roly-poly bug. The interior was compact with a folding table hooked flat against the wall, a padded bench that became a single bed, a canvas chair that completely blocked passage to the sink, a chemical toilet, and a hot plate. He opened two bottles of beer, which he'd taken from a refrigerator the size of a cardboard box, located under the sink.

He offered me the padded bench, unfolding the small table between us. A single leg flopped down to give it support. I was effectively hemmed in and could only get comfortable by turning sideways. Greg took the canvas chair, tilting back so he could study me while I studied him. He looked a lot like Laurence Fife—lank dark-brown hair, a square-cut smooth face that was clean-shaven, dark eyes, bold dark brows, square chin. He looked younger than twenty-five but his smile had the same touch of arrogance that I remembered from his father. He was darkly tanned, cheekbones tinted with sunburn. His shoulders were wide, his body lean, his feet bare. He wore a red cotton turtleneck and cutoffs that were ragged at the bottom, nearly ruffled with bleached threads. He took a sip of beer.

"You think I look like him?"

"Yes," I said. "Does that suit you?"

Greg shrugged. "Doesn't matter much at this point," he said. "We weren't anything alike."

"How so?"

"God," he said facetiously, "let's just skip over the preliminaries and get right down to the personal stuff, why don't we."

I smiled. "I'm not very polite."

"Neither am I," he said.

"So what do you want to talk about first? The weather?"

"Skip it," he said. "I know what you're here for so get to the point."

"You remember much about that time in your life?"

"Not if I can help it."

"Except for shrinks," I suggested.

"I did that to please my mom," he said and then smiled briefly as though he recognized the fact that the phrase "my mom" sounded too boyish for him at his age.

"I worked for your father a couple of times," I said.

He began to peel a strip of label with his thumbnail, feigning disinterest. I wondered what he'd heard about his father and I decided, on impulse, not to give Lau-

rence Fife any posthumous pats lest I sound conde-
scending or insincere.

I said, "I've heard he was a real bastard."

"No shit," Greg said.

I shrugged. "I didn't think he was that bad myself.
He was straight with me. I suspect he was a complicated man and I don't think many people got close to
him."

"Did you?"

"No," I said. I shifted slightly in my seat. "How'd
you feel about Nikki?"

"Not that good."

I smiled. "Try to keep your answers short so I can
get 'em on one line," I said. He didn't bite. I drank beer
for a while, then rested my chin on my fist. Sometimes
I just really do get sick of trying to coax information
out of people who aren't in the mood. "Why don't you
fold up the table and we'll go outside," I said.

"What for?"

"So I can get some fresh air, fucker, what do you
think?"

He chuckled suddenly and moved his long legs out
of my way as I slid out of the seat.

I'd surprised myself, getting snappish with him, but
I get tired of people being cute or sullen or cautious or
tight-lipped. I wanted straight answers and a lot of
them too. And I wanted a relationship based, just once,
on some sort of mutual exchange instead of me always
having to connive and manipulate. I walked aimlessly,
Greg at my heels, trying to cool myself down. It wasn't

his fault, I knew, and I'm suspicious of myself anyway when I'm feeling righteous and misunderstood.

"Sorry I snapped at you," I said.

The trailer was about two hundred yards from the water's edge. There were several larger trailers nearby, all facing the sea, like a queer band of animals that had crept down to the water to drink. I pulled off my tennis shoes and tied the laces together, hanging them around my neck. The Salton Sea has a mild to nonexistent surf, like an ocean that has been totally tamed. There is no vegetation visible in the water and few if any fish. It gives the shore a curious air, as though the tides had been brought to heel, becalmed, the life forms leeched away. What remains is familiar but subtly changed, like a glimpse into the future where certain laws of nature have been altered by the passage of time. I placed a drop of water on my tongue. The taste of salt was fierce. "Is this ocean water?"

Greg smiled, apparently unperturbed by my former outburst. In fact he seemed friendlier. "You want a lesson in geology," he said, "I'll give you one." It was the first time his voice had contained any sign of enthusiasm.

"Sure, why not?"

He picked up a rock, using it like a piece of chalk as he drew a crude map in the wet sand. "This is the California coastline and this is Baja. Over here is Mexico. Right at the tip of the Gulf of California is Yuma— southeast of here, more or less. This is us here," he said, pointing. "The Colorado River curves right up through here and then up past Las Vegas. That's

Hoover Dam. Then it goes up here and over into Utah and then to Colorado, but we can skip that part. Now," he said, tossing the rock aside. He began to draw with his fingertip, glancing up at me to see if I was listening. "This area in here is called the Salton Sink. Two hundred and seventy-three feet below sea level—something like that. If it weren't for the Colorado River forming a kind of natural dam right here, all this water from the Gulf of California would have spilled into the Salton Sink years ago—all the way up to Indio. God, that gives me the willies when I think of it. Anyway, the Salton Sea came from the Colorado River itself, so it was originally fresh water. Overflowed in 1905—the river did, billions of gallons of water pouring in over a two-year period. It was finally controlled with rock and brush dams. The salt, which has been gradually saturating the water, was probably from prehistoric times when all of this area was submerged." He stood up, brushing wet sand off his hands, apparently satisfied with his summary.

We began to walk—he on the beach side, me scuffling my bare feet through the shallows. He tucked his hands in his back pockets. "Sorry if I was a pissant before," he said lightly, "I've been in a bad mood with my boat out of the water. I was never meant to be on land."

"You sure snapped out of it quick enough," I remarked.

"Because you said 'fuck.' I always get tickled when women say that. Especially you. It was the last thing I expected to come out of your mouth."

"What do you do down here?" I asked. "Fish?"

"Some. Mostly sail. Read. Drink beer. Hang out."

"I'd go nuts."

Greg shrugged. "I started out nuts so I'm getting sane."

"Not really 'nuts,'" I said.

"Not certifiable, no."

"What kind then?"

"Don't make me tell all that stuff," he said mildly. "I get bored with myself. Ask me something else. Three questions. Like magic wishes."

"If I have to limit myself to three questions, I might as well go home," I said, but basically I was willing to play the game. I looked over at him. He was looking less like his father and more like himself. "What do you remember from the period just before he died?"

"You asked me that before."

"Yeah, and that's just about the time you turned all surly on me. I'll tell you why I'm asking. Maybe that will help. I'd like to reconstruct the events just before his death. Maybe as far back as the last six months before he was killed. I mean, maybe he was involved in some kind of legal hassle—a personal feud. Maybe he fought with a neighbor over a property line. Somebody did it, and there had to be a sequence of events."

"I wouldn't know about that stuff," he said. "I can tell you just family events, but the other I wouldn't know."

"That's okay."

"We came down here that fall. That's one of the reasons I came back."

I wanted to prompt him with another question but I was afraid he'd count it as one of my three so I kept my mouth shut. He went on.

"I was seventeen. God, I was such a jerk and I thought my father was so impossibly perfect. I didn't know what he expected of me but I figured I'd never measure up, so I was a pissant. He was supercritical and he hurt my feelings a lot, but I'd just stonewall him. Half the time I hung on his every word and the rest of the time I hated his guts. So when he died, I lost the chance to square myself with him. I mean, for all time, you know? That's it. I've got no way to take care of any old business with him, so I'm stuck. I figured if I was stuck in time, I might as well be stuck in place, too, so that's why I came here. We were out on the beach once—and he had to go back to the car for something and I remember watching him walk. Just looking at him. He had his head bent and he was probably thinking about anything but me. I felt like I should call him back, really tell him how much I loved him, but of course I didn't. So that's the way I remember him. That whole business really screwed me up."

"It was just the two of you?"

"What? No, the whole family. Except Diane. She got sick and stayed with Mom. It was Labor Day weekend. We drove to Palm Springs, first, just for the day, and then came on down here."

"How'd you feel about Colin?"

"Okay I guess, but I didn't see why the whole family had to revolve around him. The kid had a handicap and I felt bad about that, but I didn't want my life to focus on his infirmity, you know? I mean, Jesus, I would have had to develop a terminal disease to compete with him. This is me at seventeen, you understand. Now I'm a little more compassionate, but back then, I couldn't cope with that stuff. I didn't see why I should. Dad and I were never bosom buddies, but I needed time with him too. I used to have these fantasies of what it would be like. I'd really tell him something important and he'd really listen to me. Instead, all we talked about was bullshit—just *bull*shit. So six weeks later he's dead."

He glanced at me and then shook his head, smiling sheepishly.

"Shakespeare should have done a play about this stuff," he said. "I could have done the monologue."

"So he never talked to you about his personal life?"

"That's number three, you know," he remarked. "You sneaked in that little question about whether it was just Dad and me down here. But the answer is no. He never talked to me about anything. I told you I couldn't be much help. Let's knock it off for a while, okay?"

I smiled and tossed my shoes up on the beach, starting to jog.

"Do you jog?" I called back over my shoulder.

"Yeah, some," he said, catching up. He began to trot at my side.

"What happens if I work up a sweat?" I asked. "Can we get cleaned up?"

"The neighbors let me use their shower."

"Great," I said and picked up the pace.

We ran, not exchanging a word, just taking in sun and sand and dry heat. The whole time, the same question came up over and over again. How could Sharon Napier fit into this scheme? What could she possibly have known that she didn't live long enough to tell? So far, none of it made sense. Not Fife's death, not Libby's, not Sharon's death eight years later. Unless she was blackmailing someone. I glanced back at the little trailer, still visible, looking remarkably close in the odd perspective of the flat desert landscape. There was no one else around. No sign of vehicles, no boogeymen on foot. I smiled at Greg. He wasn't even panting yet.

"You're in good shape," I said.

"So are you. How long do we keep this up?"

"Thirty minutes. Forty-five."

We chunked along for a while, the sand causing mild pains in my calves.

"How about I ask you three?" he said.

"Okay."

"How'd you get along with your old man?"

"Oh great," I said. "He died when I was five. Both of them did. In a car wreck. Up near Lompoc. Big rock rolled down the mountain and smashed the windshield. Took them six hours to pry me out of the back. My mother cried for a while and then she stopped. I still hear it sometimes in my sleep. Not the sobs. The silence after that. I was raised by my aunt. Her sister."

He digested that. "You married?"

"Was." I held up two fingers.

He smiled. "Is that for 'twice' or question number two?"

I laughed. "That's number three."

"Hey come on. You cheat."

"All right. One more. But make it count."

"You ever kill anyone?"

I glanced over at him with curiosity. It seemed like a strange follow-up. "Let's put it this way," I said. "I did my first homicide investigation when I was twenty-six. A job I did for the public defender's office. A woman accused of killing her own kids. Three of them. Girls. All under five. Taped their mouths, hands, and feet, then put them in garbage cans and let them suffocate. I had to look at the glossy eight-by-ten police photographs. I got cured of any homicidal urges. Also any desire for motherhood."

"Jesus," he said. "And she really did it?"

"Oh sure. She got off, of course. Pleaded temporary insanity. She might be back on the streets again for all I know."

"How do you keep from getting cynical?" he asked.

"Who says I'm not?"

While I showered in the trailer next door, I tried to think what else I might learn from Greg. I was feeling restless, anxious to be on the road again. If I could get to Claremont by dark, I could talk to Diane first thing in the morning and then drive back to Los Angeles after lunch. I toweled my hair dry and dressed. Greg had opened another beer for me, which I sipped while I waited for him to get cleaned up. I glanced at my watch. It was 3:15. Greg came into the trailer, leaving the door open, sliding the screen door shut. His dark hair was still damp and he smelled of soap.

"You look poised for flight," he said, getting himself a beer. He popped the cap.

"I'm thinking I should try to get to Claremont before dark," I said. "You have any messages for your sister?"

"She knows where I am. We talk now and then, often enough to keep caught up," he said. He sat down in the canvas chair, propping his feet up on the padded bench next to me. "Anything else you want to ask?"

"Couple of things if you don't mind," I said.

"Fire away."

"What do you remember about your father's allergies?"

"Dogs, cat dander, sometimes hay fever but I don't know what that consisted of exactly."

"He wasn't allergic to any kind of food? Eggs? Wheat?"

Greg shook his head. "Not that I ever heard. Just stuff in the air—pollens, things like that."

"Did he have his allergy capsules with him when the family came down here that weekend?"

"I don't remember that. I would guess no. He knew we'd be out in the desert and the air down here is usually pretty clear even in late summer, early fall. The dog wasn't with us. We left him at home, so Dad wouldn't have needed the allergy medication for that, and I don't think there was anything else he needed it for."

"I thought the dog got killed. I thought Nikki told me that," I said.

"Yeah, he was. While we were gone as a matter of fact."

I felt a sudden chill. There was something odd about that, something off. "How'd you find out about it?"

Greg shrugged. "When we got home," he said, apparently not attaching much to the fact. "Mom had taken Diane over to the house to pick something up. Sunday morning I guess. We didn't get back until Monday night. Anyway, they found Bruno lying out on the side of the road. I guess he was pretty badly mangled. Mom wouldn't even let Diane see him up close. She called the animal-shelter people and they came and picked him up. He'd been dead awhile. All of us felt bad about it. He was a great beast."

"Good watchdog?"

"The best," he said.

"What about Mrs. Voss, the housekeeper? What was she like?"

"Nice enough, I guess. She seemed to get along with everybody," he said. "I wish I knew more but that's about it as far as I can tell."

I finished my beer and got up, holding out my hand to him. "Thanks, Greg. I may need to talk to you again if that's okay."

He kissed the back of my hand, pretending to clown but meaning something else, I was almost sure. "Godspeed," he said softly.

I smiled with unexpected pleasure. "Did you ever see *Young Bess*? Jean Simmons and Stewart Granger?

That's what he says to her. He was doomed, I think, or maybe she was—I forget. Ripped my heart out. You ought to watch for it on the late movie some night. It killed me when I was a kid."

"You're only five or six years older than me," he said.

"Seven," I replied.

"Same smell."

"I'll let you know what I find out," I said.

"Good luck."

As I pulled away, I glanced back out of the car window. Greg was standing in the trailer doorway, the screen creating the ghostly illusion of Laurence Fife again.

15

I reached Claremont at 6:00, driving through Ontario, Montclair, and Pomona; all townships without real towns, a peculiar California phenomenon in which a series of shopping malls and acres of tract houses acquire a zip code and become realities on the map. Claremont is an oddity in that it resembles a trim little midwestern hamlet with elms and picket fences. The annual Fourth of July parade is composed of kazoo bands, platoons of children on crepe-paper-decorated bikes, and a self-satirizing team of husbands dressed in Bermuda shorts, black socks, and business shoes doing close-order drills with power mowers. Except for the smog, Claremont could even be considered "picturesque" with Mount Baldy forming a raw backdrop.

I pulled into a gas station and called the number Gwen had given me for Diane. She was out, but her roommate said she'd be home at 8:00. I headed up Indian Hill Boulevard, turning left onto Baughman. My friends Gideon and Nell live two doors down in a house with two kids, three cats, and a hot tub. Nell I've known since my college days. She's a creature of high intellect and wry humor who's learned never to be too amazed by my appearances on her doorstep. She seemed pleased to see me nevertheless and I sat in her kitchen, watching her make soup while we talked. I called Diane again after supper and she agreed to meet me for lunch. After that, Nell and I stripped down and soaked in the hot tub out on the deck, with icy white wine and a lot more catching up to do. Gideon graciously kept the children at bay. I slept on the couch that night with a cat curled up on my chest, wondering if there was any way I could have such a life for myself.

I met Diane at one of those brown-bread-and-sprout restaurants that all look the same: lots of natural varnished wood and healthy hanging plants, macrame and leaded-glass windows and waiters who don't smoke cigarettes but would probably toke on anything else you've got. Ours was thin with receding hair and a dark mustache, which he stroked incessantly, taking our order with an earnestness that I don't think any sandwich ever deserved. Mine was avocado and bacon. Hers was a "vegetarian delite" stuffed in pita bread.

"Greg says he really treated you like shit when you first got down there," she said and laughed. Some sort of dressing was leaking out through a crack in her pita bread and she lapped it off.

"When did you talk to him? Last night?"

"Sure." She took another unwieldy mouthful and I watched her lick her fingers and wipe her chin. She had

Greg's clean good looks but she carried more weight, wide rump packed into a pair of faded jeans, and an unexpected powdering of freckles on her face. Her dark hair was parted in the center and pulled up on top with a broad leather band, pierced through with a wooden skewer.

"Did you know Nikki was out on parole?" I asked.

"That's what Mom said. Is Colin back?"

"Nikki was just on her way up to get him when I talked to her a couple of days ago," I said. I was struggling to keep my sandwich intact, thick bread breaking with every bite, but I caught the look in her eye. Colin interested her. Nikki did not.

"Did you meet Mom?"

"Yes. I liked her a lot."

Diane flashed a quick, proud smile. "Daddy was really an asshole to dump her for Nikki if you ask me. I mean, Nikki's okay, but she's kind of cold, don't you think?"

I murmured something noncommittal. Diane didn't seem to be listening anyway. "Your mother said you went into therapy right after your father died," I said.

Diane rolled her eyes, taking a sip of peppermint tea. "I've been in therapy half my life and my head's still not on straight. It's really a drag. The shrink I got now thinks I should go into analysis but nobody does that anymore. He says I need to go into my 'dark' side. He's into this real Freudian horseshit. All those old guys are. You know, they want you to lie there and tell 'em all your dreams and kinky fantasies so they can whack off mentally at your expense. I did Reichian before that but I got sick of huffing and puffing and pulling on towels. That just felt dumb to me."

I took a big bite of sandwich, nodding as if I knew what she was talking about. "I've never been in therapy," I murmured.

"Not even *group*?"

I shook my head.

"God, you must really be neurotic," she said respectfully.

"Well I don't bite my nails or wet the bed."

"You're probably the compulsive type, avoiding commitments and shit like that. Daddy was like that some."

"Like how?" I said, skipping right over the reference to my character. After all, it was just a wild guess.

"Oh. You know. Fucking around all the time. Greg and I still compare notes on that. My shrink says he was just warding off pain. My granny used to manipulate the shit out of him so he turned around and manipulated everyone else, including Greg and me. And Mom. And Nikki, and I don't even know who else. I don't think he ever loved anybody in his life except Colin maybe. Too threatening."

She finished her sandwich and spent a few minutes wiping her face and hands. Then she folded the paper napkin carefully.

"Greg told me you missed the trip to Salton Sea," I said.

"What, before Daddy died? Yeah I did. I had the flu,

really grisly stuff, so I stayed with Mom. She was great, really poured on the TLC. I never slept so much in my life."

"How did the dog get out?"

She put her hands in her lap. "What?"

"Bruno. Greg said he got hit by a car. I just wondered who let him out. Was Mrs. Voss staying at the house while the family was gone?"

Diane looked at me with care and then away. "I don't think so. She was on vacation, I think." Her eyes strayed to the clock on the wall behind me. "I've got a class," she said. Her face was suffused with pink.

"Are you okay?"

"Sure. Fine," she said, casually gathering up her purse and books. She seemed relieved to have something to do. "Oh, I nearly forgot. I've got something for Colin if you're going to see him." She held out a paper bag. "It's an album I put together for him. We had all those pictures in a box." She was all business now, her manner distracted, her attention disengaged. She gave me a brief smile. "I'm sorry I don't have any more time. How much is my part of the lunch?"

"I'll take care of it," I said. "Can I drop you someplace?"

"I've got a car," she said. All the animation had left her face.

"Diane, what's going on?" I said.

She sat down again abruptly, staring straight ahead. Her voice had dropped about six notes. "I let the dog out myself," she said, "the day they left. Nikki said to let him have a run before Mom picked me up so I did but I just felt like shit. I lay down on the couch in the living room to wait for Mom and when she honked, I just grabbed my stuff and went out the front. I never even thought about the dog. He must have been running around for two days before I remembered. That's why Mom and I drove over there. To feed him and let him in."

Her eyes finally met mine and she seemed close to tears. "That poor thing," she whispered. The guilt seemed to take possession of her totally. "It was my fault. That's why he got hit. Because I forgot." She put a trembling hand against her mouth, blinking. "I felt awful about it but I never told anyone except Mom and nobody ever asked. You won't tell, will you? They were so upset that he got killed that nobody ever even asked me how he got out and I never said a word. I couldn't. Nikki would have hated me."

"Nikki's not going to hate you because the dog got killed, Diane," I said. "That was years ago. What difference does it make now?"

Her eyes took on a haunted look and I had to lean forward to hear what she was saying. "Because someone got in. While the dog was out. Someone got into the house and switched the medication. And that's why Daddy died," she said. She fumbled in her purse for a Kleenex, her sobs sounding like a series of gasps, involuntary, quick, her shoulders hunching helplessly.

Two guys from the next table looked over at her with curiosity.

"Oh God, oh God," she whispered, her voice hoarse with grief.

"Let's get out of here," I said, grabbing up her belongings. I left too much money on the table for the check. I took her by the arm, propelling her toward the door.

By the time we got out to the parking lot, she was almost in control of herself. "God, I'm sorry. I can't believe I did that," she said. "I never fall apart that way."

"That's okay," I said. "I had no idea I'd set you off like that. It was just something that stuck in my mind after Greg mentioned it. I didn't mean to *accuse* you of anything."

"I couldn't believe you said it," she said, tears rising again. She looked at me earnestly. "I thought you knew. I thought you must have found out. I never would have admitted it otherwise. I've felt so awful about that for so long."

"How can you blame yourself? If someone wanted to get into the house, he would have let the dog loose anyway. Or killed it and made it look like an accident. I mean, who's going to get upstairs with a goddamn German shepherd barking and snarling?" I said.

"I don't know. Maybe so. It could be, I guess. I mean, he *was* a good watchdog. If he'd been in, nobody could have done anything."

She let out a deep breath, blowing her nose again on the damp twisted Kleenex. "I was so irresponsible in those days. They were always on my case, which just made things worse. I couldn't tell 'em. And nobody seemed to make the connection when Daddy died except me and I *couldn't* admit it then."

"Hey it's over," I said, "it's done. You can't beat your-

self to death with it. It's not as if you did it deliberately."

"I know, I know. But the result was the same, you
know?" Her voice lifted up and her eyes squeezed shut
again, tears running down her cheeks. "He was such a
shit and I loved him so much. I know Greg hated his
guts, but I just thought he was great. I didn't care if he
screwed around. That wasn't his fault. He was just so
messed up all his life. He really was."

She wiped her eyes with the wad of Kleenex and
then took another deep breath. She reached in her
purse for a compact.

"Why don't you skip your class and go home?" I
said.

"Maybe I will," she said. She looked at herself in the
mirror. "God, I'm a wreck. I can't go anywhere looking
like this."

"I'm sorry I triggered this. I think I feel worse than
you," I said sheepishly.

"No, that's all right. It's not your fault. It's mine. I
guess I'll even have to tell my shrink now. He'll think
it's cathartic. He loves that shit. I guess everyone will
know now. God, that's all I need."

"Hey, I may or may not have to mention it. I really
don't know yet, but I don't think it matters now. If
someone was determined to kill your father, it would
have been done one way or the other. That's just a
fact."

"I guess so. Anyway, it's nice of you to say that. I feel
better. Really. I didn't even know it was still weighing
on me, but it must have been."

"You're sure you're okay now?"

She nodded, giving me a little smile.

We said our good-byes, which took a few minutes more, and then she walked to her car. I watched while she drove off and then I tossed the album for Colin in the backseat of my car and pulled out. Actually, though I hated to admit it, she was probably right. If the dog had been in the house, no one could have messed with anything. With the dog in or out, dead or alive, it certainly wouldn't have protected Libby Glass. And at least one piece of the puzzle now fit. It didn't seem to mean much, but it did seem to establish the approximate date of entry to the house, if that's how the killer had effected the switch. It felt like the first blank I'd really filled in. Small progress but it made me feel good. I drove back to the San Bernardino Freeway and headed for L.A.

16

When I got back to the Hacienda, I went into the office to check for telephone messages. Arlette had four, but three of them turned out to be from Charlie Scorsoni. She leaned an elbow on the counter, munching on something sticky and dark brown enclosed in cookie dough.

"What is that thing?"

"Trimline Diet Snack Bar," she said. "Six calories each." Some of the filling seemed to be stuck to her teeth like dental putty and she ran a finger along her gums, popping goo into her mouth again. "Look at this label. I bet there's not one natural ingredient in this entire piece of food. Milk powder, hydrogenated fat, powdered egg, and a whole list of chemicals and additives. But you know what? I've noticed real food doesn't taste as good as fake. Have you noticed that? It's just a fact of life. Real food is bland, watered-down-tasting. You take a supermarket tomato. Now it's pathetic what that tastes like," she said and shuddered.

I was trying to sort through my messages but she was making it hard.

"I bet this isn't even real flour in this thing," she said. "I mean, I've heard people say junk food just has empty calories, but who needs full ones? I like 'em empty. That way I figure I can't gain any more weight. That Charlie Scorsoni sure kept in touch, didn't he? He called once from Denver and then he called from Tucson and last night from Santa Teresa. Wonder what he wants. He sounded cute."

"I'll be in my room," I said.

"Well all right. Good enough. You want to return those calls, you just give me a buzz up here and I'll put you through."

"Thanks," I said.

"Oh yeah, and I gave your telephone number in Las Vegas to a couple of people who didn't want to leave messages. I hope that's okay. You didn't say I couldn't refer calls."

"No, that's fine," I said. "Any idea who it might have been?"

"Male and female, one each," she said airily.

When I got to my room, I kicked my shoes off and called Charlie Scorsoni's office and talked to Ruth.

"He was supposed to get back last night," she said. "But he didn't plan to come in to the office. You might try him at home."

"Well, if I don't get him there, will you tell him I'm

back in Los Angeles? He knows where to reach me here."

"Will do," she said.

The other message was a bonus. Apparently Garry Steinberg, the accountant at Haycraft and McNiece, had come back from New York a few days early and was willing to talk to me on Friday afternoon, which was today. I called and talked to him briefly, telling him I'd be there within the hour. Then I called Mrs. Glass and told her I should be out at her place shortly after supper. There was one more call I felt I should make, though I dreaded the necessity. I sat for a moment on the edge of the bed, staring at the phone and then I said to hell with it and dialed my friend in Las Vegas.

"Jesus, Kinsey," he said through his teeth. "I wish you wouldn't do this to me. I get you the lowdown on Sharon Napier and next thing I know she's dead."

I gave him the situation as succinctly as I could but it didn't seem to ease his anxieties. Or mine. "It could have been anyone," I said. "We don't *know* that she was shot because of me."

"Yeah, but I got to cover myself anyway. Somebody remembers that I was asking around after this lady and then she's found with a bullet in her throat. I mean, how does that look?"

I apologized profusely and told him to let me know anything he found out. He didn't seem that eager to keep in touch. I changed clothes, putting on a skirt, hose, and heels, and then I drove to the Avco Embassy building and took the elevator to the tenth floor. I was feeling bad about Sharon Napier all over again, guilt sitting in my gut like a low-level colic. How could I have missed that appointment? How could that have happened to me? She knew *something* and if I'd gotten there on time, I might be wrapping this investigation up instead of being where I was—which was nowhere in particular. I made my way back into the imitation barnyard of Haycraft and McNiece, staring at the dried corn on the wall while I whipped myself some more.

Garry Steinberg turned out to be a very nice man. I guessed him to be in his early thirties, with dark curly hair, dark eyes, and a small gap between his front teeth. He was probably five feet, ten inches and his body looked soft, his waist puffing out like rising bread dough.

"You're noticing my waist, am I right?" he asked.

I shrugged somewhat sheepishly, wondering if he did or did not want me to comment. He motioned me into a chair and then sat down behind his desk.

"Let me show you something," he said, lifting a finger. He opened his top desk drawer and took out a snapshot, which he handed to me. I glanced at it.

"Who's this?"

"Perfect," he said. "That was the perfect response. That's me. When I weighed three hundred and ten pounds. Now I weigh two-sixteen."

"My God," I said and looked at the picture again. Actually I could see now that in the old days he had looked a bit like Arlette might if she decided to cross-dress. I'm crazy about "before-and-after" shots, an avid fan of all those magazine ads showing women pumped up like tires and then magically thin, one foot arranged in front of the other, as though weight loss also involved the upsurge of charm and modeling skills. I wondered if there was anyone left in California not obsessed with self-image.

"How'd you do it?" I asked, handing the snapshot back.

"Scarsdale," he said. "It was a real honest-to-God bitch but I did it. I only cheated once—well, twice. Once was when I turned thirty-five. I figured I was en-titled to a bagel and cream cheese with a birthday can-dle. And one night I binged because my girl friend got mad at me and kicked me out. I mean, lookit, when I was three-ten I never even had a girl. Now I'm having fits when she throws me out. We made up again though, so that turned out all right. I've got twenty-five pounds to lose yet but I'm giving myself a break. Strictly maintenance. Have you ever done Scarsdale?"

I shook my head apologetically. I was beginning to feel I'd never done anything. No Scarsdale, no therapy.

"No alcohol," he said. "That's the hard part. On the maintenance diet, you can have like a small glass of white wine now and then, but that's it. I figure the first fifty pounds I lost was from that. Giving up booze. You'd be surprised how much weight that adds."

"Sounds a lot better for you," I said.

"I feel good about myself," he said. "That's the im-portant thing. So. Enough of that. What do you want to know about Libby Glass? The receptionist says you came about her."

I explained what I was up to and how I came to be involved in the matter of her death. He took it all in, asking occasional questions. "What can I tell you?" he said, finally.

"How long had she handled Laurence Fife's account?"

"I'm glad you asked me that because that's one thing I looked up when I knew you were coming over. We handled his personal finances first for about a year. The law firm of Fife and Scorsoni had only been with us six months. Actually a little less. We were just putting in our own computer system and Libby was trying to get all the records straightened out for the changeover. She was a very good accountant by the way. Real conscientious and real smart."

"Were you a good friend of hers?"

"Pretty good. I was El Blimpo back then but I had a crush on her and we kind of had this brother-sister relationship—platonic. We didn't date. Just had lunch together once a week, something like that. Sometimes a drink after work."

"How many accounts did she handle?"

"All together? I'd say twenty-five, maybe thirty. She was a very ambitious girl and she really knocked herself out . . . for all the good it did."

"Meaning what?"

He got up and closed the door to his office, pointing significantly to the wall of the office next door.

"Listen, old man Haycraft was a petty tyrant, the

original male chauvinist pig. Libby thought if she worked hard, she'd get a promotion and a raise, but no such thing. And these guys aren't much better. You want to know how I get a raise? I threaten to quit. Libby didn't even do that."

"How much was she paid?"

"I don't know. I could maybe look that up. Not enough to suit her, I can tell you that. Fife and Scorsoni was a big account—not the biggest, but big. She didn't feel it was fair."

"She did more work for Fife than Scorsoni, I assume."

"At first. After that, it was half and half. A lot of the purpose of our taking over their business management was to keep track of all the estate work. That was a big part of their ongoing business from what she said. The dead guy, Fife, did a lot of messy divorce work, which paid big fees but didn't require that much in the way of bookkeeping. Also, we did accounts receivable for them, paid their office bills, kept track of profits from the firm, and made suggestions about investments. Well, at that point, we weren't doing much in the way of investment counseling because they hadn't been with us that long but that was the object of the exercise eventually. We like to hold off some until we see where our clients stand. Anyway, I can't go into details on that but I can probably answer any other general questions you might have."

"Do you know anything about where the money from the Fife's estate went?"

"The kids. It was divided equally among them. I

never saw the will but I helped settle the estate in terms of disbursements after probate."

"You don't happen to represent Scorsoni's new law firm, do you?"

"Nope," Garry said. "I met him a couple of times after Fife died. He seemed like a nice man."

"Is there any way I could look at the old books?"

"Nope," he said. "You could do it if I had Scorsoni's written permission but I don't know what good that would do you anyway unless you're an accountant yourself. Our system isn't that complicated, but I don't think it'd make sense to you."

"Probably not," I said, trying to think what else I wanted to ask him about.

"You want coffee? I'm sorry, I should have asked you sooner."

"No thanks. I'm fine," I said. "What about Libby's personal affairs. Is there any chance that she was sleeping with Laurence Fife?"

Garry laughed. "Now that I don't know. She'd been going with some creepy little guy ever since high school, and I knew she'd broken up with him. On my advice, I might add."

"How come?"

"He came in to apply for a job here. I was in charge of screening all applicants. He was just supposed to messenger stuff back and forth but he didn't even look that smart. He was belligerent, too, and if you want my honest opinion, he was high."

"You wouldn't still have his application on file, would you?" I asked, feeling a faint surge of excitement.

Garry looked at me. "We're not having this conversation, am I right?"

"Right."

"I'll see what I can find," he said promptly. "It wouldn't be here. It'd be over in the warehouse. We have all the old records stored there. Accountants are real pack rats. We never throw anything away and everything gets written down."

"Thanks, Garry," I said. "I can't tell you how much I appreciate this."

He smiled happily. "And maybe I'll look for the old Fife files as long as I'm over there. It won't hurt to take a peek. And to answer your question about Libby, my guess would be no. I don't think she was having an affair with Laurence Fife." He glanced at his watch. "I got a meeting."

I shook his hand across the desk, feeling good. "Thanks again," I said.

"No problem. Stop by again. Anytime."

I got back to my hotel room at 3:30. I put a pillow on the plastic chair, set my typewriter up on the wobbly desk, and spent an hour and a half typing up my notes. It had been a long time since I sat down to do paperwork but it had to be caught up. By the time I pecked my way through the last paragraph, I had a pain in my lower back and another one right between my shoulder blades. I changed into my running clothes, my body heat resurrecting the smell of old sweat and car fumes. I was going to have to find a Laundromat soon. I jogged south on Wilshire, just for variety, cutting across to San Vicente at Twenty-sixth

Street. Once I got on the wide grassy divider, I could feel myself hit stride. Running always hurts—I don't care what they say—but it does acquaint one with all of one's body parts. This time I could feel my thighs protest and I noticed a mild aching in my shins, which I ignored, plodding on gamely. For my bravery, I netted a few rude remarks from two guys in a pickup truck. When I got back to the motel, I showered and got back into my jeans and then I stopped by McDonald's and had a Quarter Pounder with cheese, fries, and a medium Coke. By then, it was 6:45. I filled up the car with gas and headed over the hill into Sherman Oaks.

17

Mrs. Glass answered the door after half a buzz. This time the living room had been picked up to some extent, her sewing confined now to a neatly folded pile of fabric on the arm of the couch. Raymond was nowhere in sight.

"He had a bad day," she said to me. "Lyle stopped by on his way home from work and we put him to bed."

Even the television set was turned off, and I wondered what she did with herself in the evenings.

"Elizabeth's things are in the basement," she murmured. "I'll just get the key to the storage bin."

She returned a moment later and I followed her out into the corridor. We turned left, past the stairway back to the basement door which was set into the right-hand wall. The door was locked and after she opened it, she flipped the light switch at the top of the stairs. I could already smell the dry musty scent of old window screens and half-empty cans of latex paint. I was about two steps behind her as we made our way down the narrow passageway, wooden stairs taking a sharp right-hand turn. At the landing, I caught a glimpse of concrete floor with bins of wooden lathing reaching to the low ceiling. Something wasn't right but the oddity didn't really register before the blast rang out. The light bulb on the landing shattered, spraying us both with thin flakes of glass and the basement was instantly blanketed in darkness. Grace shrieked and I grabbed her, pulling her back up the stairs. I lost my balance and she stumbled over me. There must have been an outside exit because I heard a wrenching of wood, a bang, and then someone taking the concrete steps outside two at a time. I struggled out from under Grace, jerking her up the stairs with me and then I left her in the corridor, racing out through the front and around the side of the building. Someone had left an old power mower in the driveway and I tripped in the darkness, sprawling forward on my hands and knees, cursing savagely as I scrambled back to my feet again. I reached the rear of the building, keeping low, my heart pounding in my ears. It was black-dark, my eyes just beginning to adjust. A vehicle started up one street over and I could hear it chirp out with a quick shift of gears. I ducked back, leaning against the building then, hearing nothing but the fading roar of a vehicle being driven away at high speed. My mouth was dry. I was drenched in sweat and belatedly I felt a shudder go through me. Both my palms stung where the gravel had bitten into the flesh. I trotted back to my car and got out my flashlight, tucking the little automatic into my windbreaker pocket. I didn't think there was any-one left to shoot but I was tired of being surprised.

Grace was sitting on the doorsill, her head hanging down between her knees. She was shaking from head to foot and she'd started to weep. I helped her to her feet, easing open the apartment door.

"Lyle knew I was picking the stuff up, right?" I snapped at her. She gave me a haunted, pleading look.

"It couldn't have been him. He wouldn't have done that to me," she whimpered.

"Your faith is touching," I said. "Now sit. I'll be back in a minute."

I went back to the basement stairs. The beam from the flashlight cut through the blackness. There was a second bulb at the bottom of the stairs and I pulled the chain. A flat dull light from the swinging bulb threw out a yellow arc that slowed to a halt. I turned off the flashlight. I knew which bin belonged to Mrs. Glass. It had been smashed open, the padlock dangling ineffectually where the lathing had been broken through. Cardboard boxes had been torn open, the contents strewn about in haste, forming an ankle-deep mess through which I picked my way. The emptied boxes all bore the name "Elizabeth," obligingly rendered in bold Magic Marker strokes. I wondered if we'd interrupted the intruder before or after he'd found what he was looking for. I heard a sound behind me and I whirled, raising the flashlight instantly like a club.

A man stood there staring at me with bewilderment.

"Got a problem down here?"

"Oh fuck. Who are you?"

He was middle-aged, hands in his pockets, his expression sheepish. "Frank Isenberg from apartment three," he said apologetically. "Did somebody break in? You want me to call the police?"

"No, don't do that yet. Let me check upstairs with Grace. This looks like the only bin that's been damaged. Maybe it was just kids," I said, heart still thudding. "You didn't have to sneak up on me."

"Sorry. I just thought you might need some help."

"Yeah, well thanks anyway. I'll let you know if I need anything."

He stood there surveying the chaos for a moment and then he shrugged and went back upstairs.

I checked the basement door at the rear. The glass had been broken out and someone had pulled back the bolt by reaching through. The door was wide open of course. I shut it, pushing the bolt back into place. When I turned around, Grace was creeping timidly down the stairs, her face still pale. She clung to the railing. "Elizabeth's things," she whispered. "They spoiled all of her boxes, all the things I saved."

She sank down on the steps, rubbing her temples. Her large dark eyes looked injured, perplexed, with a touch of something else that I could have sworn was guilt.

"Maybe we should call the police," I said, feeling mean, wondering just how protective of Lyle she intended to be.

"Do you really think?" she said. Her gaze flitted back and forth indecisively and she took out a handkerchief, pressing it against her forehead as though to remove beads of sweat. "Nothing might be missing," she said hopefully. "Maybe nothing's gone."

"Or maybe we won't know the difference," I said.

She pulled herself up and moved over to the bin, taking in the disastrous piles of papers, stuffed animals, cosmetics, underwear. She stopped, picking up papers randomly, trying to make stacks. Her hands still trembled but I didn't think she was afraid. Startled perhaps, and thinking rapidly.

"I take it Raymond is still asleep," I said.

She nodded, tears welling up as the extent of the vandalism became more and more apparent. I could feel myself relent. Even if Lyle had done it, it was mean-spirited, a violation of something precious to Grace. She had already suffered enough without this. I set the flashlight aside and began to pile papers back into the boxes: costume jewelry, lingerie, old issues of *Seventeen* and *Vogue*, patterns for clothing that Libby had probably never made. "Do you mind if I take these boxes with me and go through them tonight?" I asked. "I can have them back to you by morning."

"All right. I suppose. I can't see what harm it would do now anyway," she murmured, not looking at me.

It seemed hopeless to me. In this jumble, who knew what might be missing? I'd have to go through the boxes and see if I could spot anything, but the chances weren't good. Lyle couldn't have been down there long—if it had been him. He knew I was coming back for the stuff and when he'd been there earlier, Grace probably told him exactly what time I expected to arrive. He'd had to wait until dark and he probably thought we'd spend more time upstairs before coming down. Still, he was cutting it close—unless he simply didn't care. And why didn't he break in during the three days I was gone? I thought back to his insolence and I suspected that he might take a certain satisfaction in thwarting me, even if he was caught at it.

Grace helped me cart the boxes to the car, six of them. I should have taken the stuff the first time I was there, I thought, but I couldn't picture driving to Vegas with the entire backseat filled with cardboard boxes. Still, the boxes would have been intact. It was my own damn fault, I thought sourly.

I told Grace I'd be back first thing in the morning and then I pulled out. It was going to be a long night.

I bought two containers of black coffee across the street, locked the door to my motel room, and closed the drapes. I emptied the first carton onto the bed and then I started making stacks. School papers in one pile. Personal letters. Magazines. Stuffed animals. Clothing. Cosmetics. Bills and receipts. Grace had apparently saved every article Elizabeth had touched since kindergarten. Report cards. School projects. Really, six cartons seemed modest when I realized how much there was. Blue books from college. Copies of applications for work. Tax returns. The accumulation of an entire life and it was really only so much trash. Who would ever need to refer to any of this again? The original energy and spirit had all seeped away. I did feel for her. I did get some sense of that young girl, whose gropings and triumphs and little failures were piled together now in a drab motel room. I didn't even know what I was looking for. I flipped through a diary from the fifth grade—the handwriting round and dutiful, the entries dull. I tried to imagine myself dead, someone sorting carelessly through my belongings. What was there really of my life? Canceled checks. Reports all typewritten and filed. Everything of value reduced to terse prose. I didn't keep much myself, didn't hoard or save. Two divorce decrees. That was about the sum of it for me. I collected more information about other people's lives than I did about my own, as though, perhaps, in poring over the facts about other people, I could discover something about myself. My own mystery, unplumbed, undetected, was sorted into files that were neatly labeled but really didn't say much. I picked through the last of Elizabeth's boxes but there was nothing of interest. It was 4:00 in the morning when I finished. Nothing. If there had been anything there, it was gone now and I was irritated with myself again, berating myself for my own poor judgment. This was the second time I'd arrived too late—the second time some vital piece of information had slipped away from me.

I began to repack boxes, automatically rechecking as I went, sorting. Clothes in one box, stuffed animals tucked into the spaces along the sides. School papers, diaries, blue books in the next box. Back it all went, neatly catalogued this time, compulsively arranged, as though I owed Elizabeth Glass some kind of order after I'd pried into the hidden crevices of her abandoned life. I riffed through magazines, held textbooks by the spine, letting the pages fly loose. The stacks on the bed diminished. There weren't that many personal letters and I felt guilty reading them, but I did. Some from an aunt in Arizona. Some from a girl named Judy whom Libby must have known in high school. No one seemed to refer to anything intimate in her life and I had to conclude that she confided little or else that she had no tales to tell. The disappointment was acute. I was down to the last pile of books, mostly paperbacks. Such taste. Leon Uris and Irving Stone, Victoria Holt, Georgette Heyer, a few more exotic samples that I guessed had been from some literature survey course in college. The letter slipped out of the pages of a dog-eared copy of *Pride and Prejudice*. I nearly tossed it in the box with the rest of the stuff. The handwriting was a tightly stroked cursive on two sides in dark blue ink. No date. No envelope. No postmark. I picked it up by one corner and read it, feeling a cold pinching sensation begin at the base of my spine.

Darling Elizabeth . . . I'm writing this so you'll have something when you get back. I know these separations are hard for you and I wish there were some way I could ease your pain. You are so much more honest than I am, so much more open about what you feel than I allow myself to be, but I do love you and I don't want you to have any doubts about that. You're right when you say that I'm conservative. I'm guilty as charged, your Honor, but I'm not immune to suffering and as often as I've been accused of being selfish, I'm not as reckless of others as you might think. I would like to take our time about this and be sure that it's something we both want. What we have now is very dear to me and I'm not saying—please believe me—that I wouldn't turn my life around for you if it comes to that. On the other hand, I think we should both be sure that we can survive the day-to-day absurdities of being together. Right now, the intensity dazzles and it seems simple enough for us both to chuck it all and make some kind of life, but we haven't known each other that long or that well. I can't afford to risk wife, kids, and career in the heat of the moment though you know it tempts me. Please let's move slowly on this. I love you more than I can say and I don't want to lose you—which is selfish enough, I suppose, in itself. You're right to push, but please don't lose sight of what's at stake, for you as well as me. Tolerate my caution if you can. I love you. Laurence

I didn't know what to make of it. I realized, in a flash, that it wasn't just that I hadn't believed in an affair between Laurence and Elizabeth. I hadn't *wanted* to believe. I wasn't sure I believed it yet but why the resistance? It was so neat. So convenient. It fit in so nicely with what I knew of the facts and still I stared at the letter, holding it gingerly by one corner as I read it again. I leaned back against the bed. What was the matter with me? I was exhausted and I knew I'd been through too much in the last few days but something nagged at me and I wasn't sure it had so much to do with the letter as it did with myself, with something in my nature—some little niggling piece of self-illumination that I was fighting hard not to recognize. Either the letter was real or it was not, and there were ways to verify that. I pulled myself together wearily. I found a large envelope and slipped the letter inside, being careful not to smudge fingerprints, already thinking ahead to Con Dolan, who would love it since it confirmed all his nastiest suspicions about what had been going on back then. Was this what Sharon Napier had figured out? Was this what she could have corroborated if she'd lived long enough?

I lay on the bed fully dressed, body tense, brain wired. Who could she have hoped to blackmail with this information if she'd known? It had to be what she was up to. It had to be why she'd been killed. Someone had followed me to Las Vegas, knowing that I would see her, knowing that she might confirm what I hadn't wanted to believe. I couldn't prove it, of course, but I wondered if I was getting close enough to the truth to be in danger myself. I wanted to go home. I wanted to retreat to the safety of my small room. I wasn't thinking clearly yet, but I was getting close. For eight years, nothing happened and now it was all beginning again. If Nikki was innocent, then someone had been sitting pretty all this time, someone in danger of exposure now.

I saw, for an instant, the look that had flashed in Nikki's eyes, unreasoning malevolence, a harsh irrational rage. She had set this all in motion. I had to consider the possibility that Sharon Napier was blackmailing *her*; that Sharon knew something that could link Nikki to Libby's death. If Sharon had dropped out of sight, it was possible that Nikki had hired me to flush her out and that Nikki had then eliminated any threat with one quick shot. She might also have followed me back to Sherman Oaks for a frantic search through Libby's belongings for anything that might have linked Libby to Laurence Fife. There were pieces missing yet but they would fall into place and then maybe the whole of it would make sense. Assuming I lived long enough myself to figure it out . . .

18

I dragged myself out of bed at 6:00 A.M. I hadn't slept at all. My mouth felt stale and I brushed my teeth. I showered and dressed. I longed to run but I felt too vulnerable to jog down the middle of San Vicente at that hour. I packed, closing up my typewriter, shoving the pages of my report into my briefcase. I loaded the boxes into my car again, along with my suitcase. The lights in the office were on and I could see Arlette taking jelly doughnuts out of a bakery box, putting them on a plastic plate with a clear dome lid. Water was already heating for that awful, flat instant coffee. She was licking powdered sugar from her fingers when I went in.

"God, you're up awful early," she said. "You want breakfast?"

I shook my head. Even with my penchant for junk food, I wouldn't eat a jelly doughnut. "No, but thanks," I said. "I'm checking out."

"Right now?"

I nodded, almost too tired to talk. She finally seemed

to sense that this was the wrong time to chat. She got my bill ready and I signed it, not even bothering to add up the charges. She usually made a mistake but I didn't care.

I got in my car and headed for Sherman Oaks. There was a light on in Grace's kitchen, which I approached from around the side of the building. I tapped on the window and after a moment, she came into the service porch and opened the side door. She looked small and precise this morning in an A-line corduroy skirt and a coffee-colored cotton turtleneck. She kept her voice low.

"Raymond's not awake yet but there's coffee if you like," she said.

"Thanks, but I've got a breakfast meeting at eight," I said, lying without much thought. Whatever I said would be passed on to Lyle and my whereabouts were none of his business—or hers. "I just wanted to drop the boxes off."

"Did you find anything?" she asked. Her gaze met mine briefly and then she blinked, glancing first at the floor and then off to my left.

"Too late," I said, trying to ignore the flush of relief that tinted her cheeks.

"That's unfortunate," she murmured, placing a hand against her throat. "I'm . . . uh . . . sure it wasn't Lyle . . ."

"It doesn't matter much anyway," I said. I felt sorry for her in spite of myself. "I packed everything back as neatly as I could. I'll just stack the boxes in the basement near the bin. You'll probably want to have that repaired when you get the basement door fixed."

She nodded. She moved to close the door and I stepped back, watching her pad back into the kitchen in her soft-soled slippers. I felt as if I'd personally violated her life somehow, that everything was ending on a bad note. She'd been as helpful as she knew how and she'd gotten little in return. I had to shrug. There was nothing I could do at this point. I unloaded the car, making several trips, stacking boxes just inside the damaged bin. Unconsciously, I listened for Lyle. The light in the basement was cold and gray by day, but aside from the splintered lathework and the shattered window, there was no other evidence of the intruder. I went out the back way on the last trip up from the basement, checking idly for smashed cigarette butts, bloody fingerprints, a small printed business card perhaps, dropped by whoever broke in. I came up the concrete stairs outside, looking off to the right at the path the intruder had taken—across the patchy grass in the backyard, over a sagging wire fence, and through a tangle of bushes. I could see through to the next street where the car must have been parked. It was early morning yet and the sunlight was flat and still. I could hear heavy traffic on the Ventura Freeway, which was visible in glimpses through the clumps of trees off to the right. The ground wasn't even soft enough to absorb footprints. I moved around the building to the driveway on my left, noting with interest that the power mower had now been pulled off to one side. My palms were still ripped up in places, two-inch tracks where I'd skidded across the gravel on my hands. I hadn't even thought to use Bactine and I hoped I wouldn't be subject to raging gangrene, perilous infections, or blood poisoning—dangers my aunt had warned me about every time I skinned my knee.

I got back in my car and headed for Santa Teresa, stopping in Thousand Oaks for breakfast. I was home by 10:00 in the morning. I wrapped myself up in a quilt on the couch and slept for most of the day.

At 4:00, I drove out to Nikki's beach house. I had called to say I was back in town and she invited me out for a drink. I wasn't sure yet how much I would tell her or how much, if anything, I would hold back, but after my recent gnawing suspicions about her, I wanted to test my perceptions. There are moments in every investigation when my speculations about what's possible cloud and confuse any lingering sense I have of what's actually true. I wanted to check out my intuitions.

The house was situated on a bluff overlooking the ocean. The lot was small, irregular in shape, surrounded by eucalyptus trees. The house was tucked into the landscaping—laurel and yew, with pink and red geraniums planted along the path—its exterior made of cedar shingles, still a raw-looking wood brown, the roofline undulating like an ocean swell. There was a large oval window in the front, flanked by two bow windows, all undraped. The lawn was a pale green, tender blades of grass looking almost edible, curls of eucalyptus bark intermingled like wood shavings. White and yellow daisies grew in careless patches. The whole effect was of subtle neglect, a refined wilderness untended but subdued, curiously appealing with the thick scent of ocean overlaid and the dull thunder of waves crashing down below. The air was moist and smelled of salt, wind buffeting the ragged grass. Where the house in Montebello was boxy, substantial, conventional, plain, this was a whimsical cottage, all wide angles, windows, and unpainted wood. The front door had a tall oval leaded-glass window in it, filled with tulip shapes, and the doorbell sounded like wind chimes.

Nikki appeared at once. She was wearing a celery-green caftan, its bodice embroidered with mirrors the size of dimes, the sleeves wide. Her hair was pulled up and away from her face, tied with a pale-green velvet ribbon. She seemed relaxed, her wide forehead unlined, the gray eyes looking light and clear, her mouth faintly tinted with pink, curving upward as though from some secret merriment. The languidness in her manner was gone and she was animated, energetic. I had brought the photograph album Diane had given me and I handed it to her as she closed the door behind me.

"What's this?" she asked.

"Diane put it together for Colin," I said.

"Come see him," she said. "We're making bread."

I followed her through the house. There were no square rooms at all. The spaces flowed into one another, connected by gleaming pale wood floors and bright shag rugs. There were windows everywhere, plants, skylights. A free-form fireplace in the living room looked as if it had been constructed from buff-colored boulders, piled up randomly like the entrance to a cave. On the far wall, a crude ladder led up to a loft that overlooked the ocean. Nikki smiled back at me happily, placing the album on the glass coffee table as she passed.

The kitchen was a semicircle, wood and white Formica and luscious healthy houseplants, windows on three sides looking onto a deck with the ocean stretching out beyond, wide and gray in the late afternoon. Colin was kneading bread, his back to me, his concentration complete. His hair was the same pale no-color shade as Nikki's, silky like hers where it curled down on his neck. His arms looked wiry and strong, his hands capable, fingers long. He gathered the edges of the dough, pressing inward, turning it over again. He looked like he was just on the verge of adolescence, beginning to shoot up in height but not awkward yet. Nikki touched him and he turned quickly, his gaze sliding over to me at once. I was startled. His eyes were large, tilted slightly, an army-fatigue green, his lashes thick and dark. His face was narrow, chin pointed, ears coming to a delicate point, a pixie effect with the fine hair forming a point on his forehead. The two of them looked like an illustration from a faerie book—fragile and beautiful and strange. His eyes were peaceful, empty, glowing with acute intelligence. I have seen the same look in cats, their eyes wise, aloof, grave.

When I spoke to Nikki, he watched our lips, his own

lips parting breathlessly, so that the effect was oddly sexual.

"I think I just fell in love," I said and laughed. Nikki smiled, signing to Colin, her fingers graceful, succinct. Colin flashed a smile at me, much older than his years. I felt myself flush.

"I hope you didn't tell him that," I said. "We'd probably have to run off together."

"I told him you were my first friend after prison. I told him you needed a drink," she said, still signing, eyes resting on Colin's face. "Most of the time we don't sign this much. I'm just brushing up."

While Nikki opened a bottle of wine, I watched Colin work the bread dough. He offered to let me help and I shook my head, preferring to watch his agile hands, the dough developing a smooth skin almost magically as he worked. He made gruff, unintelligible sounds now and then without seeming aware of it.

Nikki gave me chilled white wine in a glass with a thin stem while she drank Perrier. "Here's to parole," she said.

"You look much more relaxed," I said.

"Oh I am. I feel great. It's so good to have him here. I follow him everywhere. I feel like a puppy dog. He gets no peace."

Her hands were moving automatically and I could see that she was translating for him simultaneously with her comments to me. It made me feel rude and clumsy that I couldn't sign too. I felt as if there were things I wanted to say to him myself, questions I wanted to ask about the silence in his head. It was like charades of some kind, Nikki using body, arms, face, her whole self totally involved, Colin signing back to her casually. He seemed to speak much more quickly than she, without deliberation. Sometimes Nikki would halt, struggling for a word, remembering, laughing at herself as she relayed to him her own forgetfulness. His smile in those moments was indulgent, full of affection, and I envied them this special world of secrets, of self-mockery, wherein Colin was the master and Nikki the apprentice. I couldn't imagine Nikki with any other kind of child.

Colin placed the smooth dough in the bowl, turning it once to coat its pale surface with butter, covering it carefully then with a clean white towel. Nikki motioned him into the living room, where she showed him the photo album. Colin settled on the edge of the couch, leaning forward, elbows on his knees, the album open on the coffee table in front of him. His face was still but his eyes took in everything and he was already engrossed in the snapshots.

Nikki and I went out onto the deck. It was getting late but there was still enough sunlight to create the illusion of warmth. She stood at the railing, staring out at the ocean that rumbled below us. I could see tangles of kelp just under the surface in places, dark strands undulating in waves of paler green.

"Nikki, did you talk to anyone about where I was and what I was up to?" I asked.

"Not at all," she said, startled. "What makes you ask?"

I filled her in on the events of the last few days—

Sharon Napier's death, my talks with Greg and Diane, the letter I'd found among Libby Glass's effects. My trust in her was instinctive.

"Would you recognize his handwriting?"

"Sure."

I took the manila envelope out of my purse, carefully removing the letter, which I unfolded for her. She glanced at it briefly.

"That's him," she said.

"I'd like you to read it," I said. "I want to see if it coincides with your intuitions about what was going on."

Reluctantly her gaze dropped back to the pale blue pages, when she finished, she seemed almost embarrassed. "I wouldn't have guessed it was that serious. His other affairs weren't."

"What about Charlotte Mercer?"

"She's a bitch. She's an alcoholic. She called me once. I hated her. And she hated him. You should have heard what she said."

I folded the letter carefully. "I didn't get it. From Charlotte Mercer to Libby Glass. That's quite a leap. I assumed he was a man of taste."

Nikki shrugged. "He was easily seduced. It was his own vanity. Charlotte *is* beautiful . . . in her own way."

"Was she in the process of divorcing? Is that how they met?"

Nikki shook her head. "We socialized with them. Judge Mercer was a sort of mentor of Laurence's at one point. I don't imagine he ever found out about the affair—it would have killed him, I think. He's the only decent judge we've got anyway. You know what the rest are like."

"I only talked to her a short time," I said, "but I can't see how she could be involved. It had to be somebody who knew where I was and how could she have come by that kind of information? Somebody had to have followed me up to Las Vegas. Sharon's murder was too closely timed to have been coincidence."

Colin appeared at Nikki's side, placing the open photograph album up on the railing. He pointed to one of the snapshots, saying something I couldn't understand at all, an indistinct blur of vowels. It was the first time I'd heard him speak. His voice was deeper than I would have imagined for a twelve-year-old.

"That's Diane's junior-high-school graduation," Nikki said to him. Colin looked at her for a moment and then pointed again more emphatically. He put his index finger in front of his mouth and moved it up and down rapidly. Nikki frowned.

" 'Who' what, honey?"

Colin placed his finger on the picture of a group of people.

"That's Diane and Greg and Diane's friend, Terri, and Diane's mother," she said to him, enunciating carefully and signing at the same time.

A puzzled smile formed on Colin's face. Colin spread his hands out, putting his thumb against his forehead and then his chin.

Nikki laughed this time, her expression as puzzled as his.

"No, *that's* Nana," she said, pointing to a snapshot one page back. "This is *Diane's* mother, not Daddy's. The mother of Greg and Diane. Don't you remember Nana? Oh God, how could he," she flashed at me. "She died when he was a year old." She looked back at him.

Colin made some guttural sounds, something negative and frustrated. I wondered what would happen to his temper when puberty really caught up with him. Again the thumb against the forehead, then the chin. Nikki shot me another look. "He keeps saying 'Daddy's mother' for Gwen. How do you explain 'ex-wife'?" She signed again patiently.

Colin shook his head slightly, suddenly unsure of himself. He watched her for a moment more as though some other explanation might be forthcoming. He took the album and backed away, eyes still fixed on Nikki's face. He signed once more, flushing uncomfortably. Apparently, he didn't want to look foolish in front of me.

"We'll go through those together in a minute," she signed to him, translating for me.

Colin moved slowly back through the sliding glass doors, pushing the screen door shut.

"Sorry for the interruption," she said briefly.

"That's all right, I've got to go anyway," I said.

"You can stay for supper if you like. I've made a big pot of beef bourguignon. It's great with Colin's bread."

"Thanks but I've got all kinds of things to do," I said.

Nikki walked me to the door, signing our final chitchat without even being aware of it.

I got in my car and sat for a moment, puzzled by Colin's puzzlement over Gwen. That was odd. Very odd.

19

When I got back to my apartment, Charlie Scorsoni was sitting on my doorstep. I felt grubby and unprepared and I realized with embarrassment that I'd been entertaining a fantasy of how we'd meet again and it wasn't like this.

"God, don't get all excited, Millhone," he said when he saw the expression on my face.

I got out my key. "I'm sorry," I said, "but you catch me at the worst possible times."

"You have a date," he said.

"No, I don't have a date. I look like shit." I unlocked the door and flipped on the desk lamp, letting him follow me in.

"At least I caught you in a good mood," he said, making himself at home. He sauntered out to the kitchen and got out the last beer. The familiarity in his manner made me cross.

"Look, I've got laundry to do. I haven't been to the grocery store for a week. My mail is piled up, the whole place is covered with dust. I haven't even shaved my legs since I saw you last."

"You need a haircut too," he said.

"No I don't. It always looks like this."

He smiled, shaking his head. "Get dressed. We'll go out."

"I don't want to go out. I want to get my life in shape."

"You can do that tomorrow. It's Sunday. I bet you always do shit like that on Sunday anyway."

I stared at him. It was true. "Wait a minute. Here's how it's supposed to go," I said patiently. "I get home. I do all my chores, get a good night's sleep, which I could sorely use, then tomorrow I call you and we see each other tomorrow night."

"I gotta be at the office tomorrow night. I have a client coming in."

"On Sunday night?"

"We've got a court appearance first thing Monday morning and this is the only thing we could work out. I just got back into town myself Thursday night and I'm up to my ass."

I stared at him some more, wavering. "Where would we go? Would I have to dress up?"

"Well I'm not going to take you anywhere looking like *that*," he said.

I glanced down. I was still wearing jeans and the shirt I'd slept in but I wasn't ready to back down yet. "What's wrong with this?" I asked perversely.

"Take a shower and change clothes. I'll pick up some

stuff at the grocery store if you give me a list. By the time I get that done, you'll be ready, yes?"

"I like to shop for my own stuff. Anyway, all I need is milk and beer."

"Then I'll take you to a supermarket after we eat," he said, emphasizing every single word.

We drove down to the Ranch House in Ojai, one of those elegant restaurants where the waiter stands at your table and recites the menu like a narrative poem.

"Shall I order for us or would that offend your feminine sensibilities?"

"Go ahead," I said, feeling oddly relieved, "I'd like that." While he and the waiter conferred, I studied Charlie's face surreptitiously. It was strong and square, good jawline, visible dent in his chin, full mouth. His nose looked like it might have been broken once but mended skillfully, leaving only the slightest trace just below the bridge. His glasses had large lenses, tinted a blue-gray, and behind them, his blue eyes were as clear as sky. Sandy lashes, sandy brows, his thick sandy hair only beginning to recede. He had big hands, big bones in his wrists, and I could see a feathering of sandy hair at the cuff. There was something else about him, too, smoldering and opaque, the same sense I'd had before of sexuality that surfaced now and then. Sometimes he seemed to emit an almost audible hum, like a line of power stations marching inexorably across a hillside, ominous and marked with danger signs. I was afraid of him.

The waiter was nodding and moving away. Charlie turned back to me, obscurely amused. I felt myself go mute, but he pretended not to notice and I felt dimly grateful, faintly flushed. I was overcome with the same self-consciousness I'd felt once at a birthday party in the sixth grade when I realized that all the other little girls had worn nylon stockings and I was still wearing stupid white ankle socks.

The waiter returned with a bottle of wine and Charlie went through the usual ritual. When our glasses were filled, he touched his rim to mine, his eyes on my face. I sipped, startled by the delicacy of the wine, which was pale and cool.

"So how's the investigation going?" he asked when the waiter had left.

I shook my head, taking a moment to orient myself. "I don't want to talk about it," I said shortly and then caught myself. "I don't mean to be rude," I said in a softened tone. "I just don't think talking about it will help. It's not going well."

"I'm sorry to hear that," he said. "It's bound to improve."

I shrugged and watched while he lit a cigarette and snapped the lighter shut. "I didn't know you smoked," I said.

"Now and then," he said. He offered me the pack and I shook my head again. He seemed relaxed, in possession of himself, a man of sophistication and grace. I felt doltish and tongue-tied, but he didn't seem to expect anything of me, talking on about inconsequential things. He seemed to operate at half speed, taking his own time about everything. It made me aware of the usual tension with which I live, that keyed-up state of raw nerve that makes me grind my teeth in my sleep. Sometimes I get so wired that I forget to eat at all, only remembering at night, even then not being hungry but wolfing down food anyway as though the speed and quantity of consumption might atone for the infrequency. With Charlie, I could feel my time clock readjust, my pace slowing to match his. When I finished the second glass of wine, I heaved a sigh and only then did I realize that I'd been holding myself tensely, like a joke snake ready to jump out of a box.

"Feel better?" he said.

"Yes."

"Good. Then we'll eat."

The meal that followed was one of the most sensual I ever experienced: fresh, tender bread with a crust of flaky layers, spread with a buttery pâté, Boston lettuce with a delicate vinaigrette, sand dabs sautéed in butter and served with succulent green grapes. There were fresh raspberries for dessert with a dollop of tart cream, and all the time Charlie's face across the table from me, shadowed by that suggestion of caution, that hint of something stark and fearful held back, pulling me forward even while I felt myself kept in check.

"How'd you end up in law school?" I asked him when coffee arrived.

"Accident I guess. My father was a drunk and a bum, a real shit. Knocked me around a lot. Not seriously. More like a piece of furniture that got in his way. He beat my mother too."

"Doesn't do much for your self-esteem," I ventured.

Charlie shrugged. "It was good for me actually. Made me tough. Let me know I couldn't depend on anyone but myself, which is a lesson you might as well learn when you're ten. I took care of me."

"You worked your way through school?"

"Every nickel's worth. I picked up money ghosting papers for jocks, sitting in on tests, writing C minus answers so no one would suspect. You'd be surprised how tricky it is to miss just enough questions to look genuine. I had regular jobs, too, but after I watched half a fraternity get into law school on my smarts, I figured I might as well try it myself."

"What'd your father do when he didn't drink?"

"Construction till his health broke down. He finally died of cancer. Took him six years. Bad stuff. I didn't give a shit and he knew it. All that pain. Served him right," he said and shook his head. "My mother died four months after he did. I thought she'd be relieved he was gone. Turns out she was dependent on the abuse."

"Why do estate law? That doesn't seem like you. I picture you doing criminal law, something like that."

"Listen, my father pissed away everything he had. I ended up with nothing—less than nothing. It took me years to pay off his hospital bills and his fucking debts. I had to pay for my mother's death, too, which at least was quick, God bless her, but hardly cheap. So now I show people how to outwit the government even in death. A lot of my clients are dead so we get along very well and I make sure their greedy heirs get more than

they deserve. Also when you're executor for somebody's estate, you get paid on time and nobody calls
you up about your bill."

"Not a bad deal," I said.

"Not at all," he agreed.

"Have you ever been married?"

"Nope. I never had time for that. I work. That's the
only thing that interests me. I don't like the idea of giving someone else the right to make demands. In exchange for what?"

I had to laugh. I felt the same way myself. His tone
throughout was ironic and the look he laid on me then
was oddly sexual, full of strange, compelling male heat
as though money and power and sexuality were all
somehow tangled up for him and fed on one another.
There was really nothing open or loose or free about
him, however candid he might seem, but I knew that it
was precisely his opacity that appealed to me. Did he
know that I was attracted to him? He gave little indication of his own feelings one way or the other.

When we finished our coffee, he signaled for the
waiter without a word and paid the check. Conversation between us was dwindling anyway and I let it lie,
feeling watchful, quiet, even wary of him again. We
moved through the restaurant, our bodies close but
our behavior polite, circumspect. He opened the door
for me. I passed through. He'd made no gesture toward me, verbally or otherwise, and, I was suddenly
disconcerted, lest my sense of his pull turned out to be
something generated in me and not reciprocal. Charlie
took my arm briefly, guiding me up a shallow step but

as soon as we were on smooth pavement again, he dropped his hand. We went around to my side of the car. He opened the door and I got in. I didn't think I'd said anything flirtatious and I was glad of that, curious still about his intentions toward me. He was so matter-of-fact, so removed.

We drove back to Santa Teresa, saying little. I was feeling mute again, not uncomfortable but languid. As we approached the outskirts of town, he reached over and took my hand noncommittally. It felt like a low-voltage current was suffusing my left side. He kept his left hand on the steering wheel. With his right hand, he was carelessly, casually rubbing my fingers, his attitude inattentive. I was trying to be as casual as he, trying to pretend there might be some other way to interpret those smoldering sexual signals that made the air crackle between us and caused my mouth to go dry. What if I was wrong, I thought. What if I fell on the man like a dog on a bone only to discover that his meaning was merely friendly, absentminded, or impersonal? I couldn't think about anything because there was no sound between us, nothing said, not anything I could react to or fix on—no way to divert myself. He was making it hard to breathe. I felt like a glass rod being rubbed on silk. Out of the corner of my eye, I thought I saw his face turn toward me. I glanced at him.

"Hey," he said softly. "Guess what we're going to do?"

Charlie shifted in his seat slightly and pressed my hand between his legs. A charge shot through me and I groaned involuntarily. Charlie laughed, a low excited sound, and then he looked back at the road.

Making love with Charlie was like being taken into a big warm machine. Nothing was required of me. Everything was attended to with such ease, such fluidity. There were no awkward moments. There was no holding back, no self-consciousness, no hesitation, no heed. It was as though a channel had been opened between us, sexual energy flowing back and forth without impediment. We made love more than once. At first, there was too much hunger, too much heat. We came at each other with a clash, an intensity that admitted of no tenderness. We crashed against one other like waves on a breakwater, surges of pleasure driving straight up, curling back again. All of the emotional images were of pounding assault, sensations of boom and buffet and battering ram until he had broken through to me, rolling down again and over me until all my walls were reduced to rubble and ash. He raised himself up on his elbow then and kissed me long and sweet and it began all over again, only this time at his pace, half speed, agonizingly slow like the gradual ripening of a peach on a limb. I could feel myself go all rosy, turn to honey and oil—a mellowing ease filtering through me like a sedative. We lay there afterward, laughing and sweaty and out of breath and then he encompassed me in sleep, the weight of his big arms pinning me to the bed. But far from feeling trapped, I felt comforted and safe, as though nothing could ever harm me as long as I stayed in the shadow of this man, this sheltering cave of flesh, where I was tucked away until morning without waking once.

At 7:00, I felt him kiss me lightly on the forehead, and after that the door closed softly. By the time I'd stirred myself awake, he was gone.

20

I got up at 9:00 and spent Sunday taking care of personal chores. I cleaned my place, did laundry, went to the supermarket, and had a nice visit in the afternoon with my landlord, who was sunning himself in the backyard. For a man of eighty-one, Henry Pitts has an amazing set of legs. He also has a wonderful beaky nose, a thin aristocratic face, shocking white hair, and eyes that are periwinkle blue. The overall effect is very sexy, electric, and the photographs I've seen of him in his youth don't even half compare. At twenty and thirty and forty, Henry's face seems too full, too unformed. As the decades pass, the pictures begin to reveal a man growing lean and fierce, until now he seems totally concentrated, like a basic stock boiled down to a rich elixir.

"Listen, Henry," I said, plunking down on the grass near his chaise. "You live entirely too idle a life."

"Sin and degradation," he said complacently, not even bothering to open his eyes. "You had company last night."

"A sleep-over date. Just like our mamas warned us about."

"How was it?"

"I'm not telling," I said. "What kind of crossword puzzle did you concoct this week?"

"An easy one. All doubles. Prefixes—'bi,' 'di,' 'bis,' 'dis.' Twin. Twain. Binary. Things like that. Try this one: six letters, 'double impression.' "

"Already, I give up."

" 'Mackle.' It's a printer's term. Kind of a cheat but the fit was so nice. Try this. 'Double meaning.' Nine letters."

"Henry, would you *quit* that?"

" 'Ambiguity.' I'll leave it on your doorstep."

"No, don't. I get those things in my head and I can't get 'em out."

He smiled. "You run yet?"

"No, but I'm on my way," I said, hopping up again. I crossed the grass, glancing back at him with a grin. He was putting suntan oil on his knees, which were already a gorgeous shade of caramel. I wondered how much it really mattered that there was a fifty-year difference in our ages. But then again, I had Charlie Scorsoni to think about. I changed clothes and did my run. And thought about him.

Monday morning, I went in to see Con Dolan at Homicide. He was talking on the phone when I got there, so I sat down at his desk. He was tipped back in his chair, feet jammed against the edge of the desk, the receiver laid loosely against his ear. He was saying, "uh-huh, uh-huh, uh-huh," looking bored. He scanned me with care, taking in every detail of my face, as though he were memorizing me all over again, running me through a computer file of known felons, looking for a match. I stared back at him. In moments, I could see the young man in his face, which was sagging now and worn, pouches beneath his eyes, hair slicked down, cheeks turning soft at the jawline as though the flesh were beginning to warm and melt. The skin on his neck had collapsed into a series of fine folds, reddened and bulging slightly over his starched shirt collar. I feel an ornery kind of kinship with him, which I never can quite identify. He's tough, emotionless, withdrawn, calculating, harsh. I've heard he's mean, too, but what I see in him is the overriding competence. He knows his business and he takes no guff and despite the fact he gives me a hard time whenever he can, I know he likes me, though grudgingly. I saw his attention sharpen. He focused on what was being said to him and it made his temper climb.

"All right now, you listen here, Mitch, because I've said all I intend to say. We're getting down to the short strokes on this and I don't want you fuckin' up my case. Yeah, I know that. Yeah, that's what you said. I just want it clear between us. I gave your boy all the breaks I mean to give so either he cooperates or we can put him right back where he was. Yeah, well you talk to him again!"

Con dropped the phone down from a height, not exactly slamming it but making his point. He was done. He looked at me through a haze of irritation. I put the manila envelope on his desk. He put his feet on the floor.

"What *is* this?" he said snappishly. He peered in through the flap, removing the letter I'd found in Libby Glass's effects. Even without knowing what it was, he held it by the edges, his eyes raking the contents once and then going back again with caution. He glanced up at me sharply. He tucked it back in the envelope.

"Where'd you get it?"

"Libby Glass's mother kept all her stuff. It was shoved in a paperback book. I picked it up Friday. Can you have it checked for fingerprints?"

The look he gave me was cold. "Why don't we talk about Sharon Napier first?"

I felt a spurt of fear, but I didn't hesitate. "She's dead," I said, reaching for the envelope. He smacked his fist down on it and I drew my hand back. We locked eyes. "A friend of mine in Vegas told me," I said. "That's how I knew."

"Horseshit. You drove up there."

"Wrong."

"God damn it, don't lie to me," he snapped.

I could feel my temper flare. "You want to read me my rights, Lieutenant Dolan? You want to hand me a certification of notification of my constitutional rights? Because I'll read it and sign it if you like. And then I'll call my attorney, and when he gets down here, we can chat. How's that?"

"You've been on this business two weeks and somebody shows up dead. You cross me up and I'll have your ass. Now you give it to me straight. I told you to keep out of this."

"Uh-uh. You told me to keep out of trouble, which I did. You said you'd like a little help making the connection between Libby Glass and Laurence Fife and I gave you that," I said, indicating the manila envelope.

He picked it up and tossed it in the trash. I knew it was just for effect. I tried another tack.

"Come on, Con," I said. "I had nothing to do with Sharon Napier's death. Not in any way, shape, or form. What do you think? That I'd run up there and kill somebody who might be of help? You're crazy! I never even went to Vegas. I was down at the Salton Sea talking to Greg Fife and if you doubt my word, call *him*!" I shut my mouth then and stared at him hotly, letting this bold admixture of truth and utter falsehood penetrate his darkened face.

"How'd you know where she was?"

"Because I spent a day and a half on a trace through a Nevada P.I. named Bob Dietz. I was going to drive to Vegas after I talked to Greg. I put a call through first and found out somebody'd put a bullet in her. How do you think *I* feel about that? She might have filled in a few blanks for me. I've got it tough enough as it is. This goddamn case is eight years old, now give me a break!"

"Who knew you intended to talk to her?"

"I don't know that. If you're implying that somebody killed her to keep her from talking to me, I think you're wrong but I couldn't swear to that. She was stepping on a lot of toes up there from what I hear. And don't ask me the particulars because I don't know. I just hear she was treading on somebody's turf."

He sat and stared at me then and I guessed that I must have hit a vein. The rumors my friend in Vegas had passed on must have lined up with whatever the Las Vegas Police Department had turned up. I was personally convinced that she'd been killed to shut her mouth, that someone had followed me and had gotten to her just in time, but I was damned if I was going to have a finger pointed at me. I couldn't see what purpose it would serve and it would only prevent me from getting on with my own inquiries. I still wasn't entirely easy about the fact that someone else had probably tipped off the Las Vegas PD about the shooting. One more minute in her apartment and I'd have been in a real jam, which might have closed down my investigation for good. Whatever regret I felt for my involvement with her death wasn't going to be expiated by my being caught up in the aftermath.

"What else have you found out about Libby Glass?" he asked me then, his tone shifting slightly along with the subject.

"Not a lot. Right now, I'm still trying to make a few pieces fall into place, and so far I'm not having much luck. If that letter really was written by Laurence Fife, then at least we can nail that down. Frankly, I hope it wasn't, but Nikki seems to think the writing is his. There's something about it that doesn't sit well with me. Can you let me know if the prints match?"

Con pushed impatiently at a stack of files on his desk. "I'll think about that," he said. "I don't want us to get buddy-buddy over this."

"Believe me, we will never be close friends," I said, and for some reason his expression softened slightly and I almost thought he might smile.

"Get out of here," he said gruffly.

I went.

I got in my car and left the downtown area, taking a left on Anaconda down to the beach. It was a gorgeous day—sunny and cool, with fat clouds squatting on the horizon. There were sailboats here and there, probably planted by the Chamber of Commerce to look picturesque for the tourists who straggled along the sidewalk taking snapshots of other tourists who were sitting in the grass.

At Ludlow Beach, I followed the hill upward and then branched off onto the steep side street where Marcia Threadgill lived. I parked and got out my binoculars, scanning her patio. All of her plants were present and accounted for and they were all looking healthier than I liked. There was no sign of Marcia or the neighbor she feuded with. I wished she would move so I could take pictures of her lugging fifty-pound cartons of books down to a U-Haul van. I'd even settle for a glimpse of her coming back from the grocery store with a big double bag of canned goods ripping across the bottom from the weight. I focused in on her patio again and noticed for the first time that there were actually four plant hooks screwed into the wooden overhang of the patio above. On the hook at the near corner was the mammoth plant I'd seen before, but the other three hooks were empty.

I put the binoculars away and went into the building, pausing at the landing between the second and third floors. I peered down through the stair railing. If I situated myself correctly, I'd be able to focus my camera at just the right angle to pick up a nice view of Marcia's front door. Having ascertained that much, I went out to my car again and drove to the Gateway supermarket. I hefted a few houseplants potted in plastic and found one that was just right for my purposes—twenty-five pounds of sturdy trunk with a series of vicious swordlike leaves protruding at intervals. I picked up some prettied gift ribbons in a fire-engine red and a get-well card with a sentimental verse. All of this was taking up precious time that I would have preferred devoting to Nikki Fife's business, but I have my rent to account for and I felt like I owed California Fidelity for at least half a month.

I went back to Marcia's apartment and parked in front. I checked my camera, tore open the packaged ribbons, and stuck several of them to the plastic pot in a jaunty fashion and then tucked the card down inside with a signature scrawled on it that even I couldn't read. I hoisted plant, camera, and myself with a slightly thudding heart up the steep concrete stairs, into the building, and up to the second floor. I set the plant down near Marcia's doorsill and then went up to the landing, where I checked my light meter, set up the camera, and adjusted the focus on the lens. Nice angle, I thought. This was going to be a work of art. I trotted back down, took a deep breath, and rang Ms. Thread-gill's bell, racing back up the stairs again at breakneck speed. I picked up the camera and checked the focus again. My timing was perfect.

Marcia Threadgill opened her front door and stared down with surprise and puzzlement. She was wearing shorts and a crocheted halter and in the background the voice of Olivia Newton-John boomed out like an audible lollipop. I hesitated a moment and then peered over the rail. Marcia was leaning over to extract the card. She read it, turned it over, and then studied its face again, shrugging with bewilderment. She glanced down the stairwell as though she might catch sight of the delivery person. I began to click off pictures, the whir of the thirty-five-millimeter camera obscured by the record being played too loudly. Marcia padded back to her doorsill and bent casually from the waist, picking up twenty-five pounds of plant without even bothering to bend her knees as we've all been in-structed to in the exercise manuals. As soon as she'd trucked the plant inside, I raced back down the stairs and out to the street, focusing again from the sidewalk below just as she appeared on the patio and placed the plant up on the rail. She disappeared. I backed up sev-eral yards, attaching the telephoto lens, waiting then with my breath held.

Back she came with what must have been a kitchen chair. I clicked off some nice shots of her climbing up.

Sure enough, she picked up the plant by the wire, heaving it up to shoulder height, muscles straining until she caught the wire loop on the overhead hook. The effort was such that her halter hiked up and I got a nice shot of Marcia Threadgill's quite large bosom peeping out. I turned away just in time, I suspect, catching only the inkling of her quick look around to see if anyone else had spotted her exposure. When I glanced back casually she was gone.

I dropped the film off to be developed, making sure it was properly dated and identified. Still photographs were not going to be much good to us, especially without a witness to corroborate my testimony as to the date, time, and circumstance, but the pictures might at least persuade the claims manager at California Fidelity to pursue the case, which was the best I could hope for at this point. With his authorization, I could go back with a video outfit and a real photographer and pick up some footage that would stand up in court.

I should have known he wouldn't see it that way. Andy Motycka is in his early forties and he still bites his nails. He was working on his right hand that day, trying to gnaw off what remained of his thumb. It made me nervous just to look at him. I kept expecting him to rip loose a big triangle of flesh at the corner of his cuticle. I could feel my face set with distaste and I had to stare just over his shoulder to the left. Before I was even halfway through my explanation, he was shaking his head.

"Can't do it," he said bluntly. "This chick doesn't even have an attorney. We're supposed to get a signed release from the doctor next week. No deal. I don't want to mess this one up. Forty-eight hundred dollars is chicken feed. It'd cost us ten grand to go into court. You know that."

"Well, I know, but—"

"But nothing. The risk is too great. I don't even know why Mac had you check this one out. Look, I know it frosts your ass, but so what? You set her off and she'll go straight out and hire a lawyer and next thing you know, she'll sue us for a million bucks. Forget it."

"She'll just do it again somewhere else," I said.

Andy shrugged.

"Why do I waste my time on this shit," I said, voice rising with frustration.

"Beats me," he said conversationally. "Let me see the pix, though, when you get 'em back. Her tits are huge."

"Screw you," I said and moved on into my office.

21

There were two messages on my answering service. The first was from Garry Steinberg. I called him back.

"Hey, Kinsey," he said when I'd been put through.

"Hi, Garry. How are you?"

"Not bad. I've got a little piece of information for you," he said. I could tell from his tone that he was feeling satisfied with himself, but what he said next still took me by surprise.

"I looked up that job application on Lyle Abernathy this morning. Apparently he worked for a while as an apprentice to a locksmith. Some old guy named Fears."

"A locksmith?"

"That's right. I called the guy this morning. You'd have loved it. I said Abernathy had applied for a job as a security guard and I was doing a background check. Fears hemmed and hawed some and finally said he'd had to fire the kid. Fears was getting a lot of complaints about missing cash on jobs where Lyle had worked and he began to suspect he was involved in petty thievery. He never could prove it, but he couldn't afford to take the chance, so he let Lyle go."

"Oh God, that's great," I said. "That means Lyle could have gotten into the Fifes' house anytime he wanted to. Libby's too."

"It looks that way. He worked for Fears for eight months and he sure picked up enough information to give it a try, judging from what Fears said. Unless they had burglar alarms or something like that."

"Listen, the only security system they had in effect was a big German shepherd that got hit by a car six weeks before Laurence Fife died. He and his wife and kids were away when the dog was killed."

"Nice," Garry said. "Nothing you could prove after all this time, but it might put you on the right track at any rate. What about the application? You want a copy?"

"I'd love it. What about Fife's accounts?"

"I've got those at my place and I'll look at 'em when I can. It's a lot of stuff. In the meantime, I just thought you might want to know about that locksmith stint."

"I appreciate your help. Jesus, what a schmuck that guy is."

"I'll say. Hey, I got another call coming in. I'll be in touch." He gave me his home phone in case I needed him.

"You're terrific. Thanks."

The second message was from Gwen at K-9 Korners. One of her assistants answered and I listened to assorted dogs bark and whine while Gwen came to the phone.

"Kinsey?"

"Yeah, it's me. I got your call. What's happening?"

"Are you free for lunch?"

"Just a minute. I'll check my appointment book," I said. I put my palm against the mouth of the receiver and looked at my watch. It was 1:45. Had I *eaten* lunch? Had I even eaten breakfast today? "Yes, I'm free."

"Good. I'll meet you at the Palm Garden in fifteen minutes if that's okay for you."

"Sure. Fine. See you shortly."

My glass of white wine had just arrived when I glanced up to see Gwen approaching from across the courtyard: tall and lean, her gray hair slicked away from her face. The blouse she wore was gray silk, long full sleeves nipped in at the wrist, the dark gray skirt emphasizing her trim waist and hips. She was stylish, confident—like Nikki in that—and I could see where both women must have appealed to Laurence Fife. I guessed that once upon a time Charlotte Mercer fit the same mold: a woman of stature, a woman of taste. I wondered idly if Libby Glass would have aged as well had she lived. She must have been much less secure at twenty-four, but bright—someone whose freshness and ambition might have appealed to Laurence as he neared the age of forty. God save us all from the consequences of male menopause, I thought.

"Hello. How are you," Gwen said briskly, sitting down. She removed the napkin beside her plate and ordered wine as the waitress passed. Close up, her image softened, the angularity of her cheekbones offset by the large brown eyes, the purposeful mouth tinted with soft pink. Most of all, there was her manner: amused, intelligent, feminine, refined.

"How are all the dogs?" I said.

She laughed. "Filthy. Thank God. We're swamped today, but I wanted to talk to you. You've been out of town."

"I just got back Saturday. Have you been trying to get in touch?"

She nodded. "I called the office on Tuesday, I think. Your answering service said you were in Los Angeles so I tried to reach you there. Some total nitwit answered—"

"Arlette."

"Well, whoever it was, she got my name wrong twice so I hung up."

The waitress arrived with Gwen's wine.

"Have you ordered yet?"

I shook my head. "I was waiting for you."

The waitress got out her order card, glancing at me.

"I'll have the chef's salad," I said.

"Make that two."

"Dressing?"

"Blue cheese," I said.

"I'll have oil and vinegar," Gwen said and then

handed both menus to the waitress, who moved away. Gwen turned her attention to me.

"I've decided I should level with you."

"About what?"

"My old lover," she said. Her cheeks had flushed mildly. "I realized that if I didn't tell you who he was, you'd be off on some wild-goose chase, wasting a lot of time trying to find out his name. It really amounts to more mystery than it's worth."

"How so?"

"He died a few months ago of a heart attack," she said, her manner turning brisk again. "After I talked to you, I tried tracking him down myself. His name was David Ray. He was a schoolteacher. Greg's, as a matter of fact, which is how we met. I thought he should know that you were asking questions about Laurence's death, or at any rate that your curiosity might lead you to him."

"How'd you find him?"

"I'd heard that he and his wife had moved to San Francisco. Apparently he was living in the Bay Area, where he was a principal of one of the Oakland public schools."

"Why not tell me before?"

She shrugged. "Misplaced loyalty. Protectiveness. That was a very important relationship and I didn't want him involved at this late date."

She looked at me and she must have read the skepticism in my face. The flush in her cheeks deepened almost imperceptibly.

"I know how it looks," she said. "First I refuse to

give you his name and then he's dead and out of reach, but that's exactly the point. If he were still alive, I don't know that I'd be telling you this."

I thought that was probably true, but there was something else going on and I wasn't sure what it was. The waitress arrived with our salads and there was a merciful few minutes in which we busied ourselves with melba rounds. Gwen was rearranging her lettuce but she wasn't eating much. I was curious to hear what else she had to say and too hungry to worry about it much until I'd eaten some.

"Did you know he had heart trouble?" I asked finally.

"I had no idea, but I gather he was ill for years."

"Did he break off the relationship or did you?"

Gwen smiled bitterly. "Laurence did that but I wonder now if David might have engineered it to some extent. The whole affair must have complicated his life unbearably."

"He'd told his wife?"

"I think so. She was very gracious on the phone. I told her that Greg had asked me to get in touch and she played right along. When she told me that David was dead, I was . . . I didn't even know what to say to her but of course, I had to babble right on—how sorry, how sad . . . like some disinterested bystander making the right noises somehow. It was awful. Terrible."

"She didn't mention your relationship herself?"

"Oh no. She was much too cool for that, but she did know exactly who I was. Anyway, I'm sorry I didn't tell you to begin with."

"No harm done," I said.

"How's it going otherwise?" she asked.

I felt myself hesitate. "Bits and pieces. Nothing concrete."

"Do you really expect to turn up anything after all this time?"

I smiled. "You never know. People get careless when they're feeling safe."

"I guess that's true."

We talked briefly about Greg and Diane and my visits with them, which I edited heavily. At 2:50 Gwen glanced at her watch.

"I've got to get back," she said, fishing in her purse for her billfold. She took out a five-dollar bill. "Will you keep in touch?"

"Sure," I said. I took a sip of wine, watching her get up. "When did you last see Colin?"

She focused abruptly on my face. "Colin?"

"I just met him Saturday," I said as though that explained it. "I thought maybe Diane might like to know he's back. She's fond of him."

"Yes, she is," Gwen said. "I don't know when I saw him last myself. Diane's graduation, I guess. Her junior-high-school graduation. What makes you ask?"

I shrugged. "Just curious," I said. I gave her what I hoped was my blandest look. A mild pink patch had appeared on her neck and I wondered if that could be introduced in court as a lie-detecting device. "I'll take care of the tip," I said.

"Let me know how it goes," she said, all casual again.

She tucked the money under her plate and moved off at the same efficient pace that had brought her in. I watched her departure, thinking that something vital had gone unsaid. She could have told me about David Ray on the phone. And I wasn't entirely convinced she hadn't known about his death to begin with. Colin popped into my head.

I walked the two blocks to Charlie's office. Ruth was typing from a Dictaphone, fingers moving lightly across the keyboard. She was very fast.

"Is he in?"

She smiled and nodded me on back, not missing a word, gaze turned inward as she translated sound to paper with no lag time in between.

I stuck my head into his office. He was sitting at his desk, coat off, a law book open in front of him. Beige shirt, dark brown vest. When he saw me, a slow smile formed and he leaned back, tucking an arm up over the back of his swivel chair. He tossed the pencil on his desk.

"Are you free for dinner?" I said.

"What's up?"

"Nothing's up. It's a proposition," I said.

"Six-fifteen."

"I'll be back," I said and closed his office door again, still thinking about that pale shirt and the dark brown vest. Now *that* was sexy. A man in a nylon bikini, with that little knot sticking out in front, isn't half as interesting as a man in a good-looking business suit. Charlie's outfit reminded me of a Reese's

Peanut Butter Cup with a bite taken out and I wanted the rest.

I drove out to Nikki's beach house.

22

Nikki answered the door in an old gray sweatshirt and a pair of faded jeans. She was barefoot, hair loose, a paintbrush in one hand, her fingers stained the color of pecan shells.

"Oh hi, Kinsey. Come on in," she said. She was already moving back toward the deck and I followed her through the house. On the other side of the sliding glass doors, I could see Colin, shirtless, in a pair of bib overalls sitting cross-legged in front of a chest of drawers, which the two were apparently refinishing. The drawers were out, leaning upright along the balcony, hardware removed. The air smelled of stripper and turpentine, which mingled not incompatibly with the smell of eucalyptus bark. Several sheets of fine sandpaper were folded and tossed aside, creases worn white with wood dust, looking soft from hard use. The sun was hot on the railings and newspapers were spread out under the chest to protect the deck.

Colin glanced up at me and smiled as I came out. His nose and cheeks were faintly pink with sunburn, his eyes green as sea water, bare arms rosy, there wasn't even a whisper of facial hair yet. He went back to his work.

"I want to ask Colin something but I thought I'd try it out on you first," I said to Nikki.

"Sure, fire away," she replied. I leaned against the railing while she dipped the tip of her brush back into a small can of stain, easing the excess off along the edge. Colin seemed more interested in the painting than he was in our exchange. I imagined that it was a bit of a strain to try to follow a conversation even if his lip-reading skills were good or maybe he thought adults were a bore.

"Can you remember offhand if you were out of town for any length of time in the four to six months before Laurence died?"

Nikki looked at me with surprise and blinked, apparently not expecting that. "I was gone once for a week. My father had a heart attack that June and I flew back to Connecticut," she said. She paused then and shook her head. "That was the only time, I think. What are you getting at?"

"I'm not sure. I mean, this is going to seem far-fetched, but I've been bothered by Colin's calling Gwen 'Daddy's mother.' Has he mentioned that since?"

"Nope. Not a word."

"Well, I'm wondering if he didn't have occasion to see Gwen at some point while you were gone. He's too smart to get her mixed up with his own grandmother unless somebody identified her to him that way."

Nikki gave me a skeptical look. "Boy, that *is* a

stretch. He couldn't have been more than three and a half years old."

"Yeah, I know, but a little while ago I asked Gwen when she saw him last and she claims it was at Diane's junior-high-school graduation."

"That's probably true," Nikki said.

"Nikki, Colin must have been fourteen months old at the time. I saw those snapshots myself. He was still a babe in arms."

"So?"

"So why did he remember her at all?"

Nikki applied a band of stain, giving that some thought. "Maybe she saw him in a supermarket or ran into him with Diane. She could have seen him or he could easily have seen her without any particular significance attached to it.

"Maybe. But I think Gwen lied to me about it when I asked. If it was no big deal, why not just say so. Why cover up?"

Nikki gave me a long look. "Maybe she just forgot."

"Mind if I ask him?"

"No, go ahead."

"Where's the album?"

She gestured over her shoulder and I went back into the living room. The photograph album was sitting on the coffee table and I flipped through until I found the snapshot of Gwen. I slipped it out of the four little corners holding it down and went back out to the deck. I held it out to him.

"Ask him if he can remember what was happening when he saw her last," I said.

Nikki reached over and gave him a tap. He looked at her and then at the snapshot, eyes meeting mine inquisitively. Nikki signed the question to him. His face closed up like a day lily when the sun goes down.

"Colin?"

He started to paint again, his face averted.

"The little shit," she said good-naturedly. She gave him a nudge and asked him again.

Colin shrugged her off. I studied his reaction with care.

"Ask him if she was here."

"Who, Gwen? Why would she be here?"

"I don't know. That's why we're asking him."

The look she gave me was half doubt, half disbelief. Reluctantly, she looked back at him. She signed to him, translating for my benefit. She didn't seem to like it much.

"Was Gwen ever here or at the other house?"

Colin watched her face, his own face a remarkable mirror of uncertainty and something else—uneasiness, secrecy, dismay.

"I don't know," he said aloud. The consonants blurred together like ink on a wet page, his tone conveying a sort of stubborn distrust.

His eyes slid over to me. I thought suddenly of the time in the sixth grade when I first heard the word *fuck*. One of my classmates told me I should go ask my aunt what it meant. I could sense the trap though I had no idea what it consisted of.

"Tell him it's okay," I said to her. "Tell him it doesn't matter to you."

"Well it certainly does," she snapped.

"Oh come on, Nikki. It's important and what difference does it make after all this time."

She got into a short discussion with him then, just the two of them, signing away like mad—a digital argument. "He doesn't want to talk about it," she said guardedly. "He made a mistake."

I didn't think so and I could feel excitement stir. He was watching us now, trying to get an emotional reading from our interchange.

"I know this sounds weird," I said to her tentatively, "but I wonder if Laurence told him that—that she was his mother."

"Why would he do that?"

I looked at her. "Maybe Colin caught them embracing or something like that."

Nikki's expression was blank for a moment and then she frowned. Colin waited uncertainly, looking from her to me. Nikki signed to him again. He seemed embarrassed now, head bent. She signed again more earnestly. Colin shook his head but the gesture seemed to come out of caution, not ignorance.

Nikki's expression underwent a change. "I just remembered something," she said. She blinked rapidly, color mounting in her face. "Laurence did come out here. He told me he brought Colin out the weekend I was back east. Greg and Diane stayed at the house with Mrs. Voss. Both had social plans or something, but Laurence said the two of them—he and Colin—came out to the beach to get away for a bit."

"Nice," I said with irony. "At three and a half, none

of it would have made sense to him anyway. Let's just assume it's true. Let's assume she was out here—"

"I really don't care to go on with this."

"Just one more," I said. "Just ask him why he called her 'Daddy's mother.' Ask him why the 'Daddy's mother' bit."

She relayed the question to Colin reluctantly but his face brightened with relief. He signed back at once, grabbing his head.

"She had gray hair," she reported to me. "She *looked* like a grandmother to him when she was here."

I caught a glint of temper in her voice but she recovered herself, apparently for his sake. She tousled his hair affectionately.

"I love you," she said. "It's fine. It's okay."

Colin seemed to relax but the tension had darkened Nikki's eyes to a charcoal gray.

"Laurence hated her," she said. "He *couldn't* have—"

"I'm just making an educated guess," I said. "It might have been completely innocent. Maybe they met for drinks and talked about the kids' schoolwork. We really don't know anything for *sure*."

"My ass," she murmured. Her mood was sour.

"Don't get mad at me," I said. "I'm just trying to put this thing together so it makes some sense."

"Well I don't believe a word of it," she said tersely.

"You want to tell me he was too nice a man to do such a thing?"

She put the paintbrush on the paper and wiped her hands on a rag.

"Maybe I'd like to have a few illusions left."

"I don't blame you a bit," I said. "But I don't understand why it bothers you. Charlotte Mercer was the one who put it into my head. She said he was like a tomcat, always sniffing around the same back porch."

"All right, Kinsey. You've made your point."

"No, I don't think I have. You paid me five grand to find out what happened. You don't like the answers, I can give you your money back."

"No, never mind. Just skip it. You're right," she said.

"You want me to pursue it or not?"

"Yes," she said flatly, but she didn't really look at me again. I made my excuses and left soon after that, feeling almost depressed. She still cared about the man and I didn't know what to make of that. Except that nothing's ever cut-and-dried—especially where men and women are concerned. So why did I feel guilty of doing my job?

I went into Charlie's office building. He was waiting at the top of the stairs, coat over one shoulder, tie loose.

"What happened to you," he said when he saw my face.

"Don't ask," I said. "I'm going to try to get a scholarship to secretarial school. Something simple and nice. Something nine-to-five."

I came up level with him, tilting my face slightly to look at him. It was as though I had suddenly entered a magnetic field like those two little dog-magnets when I was a kid—one black, one white. At the positive poles, if you held them half an inch apart, they would suck together with a little click. His face was solemn, so close, eyes resting on my mouth as though he might will me forward. For a full ten seconds we seemed caught and then I pulled back slightly, unprepared for the intensity.

"Jesus," he said, almost with surprise, and then he chuckled, a sound I knew well.

"I need a drink," I said.

"That's not all you need," he said mildly.

I smiled, ignoring him. "I hope you know how to cook because I don't."

"Hey listen, there is one slight kink," he said. "I'm house-sitting for my partner. He's out of town and I've got his dogs to feed. We can grab a bite to eat out there."

"Fine with me," I said.

He locked the office then and we went down the back stairs to the small parking lot adjacent to his office building. He opened his car door but I was already moving toward mine, which was parked out on the street.

"Don't you trust me to drive?"

"I'm courting a ticket if I stay parked out here. I'll follow you. I don't like to be stuck without my own wheels."

" 'Wheels'? Like in the sixties, you refer to your car as 'wheels'?"

"Yeah, I read that in a book," I said dryly.

He rolled his eyes and smiled indulgently, apparently resigned. He got in his car and waited pointedly until I had reached mine. Then he pulled out, driving slowly so that I could follow him without getting lost. Once in a while, I could see him watching me in his rearview mirror.

"You sexy bastard," I said to him under my breath and then I shivered involuntarily. He had that effect.

We proceeded to John Powers's house at the beach, Charlie driving at a leisurely pace. As usual, he was operating at half speed. The road began to wind and finally his car slowed and he turned left down a steep drive, a place not far from Nikki's beach house, if my calculations were correct. I pulled my car in beside his, nose down, hoping my handbrake would hold. Powers's house was tucked up against the hill to the right, with a carport dead ahead and parking space for two cars. The carport itself had a white picket fence across it, the two halves forming a gate, locked shut, with what I guessed to be his car parked inside.

Charlie got out, waiting as I came around the front of my car. As with Nikki's property, this was up on the bluff, probably sixty or seventy feet above the beach. Through the carport, I could see a patchy apron of grass, a crescent of yard. We went along a narrow walkway behind the house and Charlie let us into the kitchen. John Powers's two dogs were of the kind I hate: the jumping, barking, slavering sort with toenails like sharks' teeth. They reeked of bad breath. One was black and the other was the color of moldering whale washed up on the beach for a month. Both were large and insisted on standing up on their hind legs to stare into my face. I kept my head back, lips shut lest wet, sloppy kisses be forthcoming.

"Charlie, could you help me with this?" I ventured through clenched teeth. One licked me right in the mouth as I spoke.

"Tootsie! Moe! Knock it off!" he snapped.

I wiped my lips. "Tootsie and Moe?"

Charlie laughed and dragged them both by neck chains to the utility room, where he shut them in. One began to howl while the other barked.

"Oh Jesus. Let 'em out," I said. He opened the door and both bounded out, tongues flapping like slivers of corned beef. One of the dogs galummoxed into the other room and came trotting back with a leash in its mouth. This was supposed to be cute. Charlie put leashes on both and they pranced, wetting the floor in spots.

"If I walk them, they calm down," Charlie remarked. "Sort of like you."

I made a face at him but there seemed to be no alternative but to follow him out the front. There were various dog lumps in the grass. A narrow wooden stairway angled down toward the beach, giving way in places to bare ground and rock. It was a hazardous descent, especially with two ninety-five-pound lunkheads doing leaps and pirouettes at every turn.

"John comes home at lunch to give 'em a run," Charlie said back over his shoulder.

"Good for him," I said, picking my way down the cliffside, concentrating on my feet. Fortunately, I was wearing tennis shoes, which provided no traction but at least didn't have heels that would catch in the rotting steps and pitch me headfirst into the Pacific.

The beach below was long and narrow, bounded by precipitious rocks. The dogs loped from one end to the other, the black one pausing to take a big steaming dump, backside hunched, eyes downcast modestly. Jesus, I thought, is that all dogs know how to do? I averted my gaze. Really, it was all so *rude*. I found a seat on a rock and tried to turn my brain off. I needed a break, a long stretch of time in which I didn't have to worry about anybody but myself. Charlie threw sticks, which the dogs invariably missed.

Finally, the dog romp at an end, we staggered back up the steps together. As soon as we were inside, the dogs flopped happily on a big oval rug in the living room and began to chew it to shreds. Charlie went into the kitchen and I could hear ice trays cracking.

"What do you want to drink?" he called.

I moved over to the kitchen doorway. "Wine if you have it."

"Great. There's some in the fridge."

"You do this often?" I asked, indicating the pups.

He shrugged, filling ice trays again. "Every three or four weeks. It depends," he said and then smiled over at me. "See? I'm a nicer guy than you thought."

I twirled an index finger in the air just to show how impressed I was, but I did, actually, think it was nice of him to sit the dogs. I couldn't imagine Powers finding a kennel to keep them. He'd have to take them to the zoo. Charlie handed me a glass of wine, pouring a bourbon on the rocks for himself. I leaned against the doorframe.

"Did you know that Laurence had an affair at one time with Sharon Napier's mother?"

He gave me a startled look. "You're making a joke."

"No I'm not. Apparently it happened some time before Sharon went to work for him. From what I gather, her 'employment' was a combination extortion and revenge. Which might explain the way she treated him."

"Who told you this stuff?"

"What difference does that make?"

"Because it sounds like crap," he said. "The name Napier never meant anything to me and I knew him for years."

I shrugged. "That's what you said about Libby Glass," I replied.

Charlie's face began to fade. "Jesus, you don't forgive a thing, do you?" He moved into the living room and I followed. He sat down in a wicker chair, which creaked beneath his weight.

"Is that why you're here? To work?" he asked.

"Actually, it's not. Actually, it's just the opposite."

"Meaning what?"

"I came out here to get away from it," I said.

"Then why the questions? Why the third-degree? You know how I feel about Laurence and I don't like to be used."

I felt my own smile fade, my face setting with embarrassment.

"Is that what you think?" I asked.

He looked down at his glass, speaking carefully. "I can appreciate the fact you have a job to do. That's fine with me and I'm not complaining about that. I'll help you where I can, but I can do without the interrogation at every step. I don't think you have any idea what it's like. You ought to see the change that comes over you when you start talking homicide."

"I'm sorry," I said stiffly. "I don't mean to do that to you. I get information and I need to have it verified. I can't afford to take things at face value."

"Not even me?"

"Why are you doing this?" I said, and my voice seemed to have dropped to a hush.

"I'm just trying to get a few things clarified."

"Hey. You were the one who came after me. Remember that?"

"Saturday. Yes. And you were the one who came after me today. And now you're pumping me and I don't like that."

I stared down at the floor, feeling fragile and mortified. I didn't like being smacked down and it was pissing me off. A lot. I began to shake my head. "I had a hard day," I said. "I really don't need this shit."

"I had a hard day too," he said. "So what?"

I set my wineglass on the table and grabbed up my purse.

"Fuck off," I said mildly. "Just go fuck yourself."

I moved toward the kitchen. The dogs raised their heads and watched me pass. I was hot and they lowered their eyes meekly as though I had communicated that much at any rate. Charlie didn't move. I banged out the back door and got into my car, starting it up with energy, peeling back up the driveway with a chirp. As I backed out onto the road, I caught a glimpse of Charlie standing near the carport. I put the car into first and pulled away.

23

I've never been good at taking shit, especially from men. It was an hour after I got home before I cooled down. Eight o'clock and I still hadn't eaten anything. I poured myself a big glass of wine and sat down at my desk. I took out some blank index cards and began to work. At 10:00 I had dinner—a sliced hard-boiled-egg sandwich, which I ate hot on wheat bread with a lot of mayonnaise and salt, popping open a Pepsi and a package of corn chips. By then I'd consigned all the information I had to the index cards, which I'd tacked up on my bulletin board.

I sketched the story out, allowing myself to speculate. I mean, why now? I didn't have much else to go on at this point. It seemed likely that someone had broken into the Fifes' house the weekend the German shepherd was killed, while Nikki and Laurence were off at the Salton Sea with Colin and Greg. It also seemed likely that Sharon Napier had come up with something after Laurence died—which was (maybe) why she had gotten herself killed. I started making lists, systematizing the information I had, along with the half-formed ideas that were simmering at the back of my head. I typed up my sheets and arranged them in alphabetical order, starting with Lyle Abernathy and Gwen.

I didn't dismiss the idea that Diane and Greg were possibly involved, though I couldn't make any sense of the notion that either could have killed him, let alone Libby Glass. I included Charlotte Mercer on my list. She was spoiled and spiteful and I didn't think she would spare any energy or expense in seeing that the world was arranged exactly as she wanted it. She could have hired someone if she didn't want to go to the trouble of murdering him herself. And if she killed him, why not Libby Glass? Why not Sharon Napier, if Sharon had figured it out? I decided it might be smart to check with the airlines to see if her name appeared on any of the passenger lists for Las Vegas at the time Sharon died. That was one angle I hadn't thought of. I made a note to myself. Charlie Scorsoni was still on my list and the realization had a disturbing effect.

There was a knock at the door and I jerked involuntarily, adrenaline shooting through me. I glanced at my watch: 12:25. My heart was thumping so hard it made my hands shake. I crossed to the door and bent my head.

"Yes?"

"It's me," Charlie said. "Can I come in?"

I opened the door. Charlie was leaning against the frame. No jacket. No tie. Tennis shoes with no socks.

His square handsome face looked solemn and subdued. He searched my face and then looked away. "I
came down on you too hard and I'm sorry," he said.

I studied his face. "You had a legitimate complaint,"
I said. I knew that my tone of voice was unrelenting,
regardless of the content, and I knew that my purpose
was punitive. He only had time to look at me to guess
my real attitude and it frosted him some.

"Jesus Christ, could we just talk?" he said.

I glanced at him briefly and then moved away from
the door. He came in, closing it behind him. He leaned
on the door, hands in his pockets, watching me prowl
the room, circling back to my desk, where I began to
take cards down, packing papers away.

"What do you want from me?" he said helplessly.

"What do you want from *me*?" I snapped back. I
caught myself and raised a hand. "I'm sorry. I didn't
mean to use that tone."

He stared down at the floor as though trying to figure out where to go next. I sat down in the upholstered chair near the couch, flinging my legs over the
padded arm.

"Want a drink?" I asked.

He shook his head. He moved over to the couch and
sat down heavily, leaning his head back. His face
looked lined, his brow furrowed. His sandy hair
looked as though he'd run a hand through it more than
once. "I don't know what to do with you," he said.

"What's to do?" I asked. "I know I'm a bitch sometimes, but why not? I'm serious, Charlie. I'm too old to
take any guff from anyone. And truly, in this case, I

don't know who did what to whom. Did you generate that fight or did I?"

He smiled slightly. "Okay, so we're both touchy now and then. Is that fair enough?"

"I don't know from fair anymore. I don't know from any of this stuff."

"Haven't you ever heard of compromise?"

"Oh sure," I said. "That's when you give away half the things you want. That's when you give the other guy half of what's rightfully yours. I've done that lots of times. It sucks."

He shook his head, smiling wearily. I stared at him, feeling stubborn and belligerent. He'd already given more than I, and I still couldn't bend. He regarded me skeptically.

"Where do you go when you look at me that way?" he asked. I didn't know what to say so I kept my mouth shut. He reached over and waggled my bare foot as though to get my attention.

"You know you keep me at arm's length," he said.

"Really? Saturday night you think I did that?"

"Kinsey, sex was the only time you let me get close. What am I supposed to do with that? Chase around after you with my dick hanging out?"

I smiled inside, hoping it wouldn't show on my face. He read it anyway in my eyes. "Yeah, why not?" I said.

"I don't think you're used to men," he said, not making eye contact, and then he corrected himself. "Not men," he said. "I don't think you're used to having anyone in your life. I think you're used to being free-wheeling. And that's okay. Essentially I live the same way, but this is different. I think we should be careful of this."

"This what?"

"This relationship," he said. "I don't want you shutting me out. You're not that hard to read. Sometimes you disappear like a shot and I can't cope with that. I will try to tread easy. I'll try not to be a horse's ass myself, I promise you that. Just don't run off. Don't back away. You do this kind of knee-jerk retreat, like a clam—" He broke off then.

I softened, wondering if I'd misjudged him. I was too tough, too quick. I am hard on people and I know that.

"I'm sorry," I said. I had to clear my throat. "I'm sorry. I know I do that. I don't know who was at fault, but you ticked me off and I blew."

I held my hand out and he took it, squeezing my fingers. He looked at me for a long time. He took my fingertips and kissed them lightly, casually, looking at me the whole time. I felt like a switch was being turned on at the base of my spine. He turned my hand over and pressed his mouth into my palm. I didn't want him to do that but I noticed I wasn't pulling my hand away. I watched him, hypnotically, my senses dulled by the heat that was raging way down, way deep. It was like a pile of rags beginning to smolder, some dark part of me hidden away under the stairs, something firemen had warned us about in grade school. Paint cans, jars of gasoline—fumes in compression. All it needed was a spark, sometimes not even that. I could feel my eyes close, mouth coming open against my will. I sensed that Charlie was moving but I couldn't take that in and the next thing I was aware of, he was on his knees between mine, pulling the neck of my T-shirt down, his mouth on my bare breast. I clutched at him convulsively, slid down and forward against him and he half lifted me, hands cupped under my ass. I hadn't known how much I wanted him until then, until that point, but the sound I made was primitive and his response was fierce and immediate and after that, in the half-light, with the table pushed aside, we made love on the floor. He did things to me that I'd only read about in books, and at the end of it, legs trembling, heart thudding, I laughed and he buried his face against my belly, laughing too.

He was gone again by 2:00 A.M. He had work to do the next day and so did I. Even so, I missed him as I brushed my teeth, smirking at my own reflection in the bathroom mirror. My chin was pink from whisker burn. My hair seemed to be standing straight up on end. There is nothing quite as smug as the self-congratulation that abounds when one has been thoroughly and proficiently screwed, but I was a little bit embarrassed with myself nevertheless. This was not good, not cool. As a rule, I scrupulously avoid personal contact with anyone connected with a case. My sexual wrangling with Charlie was foolish, unprofessional, and in theory, possibly dangerous. In some little nagging part of my head, it didn't feel right to me, but I did love his *moves*. I couldn't think when I'd last run into a man quite so inventive. My reaction to him was gut-level chemistry—like crystals of sodium flung in a swimming pool, throwing off sparks, dancing across the water like light. I had a friend once who said to me, "Wherever there is sex, we work to create a relationship that's worthy of it." I thought about that now, sensing that soon I would do that with him—start to bond, start to fantasize, start to throw out emotional tendrils like snow peas curling up a string. I was wary of it too. The sex was very good and very strong but the fact remained that I was still in the middle of an investigation and he still had not been crossed off my list. I didn't think our physical relationship had clouded my judgment about him, but how could I tell? I couldn't really afford to take the chance. Unless, of course, I was just rationalizing my own inclination to hold back. Was I *that* careful with myself these days? Was I really just sidestepping intimacy? Did I long to relegate him to the role of "possible suspect" in order to justify my own reluctance to take a risk? He was a nice man—smart, caring, responsible, attractive, perceptive. What in God's name did I want?

I turned the bathroom light out and made up my bed, which really just amounted to a quilt folded lengthways on the couch. I could have opened out the sofa bed and done it right—sheets, pillow case, a proper nightgown. Instead I'd pulled the same T-shirt over my head and tucked myself into the fold of the quilt. My body heat was making a sexual perfume waft up from between my legs. I turned out the lamp on the desk and smiled in the dark, shivering with the recollection of his mouth on me. Maybe this wasn't the time to get analytical, I thought. Maybe this was just a time to reflect and assimilate. I slept like the dead.

In the morning, I showered, skipping breakfast, reaching the office by 9:00. I let myself in and checked with the service. Con Dolan had called. I dialed the Santa Teresa Police Department and asked for him.

"What," he barked, already annoyed with the world.

"Kinsey Millhone here," I said.

"Oh yeah? What do you want?"

"Lieutenant, you called me!" I could hear him blink.

"Oh. Right. I got a report here from the lab on that letter. No prints. Just smudges, so that's no good."

"Rats. What about the handwriting? Does that match?"

"Enough to satisfy us," he said. "I had Jimmy go over it and he says it's legitimate. What else you got?"

"Nothing right now. I may come in and talk to you, though, in a couple of days if that's okay."

"Call first," he said.

"Trust me," I replied.

I went out on the balcony and stared down at the street. Something wasn't right. I'd been half convinced that letter was a fake but now it was confirmed and verified. I didn't like it. I went back in and sat down in my swivel chair, tipping back and forth slightly, listening to it creak. I shook my head. Couldn't figure it out. I glanced at the calendar. I'd been working for Nikki for two weeks. It felt like she'd hired me a minute ago and it felt like I'd been on the case all my life. I tilted forward and grabbed a scratch pad, totaling the time I'd put in, adding expenses on top of that. I typed it all up, made copies of my receipts, and stuck the whole batch in an envelope, which I mailed to her out at the beach. I went into the California Fidelity offices and shot the shit with Vera, who processes claims for them.

I skipped lunch and knocked off at 3:00. I stopped on the way home and picked up the eight-by-ten color photographs of Marcia Threadgill and I sat in my car for a moment to survey my handiwork. It isn't often that I have such a captivating spectacle of avarice and fraud. The best shot (which I might have called "Portrait of a Chiseler") was of Marcia standing up on her kitchen chair, shoulders strained by the weight of the plant as she lifted it up. Her boobs, in the crocheted halter top, sagged down like flesh melons bursting through the bottom of a string bag. The image was so clear that I could see where her mascara had left little black dots on her upper lids like tracks of some tiny beast. Such a jerk. I smiled to myself grimly. If that's the way the world works, then let me not forget. I was resigned by now to the fact that Ms. Threadgill would have her way. Cheaters win all the time. It wasn't big news but it was worth remembering. I slid all the pictures back into the manila envelope. I started the car and headed toward home. I didn't feel like running today. I wanted to sit and brood.

24

I pinned the photograph of Marcia Threadgill up on my bulletin board and stared at it. I kicked my shoes off and walked around. I'd been thinking all day and it was getting me nowhere, so I took out the crossword puzzle Henry had left on my doorstep. I stretched out on the couch, pencil in hand. I did manage to guess 6 Down—"disloyal," eight letters, which was "two-faced," and I got 14 Across, which was "double-reed instrument," four letters—"oboe." What a whiz. I got stuck on "double helix," three letters, which turned out later to be "DNA," a cheat if you ask me. At 7:05, I had an idea that jumped out of the dim recesses of my brain with a little jolt of electricity.

I looked up Charlotte Mercer's telephone number and dialed the house. The housekeeper answered and I asked for Charlotte.

"The judge and Mrs. Mercer are having dinner," she said disapprovingly.

"Well, would you mind interrupting please? I just have a quick question. I'm sure she won't mind."

"Who shall I say is calling?" she asked. I gave her my name.

"Just one moment." She put the receiver down.

I corrected her mentally. *Whom*, sweetheart. *Whom* shall I say is calling . . .

Charlotte answered, sounding drunk. "I don't appreciate this," she hissed.

"I'm sorry," I said. "But I need a piece of information."

"I told you what I know and I don't want you calling when the judge is here."

"All right. All right. Just one thing," I said hurriedly before she could hang up. "Do you happen to remember Mrs. Napier's first name."

Silence. I could practically see her hold the receiver out to look at it.

"Elizabeth," she said and slammed down the phone.

I hung up. The piece I was looking for had just clicked into place. The letter wasn't written to Libby Glass at all. Laurence Fife had written it to Elizabeth Napier years ago. I was willing to bet on that. The real question now was how Libby Glass had gotten hold of it and who had wanted it back.

I took out my note cards and went back to work on my list. I had deliberately deleted Raymond and Grace Glass. I didn't believe either of them would have killed their own child, and if my guess about that letter could be verified, then it was possible that Libby and Laurence had never been romantically involved. Which meant that the reasons for their dying had to be something else. But what? Suppose, I said to myself, just suppose Laurence Fife and *Lyle* were involved in something. Maybe Libby stumbled on to it and Lyle killed them both to protect himself. Maybe Sharon got wind of it and he'd killed her too. It didn't quite make sense to me from that angle, but after eight years much of the real proof must have been lost or destroyed. Some of the obvious connections must have faded by now. I jotted down a couple of notes and checked the list.

When I came to Charlie Scorsoni's name, I felt the same uneasiness I'd felt before. I'd checked him out two weeks ago, before I'd even met with him and he was clean, but appearances are deceptive. As squeamish as it made me feel, I thought I'd better verify his whereabouts the night Sharon died. I knew he'd been in Denver because I'd called him there myself but I wasn't really sure where he'd gone after that. Arlette said he'd left messages from Tucson and again from Santa Teresa but she only had his word for that. When it came to Laurence Fife he did have opportunity. From the first, this had been a case where motive and alibi were oddly overlapped. Ordinarily, an alibi is an account of a suspect's whereabouts at the time a crime was committed and it's offered up as proof of innocence, but here it didn't matter where anyone was. With a poisoning, it only mattered if someone had *reason* to want someone else dead—access to the poison, access to the victim, and the intent to kill. That's what I was still sorting through. My impulse was simply to take Charlie off my list but I had to question myself on that. Did I really believe he was innocent or did I simply want to relieve myself of my own uneasiness? I tried to think about something else. I tried to move on, but my mind kept drifting back to the same point. I didn't think I was being smart. I wasn't sure I was being honest with myself. And suddenly, I didn't like the idea that my thinking might not be clear. The whole setup gave me a sick feeling down in my bones. I looked up his home phone number in the telephone book. I hesitated and then I shook myself free and dialed. I had to do it.

The phone rang four times. I thought he might be out at Powers's house at the beach but I didn't have that number. I was rooting for him to be out, gone. He picked up on the fifth ring and I felt my stomach churn. There was no point in putting it off.

"Hi, it's Kinsey," I said.

"Well hello," he said softly. The pleasure in his voice was audible and I could picture his face. "God, I was hoping I'd hear from you. Are you free?"

"No, actually I'm not. Uh, listen, Charlie. I'm thinking I shouldn't see you for a while. Until I get this wrapped up."

The silence was profound.

"All right," he said finally.

"Look, it's nothing personal," I said. "It's just a matter of policy."

"I'm not arguing," he said. "Do what you want. It's too bad you didn't think about 'policy' before."

"Charlie, it's not like that," I said desperately. "It may work out fine and it's no big deal, but it's been bothering me. A lot. I don't do this. It's been one of my

cardinal rules. I can't keep on seeing you until I understand how this thing ties up."

"Babe, I understand," he said. "If it doesn't feel right
to you, then it's no good anyway. Call me if you ever
change your mind."

"Wait," I said. "God damn it, don't do that to me.
I'm not rejecting you."

"Oh really," he said, his tone flat with disbelief.

"I just wanted you to know."

"Well. Now I know. I appreciate your honesty," he
said.

"I'll be in touch when I can."

"Have a good life," he said and the phone clicked
quietly in my ear.

I sat with a hand on the phone, doubts crowding in,
wanting to call him back, wanting to erase everything
I'd just said. I'd been looking for relief, looking for a
way to escape the discomfort I felt. I think I'd even
wanted him to give me a hard time so that I could resist
and feel righteous. It was a question of my own integrity. Wasn't it? The injury in his voice had been awful after what we'd been through. And maybe he was
right in his assumption that I was rejecting him. Maybe
I was just being perverse, pushing him away because I
needed space between me and the world. The job does
provide such a perfect excuse. I meet most people in
the course of my work and if I can't get emotionally
involved there, then where else can I go? Private investigation is my whole life. It is why I get up in the
morning and what puts me to bed at night. Most of the
time I'm alone, but why not? I'm not unhappy and I'm

not discontented. I had to free up until I knew what was going on. He would just have to misunderstand and to hell with him until I got this goddamn case nailed down and then maybe we could see where we stood—if it wasn't too late. Even if he was right, even if my breaking with him was an excess of conscience, a cover for something else—so what? There were no declarations between us, no commitments. I'd been to bed with him twice. What did I owe him? I don't know what love is about and I'm not sure I believe in it anyway. "Then why so defensive?" came a little voice in reply, but I ignored it.

I had to push on. There was no other way to get out of this now. I picked up the phone and called Gwen.

"Hello?"

"Gwen. This is Kinsey," I said, keeping my voice neutral. "Something's come up and I think we should talk."

"What is it?"

"I'd rather talk to you in person. Do you know where Rosie's is, down here at the beach?"

"Yes. I think I know the place," she said with uncertainty.

"Can you meet me there in half an hour? It's important."

"Well sure. Just let me get my shoes on. I'll be there as soon as I can."

"Thanks," I said.

I checked my watch. It was 7:45. I wanted her on my turf this time.

Rosie's was deserted, the lights dim, the whole place smelling of yesterday's cigarette smoke. I used to go to a movie theater when I was a kid and the ladies' rest room always smelled like that. Rosie was wearing a muumuu in a print fabric that depicted many flamingos standing on one leg. She was seated at the end of the bar, reading a newspaper by the light of a small television set, which she'd placed on the bar, sound off. She looked up as I came in and she set the paper aside.

"It's too late for dinner. The kitchen is closed. I gave myself the night off," she announced from across the room. "You want something to eat, you gotta fix it yourself at home. Ask Henry Pitts. He'll do you something good."

"I'm meeting someone for a drink," I said. "Big crowd you got."

She looked around as though maybe she'd missed someone. I went over to the bar. She looked as though she'd just redyed her hair because her scalp was faintly pink. She was using a Maybelline dark brown eyeliner pencil on her brows, which she seemed to draw closer together every time, coquettishly arched. Pretty soon, she could take care of the whole thing with one wavy line.

"You got a man yet?" she asked.

"Six or eight a week," I said. "Do you have any cold chablis?"

"Just the crummy stuff. Help yourself."

I went around behind the bar and got a glass, taking the big gallon jug of white wine out of the refrigerator under the bar. I poured a tumblerful, adding ice. I went over to my favorite booth and sat down, preparing myself mentally like an actor about to go on stage. It was time to stop being polite.

Gwen arrived forty minutes later, looking crisp and capable. Her greeting to me was pleasant enough, but under it I thought I could detect the tension, as though she had some inkling of what I was about to say. Rosie shuffled over, giving Gwen a brief appraising look. She must have thought Gwen looked okay because she honored her with a direct question.

"You want something to drink?"

"Scotch on the rocks. And could I have a glass of water, too, please?"

Rosie shrugged. She didn't care what people drank. "You want to run a tab?" she said to me.

I shook my head. "I'll take care of it now," I said. Rosie moved off toward the bar. The look Gwen and I exchanged inadvertently indicated that both of us remembered her first reference to drinking Scotch in the days long past, when she was married to Laurence Fife and playing the perfect wife. I wondered what she was playing now.

"I revert now and then to the hard stuff," she said, picking up my thought.

"Why not?" I replied.

She studied me briefly. "What's up?"

The question was brave. I didn't think she really

wanted to know, but she'd always struck me as the type to plunge right in. She probably whipped off big pieces of adhesive tape, too, with the same decisive thrust, just to get it over with.

"I talked to Colin," I said. "He remembered you."

The modification in her manner was slight and a look, not of apprehension, but of wariness flickered in her eyes.

"Well that's nice," she said. "I haven't seen him for years, of course. I told you that." She reached into her purse and took out a compact, checking her reflection quickly in the mirror, running a hand through her hair. Rosie came back with her Scotch and a glass of water. I paid the tab. Rosie tucked the money in the pocket of her muumuu and wandered back to the bar while Gwen took a sip of water. She seemed to be holding herself in check, not trusting herself to pick up the conversation where we'd left off. I bumped her along for the sake of surprise.

"You never mentioned that you had an affair with Laurence," I said.

A laugh burbled out. "Who, me? With him? You can't be *serious*."

I had to interrupt her merriment. "Colin saw you out at the beach house that weekend when Nikki was out of town. I don't know all the details, but I can make a guess."

I watched her compute that and shift gears. She was a very good little actress herself, but the slick cover she'd constructed was getting shabby from disuse. It had been a long time since she'd had to play this game and her timing was slightly off. She knew all the right lines, but the pretense was hard to sustain after an eight-year gap. She didn't seem to recognize the bluff and I kept my mouth shut. I could almost see what was happening inside her head. The terrible need to confess and be done with it, the pressure to spill it all out was too tempting to resist. She'd gone a few rounds with me and she'd pulled it off beautifully but only because I hadn't known which buttons to push.

"All right," she blurted out rebelliously, "I went to bed with him once. So what? I ran into him at the Palm Garden as a matter of fact. I nearly told you the other day. He was the one who told me Nikki was out of town. I was shocked that he'd even speak to me." She switched to the Scotch, taking a big drink.

She was fabricating as fast as she could and it sounded nice but it was like listening to a record album. I decided to skip the cuts I didn't want to hear. I bumped her again.

"It was more than once, Gwen," I said. "You had a full-blown affair with him. Charlotte Mercer was screwing his head off back then but he broke it off with her. She says he was into something very hush-hush. 'Very hot,' to quote her. I think it was you."

"What difference does it make if we had an affair. He'd been doing that for years."

I let a little time elapse and when I spoke I kept my voice low, leaning forward slightly just to give her the full effect.

"I think you killed him."

The animation drained out of her face as though a plug had been pulled. She started to say something but she couldn't get it out. I could see her mind working, but she couldn't put anything together quickly enough. She was struggling and I pressed.

"You want to tell me about it?" I said. My own heart was pounding and I could feel damp rings of sweat forming under my arms.

She shook her head but that was all she could manage. She seemed transfixed. Her face had changed, taking on that look people get in their sleep when all the guards are down. Her eyes were luminous and dark and two bright patches of pink appeared now in the pale of her cheeks, a clownish effect, as though she'd applied too much blusher in an artificial light. She blinked back tears then, propping her chin on her fist, looking off beyond me, fighting for self-control, but the last defense was breached and the guilt was pushing against that gorgeous façade. I'd seen it happen before. People can hold out just so long and then they fold. She was really an amateur at heart.

"You got pushed too hard and you broke," I said, hoping I wasn't overplaying my hand. "You waited until he and Nikki left town and then you used Diane's keys to get into the house. You put the oleander capsules in his little plastic vial, being careful to leave no prints, and then you left."

"I hated him," she said, mouth trembling. She blinked and a tear splashed on her shirt like a drop of rain. She took a deep breath, words coming out in a rush. "He ruined my life, took my kids, robbed me blind, insulted, abused—oh my God, you have no idea. The *venom* in that man . . ."

She snatched up a napkin and pressed it to her eyes. Amazingly, Rosie didn't seem to notice her distress. She sat at the bar, probably reading Ann Landers, thinking At Wit's End should have turned hubby in for the obscene calls he made, while a customer confessed to murder right under her nose. To her right, the little television set flickered a Muppets rerun.

Gwen sighed, staring down at the tabletop. She reached over and picked up her glass, taking in a big slug of Scotch, which made her shudder as it went down. "I didn't even feel bad about it, except for the kids. They took it hard and that surprised me. They were far better off with him gone."

"Why the affair?" I probed.

"I don't know," she said, folding and refolding the paper napkin. "I guess it was my revenge. He was such an egotist. I knew he couldn't resist. After all, I'd insulted the hell out of him by having an affair with someone else. He couldn't tolerate that. I knew he'd want his own back. It wasn't even that hard to engineer. He wanted to prove something to himself. He wanted to show me what I'd passed up. There was even a certain amount of jazz to the sex for once. The hostility was so close to the surface that it gave us both a sick charge. God, I loathed him. I really did. And I'll tell you something else," she said harshly. "Killing him once just wasn't enough. I wish I could kill him again."

She looked at me fully then and the enormity of what she was saying began to sink in.

"What about Nikki? What did she ever do to you?"

"I thought they'd acquit her," she said. "I never thought she'd go to jail, and when the sentence was handed down I wasn't going to stand up and take her place. By then it was too late."

"So what else?" I said and I noticed that my tone was getting sullen. "Did you kill the dog too?"

"I had nothing to do with that. He got hit Sunday morning. I drove Diane over there because she'd remembered that she'd left him out and she was upset. He was already lying in the street. My God, I wouldn't run over a *dog*," she said emphatically, as though I should appreciate the delicacy of her sentiments.

"And the rest just fell into place? The oleander in the yard? The capsules upstairs?"

"One capsule. I doctored *one*."

"Bullshit, Gwen. That's bullshit."

"It's not. I'm telling the truth. I swear to it. I'd thought about it for a long time but I couldn't see a way to make it work. I wasn't even sure it would kill him. Diane was a wreck about the dog anyway so I drove her to my place and put her to bed. As soon as she was asleep, I took her keys and went back and that's all it was." She spoke with an edge of defiance, as though having opened up this far there was no point in mincing words.

"What about the other two?" I snapped. "What about Sharon and Libby Glass?"

She blinked at me, pulling back. "I don't know what you're talking about."

"Oh the hell you don't," I said, getting up. "You've

lied to me since the first minute we met. I can't believe a goddamn word you say and you know it."

She seemed startled by my energy. "What are you going to do?"

"Give the information to Nikki," I said. "She paid for it. We'll let her decide."

I moved away from the table, heading toward the door. Gwen grabbed her jacket and purse, keeping pace with me.

Out on the street, she snatched at my arm and I shook her off.

"Kinsey wait . . ." Her face was remarkably pale.

"Blow it out your ass," I said. "You'd better hire yourself a hot attorney, babe, because you're going to need one."

I moved off down the street, leaving Gwen behind.

25

I locked the door to my place and tried dialing Nikki out at the beach. The phone rang eight times and I hung up, pacing the room after that with an unsettled sensation in my chest. There was something off. There was something not right and I couldn't put my finger on what was bothering me. There was no feeling of closure. None. This should have been the end of it. The big climax. I'd been hired to find out who killed Laurence Fife and I had. The end. Finis. But I was left with half a case and a lot of loose ends. Gwen's killing of Laurence had been part premeditation and part impulse, but the rest of it didn't seem to fit. Why wasn't everything falling into place? I couldn't picture Gwen killing Libby Glass. Gwen had hated Laurence Fife for years, titillating herself perhaps with ways of killing him, maybe never even dreaming that she'd actually do it, never imagining that she could actually pull it off. She'd come up with the oleander scheme and suddenly she'd seen a way to make it work. A perfect opportunity had presented itself and she'd acted. Surely Libby

Glass's death couldn't have been that easy to arrange. How did Gwen know about her? How did she know where she lived? How could she have gotten into that apartment? And how could she have counted on her taking medication of any kind? I couldn't picture Gwen driving to Vegas either. Couldn't imagine her shooting Sharon in cold blood. For what? What was the point? Killing Laurence had wiped out an old grudge, satisfied an ancient and bitter hatred between them, but why kill the other two? Blackmail? Threat of exposure? That might account for Sharon but why Libby Glass? Gwen had seemed truly self-righteous in her bewilderment. Like her denial of any responsibility for killing the dog. There was just that odd note of genuine outrage in her voice. It didn't make sense.

Unless there was someone else involved. Someone else who killed.

I felt a chill.

Oh my God. Lyle? Charlie? I sat down, blinking rapidly, hand across my mouth. I'd bought into the notion that one person killed all three, but maybe not. Maybe there was another possibility. I tried it out. Gwen had murdered Laurence Fife. Why couldn't someone else have spotted the opening and taken advantage of it? The timing was close, the method the same. Of course it was going to look like it was all part of the same setup.

I thought about Lyle. I thought about his face, the strange imperceptibly mismatched eyes: sullen, watchful, belligerent. He said he'd been with Libby three days before she died. I knew he'd heard about Laurence's death. He was not a man who possessed a giant intellect, but he could have managed that much, imitating the cunning of someone else—even stoned.

I called my answering service. "I'm going down to Los Angeles," I said. "If Nikki Fife calls, I want you to give her the telephone number of the Hacienda motel down there and tell her it's important that she get in touch. But no one else. I don't want it known that I'm out of town. I'll check in with you often enough to pick up whatever calls come in. Just say I'm tied up and you don't know where I am. You got that?"

"All right, Miss Millhone. Will do," she said cheerfully and then clicked off. God. If I'd said to her, "Hold the calls. I'm slitting my throat," she'd have responded with the same blank good will.

The drive to Los Angeles was good for me—soothing, uneventful. It was after nine and there wasn't that much traffic on the darkened road south. On my left, hills swelled and rolled, covered with low vegetation—no trees, no rocks. On my right, the ocean rumbled, almost at arm's length, looking very black except for a ruffle of white here and there. I passed Summerland, Carpinteria, passed the oil derricks and the power plant, which was garlanded with tiny lights like a decorative display at Christmastime. There was something restful about having nothing to worry about except having a wreck and getting killed. It freed my mind for other things.

I had made a mistake, a false assumption, and I felt

like a novice. On the other hand, I'd made the very assumption that everyone else had made: same M.O., same murderer. But now I didn't think that was true. Now it seemed to me the only explanation that made any sense was that someone else had killed Libby Glass—and Sharon too. I drove through Ventura, Oxnard, Camarillo, where the state mental asylum was located. I've heard that there is less tendency to violence among the institutionalized insane than there is in the citizenry at large and I believe that. I thought about Gwen without surprise or dismay, my mind jumping forward and back randomly. Somehow I was more offended by the minor crimes of a Marcia Threadgill who tried for less, without any motivation at all beyond greed. I wondered if Marcia Threadgill was the new standard of morality against which I would now judge all other sins. Hatred, I could understand—the need for revenge, the payment of old debts. That's what the notion of "justice" was all about anyway: settling up.

I went over the big hill into Thousand Oaks, with traffic picking up; tract housing stretched out on either side of the road, then shopping malls packed end to end. The night air was damp and I kept the windows rolled down. I felt over into the backseat for my briefcase and fumbled with the catch. I tucked my little automatic into my jacket pocket, encountering a wad of papers. I pulled them out and glanced down. Sharon Napier's bills. I'd stuck them in my windbreaker on the way out of her place and I hadn't thought about them since. I'd have to go through them. I tossed them on the passenger seat and looked at my watch by the icy wash of highway light. It was 10:10—forty-five minutes of driving left, maybe more given traffic on the surface roads once I got off the freeway. I thought about Charlie, wondering if I'd blown a perfectly nice relationship. He didn't seem like the type to forgive and forget, but who knew. He was a lot more yielding than I was, that was for sure. My thoughts rambled on disjunctively. Lyle had known I was driving to Vegas. I wasn't sure how Sharon connected, but I'd figure that out. Blackmail still seemed like the best bet. The letter I couldn't figure at all. How had Libby come by that? Or had she? Maybe Lyle and *Sharon* were in cahoots. Maybe Lyle got the letter from her. Maybe he was *planting* the letter among Libby's effects, not trying to take it away. It was certainly to his advantage to reinforce the idea of Libby's romantic tie to Laurence Fife. He had known I was stopping back through to pick up her boxes. He could have made it back to Los Angeles well in advance of me since I'd stopped for the night to see Diane. Maybe he had deliberately timed it closely to incite my curiosity about what might have been tucked away there. My mind veered off that and I thought about Lieutenant Dolan with a faint smile. He was so sure Nikki had killed her husband, so satisfied with that. I'd have to put a call through to him when I got back. I thought about Lyle again. I didn't intend to see him that night. He wasn't as smart as Gwen, but he might be dangerous. *If* it was him. I didn't think I should jump to conclusions again.

I checked into the Hacienda at 11:05, went straight to room #2, and put myself to bed. Arlette's mother was on the desk. She is twice as fat.

In the morning, I showered and got back into the same clothes, staggering out to the car to retrieve the overnight case I kept in the crowded backseat. I went back to my room and brushed my teeth—oh blessed relief—and ran a comb through my hair. I went down to a delicatessen on the corner of Wilshire and Bundy, where I ordered scrambled eggs, sausage links, a toasted bagel with cream cheese, coffee, and fresh orange juice. Whoever invented breakfast really did it good.

I walked back up to the Hacienda to find Arlette waving a massive arm out the office door for me. Her round face was flushed, her little cap of blonde curls in a flyaway state, her eyes squeezed almost to invisibility by the heavy cheeks. I wondered when she'd last seen her own neck. Still, I liked her, irksome as she was at times.

"There's someone on the phone for you and she sounds real upset. I told her you were out but I said I'd flag you down. Thank goodness you're back," she said to me, out of breath and wheezing hard.

I hadn't seen Arlette so excited since she found out that panty hose came in queen-size. I went into the office with Arlette hard on my heels, breathing heavily. The receiver was on the counter and I picked it up.

"Hello?"

"Kinsey, this is Nikki."

Why the dread in her voice, I thought automatically. "I tried calling you last night," I said. "What's the matter? Are you okay?"

"Gwen's dead."

"I just talked to her last night," I said blankly. Killed herself. She'd killed herself. Oh shit, I thought.

"It happened this morning. Hit-and-run driver. I just heard it on the news. She was jogging along Cabana Boulevard and someone ran her down and then skipped."

"I don't believe it. Are you sure?"

"Positive. I tried calling you and the service said you were out of town. What are you doing in L.A.?"

"I've got to check out something down here but I should be back tonight," I said, thinking fast. "Look, would you see if you can find out the details?"

"I can try."

"Call Lieutenant Dolan at Homicide. Tell him I told you to ask."

"Homicide," she said, startled.

"Nikki, he's a *cop*. He'll know what's going on. And it may not be an accident anyway, so see what he has to say and I'll call you as soon as I get back."

"Well, okay," she said dubiously, "I'll see what I can do."

"Thanks." I hung up the phone.

"Is someone dead?" Arlette asked. "Was it someone you knew?"

I looked right at her but I drew a blank. Why Gwen? What was happening?

She followed me out of the office and toward my room.

"Is there anything I can do to help? Do you need anything? You look awful, Kinsey. You're pale as a ghost."

I closed the door behind me. I thought about that last image of Gwen, standing on the street, her face white. *Could* it have been an accident? Coincidence? Things were moving too quickly. Someone was beginning to panic and for reasons I still couldn't quite understand.

A possibility flashed into my head and out. I stood stock-still, running it by me again like an old film clip. Maybe so. Maybe yes. It was all going to come together soon. It was all going to fit.

I threw everything into the backseat of my car, not even bothering to check out. I'd mail Arlette the damn twelve bucks.

The drive to the Valley was a blur, the car moving automatically, though I paid no attention whatever to road, sun, traffic, smog. When I reached the house in Sherman Oaks where Lyle was laying brick, I saw his battered truck parked out front. I didn't have any more time to waste and I didn't want to play games. I locked the car and went up the drive, going around the side of the house to the back. I caught sight of Lyle before he caught sight of me. He was bending over a pile of two-by-fours: faded jeans, work boots, no shirt, a cigarette in the corner of his mouth.

"Lyle."

He turned around. I had the gun out and trained on him. I held it with two hands, legs apart, meaning busines. He froze instantly where he stood, not saying a word.

I felt cold and my voice was tight, but the gun never wavered an inch. "I want some answers and I want them now," I said. I saw him glance to his right. There was a hammer lying on the ground but he made no move.

"Back up," I said, stepping forward slightly until I was between him and the hammer. He did as instructed, the pale blue eyes sliding back to mine, hands coming up.

"I don't want to shoot you, Lyle, but I will."

For once, he didn't look sullen or sly or arrogant. He stared straight at me with the first sign of respect I'd seen from him.

"You're the boss," he said.

"Don't fuckin' smart-mouth *me*," I snapped. "I'm not in the mood. Now sit down in the grass. Out there. And don't move a muscle unless I tell you to."

Obediently, he moved out to a small stretch of grass and sat down, eyes on me the whole time. It was quiet and I could hear birds chirping stupidly but we seemed to be alone and I liked it that way. I kept the gun pointed right at his chest, willing my hands not to shake. The sun was hot and it made him squint.

"Tell me about Libby Glass," I said.

"I didn't kill her," he shot back uneasily.

"That's not the point. I want to know what went on.

I want to know what you haven't told me yet. When did you see her last?"

He shut his mouth.

"Tell me!"

He didn't have Gwen's poise and he didn't have her smarts. The sight of the gun seemed to help him make up his mind.

"Saturday."

"The day she died, right?"

"That's right, but I didn't do anything. I went over to see her and we had a big fight and she was upset."

"All right, all right. Skip the buildup. What else?"

He was silent.

"Lyle," I said warningly. The muscles in his face seemed to pull together like a drawstring purse and he started to weep. He put his hands up over his face pathetically. He'd kept it in for a long time. If I was wrong about this, I was wrong about everything. I couldn't let him off the hook.

"Just tell me," I said, tone dead, "I need to know."

I thought he was coughing but I knew what I heard were sobs. He might have been nine years old, looking squeezed up and frail and small.

"I gave her a *tranq*," he said with anguish. "She asked for one and I found this bottle in the medicine cabinet and gave it to her. God, I even gave her a glass of water. I loved her so much."

The first rush subsided and he dashed at the tears on his face with a grubby hand, leaving streaks of dirt. He hugged himself, rocking back and forth in misery, tears streaming down his bony cheeks again.

"Go on," I said.

"I left after that but I felt bad and I went back later and that's when I found her dead on the bathroom floor. I was afraid they'd find my fingerprints and think I'd done something to her so I wiped the whole place down."

"And you took the tranquilizers with you when you left?"

He nodded, pressing his fingers into his eye sockets as though he could force the tears back. "I flushed 'em down the toilet when I got home. I smashed up the bottle and threw it away."

"How'd you know that's what it was?"

"I don't know. I just knew. I remembered that guy, the one up north and I knew he'd died that way. She might not have taken the goddamn thing if it weren't for me, but we had that screaming fight and she was so mad, she shook. I didn't even know she had any tranqs till she asked for one and I didn't see anything wrong with that. I went back to apologize." The worst of it seemed to be over with and he sighed deeply, his voice almost normal again.

"What else?"

"I don't know. The phone was unplugged. I plugged it back in and wiped that down too," he said woodenly. "I didn't mean any harm. I just had to protect myself. I wouldn't poison her. I wouldn't have done that to her, I swear to God. I didn't have anything to do with that or anything else except I cleaned the place. In case there were fingerprints. I didn't want anything pointing to me. And I took the bottle the pills were in. I did that."

"But you didn't break into the storage bin," I said.

He shook his head.

I lowered the gun. I'd half known but I had to be sure.

"Are you going to turn me in?"

"No. Not you."

I went back to the car and sat blankly, wondering in some vague irrational way if I really would have used the gun. I didn't think so. Tough. I'm tough, scaring the shit out of some dumb kid. I shook my head, feeling tears of my own. I started the car and put it into gear, heading back over the hill toward West L.A. I had one more stop and then I could drive back to Santa Teresa and clean it up. I thought I knew now who it was.

26

I caught sight of my reflection in one of the mirrored walls across from the entrance to Haycraft and Mc-Niece. I looked like I was ready for the last round-up: seedy, disheveled, mouth grim. Even Allison, in her buckskin shirt with the fringes on the sleeves, seemed alarmed by the sight of me, and her prerehearsed receptionist's smile dropped from sixty watts to twenty-five.

"I have to talk to Garry Steinberg," I said, my tone apparently indicating that I wouldn't take much shit.

"He's back in his office," she said timidly. "Do you know which one it is?"

I nodded and pushed through the swinging doors. I caught sight of Garry walking down the narrow interior corridor toward his office, slapping a batch of unopened mail against his thigh.

"Garry?"

He turned, his face lighting up at the sight of me and then turning hesitant. "Where'd you come from? You look exhausted."

"I drove down last night. Can we talk?"

"Sure. Come on in."

He turned left into his office, gathering up a stack of files on the chair in front of his desk. "You want some coffee? Can I get you anything?" He tossed the mail on the file cabinet.

"No, I'm fine but I need to check out a hunch."

"Fire away," he said, sitting down.

"Didn't you tell me once upon a time—"

"Last week," he inserted.

"Yeah, I guess it was. You mentioned that Fife's accounts were being put on computer."

"Sure, we were converting everything. Makes it a hell of a lot easier on us and it's better for the client too. Especially at tax time."

"Well what if the books had been fiddled with?"

"You mean embezzlement?"

"In a word," I said with irony. "Wouldn't that have shown up pretty quickly?"

"Absolutely. You think Fife was milking his own accounts?"

"No," I said slowly, "I think Charlie Scorsoni was. That's part of what I need to ask you about. Could he have skimmed money out of the estates he was representing back then?"

"Sure. It can be done and it's not that hard," Garry said appreciatively, "but it might be a bitch to track. It really depends on how he did it." He thought for a moment, apparently warming to the idea. He shrugged. "For instance, he could have set up some kind of special account or an escrow account for all his estates—

maybe two or three phony accounts within this overall account. A large dividend check comes in, he diverts a percentage of the check from the estate it's supposed to be credited to, and he credits it to a phony account instead."

"Could Libby have realized something was wrong?"

"She might have. She had a head for that kind of thing. She'd have had to trace the dividends through Moody's Dividend Book, which gives the amount of each dividend by company. Then if there was some kind of discrepancy, she might have asked for records or documentation—bank statements, canceled checks, stuff like that."

"Yeah, well Lyle told me last week that there were lots of phone calls back and forth, some attorney driving down for dinner. It finally occurred to me that Charlie might have engineered an affair with her in the hopes that she'd cover for him . . ."

"Or maybe he offered her a cut," Garry said.

"Oh God, would she have done that?"

Garry shrugged. "Hey, who knows? Would *he*?"

I stared down at his desk top. "Yeah, I think so," I said. "You know, everybody kept saying that she was involved with some Santa Teresa attorney and we all assumed it was Fife because both died the same way. But if I'm right about this embezzlement business then I need proof. Are the files still at your place?"

"No, I've got 'em right here as a matter of fact. I thought I'd take a look at 'em during my lunch hour. I've been having cottage cheese but I don't think that counts as food so I thought I'd do without. I brought 'em in yesterday and then I got tied up. Now that you mention it, I do think she was working on that account when she died, because the cops found her briefcase at her place," he said. He gave me a curious look. "How'd you fix on him?"

I shook my head. "I don't know. It just popped into my brain and it fit. Charlie told me that Fife made a trip to Los Angeles sometime in the week before he died, but I don't think that's true. I think probably Charlie made the trip himself and it would have been within a day or two after Laurence died. Libby had a bottle of tranqs and I think he doctored some—who knows, maybe all of 'em. We'll never know about that."

"Jesus. He killed Fife too?"

I shook my head. "No, I know who killed Fife. My guess is that Charlie saw a way to bail himself out. Maybe Libby wouldn't play ball with him or maybe she'd threatened to turn him in. Not that I've got any evidence one way or the other."

"Hey, it'll come," he said soothingly. "If it's there, we'll find it. I'll start on the files this afternoon."

"Good," I said, "I'd like that."

"Take care."

We shook hands across the desk.

I drove back to Santa Teresa, resolutely refusing to think of Gwen. Thinking about Charlie Scorsoni was depressing enough. I would have to check his whereabouts at the time Sharon died, but he could easily have checked out of the hotel in Denver and flown straight to Las Vegas, picking up my location from the answering service, finding my motel, and then following me to the Fremont. I thought about Sharon—that moment in the coffee shop when I thought she'd seen someone she knew. She'd said it was the pit boss signaling the end of her break, but I was sure she was lying. Charlie may have put in an appearance then, pulling back when he spotted me. Maybe she thought he had shown up to pay her off. I was relatively certain she'd been leaning on him for bucks, but then again, I'd have to pin that down. Sharon must have known that Fife was never involved with Libby Glass sexually. It was Charlie who'd been making the trips down to Los Angeles to discuss the accounts. Sharon must have kept her mouth shut during the trial, watching the whole tale unfold, biding her time, eventually cashing in on whatever information she had. It was also possible that Charlie Scorsoni hadn't known where she was—that I'd led him straight down the path to her door. I was aware, as I went over the sequence of events, that much of it sounded like a lot of fancy guesswork, but I felt I was headed in the right direction and I could probe now for corroborating evidence.

If Charlie had killed Gwen in that hit-and-run accident, there were bound to be ways to trace it back to him: hair and fibers on the fender of his car, which probably sustained some damage that would have to be repaired; paint flakes and glass fragments on Gwen's clothes. Maybe even a witness somewhere. It would have been much wiser if Charlie'd never made a move—just held tight and kept his mouth shut, lying low. It probably would have been impossible to put a case together against him after all these years. There was an arrogance in his behavior, a hint that he considered himself too smart and too slick to get caught. No one was *that* good. Especially at the rate he'd been operating these days. He had to be making mistakes.

And why not just go down for the count on the original embezzlement? He must have been desperately trying to cover for himself in Laurence Fife's eyes. But even if he'd been exposed, even if he'd been caught, I didn't believe Laurence would have turned him in. As sleazy as Fife had been in his personal life, I knew he was scrupulously honest in business matters. Still, Charlie was his best friend and the two went a long way back together. He might have warned Charlie off or smacked his hand—perhaps even dissolved the partnership. But I didn't think Charlie would have gone to jail or been disbarred from the practice of law. His life probably wouldn't have been ruined and he probably wouldn't have lost what he'd worked so hard to achieve. He would have lost Laurence Fife's good opinion and his trust perhaps, but he must have known that when he first put his hand in the cookie jar. The ludicrous fact of the matter is that in this day and age, a white-collar criminal can become a celebrity, a hero, can go on talk shows and write bestselling books. So what was there to sweat? Society will forgive just about anything except homicide. It was hard to shrug that one off, hard to rationalize that one away and whereas before, Charlie might have come out somewhat tarnished but intact, he was in big trouble now and things just seemed to be getting worse.

I didn't even address myself to the matter of his relationship to me. He'd played me for a sucker, just as he'd done with Libby Glass, and she, in her innocence, at least had a better excuse for the tumble than I did. It had been too long since I'd cared about anyone, too long since I'd taken that risk and I'd already invested too much. I just had to slam the gate shut emotionally and move on, but it didn't sit well with me.

When I reached Santa Teresa, I went straight to the office, taking with me the sheaf of bills from Sharon Napier's apartment. For the first time, I was beginning to think those might be significant. I went through them with an abstract curiosity that felt ghoulish nevertheless. She was dead and it seemed obscene now to note that she'd bought lingerie that had gone unpaid for, cosmetics, shoes. Her utilities were a month behind, with dunning notices from several small businesses including her tax man, a chiropractor, and a health spa membership renewal. Visa and Mastercharge had gotten churlish and American Express wanted its card back in no uncertain terms, but it was her telephone bill that interested me. In the area code that included Santa Teresa, there were three calls in the month of March, not an excessive number but telling. Two of the calls were to Charlie Scorsoni's office—both on the same day, ten minutes apart. The third number she'd called I didn't immediately recognize but the Santa Teresa exchange was the same. I picked up my Cross-Reference Directory. The number was for John Powers's house at the beach.

I dialed Ruth, not allowing myself to hesitate. Surely Charlie hadn't told her I'd broken with him. I couldn't picture him confiding his personal affairs to anyone. If he was there, I'd have to think fast and I wasn't sure what I intended to say. The information I needed was from her.

"Scorsoni and Powers," she sang.

"Oh hi, Ruth. This is Kinsey Millhone," I said, heart in my throat. "Is Charlie there?"

"Oh hi, Kinsey. No he's not," she said with a hint of regret in my behalf. "He's in court up in Santa Maria for the next two days."

Thank God for that, I thought, and took a deep breath. "Well maybe you can help me instead," I said. "I was just going over some bills for a client and it looks like she was in touch with him. Do you happen to remember someone calling him a couple of times maybe six, eight weeks ago? Her name was Sharon Napier. Long-distance."

"Oh, the one who used to work for him. Yes, I remember that. What did you need to know?"

"Well I can't quite tell from this if she actually got through to him or not. It looks like she called on a Friday—the twenty-first of March. Does that ring a bell?"

"Oh yes. Absolutely," Ruth said efficiently. "She

called asking for him and he was out at Mr. Powers's house. She was very insistent that I put her through but I didn't feel I should give out the number without checking with him, so I told her to call me back and then I checked with him out at the beach and he said it was fine. I hope that's all right. I hope she hasn't hired you to pester him or anything."

I laughed. "Oh heavens, Ruth, would I do that to him? I did see the number for John Powers and I just thought maybe she talked to him instead."

"Oh no. He was out of town that weekend. He's usually gone around the twenty-first for a couple of days. I have it right here on my calendar. Mr. Scorsoni was taking care of his dogs."

"Oh well, that would explain it," I said casually. "God, that's been a great help. Now the only other thing I need to check is that trip to Tucson."

"Tucson?" she said. Doubt was beginning to creep into her voice, that protective tone secretaries sometimes take when it suddenly occurs to them that someone wants something they're not supposed to get. "What is this about, Kinsey? Maybe I could be of more help if I understood what this has to do with a client of yours. Mr. Scorsoni's pretty strict about things like that."

"Oh no, that's something else. And I can check that out myself so don't worry about it. I can always give Charlie a buzz when he gets back and ask him."

"Well, I can give you his motel number in Santa Maria if you want to call him yourself," she said. She was trying to play it both ways—helpful to me if my questions were legitimate, helpful to Charlie if they weren't—but in any case, dumping the whole matter in his lap. For an old lady, she was adroit.

I jotted the number down dutifully, knowing I'd never call him but glad to get a fix on him anyway. I wanted to tell her not to mention my call but I didn't see how I could do it without tipping my hand. I just had to hope that Charlie wouldn't check in with her anytime soon. If she told him what I'd been asking about, he would know like a shot that I was on his tail and he wouldn't like that a bit.

I put in a call to Dolan at Homicide. He was out but I left a message, "important" underlined, that he should call me back when he got in. I tried Nikki at the beach and got her on the third ring.

"Hi, Nikki, it's me," I said. "Is everything okay?"

"Oh yeah. We're fine. I still haven't quite recovered from the shock of Gwen's death, but I don't know what to do about that. I never even knew the woman and it still seems a shame."

"Did you get any details from Dolan? I just tried to call him and he's out."

"Not a lot," she said. "He was awfully rude. Worse than I remember him and he wouldn't tell me much except the car that hit her was black."

"Black?" I said with disbelief. I was picturing Charlie's pale blue Mercedes and I'd fully expected some detail that would tie that in. "Are you sure?"

"That's what he said. I guess the detectives have been checking with the body shops and garages but so far nothing's turned up."

"That's odd," I said.

"Are you coming out for a drink? I'd love to hear what's going on."

"Maybe later. I'm trying to clean up a couple of loose ends. I'll tell you what else I need. Maybe you can answer this. Remember the letter I showed you that Laurence wrote—"

"Sure, the one to Libby Glass," she broke in quickly.

"Yeah, well I'm almost sure now that the letter was written to Elizabeth Napier instead."

"Who?"

"I'll fill you in on that later. I suspect that Elizabeth Napier was the one he got involved with when he was married to Gwen. Sharon Napier's mother."

"Oh, the *scandal*," she said, light breaking. "Oh sure, it could well be. He never would tell me much about that. Messy business. I know the story because Charlotte Mercer filled me in on that, but I was never really sure of the name. God, that would have been way back in Denver, just after his law-school days."

I hesitated. "Can you think who else would have known about that letter? Who could have had access to it? I mean, could Gwen?"

"I suppose so," she said. "Certainly Charlie would. He was working as a law clerk in the firm that represented the husband in that divorce and he lifted the letter from what I heard."

"He what?"

"Stole it. Oh I'm sure that's the one. Didn't I ever tell you the end of that? Charlie snitched the letter, just cleaned out all the evidence, and that's why they ended up settling out of court. She didn't do that well but at least it got Laurence off the hook."

"What happened to the letter? Could Charlie have kept the letter himself?"

"I don't know. I always assumed it had been destroyed but I guess he could have hung on to it. He never did get caught and I don't think the husband's attorney ever figured it out. You know how things disappear in offices. Probably some secretary got fired."

"Could Gwen have testified to any of this?"

"What *am* I, the district attorney's office?" she said with a laugh. "How do I know what Gwen knew?"

"Well, whatever it was, she's quiet now," I said.

"Oh," she said and I could tell her smile had faded fast. "Oh, I don't like that. That's a terrible thought."

"I'll tell you the rest when I see you. If I can get out there, I'll call first and make sure you're home."

"We'll be here. I take it you're making progress."

"Rapidly," I said.

Her good-byes were puzzled and mine were brief.

I hauled out my typewriter and committed everything I knew to paper in a lengthy and detailed report. Another piece had fallen into place. The night the storage bin was broken into, it was Charlie, not Lyle, who was planting the letter among Libby's belongings, hoping I'd find it, hoping he could shore up his own tale about Laurence Fife's "affair" with Libby Glass. Which probably also explained the key to her apartment that had been found on Laurence's key ring in the office. It wouldn't have been hard for Charlie to plant that one too. I typed on, feeling exhausted but determined to get it all down. In the back of my mind, I kept thinking of it as a safeguard, an insurance policy, but I wasn't sure what kind of coverage I needed. Maybe none. Maybe I didn't need protection, I thought. As it turned out, I was wrong.

27

I finished my report and locked it in my desk drawer. I went out to the parking lot and retrieved my car, heading north toward Charlie's house on Missile Avenue. Two doors down from his place was a house called Tranquility for reasons unknown. I parked in front of it and walked back. Charlie's house was a two-story structure with a painted-yellow-shingle exterior and a dark shingled roof, a bay window in front, a long narrow driveway to the left. It was the sort of house that might appear in an establishing shot for a television family show, something that might come on at 8:00 P.M., everything looking regular and wholesome and suitable for kids. There was no sign of his car in the drive, no sign of occupants. I eased along the driveway toward the garage, looking back over my shoulder as I went. There weren't even any nosy neighbors peering out at me. When I reached the one-car garage, I went around to the side, cupping my hands so that I could peer into the window. It was empty: a woodworking bench along the back wall, old lawn furniture, dust. I looked around, wondering whose black car it was and why the cops hadn't gotten a line on it yet. If I could fill in that blank, then I'd have something to talk to Con Dolan about. I was going to have something concrete.

I walked back up the drive to my car and sat, a favorite occupation of mine. It was getting dark. I glanced at my watch. It was 6:45 and that startled me. I desperately longed for a glass of wine and I decided to drive on out to Nikki's. She had said she'd be home. I turned the car around, making an illegal U, and drove back down Missile to the freeway, heading north. I got off at La Cuesta, heading toward the beach by way of Horton Ravine, a large sprawling expanse of land that is known as "a luxury residential development." Horton Ravine once belonged to one family, but it is now divided into million-dollar parcels to accommodate the housing of the nouveau riche. In Santa Teresa, Montebello is considered "old" money, Horton Ravine the "new"—but nobody really takes the distinction seriously. Rich is rich and we all know what that means. The roads through Horton Ravine are narrow and winding, overhung with trees, and the only difference I could see was that here, some houses are visible from the road whereas in Montebello, they are not. I came out at Ocean Way and swung left, the road running parallel now to the bluffs, with a number of elegant properties tucked into the selvage of land that lay between the road and the cliffs.

I passed John Powers's house, almost missing the place since I'd come at it before from the other direction. I caught a quick glimpse of the roof, which was almost level with the road. I had a sudden thought and I slammed on the brakes, pulling over to the side. I sat for a moment, heart thudding with excitement. I turned the key off and stuck my little automatic in my jeans, taking the flashlight out of the glove compartment. I flicked it on. The light was good. There were very few streetlamps along this stretch and those I could see were ornamental, as dim and misty-looking as a lithograph, casting ineffectual circles of light that scarcely penetrated the dark. I got out of the car and locked it.

There were no sidewalks, just tangles of ivy along the road. The houses were widely spaced with wooded lots in between, ratcheting now with crickets and other night-singing insects. I walked back along the road to the Powers place. There were no houses at all across from it. No cars in either direction. I paused. There were no lights visible in the house. I headed down the driveway, shining the light in front of me. I wondered if Powers was still out of town, and if so where the dogs were. If Charlie was going to be up in Santa Maria for two days he wouldn't have left them unattended.

The night was still, the ocean pounding, a recurrent thunder like a storm about to break. There was only a faint crust of moon against the hazy night sky. It was chilly, too, the air smelling lush and damp. The flashlight cut a narrow trail down the drive, illuminating in a sudden band of white the gateway across the carport. Beyond it was John Powers's car, face-in, and even from where I stood I could see that it was black. I wasn't surprised. The white picket fencing that comprised the gate was padlocked but I eased around to the left of the carport toward the front of the house. I shone the light on the car. It was a Lincoln. I couldn't tell what year but the car wasn't old. I checked the fender on the left-hand side and it was fine. I could feel my heart beginning to thump dully with dread. The right-hand fender was crumpled, the headlight broken out, metal rim crimped and pulled away, bumper indented slightly. I tried not to think of Gwen's body at the moment of impact. I could guess what it must have been like.

I heard an abrupt squealing of brakes on the road above, the high whine of a car backing up at high speed. There was a sudden wash of bright light as a car pulled into the drive. I ducked automatically, flicking out the flashlight. If it was Charlie, I was dead. I caught a glimpse of blue. Oh shit. He'd called Ruth. He was back. He knew. The Mercedes's headlights were directed straight into the carport, with only Powers's vehicle shielding me from complete exposure. I heard the car door slam and I ran.

I flew across the yard, fairly skimming the rough cut grass. Behind me, almost soundlessly, came the low scuffling of the dogs in long loping strides. I started down the narrow wooden steps to the beach, my vision inky after the harsh glare of the headlights. I missed a step and half slid my way down to the next, groping blindly. Above me, only yards away, the black dog grumbled and started down, panting, toenails scrambling on the steps. I glanced up and back. The black one was just above my head. Without even thinking about it, I reached back and grabbed at one of his long bony forelegs, yanking abruptly. The dog let out a yelp of surprise and I shoved it forward, half flinging it down the steep rocky embankment. The other dog was whining, a ninety-five-pound sissy, picking its way down the stairs with trepidation. I nearly lost my balance but I righted myself, loosened soil tumbling down into the darkness in front of me. I could hear the black dog lunging at the cliffside but he couldn't seem to get a purchase, prowling back and forth restlessly. I was nearly lying on my side as I slid down the last few feet, tumbling onto the soft sand. The gun popped out of my hand and I scrambled frantically until my fingers closed over the butt again. The flashlight was long gone. I didn't even remember when I'd lost my hold on it. The black dog was loping toward me again. I waited until he was almost on me and then I lifted a foot, kicking viciously, bringing the gun down on his head. He yelped. He'd clearly never been trained to attack. My advantage was that I knew he was a danger to me and he was just beginning to figure out how treacherous I was. He backed off, barking. I made a quick choice. North along the beach, the steep cliffs continued for miles, interrupted only by Harley's Beach, which was too isolated for sanctuary. North, the dog was blocking my path. The beach to my right would eventually straggle past the town and it couldn't be more than a couple of miles. I began to move backward, away from the dog. He stood there, head down, barking vigorously. The waves were already washing up over my shoes and I began to lift my feet, trudging backward through the surf. I turned, holding the gun up, beginning to wade. The dog paced back and forth, barking only occasionally now. The next big surge of waves crashed against my knees, drenching me to the waist. I gasped from the shock of cold, glancing back with a burble of fear as I caught sight of Charlie at the top of the cliff. The outside lights were on now, his big body sculptured in shadow, his face blank. He was staring straight down at me. I propelled myself forward, nearly flinging myself through the waist-high water, edging toward the rocks at the extreme southern limits of the beach. I reached the rocks, slippery and sharp, a mass of granite that had broken loose from the cliff and tumbled into the sea. I scrambled across, hampered by my soggy jeans, which clung to my legs, by my shoes weighted down with water, hampered by the gun, which I didn't dare relinquish. Jagged barnacles and slime alternated under me. I slipped once and something bit into my left knee, right through my jeans. I pushed on, reaching hard-packed sand again, the beach widening slightly.

There was no sign of the Powers house around the bend. No sign of either dog. I had known they couldn't follow this far even if they'd tried, but I wasn't sure about Charlie. I didn't know if he'd come down the wooden stairs and trail me along the beach or simply wait. I glanced back with dread, but the hill projected, obscuring even the light. All he had to do was get back in his car. If he took a parallel path to mine, he could intercept me easily on the other end. Eventually we'd both end up at Ludlow Beach, but I couldn't turn back. Harley's Beach was worse, too far from streetlights and residential help. I began to run in earnest, uncertain how far I had to go yet. My wet clothes stuck to me, clammy and cold, but my prime concern was the gun. I'd already dropped it once and I knew sea water had curled up toward it as I crossed the rocks. I didn't think it had gotten wet but I wasn't sure. I could see somewhat better now, but the beach was littered with rocks and kelp. I prayed I wouldn't twist an ankle. If I couldn't run, then Charlie could track me at his own pace and I'd have no way out. I glanced back: no sign of him, sound masked by the breaking surf. I didn't think he was there. Once I got to Ludlow Beach, there were bound to be other people, passing motorists. As long as I was running, the fear seemed contained, adrenaline driving out every sensation except the urge to flee. The wind was down, but it was cold and I was wet to the bone.

The beach narrowed again and I found myself running in shallow water, slogging my way through the churning surf. I tried to get my bearings but I'd never been up this far. I caught sight of a wooden stairway zigzagging up the cliff to my left, the wind-bleached railing showing white against the dark tangle of vegetation clinging to the cliff. I followed the line up with my eyes. I guessed that it was Sea Shore Park, which ran along the bluff. Parking lot. Houses across the road. I grabbed the rail and started up, knees aching as

I climbed, chest heaving. I reached the top and peered over the rim, heart stopping again.

Charlie's 450 SL was parked above, headlights raking the fence. I ducked back and started down the stairs again, a mewing sound in my throat that I couldn't control. My breathing was ragged, my chest afire. I hit the sand again and ran on, accelerating my pace. The sand was sluggish now, too soft, and I cut to my right, searching out the wet sand that was packed hard. At least I was getting warmer now, wet clothes chafing, water dripping from strands of hair matted with salt. My left knee was stinging and I could feel something warm ooze through my pantleg. The beach was interrupted not by rocks this time but by the sheer fear of the cliff, jutting out like a pie-shaped wedge into the black of the sea. I waded out into the waves, undercurrent tugging at me as I rounded the bend. Ludlow Beach was visible just ahead. I nearly wept with relief. Painfully, I began to run again, trying for a pace I could live with. I could make out lights now, dark patches of palm against gray sky. I slowed to a jog, trying to catch my breath. I stopped finally, bending from the waist, my mouth dry, sweat or salt water streaking down my face. My cheeks were hot and my eyes stung. I wiped my mouth on the back of my hand and moved on, walking this time, fear creeping up again until my heart was battering my ribs.

This stretch of beach was gentle and clean, looking pale gray, widening to the left where the high cliff finally dwindled away into sloping hillside, slipping down to the flat of the sand. Beyond, I could see the long stretch of parking lot and beyond that, the street, well lighted, empty, and inviting. The beach park closed at 8:00 and I thought the parking lot would probably be chained and locked. Still the sight of Charlie's pale blue 450 SL was a jolt—that single vehicle in the whole expanse of empty asphalt. His car lights were on, slanting forward into the palms. There was no way I could cut across the sand to the street without his seeing me. The darkness, which had seemed to lift before, now felt like a veil. I couldn't see clearly. I couldn't pick out anything in that smoky wash of darkness. The streetlights at that distance seemed pointless and whimsical and cruel, illuminating nothing, marking a path to safety that I couldn't reach. And where was he? Sitting in his car, his eyes scanning the park, waiting for me to crash through to him? Or out among the palms much closer to the beach?

I moved to the right again, wading out into the ocean. The icy water was making my blood congeal but I crept on, waves splashing against my knees. Out here, I would be harder to spot and if I couldn't see him, at least he couldn't see me. When I was out far enough, I sank down, half walking, half drifting through the undulating depths beyond the breakers. It cost me everything to keep the gun up. I was obsessed with that, arm aching, fingers numb. My hair floated around my face like wet gauze. I watched the beach, seeing little, searching for Charlie. Car lights still on. Nothing. No one. I had moved perhaps two hundred yards past the far-left extreme of the parking lot, almost even now with the concession stand: a small oasis of palms and picnic tables, trash cans, public telephones. I put my feet down, easing into a standing position, still angling to the right. He could be anywhere, standing in any shadow. I waded toward the shallows, waves curling at knee height, washing forward then across my shoes. Finally I was on wet sand again, moving quickly toward the lot, straining through the darkness for sight of him. He couldn't be looking everyplace at once. I crouched, shifting my gaze to the left. Now that I was forced into immobility, the fear took up where it had left me, ice spreading across my lungs, pulse beating in my throat. I slipped out of my wet jeans and shoes—lightly, quietly.

The concession stand was dead ahead: squat structure of cinder block, windows boarded over for the night. I moved to the right, through powdery sand, sinking down to my ankles, working harder on land than I had in water. I jumped. There he was—just a flash to my left. I dropped to a crouch again, wondering how visible I was. I eased down flat on my belly, pulled myself forward on my elbows. I reached the dark shade of the palms, which even at this hour cast clear shadows against the gray of night. I peered to the left, spotting him again. He wore a white shirt, darker pants. He disappeared into the shadows, passing into the grove of palm trees where the picnic tables were set out. Behind me, the ocean was hushed, a sibilant backdrop to our little cat-and-mouse. To my right, there was an oblong metal trash bin, chest-height with a hinged metal lid. I heard Charlie's car start up and I glanced back with surprise. Maybe he was leaving.

Maybe he thought he had missed me and was moving now to intercept me farther down the beach. As he swung back to turn around, I darted toward the trash bin, lifted the lid with one thrust, and pulled myself over the metal lip into the crush of paper cups, discarded picnic sacks, debris. I wrestled out a place for myself with my backside, shifting my bare legs down into the garbage, wrinkling my nose with disgust. My right foot was touching something cold and gooey and the trash beneath me felt warm, like a compost heap, smoldering with bacteria. I pushed up slightly and peered over my shoulder through the crack, the metal lid tilted slightly ajar by the mountain of accumulated trash. Charlie's car was moving toward me, headlights slicing straight across my hiding place. I ducked down, heartbeat making my eyes bulge.

He got out of the car, leaving the lights on. I could still see a slice of light reflected from where I crouched. He slammed the car door. I could hear his footsteps scratch across the concrete.

"Kinsey, I know you're here someplace," he said.

I tried not to move. Tried not to breathe.

Silence.

"Kinsey, you don't have to be afraid of me. My God, don't you know that?" His tone was insistent, gentle, persuasive, hurt.

Was I just imagining everything? He sounded like he always did. Silence. I heard his footsteps moving away. I eased up slowly, peering out through the crack. He was standing ten feet away from me, staring out toward the ocean, his body still, half turned away. He started back and I ducked down. I could hear footsteps approaching. I shrank, pulling the gun up, hands shaking. Maybe I was crazy. Maybe I was making a fool of myself. I hated hide-and-seek. I'd never been good at that as a kid. I always jumped right out when anyone got close because the tension made me want to wet my pants. I felt tears rising. Oh Jesus, not *now*, I thought feverishly. The fear was like a sharp pain. My heart hurt me every time it beat, making the blood pound in my ears. Surely he could hear that. Surely he knew now where I was.

He lifted the lid. The beams from his headlights shone against his golden cheek. He glanced over at me. In his right hand was a butcher knife with a ten-inch blade.

I blew him away.

Epilogue

The Santa Teresa police conducted a brief investigation but in the end no charges were filed. The folder on Laurence Fife contains the report I sent to the chief of the Bureau of Collection and Investigative Services regarding the discharge of my firearm "while acting within the course and scope" of my employment. There is also a copy of the refund check I sent to Nikki for the unused portion of the $5000 she advanced on account. All together, I was paid $2978.25 for services rendered in the course of that sixteen days and I suppose it was fair enough. The shooting disturbs me still. It has moved me into the same camp with soldiers and maniacs. I never set out to kill anyone. But maybe that's what Gwen would say, and Charlie too. I'll recover, of course. I'll be ready for business again in a week or two, but I'll never be the same. You try to keep life simple but it never works, and in the end all you have left is yourself.

—Respectfully submitted,
Kinsey Millhone

B is for Burglar

For Steven,
who sees me through

The author wishes to acknowledge the invaluable assistance of the following people: Steven Humphrey; John Carroll; Brenda Harman, D.D.S.; Billie Moore Squires; De De La Fond; William Fezler, Ph.D.; Sydney Baumgartner; Frank E. Sincavage; Milton Weintraub; Jay Schmidt; Judy Cooley; Bill Pronzini and Marcia Muller; and Joe Driscoll of Driscoll and Associates Investigations, Columbus, Ohio.

Prologue

After it's over, of course, you want to kick yourself for all the things you didn't see at the time. The Had-I-But-Known school of private investigation perhaps. My name is Kinsey Millhone and most of my reports begin the same way. I start by asserting who I am and what I do, as though by stating the same few basic facts I can make sense out of everything that comes afterward.

This is what's true of me in brief. I'm female, age thirty-two, single, self-employed. I went through the police academy when I was twenty, joining Santa Teresa Police Department on graduation. I don't even remember now how I pictured the job before I took it on. I must have had vague, idealistic notions of law and order, the good guys versus the bad, with occasional court appearances in which I'd be asked to testify as to which was which. In my view, the bad guys would all go to jail, thus making it safe for the rest of us to carry on. After a while, I realized how naïve I was. I was frustrated at the restrictions and frustrated because back then, policewomen were viewed with a mixture of curiosity and scorn. I didn't want to spend my days defending myself against "good-natured" insults, or having to prove how tough I was again and again. I wasn't getting paid enough to deal with all that grief, so I got out.

For two years, I tried an assortment of occupations, but none had the same pull. Whatever else is true of police work, it does entail the intermittent sick thrill of life on the edge. I was hooked on the adrenal rush, and I couldn't go back to the commonplace.

Eventually, I joined a small firm of private investigators and spent another two years learning the business, after which I opened an office of my own, duly licensed and bonded. I've been at it for five years, supporting myself in a modest way. I'm wiser now than I used to be and I'm more experienced, but the fact remains that when a client sits down in the chair across the desk from me, I never know what's going to happen next.

1

I'd been in the office no more than twenty minutes that morning. I'd opened the French doors out onto the second-floor balcony to let in some fresh air and I'd put on the coffee pot. It was June in Santa Teresa, which means chill morning fog and hazy afternoons. It wasn't nine o'clock yet. I was just sorting through the mail from the day before when I heard a tap at the door and a woman breezed in.

"Oh good. You're here," she said. "You must be Kinsey Millhone. I'm Beverly Danziger."

We shook hands and she promptly sat down and started rooting through her bag. She found a pack of filter-tipped cigarettes and shook one out.

"I hope you don't mind if I smoke," she said, lighting up without waiting for a response. She inhaled and then extinguished the match with a mouthful of smoke, idly searching about for an ashtray. I took one from the top of my file cabinet, dusted it off, and passed it over to her, offering her coffee at the same time.

"Oh sure, why not?" she said with a laugh, "I'm already hyper this morning so I might as well. I just drove up from Los Angeles, right through the rush-hour traffic. Gawd!"

I poured her a mug of coffee, doing a quick visual survey. She was in her late thirties by my guess; petite, energetic, well groomed. Her hair was a glossy black and quite straight. The cut was angular and perfectly layered so that it framed her small face like a bathing cap. She had bright blue eyes, black lashes, a clear complexion with just a hint of blusher high on each cheekbone. She wore a boat-necked sweater in a pale blue cotton knit, and a pale blue poplin skirt. The bag she carried was quality leather, soft and supple, with a number of zippered compartments containing God knows what. Her nails were long and tapered, painted a rosy pink and she wore a wedding ring studded with rubies. She projected self-confidence and a certain careless attention to style, conservatively packaged like the complimentary gift wrap in a classy department store.

She shook her head to the offer of cream and sugar so I added half-and-half to my own mug and got down to business.

"What can I help you with?"

"I'm hoping you can locate my sister for me," she said.

She was searching through her handbag again. She took out her address book, a rosewood pen-and-pencil set, and a long white envelope, which she placed on the edge of my desk. I'd never seen anyone so self-absorbed, but it wasn't unattractive stuff. She gave me a quick smile then, as though she knew that. She opened the address book and turned it so that it faced me, pointing to one of the entries with a rosy fingertip.

"You'll want to make a note of the address and telephone number," she said. "Her name is Elaine Boldt. She has a condo on Via Madrina and that second one is her address in Florida. She spends several months a year down in Boca."

I was feeling somewhat puzzled, but I noted the addresses while she took a legal-looking document out of the long white envelope. She studied it briefly, as though the contents might have changed since she'd last seen it.

"How long has she been missing?" I asked.

Beverly Danziger gave me an uncomfortable look. "Well, I don't know if she's 'missing' exactly. I just don't know where she is and I've got to get these papers signed. I know it sounds dumb. She's only entitled to a ninth interest and it probably won't come to more than two or three thousand dollars, but the money can't be distributed until we have her notarized signature. Here, you can see for yourself."

I took the document and read through the contents. It had been drawn up by a firm of attorneys in Columbus, Ohio, and it was full of whereases, adjudgeds, ordereds, and whatnots, which added up to the fact that a man named Sidney Rowan had died and the various people listed were entitled to portions of his estate. Beverly Danziger was the third party listed, with a Los Angeles address, and Elaine Boldt was fourth, with an address here in Santa Teresa.

"Sidney Rowan was some kind of cousin," she went

on garrulously. "I don't believe I ever met the man, but I got this notice and I assume Elaine got one too. I signed the form and got it notarized and sent off and then didn't think any more about it. You can see from the cover letter that this all took place six months ago. Then, lo and behold I got a call last week from the attorney . . . what's his name again?"

I glanced at the document. "Wender," I said.

"Oh, that's right. I don't know why I keep blocking that. Anyway, Mr. Wender's office called to say they'd never heard from Elaine. Naturally, I assumed she'd gone off to Florida as usual and just hadn't bothered to have her mail sent, so I got in touch with the manager of her condominium here. She hasn't heard from Elaine in months. Well, she did at first, but not recently."

"Have you tried calling the Florida number?"

"From what I understand, the attorney tried several times. Apparently, she had a friend staying with her and Mr. Wender left his name and number, but Elaine never called back. Tillie had about the same luck."

"Tillie?"

"The woman who manages the building here where Elaine has her permanent residence. Tillie's been forwarding the mail and she says Elaine usually drops her a little note every other week or so, but she hasn't heard anything since March. Frankly, it's a nuisance more than anything else, but I don't have time to track her down myself." Beverly took a final drag of the cigarette and stubbed it out with a series of pecking motions.

I was still taking notes, but I suppose the skepticism was showing in my face.

"What's the matter? Isn't this the sort of work you do?"

"Sure, but I charge thirty dollars an hour, plus expenses. If there's only two or three thousand dollars involved, I wonder if it's going to be worth it to you."

"Oh, I fully intend to have the estate reimburse me out of Elaine's share since she caused all this trouble to begin with. I mean, everything's come to a screeching halt until her signature can be obtained. I must say it's typical of the way she's behaved all her life."

"Suppose I end up flying down to Florida to look for her? Even if I only charge you half my usual hourly rate for travel time, it'll cost a fortune. Look, Mrs. Danziger—"

"Beverly, please."

"All right, Beverly. I don't want to discourage your business, but in all honesty it sounds like something you could handle yourself. I'd even be happy to suggest some ways to go about it."

Beverly gave me a smile then, but it had a hard edge to it and I realized, at long last, that she was used to getting her way. Her eyes had widened to a china glaze, as blue and unyielding as glass. The black lashes blinked mechanically.

"Elaine and I are not on the best of terms," she said smoothly. "I feel I've already devoted quite enough time to this, but I promised Mr. Wender I'd find her so the estate can be settled. He's under pressure from the other heirs and he's putting pressure on me. I can give you an advance if you like."

She was back in her bag again, coming up with a

checkbook this time. She uncapped the rosewood pen and stared at me.

"Will seven hundred and fifty dollars suffice?"

I reached into my bottom drawer. "I'll draw up a contract."

I walked the check over to the bank and then I retrieved my car from the lot behind the office and drove over to Elaine Boldt's address on Via Madrina. It wasn't far from the down-town area.

I figured this was a routine matter I could settle in a day or two and I was thinking with regret that I'd probably end up refunding half the money I'd just deposited. Not that I was doing much else anyway—things were slow.

The neighborhood Elaine Boldt lived in was composed of modest 1930s bungalows mixed with occasional apartment complexes. So far, the little frame and stucco cottages were predominant but the properties were being converted to commercial use one by one. Chiropractors were moving in, and cut-rate dentists who were willing to give you twilight sleep so you could have your teeth cleaned without cringing. ONE-DAY DENTURES—CREDIT. It was worrisome. What did they do to you if you missed a payment on your upper plate? The area was still largely intact—old-age pensioners stubbornly propping up their hydrangea bushes—but real-estate syndicates would eventually mow them all down. There's a lot of money in Santa Teresa and much of it is devoted to maintaining a certain "look" to the

town. There are no flashing neon signs, no slums, no
fume-spewing manufacturing complexes to blight the
landscape. Everything is stucco, red tile roofs, bougainvillea, distressed beams, adobe brick walls, arched windows, palm trees, balconies, ferns, fountains, paseos,
and flowers in bloom. Historical restorations abound.
It's all oddly unsettling—so lush and refined that it ruins
you for anyplace else.

When I reached Mrs. Boldt's address, I parked my car
out front and locked it, taking a few minutes then to
survey the premises. The condominium was a curiosity.
The building itself was shaped like a horseshoe with
broad arms opening onto the street; three stories high,
parking level underneath, a strange combination of
modern and mock-Spanish. There were arches and balconies along the front, with tall wrought-iron gates
sweeping inward to a palm-planted courtyard, but the
sides and back of the building were flat and unadorned,
as though the architect had applied a Mediterranean veneer to a plain plywood box, adding a lip of red tile at
the top to suggest an entire roof when there was none.
Even the palms looked like cardboard cutouts, propped
up with sticks.

I passed through the courtyard and found myself in a
glass-enclosed lobby with a row of mailboxes and door
buzzers on the right. On my left, through another set of
glass doors, apparently kept locked, I could see a set of
elevator doors and an exit leading to a set of fire stairs.
Huge potted plants had been artfully arranged throughout the entranceway. Straight ahead, a door led out into
a patio where I caught sight of a pool surrounded by

bright yellow canvas deck chairs. I checked the tenants' names, which were punched out on strips of plastic tape and pasted alongside each apartment buzzer. There were twenty-four units. The manager, Tillie Ahlberg, occupied apartment 1. An "E. Boldt" was listed at apartment 9, which I guessed was on the second floor.

"I gave "E. Boldt" a buzz first. For all I knew, she'd answer on the intercom and then my job would be done. Stranger things had happened and I didn't want to make a fool of myself looking high and low for a lady who might well by now be at home. There was no response so I tried Tillie Ahlberg.

After ten seconds, her voice crackled into the intercom as though the sound were being transmitted from outer space.

"Yes?"

I placed my mouth near the box, raising my voice slightly.

"Mrs. Ahlberg, my name is Kinsey Millhone. I'm a private detective here in town. Elaine Boldt's sister asked me to see if I could locate her and I wondered if I might talk to you."

There was a moment of white noise and then a reluctant reply.

"Well, I suppose. I was on my way out, but I guess ten minutes won't hurt. I'm on the ground floor. Come through the door to the right of the elevator and it's down at the end of the hall to the left." The buzzer sounded and I pushed through the glass doors.

Tillie Ahlberg had left her front door ajar while she

collected a lightweight jacket, her purse, and a collapsible shopping cart that rested against the hall table. I tapped on the doorframe and she appeared from my left. I caught a glimpse of a refrigerator and a portion of kitchen counter.

Tillie Ahlberg was probably in her sixties, with apricot-tinted hair in a permanent wave that looked as if it had just been done. The curl must have been a little frizzier than she liked because she was pulling on a crocheted cotton cap. An unruly fringe of apricot hair was still peeking out, like Ronald McDonald's, and she was in the process of tucking it away. Her eyes were hazel and there was a powdery patina of pale ginger freckles on her face. She wore a shapeless skirt, hose, and running shoes, and she looked like she was capable of covering ground when she wanted to.

"I hope I didn't seem unsociable," she said comfortably. "But if I don't get to the market first thing in the morning, I lose heart."

"It shouldn't take long anyway," I said. "Can you tell me when you last heard from Mrs. Boldt? Is she Miss or Mrs.?"

"Mrs. She's a widow, though she's only forty-three years old. She was married to a man who had a string of manufacturing plants down south. As I understand it, he dropped dead of a heart attack three years ago and left her a bundle. That's when she bought this place. Here, have a seat if you like."

Tillie moved off to the right, leading the way into a living room furnished with antique reproductions. A gauzy golden light came through the pale yellow sheers and I could still smell the remnants of breakfast: bacon and coffee and something laced with cinnamon.

Having established that she was in a hurry, she seemed ready to give me as much time as I wanted. She sat down on an ottoman and I took a wooden rocking chair.

"I understand she's usually in Florida this time of year," I said.

"Well, yes. She's got another condominium down there. In Boca Raton, wherever that is. Near Fort Lauderdale, I guess. I've never been to Florida myself, so these towns are all just names to me. Anyhow, she usually goes down around the first of February and comes back to California late July or early August. She likes the heat, she says."

"And you forward mail to her while she's gone?"

Tillie nodded. "I do that about once a week in batches, depending on how much has accumulated. Then she sends me back a note every couple of weeks. A postcard, you know, just to say hi and how the weather is and if she needs someone let in to clean the drapes or something of that nature. This year she wrote me through the first of March and since then I haven't heard a word. Now, that's not like her a bit."

"Do you still have the postcards by any chance?"

"No, I just threw 'em out like I always do. I'm not much for collecting things like that. There's too much paper piling up in the world if you ask me. I read 'em and tossed 'em and never thought a thing of it."

"She didn't mention taking a side trip or anything like that?"

"Not a word. Of course, it's none of my business in the first place."

"Did she seem distressed?"

Tillie smiled ruefully. "Well, it's hard to seem upset on the message side of a postcard, you know. There isn't but that much room. She sounded fine to me."

"Do you have any guesses about where she might be?"

"Not a one. All I know is it's not like her not to write. I tried calling four or five times. Once some woman friend of hers answered but she was real abrupt and after that, there wasn't anything at all."

"Who was the friend? Anyone you knew?"

"No, but now I don't know who she knows in Boca. It could have been anyone. I didn't make a note of the name and wouldn't know it if you said it to me right this minute."

"What about the mail she's been getting? Are her bills still coming in?"

She shrugged at that. "It looks that way to me. I haven't paid much attention. I just shipped on whatever came in. I do have a few I was about to forward if you'd like to see them." She got up and crossed to an oak secretary, opening one of the glass doors by turning the key in the lock. She took out a short stack of envelopes and sorted through them, then handed them to me. "This is the kind of thing she usually gets."

I did the same quick sorting job. Visa, MasterCard, Saks Fifth Avenue. A furrier named Jacques with an address in Boca Raton. A bill from a John Pickett, D.D.S., Inc., right around the corner on Arbol. No personal letters at all.

"Does she pay utility bills from here too?" I asked.

"I already sent those this month."

"Could she have been arrested?"

That sparked a laugh. "Oh no. Not her. She wasn't anything like that. She didn't drive a car, you know, but she wasn't the type to get so much as a jaywalking ticket."

"Accident? Illness? Drink? Drugs?" I felt like a doctor interviewing a patient for an annual physical.

Tillie's expression was skeptical. "She could be in the hospital I suppose, but surely she would have let us know. I find it very peculiar to tell you the truth. If that sister of hers hadn't come along, I might have gotten in touch with the police myself. There's just something not right."

"But there are lots of explanations for where she might be," I said. "She's an adult. Apparently she's got money and no pressing business. She really doesn't have to notify anybody of her whereabouts if she doesn't want to. She might be on a cruise. Or maybe she's taken a lover and absconded with him. Maybe she and this girl friend of hers took off on a toot. It might never occur to her that anyone was trying to get in touch."

"That's why I haven't really done anything so far, but it doesn't sit well with me. I don't think she'd leave without a word to anyone."

"Well, let me look into it. I don't want to hold you up right now, but I'll want to see her apartment at some point," I said. I got up and Tillie rose automatically. I shook her hand and thanked her for her help.

"Hang on to the mail for the time being, if you would," I said. "I'm going to chase down some other possibilities, but I'll get back to you in a day or two and let you know what I've come up with. I don't think there's any reason to worry."

"I hope not," Tillie said. "She's a wonderful person."

I gave Tillie my card before we parted company. I wasn't worried yet myself, but my curiosity had been aroused and I was eager to get on with it.

2

On the way back to the office, I stopped off at the public library. I went to the reference department and pulled the city directory for Boca Raton, checking the address I had for Elaine Boldt against the addresses listed. Sure enough, she was there with a telephone number that matched the one I'd been given. I noted the names of several other owners of adjacent condominiums, jotting down telephone numbers. There seemed to be a number of buildings in the same complex and I guessed that it was an entire "planned community." There was a general sales office, a telephone number for tennis courts, a health spa, and a recreational facility. I made notes of everything just to save myself a possible trip back.

When I reached the office, I opened a file on Elaine Boldt, logging the time I'd put in so far and the information I had. I tried the Florida number, letting it ring maybe thirty times without luck, and then I put in a call to the sales office of the Boca Raton condominium. They gave me the name of the resident manager in

Elaine Boldt's building, a Roland Makowski, apartment 101, who picked up on the first ring.

"Makowski here."

I told him as briefly as possible who I was and why I was trying to get in touch with Elaine Boldt.

"She didn't come down this year," he said. "She's usually here about this time, but I guess she had a change of plans."

"Are you sure?"

"Well, I haven't seen her. I've been up and down and around this building day in and day out and I never laid eyes on her. That's all I know. I guess she could be here if she's always someplace where I'm not," he said. "That friend of hers, Pat, is here, but Mrs. Boldt went off someplace else is what I was told. Maybe she could tell you where. I just bumped into her hanging towels out on the rail which we don't allow. The balcony's not a drying rack and I told her as much. She kinda went off in a huff."

"Can you tell me her last name?"

"What?"

"Can you tell me Pat's last name? Mrs. Boldt's friend."

"Oh. Yes."

I waited a moment. "I've got a pencil and paper," I said.

"Oh. It's Usher. Like in a movie theater. She's sublet, she said. What's your name again?"

I gave him my name again and my office number in case he wanted to get in touch. It was not a satisfactory conversation. Pat Usher seemed to be the only link to

Elaine Boldt's whereabouts and I thought it essential to talk to her as soon as possible.

I put in another call to Elaine's Florida number, letting it ring until *I* got annoyed with the sound. Nothing. If Pat Usher was still in the apartment, she was resolutely refusing to answer the phone.

I checked the list I'd made of neighboring apartments and tried the telephone number of a Robert Perreti, who apparently lived right next door. No answer. I tried the number for the neighbor on the other side, dutifully letting the phone ring ten times as the telephone company advises us. At long last, someone answered—a very old someone by the sound of her.

"Yes?" She sounded as if she were feeble and might want to weep. I found myself speaking loudly and carefully as though to the hearing-impaired.

"Mrs. Ochsner?"

"Yes."

"My name is Kinsey Millhone. I'm calling from California and I'm trying to reach the woman who's staying next door to you in apartment 315. Do you happen to know if she's in? I've just called and I let the phone ring about thirty times with no luck."

"Do you have a hearing problem?" she asked me. "You're speaking very loudly, you know."

I laughed, bringing my tone down into a normal range. "I'm sorry," I said. "I wasn't sure how well you could hear me."

"Oh, I can hear perfectly. I'm eighty-eight years old and I can't walk a step without help, but there's nothing wrong with my ears. I counted every one of those thirty rings through the wall and I thought I'd go crazy if it went on much longer."

"Has Pat Usher stepped out? I was just on the line to the building manager and he said she was there."

"Oh, she's there all right. I know she is because she slammed the door not moments ago. What was it you wanted, if it's not too impertinent of me to ask?"

"Well, actually I'm trying to locate Elaine Boldt, but I understand she didn't make it down this year."

"That's true and I was awfully disappointed. She's part of a bridge foursome when Mrs. Wink and Ida Rittenhouse are here and we count on her. We haven't been able to play a hand since last Christmas and it's made Ida very cranky if you want to know the truth."

"Do you have any idea where Mrs. Boldt might be?"

"No, I don't and I suspect the woman in there is on her way out. The condominium bylaws don't permit sublets and I was surprised that Elaine agreed to it. We've complained aplenty to the association and I believe Mr. Makowski has asked her to vacate. The woman has her back up, of course, claiming her agreement with Elaine covers through the end of June. If you want to have a conversation with her yourself, you'd do well to get down here soon. I saw her bringing up some cartons from the liquor store and I believe . . . well, I should say *I hope* she's packing up even as we speak."

"Thanks. I may do that. You've been a big help. If I get down there, I'll stop by."

"I don't suppose you play bridge, do you, dear? We've been reduced to playing hearts now for the last six months and Ida's developing quite a mean mouth. Mrs. Wink and I can't take too much more of this."

"Well, I've never played but maybe I could give it a try," I said.

"A penny a point," she said brusquely, and I laughed.

I put in a call to Tillie. She sounded out of breath, as though she'd had to run for the phone.

"Hi, Tillie," I said. "It's me again. Kinsey."

"I just got back from the market," she panted. "Hang on until I catch my breath. Whew! What can I do for you?"

"I think I better go ahead and take a look at Elaine's apartment."

"Why? What's going on?"

"Well, the people in Florida say she's not there, so I'm hoping we can figure out where else she might have gone. If I come back over there, could you let me in?"

"I guess so. I'm not doing anything except unloading groceries and that won't take but two shakes."

When I reached the condominium again, I called her on the intercom and she buzzed me through and then met me at the elevator door with a key to Elaine's apartment. I told her the details of my conversation with Elaine's building manager down in Florida, filling her in as we rode up to the second floor.

"You mean nobody down there has seen her at all? Well, something's wrong then," she said. "Definitely. I know she left and I know she fully intended to go down to Florida. I was looking out the window when the cab pulled up out front and gave a toot and she got in. She had on her good fur coat and that fur turban that matched. She was traveling at night, which she didn't like to do, but then she wasn't feeling good and she thought the change in climate might help."

"She was sick?"

"Oh, you know. Her sinuses were acting up and she'd had that awful head cold or allergy or whatever it was. I don't mean to criticize, but she was a bit of a hypochondriac. She called me and said she'd decided to go ahead and fly on down, almost on the spur of the moment. She wasn't really scheduled to go for nearly two weeks, but then the doctor said it might do her good and I guess she booked the first flight she could get."

"Do you know if she used a travel agent?"

"I'm almost sure she did. Probably one close by. Since she didn't drive, she liked to deal with businesses within walking distance where she could. Here it is."

Tillie had paused outside of apartment 9, which was on the second floor, directly above hers. She unlocked the door and then followed me in.

The apartment was dim, drapes drawn, the air dry and still. Tillie crossed the living room and opened the drapes.

"Nobody's been in since she left?" I asked. "Cleaning lady? Tradesmen?"

"Not as far as I know."

Both of us seemed to be using our public-library tones, but there's something unsettling about being in someone else's place when you're not supposed to be. I could feel a low-level electrical current surging through my gut.

We did a quick tour together and Tillie said it looked all right to her. Nothing unusual. Nothing out of place. She left then and I went through on my own, taking my time so I could do it right.

This was a corner apartment, second-floor front, with windows running along two sides. I took a minute to stare down at the street. There were no cars passing. A boy with a Mohawk haircut was leaning up against a parked car directly below. The sides of his head were shaved to a preexecution gray and the strip of hair that remained stood up like a dry brush in the center divider of a highway. It was dyed a shade of pink that I hadn't seen since hot pants went out of style. He looked to be sixteen or seventeen, wearing a pair of bright red parachute pants tucked down into combat boots, and an orange tank top with a slogan on the front that I couldn't read from where I stood. I watched him roll and light a joint.

I moved to the side windows which looked down at an angle through the ground-floor windows of the small frame house next door. The roof had been gnawed by fire, the eaves of the house showing through like the frail bones of an overcooked fish. The door was boarded up, the glass broken out of the windows, apparently by the heat. A FOR SALE sign was jammed into the dead grass like a flimsy headstone. Not much of a view for a condominium that I estimated must have cost Elaine more than a hundred thousand dollars. I shrugged to myself and went into the kitchen.

The counters and appliances gleamed. The floor had apparently been washed and waxed. The cupboards were neatly stacked with canned goods, including some 9-Lives Beef and Liver Platter. The refrigerator was empty, except for the usual door full of olives and pickles and mustards and jams. The electric stove had been unplugged, the cord dangling across the clockface, which read 8:20. An empty brown paper sack had been inserted in the plastic wastebasket under the sink, a cuff neatly turned down at the top. It looked as if Elaine Boldt had systematically prepared the apartment for a long absence.

I left the kitchen and wandered out into the entrance hall. The layout seemed to be a duplicate of Tillie's apartment downstairs. I moved down a short corridor, glancing to my right into a small bathroom with a sink shaped like a sunken marble shell, gold-plated fixtures, gold-flecked mirrored tiles on one wall. The small wicker wastebasket under the sink was empty except for a delicate gray-brown clump of hair clinging to the side like the light matting when a hairbrush has been cleaned.

Across from the bathroom was a small den, with a desk, a television set, an easy chair, and a sofa bed. The desk drawers contained the usual assortment of pens, paper clips, note cards, and files, which for the moment I saw no reason to examine more closely. I did come across her social-security card and I made a note of the number. I left the den and moved into a master suite with an adjoining bathroom.

The bedroom was gloomy with the drapes pulled, but

again everything seemed in order. To the right, there was a walk-in closet large enough to rent out. Some of the hangers were empty and I could see gaps in the articles lined up on the shelves where she'd probably packed an item. A small suitcase was still tucked down in one corner, one of the expensive designer types covered with somebody else's name all done in curlicues.

I checked dresser drawers randomly. Some still contained wool sweaters in plastic cleaner's bags. A few were empty except for a sachet or two left behind like tiny scented pillows. Lingerie. A few pieces of costume jewelry.

The master bath was spacious and orderly, the medicine cabinet stripped of all but a few over-the-counter remedies. I moved back to the door and stood there for a moment, surveying the bedroom. There was nothing to suggest foul play or haste, burglary, vandalism, illness, suicide, drunkenness, drug abuse, confusion, or recent occupancy. Even the faint powdering of household dust on the glossy surfaces seemed undisturbed.

I left, locking the door behind me. I took the elevator down to Tillie's and asked her if she had any photographs of Elaine.

"Not that I know," she said, "but I can describe her if you like. She's just about my size, which would make her five foot five, a hundred and thirty pounds. She has streaked blond hair which she wears pulled back. Blue eyes." Tillie stopped. "Oh wait, maybe I do have a picture. I just remembered one. Hold on."

She disappeared in the direction of the den and after a few moments returned with a Polaroid snapshot that she handed to me. The picture had an orange cast to it and seemed sticky to the touch. Two women stood in the courtyard, a full-length shot, taken from perhaps twenty feet back. One I guessed immediately was Elaine, smiling happily, trim and elegant in a pair of well-cut slacks. The other woman was thick through the middle, with blue plastic eyeglass frames and a hairdo that looked as if it could be removed intact. She appeared to be in her forties, squinting into the sun self-consciously.

"This was taken last fall," Tillie said. "That's Elaine on the left."

"Who's the other woman?"

"Marty Grice, a neighbor of ours. Now that was an awful thing. She was killed . . . oh gosh, I guess six months back. It doesn't seem that long ago."

"What happened to her?"

"Well, they think she interrupted a burglar breaking into the house. I guess he killed her on the spot and then tried to burn the place down to cover it up. It was horrible. You might have read about it in the paper."

I shook my head. There are long periods when I don't read the paper at all, but I remembered the house next door with its charred roof and windows broken out. "That's too bad," I said. "Do you mind if I keep this?"

"Go right ahead."

I glanced at it again. The image was faintly disturbing, capturing a moment not that long ago when both women grinned with such ease, unaware that anything unpleasant lay ahead. Now, one was dead and the other missing. I didn't like that combination at all.

"Were Elaine and this woman good friends?" I asked.

"Not really. They played bridge together now and then, but they didn't socialize aside from that. Elaine is a bit standoffish where most people are concerned. Actually, Marty used to get a little snippy about Elaine's attitude. Not that she ever said anything much about it to me, but I can remember her being a bit snide once in a while. Elaine does treat herself well—there's no doubt about *that*—and she tends to be insensitive to the idea that people really can't afford to live as well as she does. That fur coat of hers is a case in point. She knew Leonard and Marty were in financial straits, but she'd wear the coat over there to play bridge. To Marty, that was just like waving a red flag in front of a bull."

"That's the same coat she was wearing when you saw her last?"

"Yes, indeed. A twelve-thousand-dollar lynx fur coat with a matching hat."

"Wow," I said.

"Oh, it's beautiful. I'd give my eyeteeth to have a coat like that."

"Can you remember anything else about her departure that night?"

"I can't say that I do. She was carrying some sort of luggage—I guess a carry-on—and the cab driver brought down the rest."

"Do you remember what cab company?"

"I really didn't pay much attention at the time, but she usually called City Cab or Green Stripe, sometimes Tip Top, though she didn't like them much. I wish I could be more help. I mean, if she left here on her way to Florida and never got there, where did she end up?"

"That's what I want to know," I said.

I gave Tillie what I hoped was a reassuring smile, but I was feeling uneasy.

I went back to the office and did a quick calculation of the expenses I'd run up so far; maybe seventy-five bucks for the time spent with Tillie and the time going through Elaine's apartment, plus the time in the library and on the telephone and the long-distance charges. I've known P.I.s who conduct entire investigations on the phone, but I don't think it's smart. Unless you're dealing with people face-to-face, there are too many ways to be deceived and too many things to miss.

I called a travel agent and got myself booked round-trip to Miami. The fare was ninety-nine bucks each way if I flew in the dead of night and didn't eat, drink, or go to the john. I also reserved a cheap rental car on the far end.

My plane didn't leave for hours yet, so I went home and got in a three-mile jog, then stuck a toothbrush and toothpaste in my purse and called it packing. At some point, I was going to have to track down Elaine's travel agent and find out what airline she had taken and whether perhaps she'd booked herself through to Mexico or the Caribbean. In the meantime, I hoped I could catch Elaine's friend in Florida before she flew the coop, taking with her my only link to Elaine's whereabouts.

3

It was still dark when the plane touched down in Miami at 4:45 A.M. The airport was sparsely populated at that hour, the lighting as subdued as a funeral home's. In the baggage claim area, stacks of abandoned suitcases were piled together in shadowy glass-fronted cabinets. All the airport shops were closed. Travelers slept here and there on the unyielding plastic seats, resting their heads on bulging canvas totes, their jackets hunched up over their shoulders. The intercom paged a passenger to the white courtesy telephone, but the name was garbled and I didn't think anyone would respond. I had only managed to sleep for about an hour on the plane and I felt rumpled and out of sorts.

I picked up my rental car and a sheet map and by 5:15 was headed north on U.S. 1. Twenty miles to Fort Lauderdale, another fifteen to Boca Raton. Dawn was turning the sky a pearly translucent gray and clouds were piled up like heads of cauliflower in a roadside stand. The land on either side of the highway was flat, with white sand creeping up to the edges of the road.

Patches of saw grass and stunted cypress cut into the horizon and Spanish moss hung from the trees like tattered rags. The air was already moist and balmy and the streaks of orange from the rising sun hinted at a hot day to come. To kill some time, I stopped at a fast-food place and ate some brown and yellow things that I washed down with a carton of orange juice. All of it tasted like something the astronauts would have to reconstitute.

By the time I reached the community where Elaine Boldt had her Florida condominium, it was nearly seven o'clock and the sprinkler system was sending out jets of water across the closely clipped grass. There were six or seven buildings of poured concrete, each three stories high, with screened-in porches punctuating the low clean lines. Hibiscus bushes added touches of bright red and pink. I circled through the area, driving slowly along the wide avenues that curved back as far as the tennis courts. Each building seemed to have its own swimming pool cradled close and there were already people stretched out on plastic chaise longues sunning themselves. I spotted the street number I was looking for and pulled into a small parking lot out in front. The manager's apartment was on the ground floor, the front door standing open, the screen door secured against the onslaught of big Florida bugs that were already making warning sounds in the grass.

I knocked against the aluminum frame.

"I'm right here." It was a woman's voice, disconcertingly close.

I cupped one hand, shading my eyes so that I could see who I was talking to through the screen door.

"Is Mr. Makowski here?"

The woman seemed to materialize on the other side, her face level with my knees.

"Hold on. I've been doing my sit-ups and I can't get to my feet yet. Lord, that hurts." She hauled herself into a kneeling position, clinging to the arm of a chair. "Makowski's off fixing the toilet in 208. What can I do you for?"

"I'm trying to get in touch with Elaine Boldt. Do you have any idea where she might be?"

"You that investigator who called from California?"

"Yes, that's me. I thought I should talk to someone down here and see if I could get a lead on her. Did she leave a forwarding address?"

"Nope. I wish I could help you out, but I don't know much more than you do. Here, come on in." She lurched to her feet and held the screen door open. "I'm Charmaine Makowski, or what's left of her. Do you exercise?"

"Well, I jog, but that's about it," I said.

"Good for you. Don't ever do sit-ups. That's my advice. I do a hundred a day and it always hurts." She was still winded, her cheeks tinted pink from the effort. She was in her late forties, wearing a bright yellow sweat suit, her belly protruding in pregnancy. She looked like a ripe Florida grapefruit.

"You got it," she said. "Another one of life's little jokes. I thought it was a tumor 'til it started to kick. Know what that is?"

She was pointing to a bump just below her waist. "That's what a belly button looks like turned inside out. It's embarrassing. Makowski and I didn't think we could have any kids. I'm almost fifty and he's sixty-five. Oh hell, what difference does it make? It's more fun than menopause, I guess. Have you talked to that woman up in 315? Her name is Pat Usher, but you probably know that. She claims Elaine let her sublet, but I doubt that."

"What's the story on that? Mrs. Boldt never talked to you about the arrangement?"

"Nope. Not a word. All I know is this Usher woman showed up a few months ago and moved in. At first nobody objected because we all just figured it was a two-week visit or something like that. People in the building can have any kind of company they want for short periods of time, but the rules say you can't sublet. Prospective buyers are screened real carefully and if we allowed sublets it would just be an invitation for any Tom, Dick, or Harry to move in here. The whole community would start to deteriorate. Anyway, after a month, Makowski went up to have a little chat with her and she claims she paid Elaine for six months and doesn't intend to move. It's driving Makowski around the bend."

"Does she have a signed lease?"

"She has a receipt showing she's paid Elaine some money, but it doesn't say for what. Makowski's had her served with an eviction notice, but she's taking her sweet time getting out. You haven't met her yet, I take it."

"I'm just on my way up. Do you know if she's in?"

"Probably. She doesn't go out much except to the pool to work on her tan. Tell her 'drop dead' from the management."

Three-fifteen was located on the third floor in the crook of the L-shaped building. Even before I rang the bell, I had the feeling that I was being inspected through the fish-eye spy hole in the middle of the door. After a moment, the door opened to the width of the burglar chain, but no face appeared.

"Pat Usher?"

"Yes."

"My name is Kinsey Millhone. I'm an investigator from California. I'm trying to locate Elaine Boldt."

"What for?" Her tone was flat, guarded, no lilt at all and no graciousness.

"Her sister's been trying to get in touch with her to sign a legal document. Can you tell me where she is?"

There was a cautious silence. "Are you here to serve me papers?"

"No." I took out the photostatic copy of my license and passed it through the crack. The license disappeared smoothly, like a bank card being sucked into an instant-cash machine. After an interval, it came back.

"Just a minute. I'll see if I can find her address."

She left the door ajar, still secured by the chain. I felt a little flash of hope. Maybe I was making progress. If I could track Elaine down in another day or two, I'd feel pretty smug, which sometimes counts as much as money whatever business you're in. I waited, staring down at the welcome mat. The letter *B* was defined in dark bristles, surrounded by bristles in a lighter shade. Did they have enough mud in Florida to justify a mat like that? It was coarse enough to rip the bottom of your shoe off. I glanced to my left. Just off the balcony, I could see palm trees with little beaded skirts near the top. Pat Usher was back, still talking through the crack.

"I must have thrown it out. She was in Sarasota last I heard."

Already, I was tired of talking to the door and I felt a surge of irritation. "Do you mind if I come in? It's about the settlement on somebody's estate. She could pick up two or three thousand dollars if I can just get her signature." Appeal to greed, I thought. Appeal to the secret yearning for a windfall. Sometimes I use it as a ploy when I am tracking down a deadbeat who's run out on a bill. This time it was even true, so my voice had this wonderful sincere ring to it.

"Did the manager send you up here?"

"Come on, would you quit being paranoid? I'm looking for Elaine and I want to talk to you. You're the only person so far who seems to have any idea where she is."

Silence. She was pondering this as though it were an I.Q. test and she could pad the results. I had to struggle with the urge to bite. This was the only lead I had and I didn't want to blow it.

"All right," she said reluctantly, "let me get some clothes on first."

When she finally opened the door, she was wearing a float, one of those gauzy print caftans you slip over your head when you're too lazy to put on your underpants. She had adhesive tape across her nose. Her eyes were puffy and circled with bruises that were fading from blue to green. She had a strip of clear tape under each eye and her tan had dimmed to a sallow hue that made her look like she had a mild case of hepatitis.

"I was in a car accident and broke my nose," she said. "I don't like for people to see me like this."

She moved away from the door, the caftan sailing out behind her as though there were a breeze. I followed her in, closing the door behind me. The place was done in rattan and pastels and smelled faintly of mildew. Sliding glass doors on one side of the living room opened out onto the screened-in porch, beyond which there were only lush green treetops visible and clouds piling up like a bubble bath.

She took a cigarette out of a lead crystal box on the coffee table and lit it with a matching table lighter that actually worked. She sat down on the couch, propping her bare feet up on the edge of the table. Her soles were gray.

"Sit down if you want."

Her eyes were an eerie, electric green, tinted by contact lenses I had to guess. Her hair was a tawny shade, with a luster I've never been able to coax out of mine. She stared at me with interest now, her manner fairly amused. "Whose estate is it?"

She had this way of asking certain questions with no tilt at the end, soliciting information by making flat statements that I was supposed to respond to. Odd. It made me wary somehow and I found myself taking care with what I said.

"A cousin, apparently. Someone in Ohio."

"Isn't it a bit radical to hire a private detective so you can hand out three thousand bucks?"

"There are other inheritors involved," I said.

"You have some kind of form you want her to sign."

"I want to talk to her first. People are worried because they haven't heard from her. I'd like to include something in my report about where she's been."

"Oh my God, now we got a report. She was restless. She's been traveling. What's the big deal?"

"Do you mind if I ask you about your relationship with her?"

"No, I don't mind. We're friends. I've known her for years. She came down to Florida this time and she wanted some company."

"When was this?"

"Middle of January. Something like that." She paused, watching the ash on her cigarette. Her eyes came up to mine again, her expression remote.

"And you've been staying here ever since?"

"Sure, why not? I'd just lost the lease on my place and she said I could move in."

"Why'd she take off?"

"You'd have to ask her that."

"When did you last hear from her?"

"Two weeks ago, something like that."

"And she was in Sarasota then?"

"That's right. Staying with some people she met."

"Can you tell me who?"

"Look, she wanted me to keep her company, not baby-sit. It's none of my business who she hangs out with, so I don't ask."

I felt as if we were playing a parlor game that I couldn't possibly win. Pat Usher was having a better time than I was too, and I resented that. I went at it again. Was it Mrs. Peacock in the library with the rope?

"Can you tell me anything else you think might help?"

"I wasn't aware I'd helped so far," she said with a smirk.

"I was trying an optimistic approach," I snapped.

She shrugged. "Sorry to dim your little ray of hope. I've told you everything I know."

"I guess we'll have to let it go at that. I'll leave you my card. If she calls again, would you have her contact me?"

"Hey, sure. No sweat."

I took a card out of my wallet and put it on the table as I got up. "I understand you're getting some hassles from people here."

"Can you believe that? I mean, what's it to them? I've paid my rent. No parties, no loud music. I hang my laundry out and the manager comes unglued. Threw a fit. I don't get it." She got to her feet and led me to the door. The caftan billowing out behind her made her seem like a larger woman than she was. As I went past the kitchen, I caught sight of some cardboard boxes stacked up near the sink. She turned and followed my gaze.

"I'll probably find a motel close by if it comes to that. The last thing in the world I need is the sheriff on my case. That's who I thought you were, as a matter of fact. They got women sheriffs these days, did you know that? Sheriffettes."

"So I've heard."

"What about you?" she asked. "How'd you become a detective. That's a weird way to make a living, isn't it?"

She was becoming real chatty now that I was on my

way out and I wondered if I might pump her for more information. She seemed eager to prolong the contact, like someone who's been cooped up too long with a pack of preschool kids.

"I sort of backed into detective work," I said, "but it beats selling shoes. You don't work yourself?"

"Not me. I'm retired. I don't ever want to work again."

"You're lucky. I don't have much choice. If I don't work, I don't eat."

She smiled for the first time. "I used to spend my life waiting for a break. Then I figured out I better make my own luck, you know what I mean? Nobody gives you nothing in this world, that's for sure."

I feigned agreement, glancing down toward the parking lot.

"I better be on my way," I said. "But could I ask you one more thing?"

"Like what."

"Do you know Elaine's other friends? There must be someone who knows how to get in touch with her, don't you think?"

"I'm the wrong one to ask," she said. "She used to visit me down in Lauderdale, so I don't know friends of hers up here."

"How'd you connect up this time? I understand she flew down almost on impulse."

She seemed momentarily perplexed at that, but regained her composure. "Yeah, that's right, she did. She called me from the airport in Miami and then picked me up on her way through."

"In a rented car?"

"Yeah. An Oldsmobile Cutlass. White."

"How long was she here then before she took off?"

Pat shrugged again. "I don't know. Not long. A couple of days, I guess."

"Did she seem at all nervous or upset?"

She became faintly irritated at that. "Wait a minute. What are you getting at? Maybe I could come up with something if I knew what was on your mind."

"I'm not sure," I said mildly. "I'm just fishing around, trying to figure out what's going on. The people who know her in Santa Teresa think it's unusual that she'd disappear without a word."

"But she told *me*. I've been telling you that. What is she, some kind of kid that she has to call home all the time and tell someone where she is and what time she's getting in? What's the problem?"

"There isn't one. Her sister wants her to get in touch. That's all it amounts to."

"Yeah, all right. I get touchy now and then. I've been under a lot of pressure and I don't mean to take it out on you. She'll probably call at some point and I'll give her your name and number, okay?"

"Great. I'd appreciate that."

I held out my hand and she shook it briefly. Her fingers were dry and cold.

"It's been nice talking to you," I said.

"You too," she replied.

I hesitated, glancing back at her. "If you do move into a motel, how will Elaine know where to reach you?"

The smirk was back, but there was something else in

her eyes. "How about I'll leave a forwarding address with Makowski, my friendly building manager downstairs. That way you'll know how to reach me too. Will that do the trick?"

"Probably so. Thanks much."

4

I moved off toward the stairs. I could feel her eyes on my back and then I heard the door close. I continued on down to the parking lot and got in my car and drove off. I wanted to talk to Mrs. Ochsner in the next apartment, but I thought it was better to wait. Something about Pat Usher bothered me. It was not just the fact that some of what she'd told me was untrue. I'm a born liar myself and I know how it's done. You stick as close to the truth as you can. You pretend to volunteer a few bits of information, but the facts are all carefully selected for effect. Pat's problem was that she was having to wing far too much and she'd started to embroider where she should have kept her mouth shut. That business about Elaine Boldt picking her up in Fort Lauderdale in a rented white Cutlass was crap. Elaine didn't drive. Tillie had told me that. At the moment, I couldn't figure out why Pat had lied about it, but it must have been significant. What really bothered me about her was that she had no class and it struck me as odd that Elaine Boldt had chosen her for a friend. From what Tillie and Beverly told me, I had the feeling Elaine was a bit of a snob and Pat Usher didn't seem quite glossy enough to satisfy.

I found a drugstore half a block away and bought two packs of index cards so I could make some notes and then I put in a call to Mrs. Ochsner in 317. Finally, she picked up.

"Hello?"

I identified myself and told her where I was. "I've just been up there talking to Pat Usher and I don't want her to know that I'm talking to you. Is there some way we can get together?"

"Well, what fun," Mrs. Ochsner said. "What shall we do? I could take the elevator down to the laundry room. It's right near the parking lot, you know, and you could pick me up."

"Let's do that," I said. "I'll swing by in ten minutes."

"Make it fifteen. I'm slower than you think."

The woman whom I helped into the front seat of the car had hobbled out of the laundry room with a cane. She was small, with a dowager's hump the size of a backpack and off-white hair that stood out around her head like dandelion fuzz. Her face was as soft and withered as an apple doll and arthritis had twisted her hands into grotesque shapes, as though she intended to make geese heads in shadow on the wall. She was wearing a house-dress that seemed to hang on her bony frame and her ankles were wrapped in Ace bandages. She had two garments over her left arm.

"I want to drop these off at the cleaner's," she said.

"You can run them in. I want to stop by the market, too. I'm out of my cereal and half-and-half." Her manner was energetic, her voice wavering but excited.

I went around to my side of the car and got in. I started the car, glancing at the third floor to make sure Pat Usher wasn't standing there watching us. I pulled out. Mrs. Ochsner peered at me avidly.

"You don't look at all like you sounded on the phone," she said. "I thought you'd be blond with blue eyes. What are they, gray?"

"Hazel," I said. I lowered my sunglasses so she could see for herself. "Where's the cleaner's from here?"

"Right next door to that drugstore you telephoned from. What do you call that haircut?"

I glanced at myself in the rearview mirror. "I guess I don't call it anything. I do that myself with nail scissors every six weeks. I keep my hair short because I don't like to fool with it. Why, do you think it looks bad?"

"I don't know yet. It probably suits, but I don't know you well enough to say. What about me? Do I look like I sound?"

I glanced over at her. "You sound like a hell-raiser on the phone."

"I was when I was your age. Now, I have to be careful I'm not just written off as a crank like Ida. All my dear friends died and I got stuck with the crabby ones. What kind of luck are you having with Elaine?"

"Not a lot. Pat Usher says she was actually in Boca for a couple of days and then took off again."

"No, she wasn't."

"Are you sure?"

"Of course I am. She always knocked on the wall when she got in. It was like a little code. She's been doing it for years. She'd come over within the hour and make arrangements to play bridge with us because she knew how much it meant."

I parked in front of the cleaner's and picked up the two dresses she'd placed over the seat. "I'll be right back," I said.

I took care of both errands while Mrs. Ochsner waited and then we sat in the car and talked. I filled her in on my conversation with Pat Usher.

"What do you think of her?" I asked.

"She's too aggressive," Mrs. Ochsner said. "She tried to cultivate me at first, you know. Sometimes I'd sit out on the balcony in the sun and she'd talk to me. She always had that sooty smell people get when they smoke too much."

"What'd you talk about?"

"Well, it wasn't culture, I'll tell you that. She talked about food most of the time, but I never saw her put anything in her mouth except cigarettes and Fresca. She drank pop incessantly and that mouth of hers flapped all the time. So self-centered. I don't believe she ever asked me one word about myself. It simply never occurred to her. I was bored to death, of course, and began to avoid her whenever I could. Now she's rude because she knows I disapprove of her. Insecure people have a special sensitivity for anything that finally confirms their own low opinion of themselves."

"Did she mention Elaine?"

"Oh yes. She said Elaine was off on a trip, which

struck me as odd. I'd never known her to come down here only to go someplace else. What would be the point?"

"Can you tell me who else Elaine might have kept in touch with? Any other friends or relatives down here?"

"I'll have to think about that. I don't know of anyone offhand. I assume that most of her good friends are in California, since that's where she lives most of the time."

We talked on for a while, but mostly about other things. At 11:15, I thanked her and took her back to the parking lot, gave her my business card so she could call me if she needed to, and then watched her hobble to the elevator. Her gait was irregular, like a marionette's being worked from above by strings. She waved to me with her cane and I waved back. She hadn't told me much, but I was hoping she'd be able to report on what was happening here after I flew back.

I drove out to the beach and sat in the parking lot with my index cards, making notes of everything I could remember about my search to this point. It took an hour and my hand was cramped, but I needed to get it down while the details were fresh. When I finished, I took my shoes off and locked the car, walking the beach. It was too hot to jog and the lack of sleep had left me torpid anyway. The breeze coming in off the ocean was dense with the smell of salt. The surf seemed to roll in at half speed and there were no whitecaps. The ocean was a luminous blue and the sand was littered with exotic shells. All I'd ever seen on the California beaches were tangles of kelp and occasional Coke-bottle bottoms worn smooth by the sea. I longed to stretch out on the beach and nap in the hot sun, but I had to be on my way.

I ate lunch at a roadside stand built of pink cinder block while a radio station blared out Spanish-language programs as foreign to me as the food. I feasted on black-bean soup and a bolsa—a sort of pouch made of pastry holding a spicy ground meat. By four o'clock that afternoon, I was on a plane, headed for California. I'd been in Florida for less than twelve hours and I wondered if I was any closer to finding Elaine Boldt. It was possible that Pat Usher was being straight with me when she claimed Elaine was in Sarasota, but I doubted it. In any event, I was anxious to get home and I slept like the dead until the plane reached LAX.

When I got to the office at nine the next morning, I filled out a routine form for the Driver's License Records at the Department of Motor Vehicles in Tallahassee, Florida, and a second form for Sacramento on the off-chance that Elaine might have been issued a driver's license in her own name sometime in the last six months. I also sent similar requests to the Vehicle Registration Records in both places, not so much with the expectation of the inquiries paying off, but just to cover my bets. I stuck all four envelopes in my out box and then I pulled out the phone book and started checking addresses for travel agents located within walking distance of Elaine's condominium. I was hoping to establish her travel arrangements and find out if a plane ticket had been used. So far, I had only Pat Usher's word that Elaine had ever arrived in Miami. Maybe she never even reached the airport in Santa Teresa, or maybe she got off the plane at some point en route. In any event, I was going to have to check it out item by item. I felt as if I were on an assembly line, inspecting reality with a jeweler's loupe. There's no place in a P.I.'s life for impatience, faintheartedness, or sloppiness. I understand the same qualifications apply for housewives.

Most of my investigations proceed just like this. Endless notes, endless sources checked and rechecked, pursuing leads that sometimes go no place. Usually, I start in the same place, plodding along methodically, never knowing at first what might be significant. It's all detail; facts accumulated painstakingly.

It's hard to remain anonymous these days. Information is available on just about anyone: credit files on microfiche, service records, lawsuits, marriages, divorces, wills, births, deaths, licenses, permits, vehicles registered. If you want to remain invisible, pay cash for everything and if you err, don't get caught. Otherwise, any good P.I. or even a curious and persistent private citizen can find you out. It amazes me that the average person isn't more paranoid. Most of our personal data is a matter of public record. All you have to know is how to look it up. What your state and city government don't have on file, your next-door neighbor will usually share without so much as a dollar changing hands. If there was no way to get a line on Elaine Boldt directly, I'd try an oblique approach. She'd left for Boca two weeks early, traveling at night, which, according to Tillie, was something she didn't like to do. She'd told Tillie she was ill, leaving town on doctor's orders, but at this point, there was no verification of that claim. Elaine might have lied to Tillie. Tillie might be lying to me. For all I knew Elaine had left the country, planting Pat Usher behind her to promulgate the notion that she was in Sarasota instead. I hadn't any idea why she'd do such a thing, but then I had a lot of ground to cover yet.

Having narrowed the list of travel agencies to six possibilities, I put in a call to Beverly Danziger and filled her in on my excursion to Florida. I wanted to bring her up to date even though the trip hadn't netted me much. I also had a couple of questions for her.

"What about family?" I asked. "Are your parents alive?"

"Oh, they've both been gone for years. We were never a close-knit family in the first place. I don't even think there were uncles or cousins she'd kept in touch with."

"What about jobs? What sort of work has she done?"

Beverly laughed at that. "You must not have a clear sense of Elaine quite yet. Elaine never lifted a finger in her life."

"But she does have a social-security card," I said. "If she's worked at all, it gives me one more avenue to pursue. For all we know, she's waiting tables someplace for a lark."

"Well, I don't think she's ever had a job, and if she did, it's not something she'd ever do again," Beverly said primly. "Elaine was spoiled. She felt she should be handed everything and what she wasn't handed, she took right out from under your nose anyway."

I really wasn't much in the mood to listen to Beverly unload past grievances. "Look, let's skip to the bottom line here. I think we ought to file a missing persons report. That way we can open up the scope of this thing. It should also eliminate some possibilities and believe me, at this point, everything helps."

The silence was so complete, I thought she'd hung up on me.

"Hello?"

"No, I'm here," she said. "I just don't understand why you want to talk to the *police* of all people."

"Because it's the next logical step. She may well be somewhere in Florida, but suppose she's not. At the moment, we only have Pat Usher's word for that. Why not get some broadscale coverage? Let the cops put out an APB. Let the Boca Raton P.D. get some sort of inquiry routed through Sarasota and see what they come up with. They can circulate a description through the state and local police down there and at least determine that she's not ill or dead or under arrest."

"Dead?"

"Hey, I'm sorry. I know it sounds alarming, and it may be nothing like that, but the cops will have access to information I just can't get."

"I don't believe this. I just wanted her signature. I hired you because I thought it would be the quickest way to find her. I don't think it's really a police matter. I mean, I simply don't want you to do that."

"All right. What, then? You can't ask me to find your sister for you and then start cutting off lines of inquiry."

"I don't see why not if I don't think it's appropriate. I don't see why you can't just let it go at this."

This time I was silent, wondering at the nature of her uneasiness. "Beverly, did I miss something here? Are you telling me to drop it?"

"Well, I don't know. Let me think about it and I'll call you back. I just didn't think it would be a problem and I'm not sure I want you to go on with this. Maybe Mr. Wender can proceed without her. Maybe he can find some loophole that will let him hold out only her portion of the estate until she turns up."

"You didn't seem to feel that way two days ago," I said.

"Maybe I made a mistake," she said. "Let's just don't worry about it right now, okay? I'll be in touch if I want you to go on with it. In the meantime, why don't you send me a report and an itemized bill of some kind? I'll have to talk to my husband about what to do from here."

"All right," I said with puzzlement, "but I have to tell you, I'm worried."

"Well, don't be," she said and the phone clicked in my ear.

I stared at the receiver. Now what was all that about? Her anxiety had been unmistakable, but I couldn't ignore the message. She hadn't fired me outright, but she'd put me on hold and I wasn't technically supposed to proceed without her instructions to do so.

Reluctantly, I went back through my index cards and typed up a report. I was stalling for time and I knew it, but I wasn't ready to let go. I put a carbon in my files and slipped the original in an envelope, which I addressed to Beverly, enclosing an itemization of my expenses to that point. Beyond the seven-hundred-and-fifty-dollar retainer she'd given me, she'd authorized an additional two hundred and fifty dollars for a total "not to exceed one thousand dollars without further written notice"—which was contractual double-talk for the fact that so far, we were covered. With the plane fare, the rental car, long-distance calls, and approximately thirty hours of my time, the charges came to $996 plus change. She owed me two hundred and forty-six bucks. I suspected she'd pay me off and wash her hands of it. My guess was that she'd enjoyed hiring a detective, officiously stirring up trouble for Elaine, who'd annoyed her by not signing on the dotted line as she'd been asked. Now suddenly, she must have realized that she'd opened up a big can of worms.

I locked up the office and dropped the report in a mailbox on my way home. Elaine Boldt was still among the missing and that didn't sit well with me.

5

My phone rang at 2:08 A.M. I picked up the receiver automatically, my brain still blank with sleep.

"Kinsey Millhone." The voice was male and the tone was neutral, like someone reading at random from a telephone book. Somehow I knew it was a cop. They all sound like that.

"Yes. Who's this?"

"Miss Millhone, this is Patrolman Benedict of the Santa Teresa Police Department. We've been called on a 594 at 2097 Via Madrina, apartment 1, and a Mrs. Tillie Ahlberg is asking for you. Would it be possible for you to lend some assistance? We have a policewoman with her, but she's asked for you specifically and we'd appreciate it if you could respond."

I raised up on one elbow, a few brain cells switching to ignition. "What's a 594?" I said. "Malicious mischief?"

"Yes ma'am."

It was clear Patrolman Benedict didn't want to risk anything by rushing right in with a lot of facts.

"Is Tillie okay?" I asked.

"Yes ma'am. She's unharmed, but she's upset. We don't mean to disturb you, but the lieutenant okayed us to get in touch."

"I'll be there in five minutes," I said and hung up.

I pushed the quilt back and grabbed for my jeans and sweatshirt, pulling on boots without ever getting up off the couch. I usually sleep naked in a fold of quilt because it's so much easier than opening the sofa bed. I went into the bathroom, brushed my teeth and splashed water on my face, combing my unruly hair with my fingers as I snatched up my keys and moved to the car. I was wide awake by now, wondering what kind of 594 we were talking about. Tillie Ahlberg was clearly not the perpetrator or she'd have called an attorney instead.

The night air was cold and the fog had rolled in off the beach and halfway across town, filling the empty streets with a fine mist. Stoplights blinked dutifully from red to green to red again, but there was no traffic and I ran the lights every chance I got. There was a black-and-white parked out in front of 2097 and the lights in Tillie's ground-floor apartment were all on, but things seemed quiet; no flashing red lights, no neighbors gathered on the sidewalk. I announced myself on the intercom and somebody buzzed me in. I pushed through the door to the right of the elevator and moved quickly down the corridor to Tillie's apartment at the end. Several people in robes and pajamas stood in the hall near the door, but a patrolman in uniform was encouraging them to go on back to bed. When he spotted me, he approached, hands on his hips as though he didn't know what else to do with them. He looked like he'd probably still be asked for his I.D. when he ordered a drink, but up close I could see signs of age: fine lines near his eyes, a slight loosening of the taut skin along his jaw. His eyes were old and I knew he'd already seen more of the human condition than he could assimilate.

I held out my hand. "Are you Benedict?"

"Yes ma'am," he said, shaking hands with me. "You're Miss Millhone, I take it. Nice to meet you. We appreciate this." His grip was firm, but brief. He nodded toward the door to Tillie's apartment, which stood ajar. "You can go on in if you want. Officer Redfern is with her, taking down particulars."

I thanked him and moved into the apartment, glancing to my right. The living room looked like something left in the path of a tornado. I stopped and stared for a moment. Vandalism in a place like this? I moved into the kitchen. Tillie was sitting at the table with her hands tucked between her knees, the freckles standing out on her pale face like red pepper flakes. A uniformed policewoman, maybe forty years old, was seated at the table taking notes. She had short-cropped blond hair and a birthmark like a patch of rose petals on one cheek. Her name tag identified her as Isabelle Redfern and she talked to Tillie in low, earnest tones like someone trying to persuade a flier not to leap off a bridge.

When Tillie caught sight of me, tears spilled out of her eyes and she began to shake, as though my appearance were tacit permission to fall apart. I knelt down beside her, taking her hands. "Hey, it's okay," I said, "what's going on?"

She tried to speak, but nothing came out at first except a wheezing sound like someone stepping on a rubber duck. Finally, she managed to choke out a response. "Someone broke in. I woke up and saw this woman standing in the door to my room. My God, I thought my heart would stop. I couldn't even move I was so terrified. And then . . . and then, she started . . . it was like this hissing sound and she ran in the living room and started tearing everything up. . . ." Tillie put a handkerchief over her mouth and nose, closing her eyes. Officer Redfern and I exchanged a look. Bizarre stuff. I put my arm around Tillie's shoulders, giving her a little shake.

"Come on, Tillie," I said, "it's over now and you're safe."

"I was so scared. I was so scared. I thought she was going to kill me. She was like a maniac, like a totally crazy person, panting and hissing and crashing around. I slammed the bedroom door shut and locked it and then dialed 911. Next thing I knew it got quiet, but I didn't open up the door until the police got here."

"That's great. You did great. Look, I know you were scared, but you did it just right and now it's okay."

The policewoman leaned forward. "Did you get a good look at this woman?"

Tillie shook her head, beginning to shake again.

This time the policewoman took Tillie's hands. "Take a couple of deep breaths. Just relax. It's over now and everything's fine. Breathe deeply. Come on. Do you have any tranquilizers on hand or alcohol of some kind?"

I got up and moved over to the kitchen cabinets,

opening doors at random, but there didn't seem to be any liquor at all. I found a bottle of vanilla extract and poured the contents into a jelly glass. Tillie downed it without even looking.

She began to breathe deeply, calming herself. "I never saw her before in my life," she said in somewhat more ordered tones. "She was crazy. A lunatic. I don't even know how she got in." She paused. The air smelled like cookies.

The policewoman looked up from her notes. "Mrs. Ahlberg, there was no sign of forced entry. It had to be someone who had a key. Have you given a key to anyone in the past? Maybe someone who was house-sitting? Someone who watered your plants when you were away?"

At first Tillie shook her head and then she stopped and shot a look at me, her eyes filled with sudden alarm.

"Elaine. She's the only one who ever had one." She turned to the policewoman. "My neighbor in the apartment right above me. I gave her a key last fall when I took a little trip to San Diego."

I took over then, filling in the rest; Elaine's apparent disappearance and her sister's hiring me.

Officer Redfern got up. "Hold on. I want Benedict to hear this."

It was 3:30 in the morning by the time Redfern and Benedict were finished, and Tillie was exhausted. They asked her to come down to the station later that morning to sign a statement and in the meantime, I said I'd stay with her until she had herself under control again.

When the cops finally left, Tillie and I sat and stared at each other wearily.

"Could it have been Elaine?" I asked.

"I don't know," she said. "I don't think so, but it was dark and I wasn't thinking straight."

"What about her sister? Did you ever meet Beverly Danziger? Or a woman named Pat Usher?"

Tillie shook her head mutely. Her face was still as pale as a dinner plate and there were dark circles under her eyes. She anchored her hands between her knees again, tension humming through her like a wind across guitar strings.

I moved into the living room and surveyed the damage more closely. The big glass-fronted secretary had been tipped over and lay facedown on the coffee table, which looked to have collapsed on impact. The couch had been slashed, the foam hanging out now like pale flesh. Drapes were torn down. Windows had been broken, lamps and magazines and flowerpots flung together in a heap of pottery shards and water and paper pulp. This was what insanity looked like when it was on the loose. That or unbridled rage, I thought. This had to be connected to Elaine's disappearance. There was no way I'd believe it was an independent event, coincidental to my search for her. I wondered if there was a way to find out where Beverly Danziger had been tonight. With her porcelain good looks and her blinking china blue eyes, it was hard to picture her loping around all looney-tunes, but how did I know for sure?

Maybe she'd driven up to Santa Teresa the first time on an institutional pass.

I tried to imagine what it would be like to wake in the dead of night to some hissing female on the rampage. An involuntary shiver took me and I went back into the kitchen. Tillie hadn't moved, but her eyes came up to my face with a look of dependency.

"Let's get it cleaned up," I said. "We're neither of us going to sleep anyway and you shouldn't have to do this by yourself. Where do you keep your dustpan and broom?"

She pointed to the utility room and then with a sigh she got to her feet and we went to work.

When order had been restored, I told Tillie I wanted the key to Elaine's apartment. "What for?" she asked apprehensively.

"I want to check it out. Maybe she's up there."

"I'll come with you," she volunteered promptly. I wondered vaguely if she was going to follow me around for life like Yogi Bear and Boo-Boo. Still, I gave her a quick hug and told her to wait a minute while I made a quick trip to my VW. She shook her head and followed me outside.

I took my semi-automatic out of the glove compartment, hefting it in my hand. It was a nondescript .32 with a cross-hatched ivory grip and a clip that would hold eight rounds. The life of a private eye is short on gun battles, long on basic research, but there are times when a ballpoint pen just doesn't get it. I had visions of some deranged female flying out of the darkness at me like a bat. A .32 may not have much stopping power, but it can sure slow you down. I wedged the gun in the back of my jeans and headed back to the elevator with Tillie at my heels.

"I thought it was against the law to carry a concealed weapon like that," she said uneasily.

"That's why I have a permit," I said.

"But I always heard handguns were so dangerous."

"Of course they're dangerous! That's the point. What do you want me to do? Go in there with a hunk of rolled-up newspaper?"

She was still giving that one some thought when we reached the second floor. I took out the automatic and eased the safety off, pulling back the slide on the barrel to cock it. I slipped the key to Elaine's lock and then I opened the door and let it swing back. Tillie was holding on to my sleeve like a little kid. I waited a moment, staring into the gloomy interior with my heart thumping. There was no sound . . . no movement inside. I felt for the light switch and flipped it on, peering around the doorframe quickly. Nothing. I indicated that Tillie was to wait where she was and I moved through the apartment quietly, turning lights as I went, using a modified version of my best junior G-man stance every time I entered a room. As far as I could tell, there was no sign that anyone had been there. I checked the closets and took a quick peek under the bed and then sighed, realizing that I'd been holding my breath. I went back to the front door and had Tillie come in, closing and locking it behind us. I moved back down the hallway to the den.

I went through Elaine's desk quickly, checking her

files. In the third drawer down, I found her passport and flipped through the pages. It was still valid, but it hadn't been used since a trip to Cozumel one April three years back. I tucked the passport in my back pocket. If she was still around, I didn't want her using her passport to slip out of the country. There was something else knocking around in the back of my head, but I couldn't figure out what it was. I shrugged to myself, assuming it would surface in due course.

I deposited Tillie at her door.

"Look," I said, "when you have a chance, take a careful look around and see if anything's missing. When you go down to the police station, they'll want a list of stolen property if you know of any. Do you carry any homeowner's insurance that might cover the damages?"

"I don't know," she said, "I guess I can check. Would you like some tea?" Her expression was wistful and she clung to my hand.

"Tillie, I wish I could, but I've got to go. I know you're uneasy, but you'll be okay. Is there somebody in the building who can keep you company?"

"Maybe the woman in apartment 6. I know she's up early. I'll try her. And thanks, Kinsey. I mean that."

"Don't worry about it. I was glad to help. I'll talk to you later. Get some sleep if you can."

I left her looking after me plaintively as I headed toward the lobby. I got in the car and tucked the gun in the glove compartment again, and then I headed for my place. My head was full of questions, but I was too tired to think. By the time I crept back in the folds of my quilt, the sky was a predawn gray and an enterprising rooster somewhere in my neighborhood was heralding the day.

The phone shrilled again at 8:00 A.M. I'd just reached that wonderful heavy stage of sleep where your nervous system turns to lead and you feel like some kind of magnetic force has just fused you to the bed. Consistently waking someone from a sleep like that could generate psychosis in two days.

"What," I mumbled. I could hear static in the line, but nothing else. Oh goody, maybe I'd been wakened by a long-distance obscene phone caller. "Hello?"

"Oh, that's you! I thought I'd dialed the number wrong. This is Julia Ochsner down in Florida. Did I wake you up?"

"Don't worry about it," I said. "I thought I just saw you. What's happening?"

"I've come across some information I thought you might like to have. It looks like that woman next door was telling the truth when she told you Elaine flew down here in January, at least as far as Miami."

"Really?" I said, sitting up. "What makes you say that?"

"I found the plane ticket in the garbage," she said with satisfaction. "You'll never believe what I did. She was packing up to go and she'd set several boxes full of discards and trash out. I'd been down to the manager's apartment and on my way back I spotted the ticket. It was right near the top, shoved down half out of sight, and I wanted to see whose it was. I didn't think I could come right out and ask her so I waited until she made a trip down to the parking lot with a load of clothes and I just scampered out there and stole it."

"You scampered?" I said, with disbelief.

"Well, it wasn't 'scampering' exactly. More like a fast creep. I don't think she even missed it."

"Julia, what made you do that? Suppose she'd caught you!"

"What do I care? I'm having a ball. When I got back, I had to go lie down I was laughing so hard!"

"Yeah, well you'll never guess what's happened here," I said. "I got fired."

"Fired?"

"More or less. Elaine's sister told me to lay off for the time being. She got nervous when I told her I thought we should file a missing persons report with the cops."

"I don't understand. Why would she object?"

"Beats me. When did Elaine leave Santa Teresa? Do you have the date?"

"It looks like January ninth. The return was left open."

"Well, that helps some. Why don't you drop that in the mail to me if it's not too much trouble. Beverly may back down yet."

"But that's ridiculous! What if Elaine's in trouble?"

"What can I do? I'm paid to follow instructions. I can't just bop around doing anything I please."

"What if I hired you myself?"

I hesitated, taken aback by the idea but not opposed to it.

"I don't know. That could get sticky. I suppose I could terminate my relationship with her, but there's no way I could release information to you that I'd uncovered for her. You and I would have to start from scratch."

"But she couldn't *prevent* me from hiring you, could she? I mean, once you've settled your account with her?"

"God, it's too early in the morning for me to worry about this stuff, but I'll mull it over and see what I can come up with. As far as I know, I could turn around and work for you as long as it doesn't represent any conflict of interest. I'd have to advise her what's going on, but I don't see how she could interfere."

"Good, then do it."

"Are you sure you want to spend your money that way?"

"Of course I am. I have lots of it and I want to know what's happened to Elaine. Besides, I'm having the time of my life! Just tell me what we do next."

"All right. Let me nose around some and I'll call you back. And Julia, in the meantime, would you watch out for yourself?" I said, but she just laughed.

6

I stayed in the shower until the hot water ran out and then I got dressed, pulling on jeans and a cotton sweater, zipping boots up to my knees. I plopped on a soft leather hat with a wide brim and studied the effect in the bathroom mirror. It would do.

I headed for the office first and wrote a letter to Beverly Danziger, terminating our professional relationship. I was pretty sure she'd be thoroughly disconcerted by that and it gave me a nice feeling. I went next door to the offices of California Fidelity Insurance and made a photocopy of my itemized bill to her, marked it "final," and tucked it in with the letter and a copy of my final report. Then I headed over to the police station on Floresta and talked to a Sergeant Jonah Robb about a missing persons report on Elaine Boldt, watching his fingers fly across the keys as he typed the information I gave him on the form.

He looked like he was in his late thirties, his body compact in his uniform. He was maybe twenty pounds overweight, not an unattractive amount, but something he'd have to cope with soon. Dark hair trimmed very short, smooth rounded face, a dent in his left ring finger where he'd recently worn a wedding ring. He shot a look at me at that point. Blue eyes flecked with green.

"Anything you want to add to this?"

"Her next-door neighbor down in Florida is sending me a plane ticket she apparently used. I'll take a look at it and see if it tells us anything else. A friend of hers named Pat Usher swears up and down she spent a couple of days with Elaine Boldt before she went off to Sarasota, but I don't believe much of what she says."

"She'll probably show up. They usually do." He took a file folder out and inserted a clamp. "You used to be a cop, didn't you?"

"Briefly," I said. "But I couldn't make it work. Too rebellious I guess. What about you? How long have you been on the force?"

"Eight years. I was a detail man before that. Sold drugs for Smith, Kline, and French. I got tired of driving around in a late-model car, hitting up on doctors. It was all hype anyway. Just like selling anything else. Sickness is big business." He looked down at his hands, then back at me. "Well. Anyway, I hope you find your lady. We'll do what we can."

"Thanks," I said, "I'll give you a call later in the week."

I picked up my bag and moved toward the door.

"Hey," he said.

I looked back.

"I like the hat."

I smiled.

As I passed the front counter on my way out, I caught sight of Lieutenant Dolan in Identification and Records, talking to a young black clerk in uniform. His glance slid past me and then came back with a look of recognition. He broke off his conversation with her and ambled over to the counter. Lieutenant Dolan is in his fifties, with a square, baggy face and a bald spot he tries to disguise with tricky arrangements of what hair remains. It's the only evidence of any vanity on his part and it cheers me up somehow. I imagine him standing in front of his bathroom mirror every morning, trying to cope with the creeping expanse of naked scalp. He was wearing rimless bifocals, apparently new, because he couldn't quite get me in range. He peered at me first from above the little half-moons and then from below. Finally, he slipped the glasses off and tucked them in the pocket of his rumpled gray suit.

"Hello, Kinsey. I haven't see you since the shooting. How are you doing with that?"

I felt myself flush with discomfort. I'd killed someone in the course of an investigation two weeks before and I was studiously avoiding the subject. The moment he mentioned it I realized how completely I'd willed it away. It hadn't even crossed my mind and his reference to it seemed as startling as that dream where you find yourself stark-naked in a public place.

"I'm fine," I said briefly, breaking off eye contact. In a flash, I saw the beach at night, that slat of light when the big trash bin I was hiding in was opened and I looked up. My little semiautomatic had jumped in my hand like some kind of reflex test and I'd squeezed off more rounds than were really necessary for getting the job done. The blast in that confined space had been deafening and my ears had been ringing ever since, a high-pitched hiss like gas escaping from a faulty valve. In a flash, the image was gone again and Lieutenant Dolan was standing there, maybe wishing he'd kept his mouth shut judging from the look on his face.

My relationship to Con Dolan has always been adversarial, remote, based on grudging mutual respect. He doesn't like private investigators as a rule. He feels we should mind our own business, whatever *that* is, and leave law enforcement to professionals like him. My fantasy has always been that one day we'll sit down and exchange criminal gossip like little old ladies, but now that he'd introduced a personal note, I could feel myself withdraw, disconcerted by the shift. When I met his eyes again, his gaze was flat, his expression bland.

I shook my head. "Sorry," I said, "you took me by surprise. I guess I haven't quite sorted it through." Actually what took me by surprise was realizing I'd killed someone and didn't much care. No, that wasn't true. I did care, but if my life was threatened, I knew I'd do it again. I'd always believed I was a good person. Now I didn't know what "good" meant. Surely good people didn't kill other human beings, so where did that put me?

He said, "What are you doing down here?"

I shook my head again slightly and focused on the subject at hand. "I just filed a missing persons report for a client," I said. I hesitated, wondering if he'd encountered Elaine during his investigation of the incident next door. "Did you handle the Grice homicide back in January of this year?"

He stared at me, his face closing up like sea anemone. Apparently he had. "What about it?"

"I wondered if you interviewed a woman named Elaine Boldt. She lives in the condominium next door."

"I remember the name," he said carefully. "I spoke to her myself by phone. She was supposed to come down and talk to us, but I don't think she ever showed up. She your client?"

"She's the one I'm looking for."

"How long she been gone?"

I detailed the information I had and I could see him run through the possibilities in the same way I had. In Santa Teresa County, some four thousand persons, male and female, are reporting missing every year. Most are found again but a few remain somewhere out in the ether.

He shoved his hands down in his pockets, rocking on his heels. "When she does turn up, tell her I want her down here for an interview," he said.

I was startled. "That case hasn't been wrapped up yet?"

"No, and I won't discuss it with you either. Department policy," he said. His favorite phrase.

"Jesus, Lieutenant Dolan. Big deal. Who asked you?" I knew he was protecting the integrity of his case, but I get tired of his being such a tight-ass. He thinks he is entitled to any information I have, while he never gives me a thing. I was hot and he knew it.

He smiled at me. "I just thought I'd head off that tendency of yours to stick your nose where it doesn't belong."

"I'll help you out sometime too," I said. "And meanwhile, if you want to talk to Elaine Boldt, you can find her yourself."

I pushed away from the counter, heading toward the exit.

"Well, you don't need to take that attitude," he called. I glanced back. He was looking entirely too self-satisfied for my taste.

"Right," I said and pushed on out the double doors.

I came out of the police station into the flat overcast day and stood for a moment, collecting myself. The man gets to me. No doubt about it. I took a deep breath.

The temperature was in the mid-sixties. Pale remnants of sunlight shone through the clouds, tinting the neighborhood with lemon-colored light. The shrubbery had taken on a chartreuse glow and the grass seemed dry and artificial from the lack of moisture. It hadn't rained for weeks and the month of June had been a monotonous succession of foggy mornings, hazy afternoons, and chilly nights. Actually, Lieutenant Dolan had opened up a possibility and I wondered if Elaine's departure was coincidental with the murder of Marty Grice or connected in some way. If the vandalism at Tillie's was related, why not this? Could she have taken off to avoid the lieutenant's questioning? I thought it might help to pin down some dates.

I headed over to the newspaper office six blocks away and asked the clerk in the newspaper morgue to track down the file clips on Marty Grice's death. There was only one clip, a small article, maybe two inches long, stuck back on page eight of local news, dated January 4.

BURGLAR KILLS HOUSEWIFE,
THEN BURNS BODY,
POLICE SAY

A Santa Teresa housewife was bludgeoned to death during an apparent burglary in her westside residence early last night. According to homicide detectives, Martha Renée Grice, 45, of 2095 Via Madrina, was struck repeatedly with a blunt instrument and doused with flammable liquid. The victim's body was discovered, badly burned, in the foyer of the partially destroyed single-family dwelling after Santa Teresa fire fighters battled the blaze for thirty minutes. The fire was first spotted by neighbors at 9:55 P.M. Two adjacent homes were evacuated, but no other injuries were reported. Details of the arson were withheld pending further investigation.

The crime seemed pretty spectacular to get such small play. Maybe the cops hadn't had much to go on and had tried to minimize the coverage. That might explain Dolan's attitude. Maybe he wasn't being uncooperative. Maybe he had no evidence. Nothing makes a cop any tighter than that. I took down the pertinent information in my notebook and then I walked over to the public library and checked the Santa Teresa city directory that had come out last spring. Martha Grice was listed at 2095 Via Madrina along with a Leonard Grice, bldg. contrctr. I assumed he was the husband. The newspaper account had made no mention of him and I wondered where he'd been when the whole thing went down. The directory listed the neighbors next door at 2093 as Orris and May Snyder. His occupation was "retired" but the directory didn't say from what. I jotted down the names and the telephone number. It might be interesting to see if I could find what went on and whether Elaine might have seen something she didn't want to talk about. The more I thought about it, the better I liked that idea. It gave me a whole new line to pursue.

I retrieved my car from the lot behind my office and circled back around to Via Madrina. It was now twelve o'clock straight up and high-school students were spilling out onto the streets; girls in jeans, short white socks and high heels, guys in chinos and flannel shirts. The wholesome California sorts outnumbered the punkers about three to one, but most of them looked like they'd been dressed out of ragbags. Some kids were wearing outrageous designer jumpsuits and some wore whole outfits in camouflage fabric as though prepared for an air attack. About half the girls sported three to four earrings per ear. In hairstyles, they seemed to fancy the wet look, or ponytails sticking up out of the sides of their heads like waterspouts.

As I pulled up in front of the condominium, a cluster of six girls were clumping down the sidewalk, smoking clove-scented cigarettes. Shoulder pads and green nail polish, dark red lipstick. They looked like they were on their way to a USO dance in 1943.

I caught just a fragment of their conversation.

"So I'm all 'What the fuck did you think I was talking about, dick-head?!' and he goes like 'Hey, well, I never did anything to you, bitch, so I don't know what your problem is.'"

I smiled to myself, and then looked over at the Grice house with interest. It was white frame, a story and a half, with a squat L-shaped porch across the front, resting on fat red-brick pillars topped with short pyramids of wood. It looked as if it had been jacked up somehow and might, at any moment, collapse. Most of the porch roof had burned away. The yard was scrappy and a row of pale pink-and-blue hydrangea bushes crowded the porch, still looking browned and wilted from the fire, though new growth was bravely showing through. The front window frames on the first floor were capped with lintels of black soot where the fire had licked the framing. A sign had been posted warning trespassers away. I wondered if the salvage crew had already gone in to clean up. I was hoping not, but I was probably out of luck on that. I wanted to see the house as it had been on the night of the fire. I also wanted to chat with Leonard Grice, but there was no indication whatever that the house was inhabited. Even from the street, I could still pick up the six-month-old cologne of charred wood and grinding damp where the firemen's hoses had penetrated every seam and crevice.

As I headed toward Elaine's condominium, I spotted someone coming out of a small wooden utility shed in the Grices' backyard. I paused to watch. A kid, maybe seventeen. He had a Mohawk haircut, three inches of what looked like bright pink hay with a path mown on either side. He had his head down, his hands shoved into the pockets of his army fatigues. With a start, I realized I'd seen him before—from Elaine's front window the first time I searched her place. He'd been standing in the street below, rolling a joint at a leisurely pace. Now what was he up to? I veered, picking up my pace so my path would intersect his just about at the property line.

"Hello," I said.

He looked up at me, startled, flashing the sort of polite smile kids reserve for adults. "Hi."

His face didn't match the rest of him. His eyes were deepset, a jade green set off by dark lashes and dark everybows that feathered together at the bridge of his nose. His skin was clear, his smile engaging, slightly snaggle-toothed. He had a dimple in his left cheek. He glanced to one side, moving past me. I reached out and caught him by the sleeve.

"Can I talk to you?"

He looked at me and then quickly back over his shoulder.

"You talking to me?"

"Yes. I saw you coming out of that shed back there. You live around here?"

"What? Oh. Sure, couple of blocks away. This is my Uncle Leonard's house. I'm supposed to check and make sure nobody's bothering his stuff." His voice was light, almost feminine.

"What stuff is that?"

The jade-green eyes had settled on me with curiosity. He smiled and his whole face brightened. "You a cop or something?"

"Private investigator," I said. "My name is Kinsey Millhone."

"Wow, that's great," he said. "I'm Mike. You guarding the place or something like that?"

I shook my head. "I'm looking into another matter, but I heard about the fire. Your aunt was the one who was killed?"

The smile flickered. "Yeah, right. Jesus, that was terrible. I mean, her and me were never close, but my uncle really got messed up over that. He's a fuckin' basket case. Oh. Sorry 'bout that," he said sheepishly. "He's like vegged out or something, staying with this other aunt of mine."

"Can you tell me how to get in touch with him?"

"Well, my aunt's name is Lily Howe. I don't remember the number offhand, or I'd help you out."

He was beginning to blush and the effect was odd. Pink hair, green eyes, rosy cheeks, green army fatigues. He looked like a birthday cake, innocent and festive somehow. He ran a hand across his hair, which was standing straight up on top like a whisk broom.

I wondered why he was so ill at ease. "What were you doing back there?"

He glanced back at the shed with an embarrassed shrug. "I was checking the padlock. I get like really paranoid, you know? I mean, the guy pays me ten bucks a month and I like to do right by him. Did you want something else? Because I have to go grab some lunch and get back to class, okay?"

"Sure. Maybe I'll see you later."

"Right. That'd be great. Anytime." He smiled at me again and then moved away, walking backward at first, his eyes latched to mine, turning finally so that I was watching the narrow back and slim hips. There was something disturbing about him, but I couldn't think what it was. Something didn't jibe. That goody-two-shoes helpfulness and the look in his eyes. Artless and cunning . . . a kid whose conscience is clear because he doesn't have one. Maybe I'd check him out too, as long as I was at it. I went into the condominium courtyard.

7

I found Tillie spraying down the walk, a rolling tumble of leaves and debris pushed along by the force of the jet. Water dripped from the feather palms, the rubbery scent of hose mingling with the odor of wet earth. Stepping-stones were tucked in among the giant ferns, though why anyone would want to walk back in there was beyond me. It looked like a shadowy haven for daddy longlegs. Tillie smiled when she saw me and released the trigger nozzle, shutting off the spray. She was wearing jeans and a T-shirt, her spare form giving her a girlish look even in her sixties.

"Did you ever get any sleep?" I asked.

"No, and I'm not going to stay in that apartment 'til the windows are fixed. I may have an alarm system put in too. I came out here just to busy myself. Hosing the walks is restful, don't you think? It's one of the pleasures of adulthood. When I was a kid, my dad never would let me have a turn."

"Have you been down to the police station yet?"

"Oh, I'll go in a bit, but I don't look forward to it."

"I went by a little while ago and filed a missing persons report on Elaine."

"What'd they say?"

I shrugged. "Nothing much. They'll do what they can. I ran into a homicide detective who worked on Marty Grice's murder. He says Elaine was supposed to come in for an interview and never showed up. Do you remember how soon afterward she went to Florida?"

"Well, I'm not sure. It was that same week. I do know that much. She was terribly upset about the murder and that's one reason she left. I thought I mentioned that."

"You said she was sick."

"She was, but she always seemed to have something wrong with her. She said the murder had her crazy with anxiety. She thought getting out of town would help. Hang on," Tillie said. She went into the bushes and turned off the water at the faucet, using the last of the water pressure to empty the hose before she coiled it up again. She emerged from the shrubbery, wiping her damp hands on her jeans. "Are you thinking she knew something about Marty's death?"

"I think it's worth looking into," I said. "Her side window looks right down into the Grices' entryway. Maybe she saw the burglar."

Tillie made a skeptical face. "In the dark?"

I shrugged. "It doesn't seem likely, does it, but I don't know what else to think."

"But why wouldn't she have gone to the police if she knew who it was?"

"Who knows? Maybe she wasn't thinking straight.

People panic. They don't like to get involved in these things. Maybe she felt she was in jeopardy herself."

"Well, she *was* nervous," Tillie said. "But then we were all a bundle of nerves that week. You want to come in?"

"Actually I do. I think I ought to take a look at those bills of hers. At least we can see how recently she's used her charge accounts and where she was at the time. Has anything else come in?"

"Just a couple of things. I'll show you what I've got."

I followed Tillie through the lobby and into the corridor beyond.

She unlocked her front door and moved into the living room, crossing to the secretary. Since the glass had been broken out of the doors, there was no need to unlock anything, but I saw her hesitate, nonplussed, putting an index finger on the side of her cheek like someone posing for a photograph. "Now, that's odd."

"What?" I asked. I crossed to the secretary and looked in. We'd replaced the tumble of books the night before, and there was nothing else on the shelves now except a small brass elephant and a framed snapshot of a puppy with a stick in its mouth.

"I don't see Elaine's bills and they should be there," she said. "Now, isn't that strange." She glanced at the shelves again and then opened the drawers one by one, sorting through the contents.

She moved into the kitchen and dug into the big black plastic bag where we had dumped all the broken glass and debris the night before. There was no sign of them.

"Kinsey, they were in the secretary yesterday. I saw them myself. Where could they have gone?"

She looked up at me. It didn't take a massive leap of intelligence to arrive at the obvious possibility.

"Could *she* have taken them?" Tillie asked. "That woman who broke in last night? Is that what she was really up to?"

"Tillie, I don't know. Something about it bothered me at the time," I said. "It didn't make sense to think someone would break in while you were here just to tear the place apart. Are you sure you saw them yesterday?"

"Of course. I put the new batch of bills with the other ones on the shelf. They were right here. And I don't remember seeing them at all when we cleaned up. Do you?"

I thought back, chasing it around in my memory. I'd only seen the bills once, the first time I'd talked to her. But why would someone bother to steal them? It didn't make sense.

"Maybe she deliberately scared the pants off you to keep you out of the way while she searched the place," I said.

"Well, she sure had the right idea. I wouldn't have come out of my room on a dare! But why would she do that? I don't understand."

"I don't either. I can always get duplicates of the bills, but it's going to be a pain in the ass and I'd rather not do it if I don't have to."

"I want to know who has a key to my apartment. That makes my blood run cold."

"I don't blame you. Listen, Tillie. Nothing makes me

crazier than sixteen unanswered questions in a row. I'm going to see what I can find out about this murder next door. It has to be connected somehow. Have you talked to Leonard Grice recently?"

"Oh, he hasn't been there since it happened," she said. "I haven't seen him at any rate."

"What about the Snyders on the other side? Do you think they could be of any help?"

"They might. Do you want me to talk to them?"

"No, don't worry about it. I'll check with them myself. Just one more thing. Leonard Grice has a nephew . . . a kid with a pink Mohawk."

"Mike."

"Yeah, him. Is there any chance he might have been the person who broke in last night? I just talked to him outside and he's not a big guy. He might well have looked like a woman in the dark."

"I don't think so," she said, skepticism plain. "I couldn't swear to it, but I don't think it was him."

"Well. Just a thought. I don't like to make assumptions about gender. It really could have been anyone. I'm going to go next door and see what the Snyders have to say. You take care of yourself."

The house at 2093 was similar in feeling to the house that burned . . . the same-size lot, same ill proportions, the same white frame and red brick. The brick itself was roughly textured, a cunning imitation of fired clay. There was a FOR SALE sign out front with a banner pasted across it boasting SOLD! as though an auction had been enacted just before I started up the walk. A large tree shaded the yard down to a chill, and dark ivy choked the trunk, spreading out in all directions in a dense mat that nearly smothered the walk. I went up the porch steps and knocked on the aluminum screen door. The front door had a big glass panel in it, blocked by a sheer white curtain stretched between two rods. After a moment, someone moved the curtain aside and peered out.

"Mr. Snyder?"

The curtain was released and the door opened a crack. The man appeared to be in his seventies, corpulent and benign. Old age had given him back his baby fat and the same look of grave curiosity.

I held out a business card. "My name is Kinsey Millhone. Could I have a few minutes of your time? I'm trying to track down Elaine Boldt, who lives in that big condominium over there, and Tillie Ahlberg suggested I talk to you. Can you help me out?"

Mr. Snyder released the catch on the screen door. "I'll do what I can. Come on in." He held the screen door open and I followed him inside. The house was as dark as the inside of a soup can and smelled of cooked celery.

From the rear of the house, a shrill voice called out.

"What's that? Who all is out there, Orris?"

"Someone Tillie sent!"

"Who?"

"Hold on a minute," he said to me, "she's deaf as a yard of grass. Take a seat."

Mr. Snyder lumbered toward the back. I perched on an upholstered chair with wooden arms. The fabric was a dark maroon plush with a high-low pattern of foliage, some nondescript sort that I'd never seen in real life. The seat was sprung; all hard edges and the smell of dust. There was a matching couch stacked with newspapers and a low mahogany coffee table with an inset of oval glass barely visible for all the paraphernalia on top: dog-eared paperbacks, plastic flowers in a ceramic vase shaped like two mice in an upright embrace, a bronze version of praying hands, six pencils with erasers chewed off, pill bottles, and a tumbler that had apparently held hot milk which had left a lacy pattern on the sides of the glass like baby's breath. There was also an inexplicable pile of pancakes wrapped in cellophane. I leaned forward, squinting. It was a candle. Mr. Snyder could have moved the entire table outside and called it a yard sale.

From the back end of the house, I could hear his exasperated explanation to his wife. "It's nobody selling anything," he snapped. "It's some woman Tillie sent, says she's looking for Mrs. Boldt. Boldt!! That widda woman lived upstairs of Tillie, the one played cards with Leonard and Martha now and again."

There was a feeble interjection and then his voice dropped.

"No, you don't need to come out! Just keep set. I'll take care of it."

He reappeared, shaking his head, his jowls flushed. His chest was sunken into his swollen waistline. He'd had to belt his pants below his big belly and his cuffs drooped at the ankles. He hitched at them irritably, apparently convinced he'd lose them if he didn't hang on. He wore slippers without socks and all the hair had been worn away from his ankles, which were narrow and white, like soup bones.

"Switch on that light there," he said to me. "She likes to pinch on util'ties. Half the time, I can't see a thing."

I reached over to the floor lamp and pulled the chain. A forty-watt bulb came on, buzzing faintly, not illuminating much. I could hear a steady thump and shuffling in the hall.

Mrs. Snyder appeared, moving a walker in front of her. She was small and frail and her jaw worked incessantly. She stared intently at the hardwood floor and her feet made a sticky sound as she walked, as though the floor had been shellacked and had never dried properly. She paused, hanging on to her walker with shaking hands. I stood up, projecting my voice.

"Would you like to sit here?" I asked her.

She surveyed the wall with rheumy eyes, trying to discover the source of the sound. Her head was small, like a little pumpkin off the vine too long, looking shrunken from some interior softening. Her eyes were narrow inverted V's and one tooth protruded from her lower gum like a candle wick. She seemed confused.

"What?" she said, but the question had a hopeless ring to it. I didn't think anybody answered her these days.

Snyder waved at me impatiently. "She's fine. Just leave her be. Doctor wants her on her feet more anyway," he said.

I watched her uncomfortably. She continued to stand there, looking puzzled and dismayed, like a baby who's learned how to pull up itself up on the sides of a crib, but hasn't figured out how to sit down again.

Mr. Snyder ignored her, settling on the couch with his knees spread. His belly filled the space between his legs like a duffel bag, as cumbersome on him as a clown suit with a false front. He put his hands on his knees, giving me his full attention as though I might be soliciting his entire history for inclusion on "This Is Your Life."

"We been in this house forty year," he said. "Bought it back in nineteen and forty-three for four thousand dollar. Bet you never heard of a house that cheap. Now it's worth one hunnert and fifteen thousand. Just the lot we're settin' on. That don't even count the house. They can knock this place down and build anything they want. Hell, she can't even get that walker into the commode. Now Leonard, next door, nearly sold his house for a hunnert and thirty-five, had it in escroll and everything and then the deal fell out. That about done him in. He's the one I feel sorry for. House burnt. Wife dead. You know what the kids these days would say . . . his carnal was bad."

He went right on talking while I took mental notes. This was better than I'd hoped. I had thought I'd have to tell a few fibs, leading the conversation around judiciously from Elaine's whereabouts to the subject of the murder next door, but here sat Orris Snyder giving testimony extemporaneously. I realized he'd stopped. He was looking at me.

"You've sold this house? I saw the sign out front."

"Sold," he said with satisfaction. "We can move us up to that retirement place when the kids get everything here packed up. We've got a regular reservation. We're on the list and everything. She's old. She doesn't even know where she is half the time. Fire broke out in this place, she'd lay there and cook."

I glanced at his wife, who had apparently locked her knees. I was worried she would pass out, but he didn't seem to give it much thought. She might as well have been a hall tree.

Snyder went on as though prompted by questions from an unseen audience. "Yessir, I sold it. She like to have a fit, but the house is in my name and I own it free and clear. Paid four thousand dollar. Now I call that a profit, wouldn't you?"

"That's not bad," I said. I glanced over at his wife again. Her legs had begun to tremble.

"Why don't you get on back to bed, May?" he said and then looked at me with a disapproving shake of his head. "She can't hear good. Hearing comes and goes. Got tintypes of the ear and all she can see is living shapes. She got the leg of that walker hung up on the broom-closet door last week and stood there for forty-six minutes before she got loose. Old fool."

"You want me to help you get her back to bed?" I asked.

Snyder floundered on the couch, turning himself sideways so he could get up. He pushed himself to his feet and then went over to her and shouted in her face. "Go lay down awhile, May, and then I'll get you some snackin' cake," he said.

She stared steadfastly at his neck, but I could have sworn she knew exactly what he was talking about and was just feeling stubborn and morose.

"Why did you put the light on? I thought it was day," she said.

"It only cost five cent to run that bulb," he said.

"What?"

"I said it's pitch-black night outside and you got to go to bed!" he hollered.

"Well," she said, "I think I might in that case."

Laboriously, she thumped the walker around, navigating with effort. Her eyes slid past me and she seemed suddenly to discern me in the haze.

"Who's that?"

"It's some woman," Snyder broke in. "I was telling her of Leonard's back luck."

"Did you tell her what I heard that night? Tell about the hammering kept me awake. Hanging pictures . . . bang, bang, bang. I had to take a pill it made my head hurt so bad."

"That wasn't the same night, May. How many times I told you that? It couldn't have been because he wasn't home and he's the one did that kind of thing. Burglars don't hang pictures."

He looked over at me then, twirling his index finger beside his temple to indicate that she was rattlebrained.

"Banged and banged," she said, but she was only muttering to herself as she thunked away, moving the walker in front of her like a clothes rack.

"She hasn't a faculty left," he said to me over his shoulder. "Pees on herself half the time. I had to move every stick of dining-room furniture out and put her bed in there right where the sideboard stood. I told her I'd outlive her the day I married her. She gets on my nerves. She did back then too. I'd just as soon live with a side of meat."

"Who's at the door?" she said insistently.

"Nobody. I'm talkin' to myself," he said.

He shuffled into the hallway behind her. His hovering had a tender quality about it in spite of what he said. In any event, she didn't seem aware of his aggravation or his minor tyrannies. I wondered if he'd stood there and timed her for the forty-six minutes while she struggled with the broom-closet door. Is that what marriages finally come down to? I've seen old couples toddle down the street together holding hands and I've always looked on faintly misty-eyed, but maybe it is all the same clash of wills behind closed doors. I've been married twice myself and both ended in divorce. I berate myself for that sometimes but now I'm not sure. Maybe I haven't made such a bad trade-off. Personally, I'd rather grow old alone than in the company of anyone I've met so far. I don't experience myself as lonely, incomplete, or unfulfilled, but I don't talk about that much. It seems to piss people off—especially men.

8

Mr. Snyder returned to the living room and sat down heavily on the couch. "Now then."

"What can you tell me about that fire next door?" I asked. "I saw the place. It looks awful."

He nodded, preparing himself as though for a television interview, staring straight ahead. "Well now, the fire engine woke me up ten o'clock at night. Two of 'em. I don't sleep good anyhow and I heard the siren come right up here close so I got up and went out. Neighbors was runnin' from ever' which way. Black smoke outen that house like you never saw. These firemen, they bashed their way in and pretty soon flames et up the front porch. Whole backside got saved. They found Marty, that was Leonard's wife, layin' on the floor. It'd be right about over there," he said, pointing toward the front door. "I never seen her myself, but Tillie said she was charred head to foot. Just a bunch of stumps, like a piece of wood."

"Oh really. Tillie didn't mention that to me."

"She seen the smoke and called right up. Nine-one-

one it was. I was sound to sleep. Woke up when the fire engine come blastin' down the road. I thought they'd go right on by, but then I seen the lights and I got up and put a robe on and went out. Poor Leonard wasn't even home. He drove up about the time they got the fire out. Collapsed right on the street when he heard she was dead. I never saw a man so tore up. My wife, May, she never woke up at all. She'd tooken a pill and she's deaf as a broom anyway. You've seen that yourself. Fire broke out here, she'd been roast pork."

"What time was it when Mr. Grice got home?"

"I don't know the exact time. Fifteen, twenty minutes after the fire engines come as best I recollect. He was out to dinner with his sister as I hear tell and he comes home to find his own wife dead. His knees give out and down he went. Right on the sidewalk with me standin' not this far away. Turned white and dropped like a big hand had give him a thump and knocked him out. It was the awfullest thing you ever saw. They brought her out zipped up in a plastic sack—"

"How'd Tillie happen to see her?" I interrupted. "I mean, if she was zipped up in a body bag?"

"Oh, that Tillie, she sees everything. Ask her. She prob'ly pushed through when the door got bashed in and seen the body for herself. Makes me sick to think of it."

"I understand Leonard's been staying with his sister since then."

"That's what I heard, too. Her name is Howe. Lives on Carolina. It's in the book if you want to get in touch."

"Good. I'll try to see him this afternoon. I'm hoping he can tell me something about where Mrs. Boldt might have gone."

I got up and held out my hand. "You've been a big help."

Mr. Snyder struggled to his feet and shook my hand, walking to the door with me.

I looked over at him with curiosity. "What do you think your wife was referring to when she mentioned the hammering that night? Do you have any idea what she meant?"

He waved impatiently. "She don't know what she's talkin' about. She got that all confused."

I shrugged. "Well, I hope Mr. Grice is doing all right at any rate. Did he have good insurance coverage? That would be a big help, I'm sure."

He shook his head, pulling at his chin. "I don't think he come out too good on that. Him and me has the same insurance comp'ny, but his policy didn't amount to much as I understand it. Between the fire and his wife's being gone now, he's about ruined. He collects disability for a bad back, you know, and she was sole support."

"God, that's terrible. I'm sorry to hear that," I said, and then took a chance. "What insurance company?"

"California Fidelity."

Ahh. I felt my little heart go pitty-pat. This was the first break I'd had. I worked for them.

California Fidelity Insurance is a small company that handles all the ordinary coverage: life and health, homeowner's, auto, and some commercial lines, with branches in San Francisco, Pasadena, and Palm Springs. Santa Teresa is the home office, occupying the second floor of a three-story building on State Street, which cuts straight through the heart of town. My corner consists of two rooms—one inner, one outer—with a separate entrance. Early in my career, I worked for CFI, doing insurance investigations on fire and wrongful-death claims. Now that I'm out on my own, we maintain a loose association. I cover certain inquiries for them every month in exchange for office space.

I let myself into the office now and checked the answering machine. The light was blinking, but the tape was blank except for some hissing and a couple of high-pitched beeps. For a while, I had a live answering service, but the messages were usually botched. I didn't think prospective clients were that keen to confide their troubles to some twenty-year-old telephone operator who could barely spell, let alone keep the numbers straight. An answering machine is irritating, but at least it tells the caller than I am female and I pick up on the second ring. The mail wasn't in yet, so I went next door to talk to Vera Lipton, one of the California Fidelity claims adjusters.

Vera's office is located in the center of a warren of cubicles separating adjusters. Each small space is equipped with a desk, a rolling file, two chairs and a telephone, rather like a little bookie joint. Vera's niche is identifiable by the pall of smoke hovering above the shoulder-high partitions. She's the only one in the company who smokes and she does so with vigor, piling up stained white filter tips like ampules of distilled nicotine. She's also addicted to Coca-Cola and she usually has a row of empty bottles marching around her desk, accumulating them at the rate of one every hour. She's thirty-six, single, and she collects men with ease, though none of them seems to suit her. I peered into her cubicle.

"What'd you do to your hair?" I asked when I caught sight of it.

"I was up all night. It's a wig," she said. She stuck a fresh cigarette between her teeth, biting gently while she lit up. I've always admired her smoking style. It's jaunty and sophisticated, dainty and tough. She pointed to the wig, which was streaked with blond, a wind-blown effect.

"I'm thinking of dyeing my hair this shade. I haven't been a blond for months."

"I like it," I said. Her usual color was auburn, a mix of several Clairol offerings that varied in hues from Sparkling Sherry to Flame. Her glasses today had tortoiseshell rims and big round lenses tinted the color of iced tea. She wore glasses so well it made other women wish their eyesight would fail.

"You must have a new man in your life," I said.

Vera shrugged dismissively, shaking her head. "I got two actually, but I wasn't up doing what you think. I read a book on how the new technology works. Lasers and analog-to-digital converters. I got curious about electricity yesterday, you know? Turns out nobody really knows what it is, which is worrisome if you ask me.

Great terminology though. 'Pulse amplitude' and 'oscillation.' Maybe I'll run into a guy I can say that to. What's with you? You want a Coke?"

She had already opened her bottom file drawer where she kept a little cooler packed with ice. She pulled out a Coke in a bottle about the size of a Playtex nurser, and uncapped it by wedging it under the metal drawer handle and giving a quick downward snap. She proffered the bottle, but I shook my head and she drank it down herself. "Have a seat," she said then and set the bottle on the desk top with a thunk.

I moved aside a stack of files and sat down in the extra chair. "What do you know about a woman named Marty Grice who was murdered six months ago? I heard she was insured through CFI."

Vera touched daintily at the corners of her mouth with her thumb and index finger. "Sure, I was assigned to that one. I went out and took a look at the place two days after it happened. God, what a mess. I don't have the proof of loss yet, but Pam Sharkey said she'd get it to me in the next couple of weeks."

"She's the agent on it?"

Vera nodded, taking a drag of her cigarette. She blew the smoke straight up. "The big life-insurance policy lapsed, but there was a little twenty-five-hundred-dollar policy in effect. That's probably not enough to bury a dog these days. There's also a homeowner's for the fire loss, but the guy was desperately underinsured. Pam swears up and down she advised him to upgrade, but he didn't want to be saddled with the added expense. You know how people get. They try to save six bucks and end up blowing two-three hundred thousand when the bottom drops out." She tapped the cigarette on the lip of the empty Coke bottle, neatly knocking the ash into it.

"Why's the settlement taking so long?"

Vera's mouth turned down and she lowered one eyelid—a gesture that conveyed the message "big deal," though I don't know how. "Who knows?" she said. "The guy's got a year to file the claim. Pam says he's been a basket case since his wife died. He can hardly manage to sign his own name."

"Did she leave a will?"

"Not that I heard. The whole thing's been sitting in probate court for the last five months or so, in any event. What's your interest in it? Are you looking into her death?"

"Not really. I'm looking for a woman who lived next door when it happened. She left town a couple of days afterward and hasn't been seen since then by the people who count. I keep thinking there's a connection. I was hoping you'd tell me there was a great big policy in effect."

"The cops had the same idea. Your buddy Lieutenant Dolan was over here practically sitting in my lap for days. I kept saying, 'Forget it! The guy's broke. He's not going to net a dime.' I guess I finally convinced him because I haven't heard from him since. What are you thinking, that Grice and this doll next door were in cahoots?"

"It did cross my mind. I haven't met him yet and I have no idea whether there could have been a relationship between them, but it does look suspect. From what

I'm told, she left town abruptly and she was upset. My first instinct was that maybe she'd seen something and took off to avoid getting caught up in it."

"Maybe so." Vera sounded dubious.

"But you don't believe it."

"I'm just looking at his end. If the guy killed his wife for fun and profit, he sure went about it wrong. Why let a policy lapse like that? If he were smart, he'd have jacked the face value up two-three years ago, let enough time pass so it didn't look too obvious and then . . . whap, his wife is dead and he collects. If he killed her with no payoff, he's an idiot."

"Unless he just wanted her out of his way. Maybe that was all he cared about. Maybe letting the policy lapse was a ploy."

"Hey, listen, what do I know? I'm not a homicide dick."

"Me neither. I'm just trying to figure out why this woman disappeared and where she might have gone. Even if you're right and Grice had nothing to do with it, she still might have witnessed something. This burglar business sounds too tidy for words."

Vera smiled cynically. "Hell, maybe she did it herself."

"God, you're more suspicious than I am."

"Well, you want Grice's number? I got it somewhere here." Vera paused to toss the tag end of her cigarette into the Coke bottle. There was a quick spitting sound as the ember touched the thimbleful of Coke that remained. She extracted a file from the bottom of a stack and found the telephone number and the address.

"Thanks," I said.

She gave me a speculative look. "You interested in an unemployed aerospace engineer? He's got bucks. He invented some little dingus they use now in all the satellites."

"How come you don't want him?" I asked. Vera tended to offer up her rejects like hostess gifts.

She made a face. "He was fine for a while, but now he's on a health kick. Started taking algae pills. I don't want to kiss a man who eats pond scum. I thought you might not object since you live so clean. Maybe you two could jog together and nibble dried seaweed snacks. If you're interested, he's yours."

"You're too good to me," I said. "I'll keep an eye out. I might run into someone who's up for him."

"You're way too picky about men, Kinsey," she said reprovingly.

"*I'm* picky?! What about you?"

Vera stuck another cigarette between her teeth and I watched her flick a tiny gold lighter into play before she spoke.

"I figure guys are like Whitman's Samplers. I like to take a little bite out of each and then move on before the whole box gets stale."

9

It was 1:30 by now and as nearly as I could remember, I hadn't eaten lunch. I pulled into a fast-food restaurant, parked, and went in. I could have hollered my order into a clown's mouth and eaten in the car as I drove, but I wanted to show I had class. I wolfed down a cheese-burger, fries, and a Coke for a dollar sixty-nine and was back on the streets again in seven minutes flat.

The house where Leonard Grice was supposedly staying was located in a dingy tract of houses just off the freeway, a neighborhood of winding streets that had been named after states, starting with the East Coast. I rambled down Maine, Massachusetts, New York, and Rhode Island Drives, getting stuck in tricky cul-de-sacs where Vermont and New Jersey turned into dead ends. It looked like the builder had gotten as far as Colorado Avenue before the money ran out or his knowledge of geography failed. There was a long stretch of vacant lots with stakes visible at intervals, each tied with a little white rag to mark off the undeveloped parcels of land.

Most of the houses had gone up in the fifties. The

trees had flourished, overpowering the small lots. The houses were alternately pale pink and pale green stucco, mirror images of one another like a whole tray of loaf cakes on a bakery shelf. All had the same rock-covered roofs, as though some volcano nearby had erupted, raining down a thin debris. The whole tract seemed dominated by wide-mouthed garages and I was subjected to untidy views of lawn equipment and camper shells, toys, tools, dusty luggage, banged-up refrigerators. There were surprisingly few cars visible and the impression I got was of a community abandoned in the wake of some natural disaster. Maybe a plague had passed this way or maybe toxic wastes had risen up through the soil, killing all the dogs and cats and burning holes in children's feet. At the intersection of Maryland and Virginia, I turned right.

On Carolina, a few enterprising souls had faced their homes with fieldstone or cedar shingle, and some had opted for an Oriental effect—trellises of plywood with geometric cutouts that were meant to look Chinese, the roof corners tilted up for that gala 1950s pagoda look. Compared to more recent tracts on the outskirts of Santa Teresa, these houses were shabby and the evidence of poor construction floated on the surface like chicken fat on homemade soup. There were cracks in the stucco, window shutters askew. The veneer on the front doors was peeling off in strips. Even the drapes were hung crookedly and I could imagine bathroom plaster bulging out in places, faucet handles frozen with rust.

The Howes had traded their front lawn for a rock

garden, apparently burying the scruffy grass under tons of sand, topped with gravel beds in shades of mauve and green. I could still see a strip of black plastic "mulch" peeping out around the edge where some attempt had been made to suppress the weeds. The Bermuda grass had risen to the challenge and it was snaking its way through the gravel at a leisurely pace. There was a bird-bath tucked among the succulents and a poured-concrete squirrel seemed to pop up out of the cactus in an attitude of perpetual, stony optimism. I doubted there was a live squirrel within blocks.

I parked the car and walked up to the house, taking the clipboard I keep in the backseat of my car. The Howes' garage door was closed, making the place look blank and unoccupied. The long, low line of the porch was obscured with ivy, looking picturesque, but capable, I knew, of lifting the roof right off. The drapes were closed. I rang the bell, but there was no reassuring "ding-dong" within. A minute passed. I knocked.

The woman who came to the door was subdued, her faded blue eyes searching my face hesitantly.

"Mrs. Howe?"

"I'm Mrs. Howe," she said.

It felt like Lesson One on a foreign-language record. There were dark circles under her eyes and her voice was as flat and dry as a cracker.

"I understand Leonard Grice is staying here. Is that correct?"

"Yes."

I held my clipboard up. "I'm from the insurance company and I wonder if I might have a word with him." It's a marvel God doesn't reach right down and rip my tongue out by the roots for the lies I tell.

"Leonard's taking a rest. Why don't you come back another time." She was closing the door.

"I'll just take a minute," I said quickly. I stuck the clipboard into the crack. She'd never get the door shut that way.

She paused. "The doctor still has him on sedatives." A non sequitur but the point was clear.

"I see. Well, of course, I wouldn't want to disturb him, but I'd really like to see him, as long as I've driven all the way out here." I tried to sound winsome, but apparently failed.

She stared at me stubbornly and I could see the color rise in her face. She glanced sideways as though she were consulting an invisible companion. Abruptly, she moved back and let me into the house with the attitude of someone using the *f* word under her breath. Her hair was gray, shoulder-length and thin, turned under in a tight pageboy. She had bangs along her forehead in a hairstyle I hadn't seen since those June Allyson movies where she was so loving and so long-suffering. Mrs. Howe wore a plain white blouse and a sensible charcoal-gray wool skirt. She was chunky through the waist. What is it about middle age that makes a woman's body mimic pregnancy?

"I'll see if he'll talk to you," she said and left the room.

I waited just inside the front door, taking in with a quick glance the cotton shag carpeting, brick fireplace painted white, an oil painting above it of waves crashing on rocks. She'd apparently used the painting as the focal point of her decorating scheme because the couch and wing chairs were upholstered in the same passionate shade of turquoise, in a fabric that looked faintly damp. I hated this part of my job—asserting myself persistently into somebody else's pain and grief, violating privacy. I felt like a door-to-door salesman, pushing unwanted sets of nature encyclopedias complete with fake walnut case. I also hated myself vaguely for being judgmental. What did I know about hairstyles anyway? What did I know about waves crashing on rocks? Maybe the turquoise said exactly what she'd meant to say about the room.

When Leonard Grice appeared, I could feel my heart sink. He didn't look like a man who'd murdered his wife, as much as that theory appealed to me. He was probably in his early fifties, but he moved like an old man. He was not bad-looking, but his face was pallid, cheeks sunken as though he'd recently lost some weight. His manner was vacant and he held his hands in front of him when he walked as though he were blindfolded. He had all the airs of a man who has stumbled painfully over something in the dark and wants to be certain he doesn't get caught by surprise again. It was possible, of course, that he'd killed her and was consumed now by guilt and remorse, but the killers I've run into in my brief career are either cheerful or matter-of-fact, like they can't understand what all the fuss is about.

Leonard's sister walked beside him, her hand near his elbow, watching where he placed his feet. She eased him toward a chair and shot me a look, clearly hoping I was satisfied at the trouble I'd caused. I did feel crummy, I'll confess.

He sat down. He seemed to be coming to life, reaching automatically for a pack of Camels in his shirt pocket while Mrs. Howe perched on the edge of the couch.

"Sorry to have to bother you," I said, "but I've just been talking to the adjuster at California Fidelity and there were a few details we wanted to clarify. Do you mind answering some questions for me?"

"He can hardly afford not to cooperate with the insurance company," she interjected peevishly.

Leonard cleared his throat, striking a match twice without effect against a paper matchbook. His hands were trembling and I wasn't sure he'd ever manage to match the flame to the end of his cigarette even if he could conjure one up. Mrs. Howe reached over, took the packet, and struck the match for him. He inhaled deeply.

"You'll have to pardon me," he said, "the doctor has me on some medicine that does this to me. I'm on disability for my back. What is it exactly that you want?"

"I've just recently been assigned to this case and I thought it might be helpful to hear your own account of what happened that night."

"What on earth for!" Mrs. Howe said.

"That's all right, Lily," he broke in, "I don't mind. I'm sure she's got her reasons for wanting to know." His voice was stronger now, dispelling the original impression of feebleness. He took a deep drag of his cigarette, letting it rest in the fork between his index and third fingers.

"My sister's widowed," he said, as though that might explain her belligerence. "Mr. Howe died of a heart attack eighteen months ago. After that, Marty and I got in the habit of taking Lil out to dinner every week. Mostly it was a way to keep up with each other and visit back and forth. Well that night, Marty planned to go as usual, but she said she felt like she was coming down with the flu, so at the last minute she decided to stay home. It was Lil's birthday and Marty was disappointed because she knew we were going to have a little cake brought to the table and waiters singing . . . you know how they do. She wanted to see the look on Lily's face. Anyway, she felt if she wasn't well, she might spoil everybody's evening so she didn't go." He paused, taking a deep drag of his cigarette. He'd accumulated a long ash and Lily pushed an ashtray toward him just as it tumbled.

"Did you tend to go out the same night of the week each time?" I asked.

He nodded. "Tuesdays as a rule."

I made a note dutifully on the legal pad on my clipboard. I hoped I looked like I had some legitimate reason to be asking all this stuff. I pretended to consult a form or two, flipping back a page. I thought the clipboard was a nice touch. I guess Lily did too. She peered over, wanting to see me write down something she said too.

"That's the best night for me," she ventured. "I get my hair done on Tuesdays and I like to go out when it's looking nice."

"Hair on Tues.," I wrote. "How many people knew you went out on Tuesday nights?"

Leonard's eyes slid over to mine with a curious look. The medication had opened his pupils to the full, perfect black holes that looked like they'd been made with a paper punch.

"Pardon?"

"I wondered how many people knew about your nights out. If the intruder was someone you knew, he might have thought she'd be out with you as usual."

His expression flickered with uncertainty. "I don't understand what this has to do with the insurance claim," he said.

I had to be careful how I framed my reply because he'd put his finger on the flaw in my charade. My questions had nothing to do with anything except trying to figure out if Elaine could have seen a murder. So far, I didn't even know what had actually happened that night and I was trying to weasel the information out of him. Lieutenant Dolan wasn't going to tell me, that was for sure.

I smiled briefly, keeping my tone light. "Naturally we're interested in seeing this crime solved," I said. "We may need a determination on the case before the claim is paid."

Lily glanced at Leonard and then back to me, alerted by his wariness. "What kind of 'determination'?" she asked. "I don't understand what you mean."

Leonard shifted back to his original attitude. "Now, Lil, it can only help," he said. "The insurance company wants to get to the bottom of this just like we do. The police haven't done anything on it for months." He glanced at me again. "You'll have to pardon Lil. . . ."

She flashed him a look. "Don't apologize for me when I'm sitting right here," she snapped. "You're too trusting, Leonard. That's what's wrong with you. Marty was the same way. If she'd been a little more cautious, she might be alive today!"

She faltered, clamping her mouth shut, then surprised me by filling in some details. "She was on the phone to me that night and someone came to the door. She rang off to see who it was."

He chimed in. "The police said it's possible she knew the person, or it might have been someone off the street. Police said a lot of times a burglar rings the bell if the lights are on. If someone answers the door, he can act like he's got the wrong address. Nobody answers, he might go ahead and break in."

"Were there signs of a struggle?"

"I don't think so," Leonard said. "Not that I ever heard. I went through the house myself, but I couldn't see anything missing."

I looked back at Lily. "What had she called about?" I asked. "Or did you call her?"

"I called her myself when we got in," she said. "We got back here a little later than we thought and Leonard didn't want her to worry."

"And she sounded all right when you talked to her?"

Lily nodded. "She sounded fine. She sounded just like she always did. Leonard talked to her for a bit and then I got back on with her and we were just winding down when she said there was someone at the door and she had to go see who it was. I was going to offer to stay on the line, but we were done anyway so I just said good-bye and hung up."

Leonard pulled a handkerchief out of his pants pocket and pressed it to his eyes. His hands had begun to shake badly and there was a tremor in his voice. "I don't even know what her last moments were like. Police said the guy must have hit her square in the face with a baseball bat, something that size. She must have been terrified—"

He broke off.

I could feel myself squirm, but I didn't say anything. What actually occurred to me, as tacky as it sounds, is that a baseball bat in the face doesn't leave time to feel much of anything. Crack! You're gone. No terror, no pain. Just lights out, home run.

Lily reached over and place her hand on his. "They were married twenty-two years."

"Good years too," he said, his tone almost argumentative. "We never went to bed mad. That was a rule we made early. Anytime we had a quarrel, we got it settled. She was a fine woman. Smarter than me and I'm not ashamed to admit it."

Tears glittered in his eyes, but I felt oddly removed, like the only sober person at a party full of drunks.

"Did the police mention any possibility of witnesses? Someone who might have seen or heard something that night?"

He shook his head, mopping at his eyes. "No. I don't think so. I never heard that."

"Possibly someone in the building next door?" I suggested. "Or someone passing by? I understand you've got people across the street from you too. You'd think someone would have noticed *something*."

He blew his nose, recovering his composure. "I don't think so. Police never said anything to us."

"Well, I've taken up enough of your time and I'm sorry I've caused you so much distress. I'd like to go through the house and assess the fire damage if you don't mind. One of our adjusters has already been through, but I'll need to see for myself so I can make my report."

He nodded. "My neighbor has a key. Orris Snyder right next door. You go knock on his door and tell him I said it was all right."

I got up and held my hand out to him. "Thanks for talking to me."

Leonard got to his feet automatically and shook my hand. His grip was solid, his flesh almost feverishly hot.

"By the way," I said as if it had just occurred to me, "have you heard from Elaine Boldt lately?"

He focused on me, apparently perplexed by the reference.

"Elaine? No, why?"

"I was trying to get in touch with her on another matter and I realized she lived in that condominium right next door," I replied with ease. "Someone mentioned that she was a friend of yours."

"That's right. We used to play bridge together before Marty died. I haven't talked to her for months. She's usually in Florida this time of year, I believe."

"Oh, that's right. I think somebody else mentioned that. Well, maybe she'll call when she gets back," I said. "Thanks again."

By the time I got back out to my car again, both my armpits were ringed with sweat.

10

It was now nearly three o'clock and I was feeling frazzled. I'd been up since two A.M. with just a brief time-out for sleep at dawn before the long-distance call from Mrs. Ochsner had wakened me. I couldn't face the office again, so I headed for my apartment and changed into my running clothes. I use the word *apartment* here in its loosest sense. Actually I live in a converted one-car garage, maybe fifteen feet square, tricked out as living room, bedroom, kitchen, bathroom, closet, and laundry facility. I've always liked living in small spaces. For months as a child, just after my parents were killed, I spent my spare time in a cardboard box that I filled with pillows and pretended was a sailing vessel on its way to some new land. It doesn't take an analyst to interpret this excursion on my part, but it's carried over into my adult life, manifesting itself now in all sorts of things. I drive small cars and I favor "littleness" in any form, so this place suits me exactly. For two hundred dollars a month I have everything I want, including a debonair eighty-one-year-old landlord named Henry Pitts.

I peered in his back window on my way out, and spotted him in the kitchen rolling out puff pastry dough. He's a former commercial baker who supplements his social security these days doing up breads and sweets, which he sells to or trades with local merchants. I tapped on the glass and he motioned me in. Henry is what I like to think of as an octogenarian "hunk," tall and lean with close-cropped white hair and eyes that are periwinkle blue, full of curiosity. Age has boiled him down to a concentrate, all male, compassionate and prudent and wry. I can't say that the years have invested him with spirituality, or infused him with any special wisdom, second sight, profundity, or depth. I mean, let's not overstate the case here. He was smart enough when he first started out and age hasn't diminished that a whit. Despite the fifty years' difference in our ages, there's nothing of the pundit in his attitude toward me, and nothing (I hope) of the postulant in my attitude toward him. We simply eye one another across that half a century with a lively and considerable sexual interest that neither of us would *dream* of acting out.

That afternoon, he was wearing a red rag around his head pirate-style, his tanned forearms bare and powdered with flour, his fingers as long and nimble as a monkey's as he gathered the dough and turned it halfway. He was using a length of chilled pipe as a rolling pin and he paused to flour it while he worked, coaxing the pastry into a rectangle.

I perched up on a wooden stool and retied my shoes. "You making napoleons?"

He nodded. "I'm catering a tea for someone up the street. What are you up to, besides a run?"

I filled him in briefly on my search for Elaine Boldt while he folded the dough in thirds and wrapped it, returning it to the refrigerator. When I got to the part about Marty Grice, I saw his brows shoot up.

"Stay away from it. Take my advice and leave it to the homicide detectives. You're a fool if you get involved in that end of it."

"But what if she saw who killed Marty? What if that's why she took off?"

"Then let her come forward with the information. It's not up to you. If Lieutenant Dolan catches you messing around with his case, he'll have your rear end."

"Actually, that's true," I said ruefully. "But how can I back off? I'm running out of places to look."

"Who says she's lost? What makes you think she's not down in Sarasota someplace lapping up gin and tonic on the beach?"

"Because somebody would have heard from her. I mean, I don't know if she's up to something or maybe in big trouble herself, but until she shows up I'm going to beat the bushes and bang on pans and see if I can run her to ground."

"Make-work," he said. "You're chasing your own tail."

"Well, that's probably true, but I gotta do something."

Henry gave me a skeptical look. He opened a bag of sugar and weighed out a mound. "You need a dog."

"No, I don't. And what's that got to do with it? I hate dogs."

"You need protection. That business at the beach would never have happened if you'd had a Doberman."

That again. God, even my recent brush with death had taken place in a garbage bin . . . someplace small and cozy with me sobbing like a kid.

"I was thinking about that stuff today and you want to know the truth? All this talk about women being nurturing is crap. We're being sold a bill of goods so we can be kept in line by men. If someone came after me today, I'd do it again, only this time I don't think I'd hesitate."

Henry didn't seem impressed. "I'm sorry to hear that. I hope you haven't started a trend."

"I mean it. I'm tired of feeling helpless and afraid," I said.

Henry puffed his cheeks up and blew a raspberry, giving me a bored look. Big talk, his face said, but you don't fool me a bit. He cracked an egg on the counter and opened it up with one hand, letting the white slip through his fingers into a cup. He put the yolk in a bowl and took up another egg, repeating the process with his eyes pinned on me.

He said, "So defend yourself. Who's arguing with that? But you can drop the rhetoric. It's bullshit. Killing is killing and you better take a look at what you did."

"I know," I said, with less energy. The look in his eyes was making me squirm and I wasn't all that crazy about his tone. "Look, maybe I haven't really dealt with that. I just don't want to be a victim anymore. I'm sick of it."

Henry cradled the bowl in his arms, whisking the eggs with a practiced ease. When I do that, the eggs always slop out the side.

He said, "When were you ever a victim? You don't have to justify yourself to me. You did what you did. Just don't try to turn it into a philosophical statement, because it doesn't ring true. It's not as if you made a rational decision after months contemplating the facts. You killed somebody in the heat of the moment. It's not a platform for a political campaign and it's not a turning point in your intellectual life."

I smiled at him tentatively. "I'm still a good person, aren't I?" I didn't like the wistful tone. I meant to show him I was a grown-up, coping with the truth. Until the words came out of my mouth, I hadn't even known I felt so unsure.

He didn't smile back. His eyes rested on my face for a moment and then dropped back to the eggs. "What happened to you doesn't change that, Kinsey, but you have to keep it straight. Blow somebody's brains out and you don't brush that off. And you don't try to turn it into an intellectual stance."

"No, you don't," I said uneasily. I had a quick flash of the face that peered into the garbage bin just before I fired. By some remarkable distortion, I could have sworn I saw how the first bullet stretched the flesh like elastic before smashing through. I shook the image away and hopped down. "I have to run," I said, feeling anxious.

I left the kitchen without glancing back, but I know what the look was on Henry's face. Caution and sorrow and pain.

Once outside, I had to put it out of my mind again. Back the subject went, into its own little box. I did a quick stretch, concentrating on my hamstrings. I don't run fast enough or far enough to justify much of a warm-up. Other joggers, I know, would argue with that, citing injuries that result from insufficient stretching before a run, but I find exercise loathsome enough without adding contortions up front. For a time, I tried it, dutifully lying on my back in the grass with one leg straight out and the other cocked sideways toward my waist as though broken at the hip. I could never get up afterward unless I flopped about like a bug and I finally decided it was worth a possible groin-muscle pull to avoid the indignity. I've never been injured running anyway. I've never thrilled to it either. I'm still waiting for the rumored "euphoria" that apparently infuses everyone but me. I headed over to the boulevard at a brisk walk, keeping my mind blank.

I generally do three miles, jogging along the bicycle path that borders the beach. The walkway is stenciled with odd cartoons at intervals and I watch for those, counting off the quarter-miles. The tracks of some improbable bird, the mark of a single fat tire that crosses the concrete and disappears into the sand. There are usually tramps on the beach; some who camp there permanently, others in transit, their sleeping bags arranged under the palm trees like large green larvae or the skins shed by some night-stirring beast.

That afternoon the air seemed heavy and chill, the ocean sluggish. The cloud cover was beginning to break up, but the visible sky was a pale washed-out blue and there was no real sign of sun. Out on the water a speedboat ran a course parallel to the beach and the path of the wake was like a spinning ribbon of silver winding along behind. On the landward side, the mountains were dark green. At this distance, the low-growing vegetation looked like soft suede, with rock face showing through along the ridges as though the nap had worn away from hard use.

I did the turnaround at East Beach and ran the mile and a half back, then walked the block to my apartment as a cool-down. I'm big on cool-downs. I showered and dressed again and then hopped in my car and headed up to Pam Sharkey's office on Chapel. Pam was the insurance agent who'd written up the policies for Leonard Grice and I wanted to probe that issue before I set it aside. I trust Vera, but I don't like taking people's word for things. Maybe Grice had taken out a massive policy from some other company. How did I know?

The Valdez Building is located at the corner of Chapel and Feria, a Spanish word meaning "fair." I only know that because I looked it up. I've been thinking I should take a Spanish class one of these days, but I haven't gotten around to it yet. I can say *taco* and *gracias* but I'm real short on verbs. The Valdez is typical of the architecture in this town: two stories of white stucco with a red tile roof, big arches, windows faced with wrought-iron gratings. There are azure blue awnings and the landscaping consists of small plots of perfect grass. Palm trees grace the courtyard and there's a fountain capped by a small naked boy doing something wicked with a fish.

Pam Sharkey's office is on the first floor and sports the same network of cubicles I'd seen at California Fidelity. Nothing architecturally innovative for the insurance game these days. It must be like doing business in a series of playpens. The company she works for, Lambeth and Creek, is an independent agency that writes policies for a number of companies, CFI being one. I'd only dealt with Pam once, when I was bird-dogging an errant husband. His wife, my client, was in the process of divorcing him and was hoping for evidence of his philandering as a negotiating tool when it came down to the settlement. Pam had taken offense, not because I'd uncovered her affair with the man, but because I'd turned up two other women involved with him at the same time. None of this was ever brought up in court, of course, but her name was prominent in my report. She had never forgiven me for knowing too much. Santa Teresa is a small town and our paths cross now and then. We're polite to one another, but the civilities are undercut with spite on her part and sly amusement on mine.

Pam is petite, a bristly little chihuahua of a human being. She's the only woman I ever met who claims to be ten years older than she actually is so that everyone will tell her how young she looks. On that basis, she swears she's thirty-eight. Her face is small, her skin dusky and she applies pancake makeup in varying shades in a vain attempt to add "planes" to her cheeks. I got news for her. There's no way to disguise the bags under your eyes by the skillful use of "cover." From most angles anybody with a brain can see the bags sitting right there, only looking phantom white instead of gray. Who's fooled by this? Why not go for the dark circles and at least look exotic and worldly-wise . . . Anna Magnani,

Jeanne Moreau, Simone Signoret perhaps. Pam had also taken lately to a permanent wave, so her pale brown hair looked frizzy and unkempt, a style apparently billed as "the bedroom look." That afternoon she was done up in a little hunting outfit: a hacking jacket, brown knickers, pink hose, and low heels with buckles. The only hunting she did was in singles bars, bagging one-night stands as though the season were nearly over and her license about to expire. Well, wait a minute here. I can see I've been unfair about this. I don't like Pam any more than she likes me. Every time I see her, it makes me feel petty and mean—not my favorite way to experience myself. Maybe she avoids me for the same reason.

Her cubicle is near the front—a status symbol, I think. She caught sight of me and busied herself with papers and files. By the time I'd made my way over to her desk, she was on the phone. She must have been talking to a man because her manner was flirtatious. She touched herself everywhere as she talked, rolling a lock of hair around her finger, checking an earring, stroking the lapel of her jacket. She wore a series of gold necklaces and those got a workout too. Sometimes she'd rub her chin with a loop of gold chain, uttering a carefree, trilling laugh she must have practiced late at night. She glanced at me, feigning surprise, holding up a palm to indicate that I'd have to wait.

She turned away from me in her swivel chair, completing the telephone exchange with a murmured intimacy of some sort. On top of a stack of files on her desk, I could see a copy of *Cosmo*, offering articles on the G spot, cosmetic breast surgery, and social rape.

Pam hung up at long last and swiveled back, all the animation leaving her face. No point in wasting the whole show on me. "Something I can help you with, Kinsey?"

"I understand you wrote a couple of policies for Leonard and Marty Grice."

"That's right."

I smiled slightly. "Could you tell me the status of the paperwork at this point?"

Pam broke eye contact, going through another quick digital survey: earring, hair, lapel. She took up a loop of gold chain, running her index finger back and forth on it until I worried she'd saw right through the skin. She wanted to tell me Leonard Grice was none of my business, but she knew I did occasional work for California Fidelity.

"What's the problem?"

"No problem," I said. "Vera Lipton's wondering about the claim on the fire loss and I need to know if there were any other policies in effect."

"Now, wait a minute. Leonard Grice is a very dear man and he's been through a terrible six months. If California Fidelity intends to make trouble, Vera better deal directly with me."

"Who said anything about trouble? Vera can't even process the claim until the proof of loss is in."

"That goes without saying, Kinsey," she said. "I still don't see what this has to do with you."

I could feel my smile begin to set like a pan of fudge. I leaned forward, left hand flat on the desk, right hand resting on my hip. I thought it was time to clarify our relationship.

"Not that it's any of your business, Pam, but I'm in the middle of a big investigation adjunctive to this. You don't have to cooperate, but I'm just going to turn around and present a court order to the supervisor here and somebody's going to come down on you like a ton of bricks for all the trouble it'll cause. Now is that how you want to proceed on this or what?"

Under the pancake makeup, she began to show signs of sunburn. "I hope you don't think you can intimidate me," she said.

"Absolutely not." I shut my mouth then and let her assimilate the threat. I thought it sounded pretty good.

She took up a stack of papers and rapped them on the desk, aligning the edges. "Leonard Grice was insured through California Fidelity Life and California Fidelity Casualty Insurance. He collected twenty-five hundred dollars for the life insurance and he'll get twenty-five thousand for the structural damage to the house. The contents were uninsured."

"Why only twenty-five for the house? I thought that place was worth over a hundred grand? He won't have enough money to do the repairs, will he?"

"When he bought the place in 1962, it was worth twenty-five thousand and that's what he insured it for. He never increased the coverage and he hasn't taken out any other policies. Personally, I don't see how he can do anything with the house. It's a complete loss, which I think is what's broken him."

Now that she'd told me, I felt guilty for all the macho bullshit I'd laid on her.

"Thanks. That's a big help," I said. "Uh . . . by the

way, Vera wanted me to ask if you'd be interested in meeting an unattached aerospace engineer with bucks."

A wonderful look of uncertainty crossed her face: suspicion, sexual hunger, greed. Was I offering her a cookie or a flat brown turd on a plate? I knew what was going through her head. In Santa Teresa, a single man is on the market maybe ten days before someone snaps him up.

She shot me a worried look. "What's wrong with him? Why didn't you take him first?"

"I just came off a relationship," I said, "I'm in retreat." Which was true.

"Maybe I'll give Vera a buzz," she said faintly.

"Great. Thanks again for the information," I said and I gave her a little wave as I moved away from her desk. With my luck, she'd fall in love with the guy and want me to be a bridesmaid. Then I'd be stuck with one of those dumb dresses with a hunk of flounce on the hip. When I glanced back at her, she seemed to have shrunk and I felt a twinge. She wasn't so bad.

11

I ate dinner that night at Rosie's, a little place half a block, down from my apartment. It's a cross between a neighborhood bar and an old-fashioned beanery, sandwiched between a Laundromat on the corner and an appliance repair shop that a man named McPherson operates out of his house. All three of these businesses have been in operation for over twenty-five years and are now, in theory, illegal, representing zoning violations of a profound and offensive sort, at least to people who live somewhere else. Every other year, some overzealous citizen gets a bug up his butt and goes before the city council denouncing the outrage of this breach of residential integrity. In the off years, I think money changes hands.

Rosie herself is probably sixty-five, Hungarian, short, and top-heavy, a creature of muumuus and hennaed hair growing low on her forehead. She wears lipstick in a burnt-orange shade that usually exceeds the actual shape of her mouth, giving the impression that she once had a much larger set of lips. She uses a brown eyebrow pencil lavishly, making her eyes look stern and re-proachful. The tip of her nose comes close to meeting her upper lip.

I sat down in my usual booth near the back. There was a mimeographed menu sheet slipped into a clear plastic cover stuck between the ketchup bottle and the napkin box. The selections were typed in pale purple like those notices they used to send home with us when we were in grade school. Most of the items were written in Hungarian; words with lots of accent marks and z's and double dots, suggesting that the dishes would be fierce and emphatic.

Rosie marched over, pad and pencil poised, her manner withdrawn. She was feeling offended about something, but I wasn't sure yet what I'd done. She snatched the menu out of my hand and put it back, writing out the order without consulting me. If you don't like the way the place is run, you go somewhere else. She finished writing and squinted at the pad, checking the results. She wouldn't quite meet my eyes.

"You didn't come in for a week so I figured you was mad at me," she said. "I bet you been eating junk, right? Don't answer that. I don't want to hear. You don't owe me an apology. You just lucky I give you something decent. Here's what you gonna get."

She consulted the pad again with a critical eye, reading the order to me then with interest as though it were news to her too.

"Green pepper salad. Fantastic. The best. I made it myself so I know it's done right. Olive oil, vinegar, little pinch of sugar. Forget the bread, I'm out. Henry didn't bring fresh today so what do I know? He could be mad at me too. How do I know what I did? Nobody tells me these things. Then I give you sour oxtail stew."

She crossed that off. "Too much grease. Is no good for you. Instead I give you tejfeles sult ponty, some nice pike I bake in cream, and if you clean your plate, I could give you deep-fried cherries if I think you deserve it, which you don't. The wine I'm gonna bring with the flatware. Is Austrian, but okay."

She marched away then, her back straight, her hair the color of dried tangerine peels. Her rudeness sometimes has an eccentric charm to it, but it's just as often simply irritating, something you have to endure if you want to eat Rosie's meals. Some nights I can't tolerate verbal abuse at the end of the day, preferring instead the impersonal mechanics of a drive-in restaurant or the peace and quiet of a peanut butter and dill pickle sandwich at home.

That night Rosie's was deserted, looking drab and not quite clean. The walls are paneled in construction-grade plywood sheets, stained dark, with a matte finish of cooking fumes and cigarette smoke. The lighting is wrong—too pale, too generalized—so that the few patrons who do wander in look sallow and unwell. A television set on the bar usually flashes colored images with no sound, and a marlin arched above it looks like it's fashioned of plaster of Paris and dusted with soot. I'm embarrassed to say how much I like the place. It will never be a tourist attraction. It will never be a singles bar. No one will ever "discover" it or award it even half a star. It will always smell like spilled beer, paprika, and hot grease. It's a place where I can eat by myself and not even have to take a book along in order to avoid unwelcome company. A man would have to worry about any woman he could pick up in a dive like this.

The front door opened and the old crone who lives across the street came in, followed by Jonah Robb, whom I'd talked to that morning in Missing Persons. I almost didn't recognize him at first in his civilian clothes. He wore jeans, a gray tweed jacket, and brown desert boots. His shirt looked new, the package folds still evident, the collar tightly starched and stiff. He carried himself like a man with a shoulder holster tucked up under his left arm. He had apparently come in to look for me because he headed straight for my table and sat down.

I said, "Hello. Have a seat."

"I heard you hung out in here," he said. He glanced around and his brows gave a little lift as though the rumor were true but hard to believe. "Does the Health Department know about this place?"

I laughed.

Rosie, coming out of the kitchen, caught sight of Jonah and stopped dead in her tracks, retreating as though she'd been yanked backward by a rope.

He looked over his shoulder to see if he'd missed something.

"What's the matter? Could she tell I was a cop? Has she got a problem with that?"

"She's checking her makeup. There's a mirror just inside the kitchen door," I said.

Rosie appeared again, simpering coquettishly as she

brought my silverware and plunked it down on the table tightly bound in a paper napkin.

"You never said you was entertaining," she murmured. "Does you friend intend to have a little bite to eat? Some liquid refreshment perhaps? Beer, wine, a mixed drink?"

"Beer sounds good," he said. "What do you have on tap?"

Rosie folded her hands and regarded me with interest. She never deals directly with a stranger so we were forced to go through this little playlet in which I interpreted as though suddenly employed by the U.N.

"You still have Mich on tap?" I asked.

"Of course. Why would I have anything else?"

I looked at Jonah and he nodded assent. "I think we'll have a Mich then. Are you eating? The food's great."

"Fine with me," he said. "What do you recommend?"

"Why don't you just double the order, Rosie? Could you do that for us?"

"Of course." She glanced at him with sly approval. "I had no idea," she said. I could feel her mentally nudge me with one elbow. I knew what her appraisal consisted of. She favored weight in men. She favored dark hair and easygoing attitudes. She moved away from the table then, artfully leaving us alone. She isn't nearly as gracious when I come in with women friends.

"What brings you here?" I said.

"Idleness. Curiosity. I did a background check on you to save us talking about all the stupid stuff."

"So we could get right down to what?" I asked.

"You think I'm on the make or something?"

"Sure," I said. "New shirt. No wedding ring. I bet your wife left you week before last and you shaved less than an hour ago. The cologne isn't even dry on the side of your neck."

He laughed. He had a harmless face and good teeth. He leaned forward on his elbows. "Hers's how it went," he said. "I met her when I was thirteen and I was with her from that time to this. I think she grew up and I never could, at least not with her. I don't know what to do with myself. Actually she's been gone for a year. It just *feels* like a week. You're the first woman I've looked at since she went off."

"Where'd she go?"

"Idaho. She took the kids. Two," he said as though he knew I'd ask that next. "One girl ten, another one eight. Courtney and Ashley. I'd have named 'em something else. Sara and Diane, Patti and Jill, something like that. I don't even understand girls. I don't even know what they think about. I really love my kids, but from the day they were born it was like they were in this exclusive little club with my wife. I couldn't seem to get a membership no matter what I did."

"What was your wife's name?"

"Camilla. Shit. She ripped my heart out by the roots. I put on thirty pounds this year."

"Time to take it off," I said.

"Time to do a lot of things."

Rosie came back to the table with a beer for him and a glass of white table wine for me. Did I know this story or what? Men just out of marriages are a mess and I was a mess myself. I already knew all the pain, uncertainty and mismanaged emotions. Even Rosie sensed it wasn't going to fly. She looked at me like she couldn't figure out how I'd blown it so fast. When she left, I got back to the subject at hand.

"I'm not doing all that well myself," I said.

"So I heard. I thought we could help each other out."

"That's not how it works."

"You want to go up to the pistol range and shoot sometime?"

I laughed. I couldn't help myself. He was all over the place. "Sure. We could do that. What kind of gun do you have?"

"Colt Python with a six-inch barrel. It'll take a .38 or a .357 magnum cartridge. Usually I just wear a Trooper MK III but I had a chance to pick up the Python and I couldn't pass it up. Four hundred bucks. You've been married twice? I don't see how you could bring yourself to do that. I mean, Jesus. I thought marriage was a real commitment. Like souls, you know, fused all through eternity and shit like that."

"Four hundred bucks is a steal. How'd you pull that off?" I squinted at him. "What is it, are you Catholic or something?"

"No, just dumb I guess. I got my notions of romance out of ladies' magazines in the beauty shop my mother ran when I was growing up. The gun I got from Dave Whitaker's estate. His widow hates guns and never liked it that he got into 'em so she unloaded his collection first chance she got. I'd have paid the going rate, but she wouldn't hear of it. Do you know her? Bess Whitaker?"

I shook my head.

He glanced up then as Rosie put a plate down in front of each of us. I could tell by his look that he hadn't expected green peppers with a vinaigrette, even with little curlicues of parsley tucked here and there.

Usually Rosie waited until I tasted a dish and gave elaborate restaurant-reviewer-type raves, but this time she seemed to think better of it. As soon as she left, Jonah leaned forward.

"What is this shit?"

"Just eat."

"Kinsey, for the last ten years I been eating with kids who sit and pick all the onions and mushrooms out. I don't know how to eat if it's not made with Hamburger Helper."

"You're in for a big surprise," I said. "What have you been eating for the year since your wife left?"

"She put up all these dinners in the deep freeze. Every night I thaw one and stick it in the oven at three-fifty for an hour. I guess she went to a garage sale and bought up a bunch of those TV dinner tins with the little compartments. She wanted me to eat well-balanced meals even though she was fucking me over financially."

I lowered my fork and looked at him, trying to picture someone freezing up 365 dinners so she could bug out. This was the woman he apparently imagined mating with for life, like owls.

He was eating his first bite of pepper salad, his eyes turning inward. His facial expression suggested that the pepper was sitting in the middle of his tongue while he made chewing motions around it. I do that myself with those mashed candied sweet potatoes people insist on at

Thanksgiving time. Why would anyone put a marshmallow on a vegetable? Would I put licorice on asparagus, or jelly beans on Brussels sprouts? The very idea makes my mouth purse.

Jonah nodded philosophically to himself and began to fork up the pepper salad with gusto. It must have been at least as tasty as the shit Camilla cooked for him. I pictured tray after tray of frozen tuna casserole with crushed potato chips, with maybe frozen peas in one compartment, carrot coins in the next. I bet she left him six-packs of canned fruit cocktail for dessert. He was looking at me.

He said, "What's the matter? Why do you have that look on your face?"

I shrugged. "Marriage is a mystery."

"I'll second that," he said. "By the way, how's your case shaping up?"

"Well, I'm still nosing around," I said. "Right now, I'm making a little side investigation into an unsolved murder. Her next-door neighbor was killed the same week she left."

"That doesn't sound good. What's the connection?"

"I don't know yet. Maybe none. It just struck me as an interesting sequence of events that Marty Grice was murdered and Elaine Boldt disappeared within days of it."

"Was there a positive I.D.?"

"On Marty? I have no idea. Dolan's getting really anal-retentive about that stuff. He won't tell me a thing."

"Why not take a look at the files?"

"Oh come on. He's not going to let me see the files."

"So don't ask him. Ask me. I can make copies if you tell me what you want."

"Jonah, he would fire your ass. You would never work again. You'd have to sell shoes for the rest of your life."

"Why would he have to know?"

"How could you get away with it? He knows everything."

"*Bull*shit. The files are kept over in Identification and Records. I'll bet he's got a second set in his office so he probably never even looks at the originals. I'll just wait 'til he's out and Xerox whatever you need. Then I'll put it back."

"Don't you have to sign 'em out?"

He gave me a look then like I was probably the kind of person who never parked in a red zone. Actually, for someone to whom lying comes so easily, I get anxious about vehicle codes and overdue library books. Violations of the public trust. Oh hey, once in a while I might pick a lock illegally, but not if I think there's a chance I'll get *caught*. The idea of sneaking official documents out of the police station made my stomach squeeze down like I was on the verge of getting a tetanus shot.

"Oh wow, don't do that," I said. "You can't."

"What do you mean, I 'can't.' Of course I can. What do you want to see? Autopsy? Incident report? Follow-up interviews? Lab reports?"

"That'd be great. That would really help."

I looked up guiltily. Rosie was standing there waiting to pick up our salad plates. I leaned back in the booth and waited until both had been removed. "Look, I'd never ask you to do such a thing—"

"You didn't ask. I volunteered. Quit being such a candy ass. You can turn around and do me a favor sometime."

"But Jonah, he really is a nut about department leaks. You know how he gets. Please don't put yourself in jeopardy."

"Don't sweat it. Homicide detectives are full of crap sometimes. You're not going to blow his case for him. He probably doesn't even have a case, so what's to worry about?"

After dinner, he walked me back over to my place. It was only 8:15, but I had work to do and he really seemed a bit relieved that the contact between us wasn't going to be prolonged or intimate. As soon as I heard his footsteps retreat, I turned the outside lights off, sat down at my desk with some index cards and caught up with my notes.

I checked back through the cards I'd filled out before and tacked them up on the big bulletin board above my desk. I stood there for a long time, reading card after card, hoping for a flash of enlightenment. Only one curious note emerged. I'd been very meticulous about writing down every single item I remembered from my first search of Elaine's apartment. I do that routinely almost like a little game I play with myself to test my memory. In the kitchen cabinet, she'd had some cans of cat food. 9-Lives Beef and Liver Platter, said the note. Now it seemed out of place to me. What cat?

12

At nine the next morning, I drove over to Via Madrina. Tillie didn't answer my buzz so I stood for a minute, surveying the list of tenants' names on the directory. There was a Wm. Hoover in apartment 10, right next door to Elaine's. I gave him a buzz.

The intercom came to life. "Yes?"

"Mr. Hoover? This is Kinsey Millhone. I'm a private detective here in town and I'm looking for Elaine Boldt. Would you mind if I asked you a couple of questions?"

"You mean, right this minute?"

"Well, yes, if you wouldn't mind. I stopped by to talk to the building manager, but she's not here."

I could hear a murmur of conversation and then the door buzzed at me by way of consent. I had to jump to catch it while the lock would still open. I took the elevator up a floor. Apartment 10 was just across from me when the elevator door slid open. Hoover was standing in the hall in a short blue terry-cloth robe with snags. I estimated his age at thirty-four, thirty-five. He was slight, maybe five foot six, with slim, muscular legs faintly matted with down. His dark hair was tousled and he looked as if he hadn't shaved for two days. His eyes were still baggy from sleep.

"Oh God, I woke you up," I said. "I hate to do that to people."

"No, I've been up," he said. He ran a hand across his hair, scratching the back of his head while he yawned. I had to clamp my teeth so I wouldn't yawn in response. Barefoot, he moved back into the apartment and I followed him.

"I just put some coffee on. It'll be ready in a sec. Come on in and have a seat." His voice was light and reedy.

He indicated the kitchen to the right. His apartment was the flip image of Elaine's and my guess was that their two master bedrooms shared a wall. I glanced at the living room which, like hers, opened off the entryway and also looked down on the Grices' property next door. Where Elaine's apartment had a view of the street, this one didn't have much to recommend it—only a glimpse of the mountains off to the left, partially obscured by the two rows of Italian stone pines that grow along Via Madrina.

Hoover adjusted his short robe and sat down on a kitchen chair, crossing his legs. His knees were cute. "What's your name again? I'm sorry, I'm still half-unconscious."

"Kinsey Millhone," I said. The kitchen smelled of brewing coffee and the fumes of unbrushed teeth. His, not mine. He reached for a slim brown cigarette and lit it, hoping perhaps to mask his morning mouth with something worse. His eyes were a mild tobacco brown, his lashes sparse, face lean. He regarded me with all the boredom of a boa constrictor after a heavy meal of groundhog. The percolator gave a few last burps and subsided while he reached for two big blue-and-white mugs. One had an overall design of bunny rabbits humping. The other portrayed elephants similarly occupied. I tried not to look. The thing I've worried about for years is how dinosaurs mated, especially those great big spiny ones. Someone told me once they did it in water, which helped support all that weight, but I find it hard to believe dinosaurs were that smart. It didn't seem likely with those tiny pinched heads. I shook myself back to reality.

"What do you call yourself? William? Bill?"

"Wim," he said. He fetched a carton of milk from the refrigerator and found a spoon for the sugar bowl. I added milk to my coffee and watched with interest while he added two heaping tablespoons of sugar to his. He caught my look.

"I'm trying to gain a little weight," he said. "I know the sugar's bad for my teeth, but I've been doing up these torturous protein drinks in the morning—you know the kind—with egg and banana and wheat germ thrown in. Ugh. The aftertaste just cannot be disguised. Besides, I hate to eat before two in the afternoon so I guess I should resign myself to being thin. Anyway, that's why I load up my coffee. I figure anything's bound to help. You look a little on the Twiggy side yourself."

"I run every day and I forget to eat." I sipped my coffee, which was scented faintly with mint. It was really very good.

"How well did you know Elaine?" I asked.

"We spoke when we ran into one another in the hall," he said. "We've been neighbors for years. Why do you want her? Did she run out on her bills?"

I told him briefly about her apparent absence, adding that the explanation didn't have to be sinister, but that it was puzzling nevertheless. "Do you remember when you saw her last?"

"Not really. Sometime before she went off. Christmas, I guess. No, I take that back. I did see her New Year's Eve. She said she was staying home."

"Do you happen to know if she had a cat?"

"Oh sure. Gorgeous thing. A massive gray Persian named Mingus. He was actually my cat originally, but I was hardly ever home and I thought he should have company so I gave him to her. He was just a kitten at the time. I had no idea he'd turn out to be such a beauty or I never would have given him up. I mean, I've kicked myself ever since, but what can one do? A deal's a deal."

"What was the deal?"

He shrugged indifferently. "I made her swear she'd never change his name. Charlie Mingus. After the jazz pianist. Also she had to promise not to leave him by himself, or what was the point in giving him away? I might as well have kept him myself."

Wim took a careful drag of his cigarette, resting his elbow on the kitchen table. I could hear the shower running somewhere in the back of the apartment.

"Did she take him with her to Florida every year?"

"Oh sure. Sometimes right up in the cabin if the airline had the space. She said he loved it down there, thought he owned the place." He picked up a napkin and folded it in half.

"Well, it's curious he hasn't shown up someplace."

"He's probably still with her, wherever she is."

"Did you talk to her after that murder next door?"

Wim shook his head, neatly flicking ash into the folded napkin. "I did talk to the police, or rather they talked to me. My living-room windows look right down on that house and they were interested in what I could have seen. Which was nothing, I might add. That detective was the biggest macho asshole I've ever met and I didn't appreciate his antagonistic attitude. Can I warm that up for you?"

He got up and fetched the coffee.

I nodded and he topped off both our mugs, pouring from a thermos. The sound of running water had abruptly ceased and Wim took note of it, just as I did. He went back to the sink and extinguished his cigarette by running it under the tap and then he tossed it in the trash. He got out a frying pan and took a package of bacon from the refrigerator. "I'd offer you breakfast, but I don't have enough unless you want to join me in a protein drink. I'm going to make that up in a minute, disgusting as it is. I'm doing real food for a friend of mine."

"I've got to go shortly anyway," I said, getting up.

He waved at me impatiently. "Sit down, sit down.

Finish your coffee at any rate. You might as well ask whatever you want as long as you're here."

"What about a vet for the cat? Did she have someone in the neighborhood?"

Wim peeled off three strips of bacon and laid them in the pan, flipping on the gas. He leaned over, peering at the low blue flame. He had to tug his robe down in back.

He said, "There's a cat clinic around the corner on Serenata Street. She used to take Ming over in one of those cat carriers, howling like a coyote. He hated the vet."

"You have any guesses about where Elaine might be?"

"What about her sister? Maybe she's gone down to L.A. to see her."

"The sister was the one who hired me in the first place," I said. "She hasn't seen Elaine in years."

Wim looked up sharply from the bacon pan and laughed. "What a crock of shit! Who told you that? I met her up here myself not six months back."

"You met Beverly?"

"Sure," he said. He took a fork and pushed the bacon strips in the pan. He went back to the refrigerator and got out three eggs. I was starving to death just watching this stuff.

He continued chattily. "She was maybe four years younger than Elaine. Black hair, cut gamin-style, exquisite skin." He looked at me. "Am I right or am I not?"

"Sounds like the woman I met," I said. "But I wonder why she lied to me."

"I can probably guess," he said. He tore off some paper toweling and folded it, putting it near the frying pan. "They had that nasty falling-out, you know, at Christmastime. Beverly probably doesn't want the word to get out. They positively shrieked and threw things, doors slamming. Oh my God! And the language they used. It was obscene. I had no idea Elaine could swear like that, though I must say the other one was worse."

"What was it about?"

"A man, of course. What else do any of us fuss about?"

"You have any idea who it was?"

"Nope. Frankly, I suspect Elaine's one of those women who's secretly thrilled with widowhood. She gets a lot of sympathy, tons of freedom. She has all that money and no one to hassle with. Why cut some guy in on a deal like that? She's better off by herself."

"Why quarrel with Beverly if that's the case?"

"Who knows? Maybe they thought it was fun."

I finished my coffee and got up then. "I better scoot. I don't want to interrupt your breakfast, but I may want to get back to you. Are you listed in the book?"

"Of course. I do work . . . tending bar at the Edgewood Hotel near the beach. You know the place?"

"I can't afford it, but I know which one you mean."

"Pop in and visit sometime. I'm there from six until closing every night except Monday. I'll buy you a drink."

"Thanks, Wim. I'll do that. I appreciate your help. The coffee was a treat."

"Anytime," he said.

I let myself out, catching a glimpse of Wim's break-fast mate, who looked like something out of *Gentlemen's Quarterly*: sultry eyes, a perfect jawline, collarless shirt, and an Italian cashmere sweater tossed across his shoulders with the sleeves folded into a knot in front.

In the kitchen, Wim had started to sing a version of "The Man I Love." His singing voice sounded just like Marlene Dietrich's.

When I reached the lobby I ran into Tillie, who was pushing a wire cart in front of her like a stroller. It was loaded with brown paper bags.

"I feel like I go to the market twice a day," she said. "Are you here looking for me?"

"Yes, but when you weren't in, I went up and had a brief chat with Wim instead. I didn't realize Elaine Boldt had a cat."

"Oh, she's had Ming for years. I don't know why I didn't think to mention that. I wonder what she did with him?"

"You said she had some carry-on luggage that night going out to the cab. Could it have been Mingus in the cat carrier?"

"Well, it must have been. It was certainly big enough and she did take the cat with her everywhere she went. I guess he's missing too. Isn't that what you're getting at?"

"I don't know yet, but probably. Too bad he's not suffering from some rare cat disease so I could track him down through a veterinarian someplace," I said.

She shook her head. "Can't help you there. He's in

good health, as far as I ever knew. He'd be easy to recognize. Big old gray long-haired thing. He must have weighed almost twenty pounds."

"Was he purebred?"

"No and she'd had him neutered early on, so he wasn't used for breeding purposes or anything like that."

"Well," I said, "I may as well start checking up on him too, since I don't have anything else at this point. Did you talk to the police yesterday?"

"Oh yes, and told 'em we thought the woman might have stolen Elaine's bills when she broke in. The officer looked at me like he thought I was nuts, but he did write it down."

"I'll tell you something else Wim brought up. He swears Elaine's sister Beverly was up here at Christmastime and got into a big fight with her. Were you aware of that?"

"No I wasn't, and Elaine never mentioned anything about it either," she said, shifting restlessly. "I've got to go in, Kinsey. I've got some sherbet that'll leak right out if I don't pop it in the freezer soon."

"All right. I'll get back to you later if I need anything else," I said. "Thanks, Tillie."

Tillie went on through the lobby, lugging her grocery cart and I went back to my car and unlocked it. I glanced over at the Grices' house as usual, my attention drawn almost irresistibly to that half-charred ruin where the murder had taken place. On impulse, I locked my car again and trotted up to the Snyders' front door. He must have spotted me through the window because the door opened just as I raised my hand to knock. He stepped out on the porch.

"I saw you coming up the walk. You're the one was here yesterday," he said. "I don't remember your name."

"Kinsey Millhone. I talked to Mr. Grice out at his sister's house yesterday. He said you had a key to his place and would let me in so I could take a look around."

"Yes, that's right. I got it here somewhere." Mr. Snyder seemed to frisk himself and then fished a key ring out of his pocket. He sorted through the keys.

"This's it," he said. He wrestled the key off the ring and handed it to me. "That's to the back door. Front's all boarded up as you can see. For a time there, they had the whole place cordovaned off 'til them fellas from the crime-scene unit could go over everything."

From the rear, I heard, "What is it, Orris? Who's that you're talking to?"

"Hold your horses! Y'old coot. I got to go," he said, his jowls atremble.

"I'll bring this back when I'm done," I said, but he was already lumbering off toward the back of the house in a snit. I thought she could hear remarkably well for someone he claimed was as deaf as a loaf of bread.

I cut across the Snyders' yard, the ivy rustling under my feet. The Grices' front lawn was dead from neglect and the sidewalk was littered with debris. It didn't look as if it had been cleaned up since the fire trucks departed, and I was crossing my fingers that the salvage crew had never gone in to clear the place out. I went around the side, passing the padlocked double doors that were slanted up against the house and led down into the basement. At the rear of the house, I climbed five crumbling steps onto a small back porch. The back door had a big glass window in the upper half and I could see into the kitchen through ruffled curtains that were dingy now and hung crookedly.

I unlocked the door and let myself in. For once, I was in luck. The floor was covered with rubble, but the furniture was still in place; kitchen table filthy, chairs knocked askew. I left the door open behind me and surveyed the room. There were dishes on the counter, shelves of canned goods visible through an open pantry door. I was feeling a faint thrill of uneasiness as I always do in situations like these.

The house smelled richly of scorched wood and there was a heavy layer of soot on everything. The kitchen walls were gray with smoke and my shoes made a gritty sound as I moved through the hallway, crushing broken glass to a sugary consistency underfoot. As nearly as I could tell, the interior of the Grices' house was laid out like the Snyders' house next door and I could identify what I guessed was the dining room just off the kitchen, with a blackened swinging door between. This must be the counterpart to the room in the Snyders' house that Orris had now outfitted as a bedroom for his wife. There was a half-bath across the hall, just the toilet and sink. The old linoleum had blistered and buckled, showing blackened floorboards beneath. The window in the hallway was broken now, but it looked out onto a narrow walkway between the two houses and right into May Snyder's converted bedroom. I could see her clearly, lying on a hospital bed that had been cranked up to a forty-five-degree angle. She seemed to be asleep, looking small and shrunken under a white counterpane. I moved away from the window and down the hall toward the living room.

The fire had leached the color out of everything and it looked now like a black-and-white photograph. The char patterns—like dark stretches of alligator hide—covered doorframes and window sashes. The destruction became more pronounced as I moved toward the front of the house. As I passed the stairs leading to the half-story up above, I could see where the flames had chewed the treads and part of the wooden banister. The wallpaper in the stairwell was as tattered and inky as an old treasure map.

I moved on, trying to get my bearings. There was an ominous patch of missing floorboards near the front door where I imagined Marty Grice's body had been found. Flames had eaten up the walls, leaving pipes and blackened beams exposed. Across the floor here, and extending back down the hall and up the stairs, there were irregular burned trails where an accelerant of some kind had been splashed. I bypassed the gaping hole in the floor and peered into the living room, which looked as if it had been outfitted with avant-garde "works of furniture" made entirely of charcoal briquettes. Two chairs and a couch were still arranged in a conversational grouping, but the fire had gnawed the upholstery right down to the bare springs. All that remained of the coffee table was a burned frame.

I went back to the stairs and crept up with care. The fire had taken the bedroom in whimsical bites, leaving a stack of paperback books untouched while the footstool nearby had been almost completely consumed. The bed was still made, but the room had been drenched by the fire hoses and smelled now of rotting carpet fiber and soggy wallpaper, mildewed blankets, singed clothing, and clumps of insulation that had boiled out through the fire-bared lath and plaster here and there. On the bed table, there was a framed photograph of Leonard with an appointment card for a teeth cleaning and exam tucked in the edge of the glass.

I moved the card aside, peering closely at Leonard's face. I thought about the snapshot I'd seen of Marty. Such a dumpy little thing: overweight, plastic eyeglass frames, a hairdo that looked like a wig. Leonard was much more attractive and in happier times presented a trim appearance, a rather distinguished face, graying hair, a steady gaze. His shoulders were rounded, possibly because of his back problems, but it gave the impression of something weak or apologetic in his nature. I wondered if Elaine Boldt had found him appealing. Could she have come between these two?

I put the picture back and picked my way down the stairs. As I moved along the hall toward the kitchen, I noticed a door ajar and I pushed it open gingerly. Before me yawned the basement, looking like a vast, black pit. Shit. In the interest of being thorough, I knew I'd have to check it out. I made a face to myself and went out to my car to get the flashlight out of the glove compartment.

13

The basement stairs were intact. The fire had apparently been contained before it reached this far. The damage to the rooms above seemed to be the result of some accelerant that had ensured at least a superficial combustion throughout the house. The beam from my flashlight cut through the dark, illuminating a narrow, moving path filled with things I didn't want to touch. I reached the bottom of the stairs. There wasn't a lot of headroom. The house was more than forty years old and the foundation was dank and spider-pocked. The air felt dense, like the atmosphere in a greenhouse, except that everything down here was dead, exuding that fenny perfume of old fire and old damp, abandonment and rot.

I angled the light along the joists, tracing the beams to the hole where daylight spilled down. Had the floor burned through and the body tumbled into the basement? I moved closer, craning to see better. The edges of the hole looked cut to me. Maybe the fire inspector had taken samples of the boards for lab tests. To my left, I could see the furnace, a silent squat bulge of gray, with sooty ducting extending in all directions. The floor was hard-packed dirt and cracked concrete, the entire space filled with junk. Paint cans and old window screens were stacked up under the stairs and there was an ancient galvanized sink in the corner, the pipes corroded away.

I toured the perimeter, poking the light into spaces where eight-legged creatures skittered away from me, horrified. Later I was glad I'd been such a conscientious little bun, but at the time, I only wanted to get out of there as quickly as I could. An empty house always seems to make those noises that have you wondering if an ax murderer is creeping through the premises in search of prey. I shone the flashlight over to the far wall where the stairs jutted up a short distance to the bolted double doors leading out to the side yard. Daylight slanted through the cracks but the smell of fresh air didn't sift down this far. I knew the double doors were padlocked on the outside, but the wood was old and crumbly and didn't seem that secure. From what Lily Howe had said, the burglar hadn't even bothered with breaking and entering. He'd marched right up to the front door and rung the bell. Had they struggled? Had he panicked when she opened the door and killed her instantly? The intruder might have been a woman, of course, especially if the weapon had actually been a baseball bat. Ever since Title IX, women have become more adept at the sportier side arms; death by discus, javelin, shot put, bow and arrow, hockey puck . . . the possibilities are endless, one would think.

I moved back toward the stairs shivering involuntarily

with the darkness at my back. I took the steps two at a time, nearly knocking myself out when I banged into a crossbeam. I cursed soundly to myself, bursting out of the basement and into the hall again as though pursued. Something feathery caught my eye and when I realized it was a delicate centipede whiffling down my front, I did this erratic quick dance step, brushing my shirt like I'd suddenly burst into flames. God, the things I do for money, I thought savagely. I went out the back door, locking it behind me, and sat down on the porch steps. My breathing finally slowed, but it took me a few more minutes to regain my composure.

In the meantime, I had a chance to check the back-yard. I don't know what I was looking for or what I thought I might find after six months. There were only overgrown bushes and weeds, a little orange tree crip-pled by the lack of water and covered with hard fruit turning brown because it hadn't been picked. The shed was one of those prefabricated metal jobs you can order through the Sears catalogue and put up anywhere. It was secured by a nice big fat padlock that looked sturdy enough. I cross the yard and inspected it. It was actually a simple warded lock I thought I could open in a few minutes, but I didn't have my little double-headed pick key with me and I wasn't crazy about the idea of stand-ing out there fiddling with a padlock in broad daylight. Better I should come back when the sun went down and find out what Grice or his nephew kept in there. Old lawn furniture was my guess, but one can never be sure.

I took the house key back to Mr. Snyder and then got in my car and headed over to the office. I let myself in and made a pot of coffee. The mail wasn't in yet and there were no messages on my machine. I opened the French doors and stood out on the balcony. Where the fuck was Elaine Boldt? And where was Elaine Boldt's pussycat? I was running out of things to do and places to look. I typed up a contract for Julia Ochsner to sign and stuck that in my out box. When the coffee was ready, I poured myself some and sat down in my swivel chair and swiveled. When in doubt, I thought, it's best to fall back on routine.

I made a long-distance telephone call to a newspaper in Boca Raton, and another call to a paper in Sarasota, placing classified ads in the personals columns of each. "Anybody knowing the whereabouts of Elaine Boldt, female, Caucasian, age 43 . . ." etc. "Please contact . . ." with my name, address, and phone number and an invitation to call collect.

That felt productive. What else? I swiveled some more and then put a call through to Mrs. Ochsner. She was on my mind anyway.

"Hello?" she said, picking up at long last. Her voice was tremulous, but held a note of anticipation, as though despite the fact she was eighty-eight, anyone might be calling and anything might come to pass. I hoped I'd always feel that way myself. At the moment, I wasn't so optimistic.

"Hi, Julia. This is Kinsey out in California."

"Just a minute, dear, and I'll turn the television down. I'm watching my program."

"You want me to call you back in a bit? I hate to interrupt."

"No, no. I'd prefer talking to you. Hold on."

Some moments passed and I heard the volume of the background noise reduced to silence. Julia was apparently creeping back to the phone as fast as she could. I waited. Finally she picked up the receiver again. "I kept the picture on," she said, out of breath, "though it just looks like one big blur from across the room. How are you?"

"Frustrated at the moment," I said. "I'm running out of things to do, but I wanted to ask you about Elaine's cat. I don't suppose you've seen Mingus in the last six months, have you?"

"Oh goodness, no. I hadn't even thought about him. If she's gone, he'd have to be missing too, I suppose."

"Well, it looks that way. The building manager here says she left that night with what looked like a cat carrier, so if she actually got to Florida, I'm assuming she'd have had him with her."

"I'd be willing to swear he never got here any more than she did, but I could check with vets and kennels in the area," Julia said. "Maybe she boarded him out for some reason."

"Could you do that? It would really save me some time. I don't know that you'll turn up anything, but at least we'll know we tried. I'm going to see if I can trace the taxicab she took and find out if she had the cat with her when she went to the airport. Did Pat Usher ever mention him?"

"Not that I recall. She's gone, you know. Moved out lock, stock, and barrel."

"Oh, really? Well, I'm not surprised, but I would like

to know where she is. Could you get her forwarding address from the Makowskis? I'll call you back in a day or two, but don't you dare call Pat yourself. I don't want her to know you're involved. I may need you to do some more snooping later and I don't want your cover blown." I added, "How are things with you otherwise?"

"Oh, I'm fine, Kinsey. You needn't worry about me. I don't suppose you'd consider a partnership after we wrap this one up.

"I've had worse offers in my day," I said.

Julia laughed. "I'm going to start reading Mickey Spillane just to get in shape. I don't know a lot of rude words, you know."

"I think I've got us covered on that score. I'll talk to you later. Let me know if you come up with anything startling in the meantime. Oh—and I'm shipping you a contract for your signature. We might as well do this right."

"Roger. Over and out," she said and hung up.

I left my vintage VW in the parking lot behind the office and walked over to the Tip Top Cab Company on Delgado. The business office is located in a narrow strip of stores best noted for their liquidation sales: a constant round of discount shoes, car stereos, lunch counters, and motorcycle shops with an occasional beauty salon or a "fast-foto" establishment. It is not a desirable location. The one-way street runs the wrong way. The parking lot is too small and apparently the owner of the building, while not exacting outrageous rents, is also content to let the premises languish under worn paint and tatty carpeting.

Tip Top was jammed between a Humane Society Thrift Shop and a Big N' Tall Men's Shop with a suit in the window designed for the steroid enthusiast. The office itself was long and narrow, partitioned across the middle with a plywood wall with a door cut into it. The place was furnished like some kid's hideout, complete with two broken-down couches and a table with one short leg. There were drawings and hand-lettered signs Scotch-taped to the walls, trash piled up in one corner, dog-eared copies of *Road and Track* magazine in an irregular tier by the front door. The bucket seat from a car was propped against the far wall, tan upholstery slashed in one spot and mended with old Band-Aids covered with stars. The dispatcher was perched on a stool, leaning one elbow on a counter as littered as a workbench. He was probably twenty-five with curly black hair and a small dark mustache. He wore chinos, a pale blue T-shirt with a faded decal of the Grateful Dead, and a visor that made his hair stick up on the sides. The shortwave radio squawked incomprehensibly and he took up the mike.

"Seven-oh," he said, his eyes immediately focusing on the map of the city affixed to the wall above the counter. I saw a butt-filled ashtray, an aspirin bottle, a cardboard calendar from Our Lady of Sorrows Church, a fan belt, plastic packets of ketchup, and a big penciled note that read "Has Anybody Seen My Red Flash Lite?" Tacked to the wall there was a list of addresses for customers who'd passed bad checks and those in the habit of calling more than one cab to see who could get there first.

There was a short burst of squawking and the dispatcher moved a round magnet from one part of the map to another. It looked like he was playing a board game all by himself.

He rotated toward me on the stool. "Yes ma'am."

I held out my hand. "I'm Kinsey Millhone," I said. He seemed slightly disconcerted at the notion of shaking hands, but he covered himself and gamely obliged.

"Ron Coachello."

I took out my wallet and showed him my identification. "I wonder if you could check some records for me."

His eyes were very dark and bright and his look said that he could check anything he wanted if it suited him. "What's the skinny?"

I gave him the *Reader's Digest* condensed version of the tale, complete with Elaine Boldt's local address and the approximate time the taxi'd been there. "Can you go back to January ninth of this year and see if Tip Top picked up the fare? It might have been City Cab or Green Stripe. I've got some questions for the driver."

He shrugged. "Sure. It might take a day. I got that stuff at home. I don't keep it down here. Why don't I give you a call, or better yet, you buzz me back? How's that?"

The phone rang and he took a call, logging it in. Then he took up the mike and pressed the button. "Six-eight." He cocked his head, listening idly. There was static, then a squawk.

"Four-oh-two-nine Orion," he said and clicked off. I gave him my card. He glanced at it with curiosity as if he'd never known a woman with a business card before.

The radio suddenly came to life again and he turned back, taking up the mike. I waved to him and he waved back over his shoulder at me.

I went through exactly the same procedure with the other two cab companies, which were fortunately within walking distance of one another. By the time I repeated the same story twice more I felt like I was suffering from a bad case of tongue flop.

When I got into the office, there was a message from Jonah Robb on my machine.

"Ah, yeah, Kinsey. This if Officer Robb on that . . . ah . . . issue we discussed. I wonder if you could give me a call sometime . . . ah . . . this afternoon and we'll find a way to get together on it. It's now Friday and it's . . . ah . . . twelve-ten P.M. Talk to you soon. Okay. Thanks." The number he left was for the police station, with the extension for Missing Persons.

I called him back, identifying myself as soon as he came on the line. "I understand you have some information for me."

"Right," he said. "You want to stop by my place later on?"

"I could do that," I said. I took down his address and we settled on 8:15, bypassing dinner. I didn't think we should get into any little domestic numbers at this point. I thanked him for his help and rang off.

I couldn't for the life of me think of anything else to do on the case that afternoon so I locked the office and headed for home. It was only 1:20 and since I'd accomplished so little at work, I felt morally obliged to be useful at my place. I washed the cup and saucer and plate that were sitting in the sink and left them in the rack to dry until I needed them again. I put a load of towels in the washer and then scoured the bathroom and kitchen sinks, took out the trash, and vacuumed a path around the furniture. Now and then, I actually move things and suck up all the woofies underneath, but today it was sufficient to have a few vacuum-cleaner tracks here and there and the apartment smelling of that peculiar cross between hot machine oil and cooked dust. I do love tidiness. When you live by yourself, you can either get all piggy or pick up as you go, which is what I prefer. There's nothing more depressing than coming home at the end of a long day to a place that looks like it's just been tossed by the mob.

I changed into my sweat pants and did three miles with energy to burn. This was one of those rare days when the run seemed inexplicably grand.

I came home, showered, washed my hair, napped, got dressed, sneaked in a little grocery shopping, and then I sat down at my desk and worked on note cards while I drank a glass of white wine and ate a warm, sliced-hard-boiled-egg sandwich with loads of Best Food's mayo and salt, nearly swooning at the taste.

At eight, I snatched up a jacket, my handbag, and my key pick and hopped in my car, heading over to Cabana Boulevard, the wide avenue that parallels the beach. I turned right. Jonah lived in an odd little tract of houses off Primavera, maybe a mile away. I passed the marina, then Ludlow Beach, glancing to my left. Even in the gathering twilight, I could identify the big trash bin where death had almost caught up with me two weeks before. I wondered how long it would take before I could pass that area without unconsciously glancing left, without taking just that one peek at the place where I'd thought my life would end. The beach seemed to glow with the last light of day and the sky was a silver gray layered with pink and lavender, deepening to dark magenta where the near hills intersected the view. Out on the ocean, the islands retained a magical hot gold light where lingering rivulets of sunlight formed a shimmering pool.

I went up the hill, passing Sea Shore Park, turning right then into a tangle of streets across the boulevard. The proximity to the Pacific meant too much chill fog and corrosive salt air, but there was an elementary school close by. For Jonah, who had had a family to support on a cop's salary, the neighborhood was affordable, but by no means grand.

I found the street number I was looking for and pulled into the driveway. The porch light was on and the yard looked well kept. The house was a ranch-style stucco painted slate blue with dark blue trim. I guessed there would be three bedrooms with maybe a patio in back. I rang the doorbell and Jonah came to the door. He wore jeans and an L. L. Bean Oxford-cloth dress shirt with a pink pinstripe. He carried a beer bottle loosely by the neck, motioning me in with a glance at his watch.

"God, you're prompt," he said.

"Well, you're not far away. I just live at the bottom of the hill."

"I know. You want me to take that?"

He was holding his hand up for the jacket, which I shed and handed to him, along with my handbag. He tossed both unceremoniously into a chair.

For a minute neither of us could think of anything to say. He took a sip of beer. I put my hands in my back pockets. Why did this feel so awkward? It reminded me of those awful junior-high-school dates where you got driven to the movies by somebody's mother and you never knew what to talk about.

I glanced around. "Nice house," I remarked.

"Come on. I'll show you around."

I followed while he talked back over his shoulder at me.

"It was a shit heap when we first moved in. The guy'd been renting it out to these weirdos who kept a ferret in the closet and never flushed the toilet because it was against their religious beliefs. You've probably seen 'em around town. Barefoot with these red and yellow rags around their heads and outfits like something out of the Old Testament. He said they hardly ever paid their rent, but every time he came to hassle them about it, they'd start humming and hold his hand, making significant eye contact. You want some wine? I bought you some high-class stuff—no twist-off cap."

I smiled. "I'm flattered."

We detoured into the kitchen and he opened a bottle of white wine for me, pouring it into a wineglass that still had the price tag on the bottom. He grinned sheepishly when he saw it.

"All I had was plastic glasses the kids used to use in the backyard," he said. "This is the kitchen."

"I kind of figured that."

It was a nice house. I don't know what I expected, but someone had made good choices. The whole place had a stripped-down feeling: bare, gleaming wood floors, furniture with simple lines, clean surfaces. Why had Camilla left this? What else was she looking for?

He showed me three bedrooms, two baths, a deck out back and a small yard enclosed by a vine-covered stucco wall.

"I'll tell you the truth," he said. "When she walked out, I packed up all her stuff and had the Salvation Army come take it away. I wasn't going to sit around looking at her little artsy-fartsy geegaws. I kept the kids' rooms intact. Maybe she'll get tired of them like she got tired of me and send them back, but *her* stuff I don't need. She was royally irritated when she heard, but what was I supposed to do?" He shrugged, standing there holding the beer bottle by the neck.

His face was beginning to take form now that I'd seen him twice. Before, I'd only registered qualities like "bland" and "harmless." I'd been aware of the extra weight he carried, a personality made up of something nice mixed with something droll. He was direct and I responded to that, but he also had a trait I'd noticed in certain cops before: bemused self-assurance, as if he were looking at the world from a long way back but it was all okay with him. Clearly, Camilla still loomed large in his life and he smiled every time he talked about her, not with affection, but to cover his wrath. I thought he needed to go through a few more women before he got down to me.

"What is that? What's that look?" he asked.

I smiled. "Beware of dog," I said. I'm not sure if I was talking about him or me.

He smiled too, but he knew what I meant. "I got the stuff in here."

He pointed toward the dining-room table in an alcove just off the living room.

I sat down in a hot circle of light, feeling like a glutton with a napkin tucked under my chin and a knife and fork upright in each fist. Along with the reports he'd Xeroxed, he'd also managed to slip me some duplicate photographs. I was going to see the aftermath of the crime with my own eyes and I could hardly wait.

14

I read through everything quickly, just to get an overview, and then I went back and noted the details that interested me. The official version of the story, as much as I knew it, and the interviews with Leonard Grice, his sister Lily, neighbors, the fire inspector, and the first police officer on the scene more or less spelled out events in the same way I'd been told. Leonard and Marty were scheduled to go out for their traditional Tuesday-night dinner with Leonard's widowed sister, Mrs. Howe. Marty wasn't feeling well and canceled out at the last minute. Leonard and Lily went out as planned and got back to the Howes' at about nine P.M., at which point a call was put through to Marty to let her know they were home. Both Mr. Grice and his sister spoke to Marty and she finally terminated the call in order to respond to a knock at the door. According to both Lily and Leonard, they had a cup of coffee and chatted for a bit. He left at approximately ten o'clock, arriving at Via Madrina twenty-some minutes later to find that his house had burned. By then, the blaze had been brought under control and his wife's body was being removed from the partially destroyed residence. He collapsed and was revived by paramedics at the scene. Tillie Ahlberg was the one who'd spotted the smoke and she'd turned in an alarm at 9:55. Two units had responded within minutes, but the blaze was such that entry couldn't be effected through the front door. Firemen had broken in through the rear, extinguishing the fire after thirty minutes or so. The body was discovered in the entryway and removed to the morgue.

Identification had been established by full-mouth X rays supplied by Marty's local dentist and through an examination of stomach contents. She'd apparently mentioned to Leonard on the phone that she'd fixed herself some canned tomato soup and a tuna sandwich. The empty cans were found in the kitchen wastebasket. The time of death had more or less been fixed in a narrow framework between the time of the telephone call and the time the fire alarm had been turned in.

I read through the autopsy report, mentally summing up a lot of technical details. The pathologist reported no carbon granules deposited in the bronchial passages or lungs and no carbon monoxide in the blood or other tissues. It was therefore determined that she had been dead when the fire broke out. Additional lab tests had revealed no alcohol, chloroform, drugs, or poisons in the system. The cause of death was attributed to multiple skull fractures apparently caused by repeated blows with a blunt instrument. Because of the nature of the wounds, the pathologist estimated the object to be some four to five inches in width, speculating that it might have been a two-by-four wielded with great force, a baseball bat, or some kind of club, possibly metal. The murder weapon had never been found. Unless, of course, it was a big old board burned up in the fire, but there was no evidence to support that possibility.

The arson investigators didn't seem to have any doubts that the fire had been deliberately set. Lab tests showed traces of kerosene in the floorboards. Charring patterns throughout the house had borne this out. They'd seen the same blackened splash marks and the same liquid trails that I'd spotted when I went through the house earlier. They'd also used some sophisticated methods of verifying the point of origin and the course the fire had taken as it burned. Leonard Grice had been questioned about the kerosene and he said he'd been storing a quantity in the basement for use in two lamps and a cooking stove that he and Marty took on camping trips, which accounted for the intruder's having had access to a flammable liquid. It looked as if the burglar had come with a weapon in hand, but without any intention of burning the place down. The fire was apparently an afterthought, a hastily concocted plan to conceal the bludgeoning of Marty Grice. So far there was nothing to suggest that anybody knew she'd be there, so the cops were having a hard time imagining that the murder had been planned in advance.

There was no evidence that a time-delay device had been employed, which ruled out the possibility that Grice had rigged the fire before he left. Grice's nephew, Mike, had been questioned and cleared. He'd been seen by numerous impartial witnesses in a hangout called

The Clockworks in downtown Santa Teresa during the critical period when experts speculated that the fire had been set. There were no other suspects and no other witnesses. Any other hard evidence including finger-prints had been destroyed by the fire. Elaine Boldt's name was on a list of persons to be interviewed and there was a note that Lieutenant Dolan had contacted her by telephone on the fifth. He'd made an appoint-ment to see her on January 10, but she'd never ap-peared. According to the information I had, she'd left for Florida the night before.

One entry, appearing in the middle of a typed report, interested me considerably. According to a deputy at the police department, a call had come in at 9:06 on the night of the murder that might well have been placed by Marty Grice. The caller had been female, in a panic, and had blurted out a cry for help before the phone went dead. Since the call was placed to the police station instead of 911, the deputy had no way of getting a fix on the address from which the call had originated. She'd made a note of it, however, and when the murder came to light, she'd reported it to Dolan, who had included it in his report. He'd questioned Grice about that too. If it *was* Marty, why would she have called the station instead of dialing 911? Leonard had pointed out that he and Marty had a telephone answering machine with a rapid-dial function. She'd entered the telephone numbers of both the police department and the fire department. The answering machine was found, undamaged, on a table in the rear of the hallway with the numbers neatly printed on the index. It looked as if Marty had had some warning of the attack and had been able to reach the telephone, calling out at least part of a distress signal before she'd been killed. If she'd actually placed the call, it pinpointed the time of death at 9:06 or soon afterward.

For a moment, I harbored the fleeting hope that Leonard Grice might still be implicated. After all, as nearly as I could tell, the police had only Lily's word for the fact that he was still at her place at that time. I was speculating that he might have come home early, killed Marty, started the fire, and then parked around the block until the appropriate moment to arrive. If he and his sister were in cahoots, they could both simply maintain afterward that he'd been with her. I was out of luck on that one. Three interviews down, there was a short paragraph detailing a conversation that Dolan had had with some of Lily's neighbors who'd stopped by unexpectedly at nine P.M. to drop off a birthday present. The husband and wife both reported independently that Leonard was there and hadn't left for home until approximately ten. The time was noted because they'd been trying to persuade him to stay for a television program that came on at ten. It turned out to be a rerun and since he was anxious to get home to his wife anyway, he'd left.

Well, shit, I thought.

Now, why was this making me feel so cross? Ah, well, because I wanted Leonard Grice to be guilty of something. Murder, conspiracy to murder, accessory to murder. I was fond of the idea for tidiness' sake—for statistical purposes, if nothing else. California has over three thousand homicide victims annually, and of those, fully two-thirds are slain by friends, acquaintances, or relatives, which makes you wonder if you might be better off as a friendless orphan in this state. The point is, when a murder goes down, the chances are good that someone near and dear has had a hand in it.

I thought about that, reluctant to give it up. Could Grice have hired someone to kill his wife? It was always possible, of course, but it was hard to see what he might have gained. The police, not being ignorant buffoons, had pursued the line as well, but had come up with nothing. No moneys unaccounted for, no meetings with unsavory characters, no apparent motive, no visible benefit.

Which brought me back to Elaine Boldt. Could she have been involved in Marty Grice's death? Most of what I'd learned about her cried out a big resounding "no." There really wasn't a hint that she'd been attached to Leonard romantically or any other way, except as an occasional bridge partner. I didn't think Marty Grice had been killed for messing up a small slam, but with bridge partners one can never tell. Wim Hoover had mentioned that Elaine and Beverly had quarreled about a man at Christmastime, but it was hard to picture the two of them in an arm wrestle over Leonard Grice. I kept coming back to the same suspicion—that Elaine knew something or had seen something related to Marty's murder and had left town to avoid the scrutiny of the Santa Teresa police.

I turned my attention to the photographs, neatly disconnecting my brain. I needed to know how things had looked and I couldn't afford to react emotionally. Violent death is repellent. My first impulse, always, is to turn abruptly away, to shield my soul from the sight, but this was the only tangible record of that event and I had to see for myself. I turned a cold eye to the first black-and-white photograph. The color pictures would be worse and I thought I'd start with the "easy" ones.

Jonah cleared his throat. I looked up.

"I'm going to have to turn in," he said. "I'm beat."

"You are?" I glanced at my watch, startled. It was 10:45. I'd been sitting there for more than two hours without moving. "I'm sorry," I said. "I had no idea I'd been here that long."

"That's okay. I got up at five this morning to work out and I need some shut-eye. You can take that stuff if you like. Of course, if Dolan ever catches you with it, I'll deny everything and throw you to the wolves, but aside from that, I hope it helps."

"Thanks. It's already helped." I shoved the photographs and reports into a big manila envelope and tucked that, in turn, in my handbag.

I drove home, disturbed. Even now, there was an image of Marty's body graven behind my eyes: features blurred by charring, mouth open, lying in a circle of ash like a pile of gray confetti. The heat had caused the tendons in her arms to retract, pulling her fists up into a pugilistic pose. It was her last fight and she had lost, but I didn't think it was over yet.

I willed the image away, running back over what I'd learned to that point. One little detail still bothered me. Was it possible that May Snyder had been accurate when she talked about the bang-bang-bang of hammering that night? If so, what in the world could it have been?

I was almost home again when I remembered the shed in the Grices' backyard. I slammed the brakes on and hung a hard left, heading across town.

Via Madrina was dark, heavily overhung by Italian stone pines. There wasn't much traffic at that hour. The night sky was hazy and though the moon was full, the light that filtered down was partially blocked by the condominium next door. I parked and got a little penlight out of the glove compartment. I pulled on a pair of rubber gloves and locked my car, heading up the Grices' front walk. I cut around the side of the house, my tennis shoes making no sound at all on the concrete.

In my jacket pocket I fingered the key pick, shaped like a flattened metal mandolin. I had a set of five picks with me on a key ring and a second more elaborate set at home in a nice leather case. They'd been given to me by a nonresidential burglar who was currently serving ten months in the county jail. Last time he'd been caught, he'd hired me to keep an eye on his wife, whom he believed was misbehaving with the guy next door. Actually, she hadn't been doing anything and he was so grateful for the good news that he gave me the key picks and taught me how to use them. He'd paid me some cash too, but then it turned out he'd stolen it and he had to ask for it back when the judge ordered him to make restitution.

It was chilly and there was a frisky little breeze making breathy sounds in the pine boughs. The house behind the Grices' had canvas awnings that were snapping like sails, and the hollow sigh of dry grass gave the whole enterprise an eerie ambiance of its own. I was feeling jumpy anyway because I'd just been looking at pictures of a charbroiled corpse, and here I was, about to do a little breaking-and-entering number that could land me in jail and cause my license to be snatched away. If the next-door neighbors set up a howl and the cops arrived on the scene, what was I going to say? Why was I doing it anyway? Ah, because I wanted to know what was in this wee metal house and I couldn't figure out how else to get in.

I fixed a tiny beam of light on the bottom of the pad-lock. In the diagram my burglar friend had drawn of a lock like this, there is a flat, hairpin spring that latches into notches in the shackle. Usually only the tip of the key actuates the spring, so it was a question of figuring out which of my picks would spread the latch apart, releasing the mechanism. In truth, I could have tried a paper clip with a small L bent on one end but that was the shape of the first pick I used and the padlock wouldn't budge. I tried the next pick which had an H shape in the point. Nope. I tried the third, working it carefully. The lock popped open in my hand. I checked my watch. A minute and a half. I get a bit vain about these things.

The shed door made a wrenching sound when I opened it and I stood for a moment, heart thudding in my throat. I heard a motorcycle putter past in the street but I didn't pay much attention to it because I had just understood Mike's custodial relationship to his uncle's property. In the shed, along with the stack of clay pots, the hand-push lawn mover, and a weed whacker were six shelves crammed with illegal drugs: Mason jars full of reds and dexies, yellow jackets, rainbows and sopers . . . along with some fat plastic packets of grass and hashish. Well, this was all just too yummy for words. I didn't think Leonard Grice was the druggist, but I was willing to bet money his nephew had invested heavily in this little portable Rexall. I was so enamored of my discovery that I didn't know he was behind me until he let out an astonished "hey!"

I jumped back and whipped around, suppressing a shriek. I found myself face-to-face with the kid, his green eyes glowing in the dark like a cat's. He was as startled to see me as I was to see him. Fortunately, neither of us was armed or we might have had a quick duel, doing each other a lot of needless harm.

"What are you *doing*?" he said. He sounded outraged, as if he couldn't believe this was happening. His Mohawk was beginning to grow out and the wind was making it lean slightly to the left like a field of tall grass in one of those old commercials for Kotex. He had on a black leather motorcycle jacket and a rhinestone earring. His boots were knee-high and made of plastic scored to resemble cobra skin only looking more like psoriasis. It was hard to take this lad seriously, but in some odd way I did. I closed the shed door and snapped the padlock into place. What could *he* prove?

"I got curious about what you were doing back here so I thought I'd take a peek."

"You mean you just broke in?" he said. His voice had that adolescent crack left over from puberty and his cheeks were hot pink. "You can't do that!"

"Mike, sweetie, I just did," I said. "You're in big trouble."

He stared at me for a moment, his expression blank. "You gonna call the cops?"

"Shit yes!"

"But what you did is just as much against the law as this," he said. I could tell he was one of those bright boys accustomed to arguing righteously with adults.

"Oh crap," I said, "wise up. I'm not going to stand out here and argue the California penal code with you. You're dealing drugs. The cops aren't going to care what I was up to. Maybe I was passing by and thought you were breaking in yourself. You're out of business, kiddo."

His eyes took on a shrewd look and he changed his tack. "Well now, wait a minute. Don't go so fast. Why can't we talk about this?"

"Sure, why not? What's to say?"

I could practically see his brain cells scurry around forming a new thought. He was no fool, but he still surprised me with the line he took. "Are you looking into Aunt Marty's death? Is that why you're here?"

Aunt Marty. Nice touch, I thought. I smiled briefly.

"Not quite, but that's close enough."

He glanced off toward the street, then down at the toe of his cobra boot. "Because I got something . . . you know, like some information about that."

"What kind of information?"

"Something I never told the cops. So maybe we could make a trade," he said. He stuck his hands in his jacket pockets looking back at me. His face was innocent, his complexion clear, the look in his eyes so pure I'd have given him my firstborn if I'd had one. The little smile that crossed his face was engaging and I wondered how much money he'd made selling dope to his high-school friends. And I wondered if he was going to end up with a bullet in his head for cheating someone higher up in the scheme of things. I was interested in what he had to say and he knew it. I had to make quick peace with my own corruption and it wasn't that hard to do. Times like this, I know I've been in the business too long.

"What kind of trade?"

"Just give me time to clear this stuff out before you tell anyone. I was about to lay off anyway because the narcs have some undercover agents at our school and I thought I'd cool it 'til the pressure's off."

We're not talking permanent reform here, folks. We're talking simple expediency, but at least the kid wasn't trying to con me . . . too much.

We looked at each other and something shifted. I knew I could rail and stomp and threaten him. I knew I could be pious and moralistic and disapproving and it wouldn't change a thing. He knew the score as well as I did and what we had to offer each other might not be a bad bet on either side.

"All right, you got it," I said.

"Let's go somewhere and talk," he said. "I'm freezin' my nuts off."

It bothered me to realize that I'd started to like him just a little bit.

15

We went to The Clockworks on State Street; he on his motorcycle, with me following in my car. The place is a teen hangout and looks like something out of a rock video; a long, narrow room painted charcoal gray with a high ceiling and the lighting done in pink and purple neon tubing. The whole of it resembles the interior of a clock in abstract and futuristic forms. There are mobiles looking like big black gears suspended from the ceiling, the smoke in the air moving them in slow circles. There are four small tables near the door and on the left are what look like shelves at chest height in a series of standing-room-only booths where couples can neck while drinking soda pop. The menu posted on the wall is larded with side orders like dinner salad and garlic toast that kids can snack on, paying seventy-five cents for the privilege of taking up table space for hours at a time. You can also buy two kinds of beer and a house chablis if you are old enough and have tangible proof. It was now nearly midnight and there were only two other people in the place, but the owner apparently knew

Mike and his gaze slid over to me appraisingly. I tried to look like I was not Mike's date. I didn't mind a May/December romance now and then, but a seventeen-year-old is pushing it some. Also I'm not clear on the etiquette of making deals with junior dope peddlers. Who pays for the drinks? I didn't want his self-image to suffer.

"What do you want?" he asked, moving toward the counter.

"Chablis is fine," I said. He was already pulling his wallet out so I let him pay. He probably made thirty grand a year selling grass and pills. The owner looked over at me again and I waved my I.D. at him casually, indicating that he could card me, but he'd be wasting a trip across the room.

Mike came back with a plastic glass of white wine for me and a soft drink for himself. He sat down, surveying the place for narcs in disguise. He seemed strangely mature and I was having trouble dealing with the incongruity of a kid who looked like a Boy Scout and behaved like a Mafia management trainee. He turned toward me then, resting both elbows on the table. He'd taken up a sugar packet from the container on the table and he tapped it and turned it restlessly, addressing most of what he had to say to the trivia question printed on the back.

"Okay. Here's what happened," he said, "and I'm tellin' you the truth. For one thing, I didn't stash at Uncle Leonard and Aunt Marty's until after she got killed and he moved out. Once the cops got done and everything, it occurred to me the utility shed was perfect so I moved some stuff in. Anyway, I went by the house the night she got killed. . . ."

"Did she know you were coming?"

"Nuh-uh, I'm getting to that. I mean, I knew they went out on Tuesday nights and I thought they'd be gone. Like, you know, if I was hard up and needed some bucks or something, I might cruise by and pick up some loose change. They kept cash around—not a lot, but enough. Or sometimes I'd take something I could unload somewhere else. Nothing they'd miss and nobody'd ever said anything about it so I figured they hadn't tipped to it yet. Anyway what happened was I went over there that night thinking the place would be empty, but when I got there the door was open—"

"The door was standing open?"

He shook his head. "I just kind of turned the knob and it was unlocked. When I stuck my head in I knew something weird was going on. . . ."

I waited, watching him uneasily.

He cleared his throat, looking over his shoulder at the front entrance. His voice dropped.

"I think the guy was still there, you know? The light was on in the basement and I could hear someone knocking around down there and there was this rug in the hall, like an area rug that had been thrown over something. I saw a hand sticking out with blood on it. Man, I took off."

"You're pretty sure she was dead at that point?"

He nodded, hanging his head. He ran a hand along the pink center divider of hair, looking off to one side. "I should've called the cops. I knew I should, but the whole thing really freaked me out. I hate that shit. And what was I supposed to do? I couldn't tell the cops anything and I didn't want 'em looking at *me*, so I just kept my mouth shut. I mean, I couldn't see what difference it made. I didn't see who did it or anything like that."

"Do you remember anything else? A car parked out front . . ."

"I don't know. I didn't stay long. I took one look at that shit and I was gone. I could smell all these gasoline fumes or something and . . ."

He hesitated briefly. "Wait a minute, yeah, there was a brown grocery bag in the hall too. I don't know what it was doing there. I mean, I didn't know what the fuck was happening, so I just backed away real quiet and came on down here and made sure people saw me."

I took a sip of wine, running through his story. The chablis tasted like fermented grapefruit juice. "Tell me about the grocery bag. Was it empty, full, crumpled?"

"It had stuff in it, I think. I mean, I didn't see anything in particular. It was one of those brown paper bags from Alpha Beta, standing just inside the door to the right."

"Did it look like she'd been shopping? Is that what you're trying to say?"

He shrugged. "It just looked like junk, I guess. I don't know. Maybe it belonged to whoever was down in the basement."

"Too bad you didn't make an anonymous call to the cops. Maybe they could have gotten there before the place went up in smoke."

"Yeah, I know. I thought about that later and I was bummed I didn't do that, but I wasn't thinking straight."

He polished off his soft drink and rattled the ice in the cup, tilting a cube into his mouth. I could hear the ice crunching in his teeth. It sounded like a horse chewing on a bit.

"Do you remember anything else?"

"No, I guess that's it. Once I figured out what was going on, I back out of there and hightailed it down here as fast as I could."

"You have any idea what time it was?"

"Nuh-un, not exactly. It was quarter of nine when I got here and it probably took me ten minutes on the motorcycle by the time I found a place to park and all like that. I had to walk the sucker for two blocks so nobody would hear me start it up. It was probably eight-thirty or something like that when I left Uncle Leonard's house."

I shook my head. "Not eight-thirty. You must mean nine-thirty. She wasn't killed until after nine."

He took the cup away from his mouth, looking at me with puzzlement. "She wasn't?"

"Your uncle and Mrs. Howe both say they talked to her at nine and the cops took a call they think was your aunt at nine-oh-six."

"Well, maybe I got it wrong then because I thought it was quarter of nine when I got here. I looked at the clock when I walked in and then I turned around and asked this buddy of mine what time it was and he checked his watch."

"I'll see if I can check that out," I said. "By the way, how's Leonard related to you?"

"My dad and him are brothers. Dad's the youngest in his family."

"So Lily Howe is their sister."

"Something like that."

The purple neon tubes began to blink out in succession and the pink ones went dark after that. The owner of the place called over to the table. "Closing down in ten minutes, Mike. Sorry to break it up."

"That's okay. Thanks, man."

We got up, moving toward the back entrance. He was not much taller than I and I wondered if we looked like brother and sister or mother and son. I didn't say anything else until we got to the parking lot.

"You have any theories about who killed your aunt?"

"No, do you?"

I shook my head. "I'd get that shed cleaned out if I were you."

"Yeah, sure. That was the deal, wasn't it?"

He got on his cycle and did one of those jumps to start it up. "Hey, you know what? I don't remember your name."

I gave him my card, then got in my VW. He waited to make sure I was under way and then he roared off.

I intended to let the case sit for the weekend because I wasn't sure what else to do. Saturday morning, I went over the police reports again at home, added note cards to my collection up on the bulletin board, but for the time being, I simply had to sit it out. Come Monday, it was possible I'd get a response from the classified ads I'd placed in the Florida papers or maybe I'd hear from the DMV in Tallahassee or Sacramento. I was still waiting for the plane ticket Julia Ochsner had mailed, hoping it would give me information of some kind. If nothing new came to light, I was going to have to start all over again and see if I could develop a few new leads. I still had local vets to check, trying to get a rundown on the cat.

I took a few minutes to do recalls on the three cab companies. The dispatcher I'd talked to at Green Stripe said he hadn't had a chance to dig through his files yet. The owner of City Cab had looked and found nothing and Ron Coachella at Tip Top wasn't in yet, but the dispatcher on duty said he'd be in shortly. So much for that.

I went down to the office. I hadn't meant to, but I couldn't help myself. I was feeling itchy and restless and dissatisfied. I don't like not succeeding at things. California Fidelity was closed for the weekend. I unlocked my door and picked up the mail that had been shoved through the slot. There was an envelope with Julia Ochsner's return address on it. I tossed it on the desk while I checked my messages. There was only one and it had apparently just come in.

"Hello, Kinsey. This is Ron Coachella over at the cab company? I got the information you want. Tip Top did pick up the fare at 2097 Via Madrina . . . let's see—on January the ninth at ten-fourteen P.M. Driver's name was Nelson Acquistapace at 555-6317. I told him you'd be in touch. I've got the trip sheet down here and you're welcome to stop by and pick up a copy so he can look at it. Twenty bucks might help his memory, if you know what I mean. Aside from that, just remember . . . 'If you want the top ride in town, call Tip Top,' " he sang and hung up.

I smiled, making a note of the driver's name and number. I put on a pot of coffee and opened the note from Julia. Her handwriting was of the old school, surprisingly firm, a clear cursive with grand flourishes and well-formed capital letters. She said she was enclosing the ticket, that the June rains were in full force, and that Charmaine Makowski had given birth to a nine-pound nine-ounce boy the night before and wanted everyone to know that she never expected to sit down again. Charmaine and Roland had not yet named the child but were accepting suggestions. Julia said that most of the appellations proffered so far were not fit to repeat. Julia thought it was a hoot. Warmest regards, said she.

I studied the ticket, which was tucked in a TWA folder. It looked like it had been generated at the Santa Teresa airport, round-trip from Santa Teresa to LAX and from LAX to Miami. All four flight coupons had been removed but the carbon remained. The ticket had been paid for by credit card. Four flight coupons torn out. Now, that was interesting. Had she come back to town at some point? If so, why had the carbon been down in Boca Raton in Pat Usher's trash? I went back to my list of travel agents, trying to figure out which one Elaine Boldt ordinarily used. I decided on Santa Teresa Travel which has an office within easy walking distance of the condominium on Via Madrina. It was just a guess, but I had to start someplace. I put in a call, but there was no answer and I assumed the agency was shut down for the weekend.

I made a list of leads to pursue on Monday. I checked the ticket again. I didn't see any indication that she'd had the cat in tow, but I wasn't sure how that worked. Did kitty cats get tickets like everybody else? I'd have to ask. There were some luggage tags still stapled to the back of the folder, but that doesn't mean much. At the airport here in town, you can pick up your bags without anybody verifying the tags. I remembered Elaine's luggage as fairly distinctive anyway, dark red leather with the designer signature writ large on the fabric trim. I'd priced that stuff once and decided to open a Keogh account instead.

I put a call through to Nelson Acquistapace, the Tip Top cab driver. He was home in bed with a head cold, but said Ron had told him what I needed. He had to pause and blow his nose twice. "Why don't you pick up the trip sheet and bring it over here? I'm on Delgado, just half a block down from Tip Top," he said. "I'll be outside around in back."

I picked up the trip sheet and arrived at his place by 9:35. I found him sitting in the backyard of a white frame bungalow tucked into a jungle of overgrown pittosporum bushes. He was lying on a hammock in a free-standing metal frame in the only patch of sunlight. The rest of the property was in deep shade, rather chilly and uninviting. He looked to be in his sixties, balding, heavyset in a dark green velour bathrobe. He had a square of pink sprigged flannel on his chest and he smelled like Vicks VapoRub. He'd set up a small metal table with his cold remedies, a box of Kleenex, an empty juice glass, and some crossword-puzzle books that I recognized.

"I know the guy who writes those puzzles," I said. "He's my landlord."

His eyebrows shot up. "This guy lives in town here? He's a whiz! He drives me up the wall with these things. Look at this one. Eighteenth-Century English Novelists and he includes all their books and their characters and everything. I had to go read Henry Fielding and Laurence Sterne and people I never even heard about just to get through the thing. It's better than a college education. I'm tellin' you. What is he, some kind of professor?"

I shook my head, feeling absurdly proud. You'd have thought Henry was a rock star the way this guy was reacting. "He used to run that little bakery at the corner of State and Purdue. He started doing the crossword puzzles when he retired."

"Is that right? You sure it's the same guy? Henry Pitts?"

I laughed. "Sure I'm sure. He tries those things out on me all the time. I don't think I've ever finished one yet."

"You tell him I want to meet him sometime. He has a very twisted sense of humor, but I like that. He did one all made up of botanical oddities, remember that? I went crazy. I was up all night. I can't believe the guy lives here in Santa Teresa. I thought he was a full professor at MIT, someplace like that."

"I'll tell him you said that. He'll be thrilled to hear he has a fan."

"You tell him to stop by here anytime. Tell him Nelson Acquistapace is at his service. He needs a cab, just call Tip Top and ask for me."

"I'll do that," I said.

"You got the trip sheet? Ron said you were looking for some lady who disappeared. Is that right?"

I took the trip sheet out of my purse and passed it over to him.

"Don't get too close, sweetheart," he said. He took a handkerchief out of his robe pocket and dusted his nose with it, honking into it before he put it back. He unfolded the sheet, holding it at arm's length to look at it. "I left my glasses inside. Which one?"

I pointed to the Via Madrina address.

"Yeah, I remember her, I think. I took her to the airport and dropped her off. I remember she was picking up that last flight from here to L.A. Where was she going, I forget now."

"Miami, Florida."

"Yeah, that's right. I remember now."

He was studying the trip sheet as though it were a pack of Tarot cards in some tricky configuration. "You know what this is?" He was tapping the paper. "You want to know why this fare is so high? Look at that. Sixteen bucks. It doesn't cost that much to go from Via Madrina to the airport. She made a stop and had me wait maybe fifteen minutes with the meter running. An intermediate stop. Now, just let me think where it was. Not far. Some place on Chapel. Okay, yeah, I got it now. That clinic down near the freeway."

"A clinic?" That took me by surprise.

"Yeah, you know. An emergency facility. For the cat. She dropped him off for some kind of emergency treatment and then she got back in the cab and we took off."

"I don't suppose you actually saw her get on the plane, did you?"

"Sure. I was done for the night. You can see for yourself from the trip sheet. She was my last fare so I went upstairs to the airport bar and had a couple of beers out on the patio. I told her I was gonna be up there so she even turned around and waved at me when she was walkin' out to the plane."

"Was she alone?"

"As far as I could tell."

"Had you ever picked her up before?"

"Not me. I just moved up here from L.A. in November last year. This is paradise. I love this town."

"Well," I said, "I appreciate your help. At least, we know she got on the plane. I guess now the question is, did she ever reach Boca Raton?"

"That's where she said she was going," he said, "though I tell you somethin'. With that fur coat, I told her she ought to head someplace cold. Get some use out of it. She laughed."

I felt myself hit the pause button mentally, a quick freeze frame. It was odd, that image, and it bothered me. I pictured Elaine Boldt with her fur coat and turban, on her way to warmth and sunshine, waving back over her shoulder to the taxi driver who'd taken her to the airport. It was disturbing somehow, that last glimpse of her, and I realized that until now I hadn't really pictured that at all. I'd been weighing the possibility that she was on the run, but in my heart of hearts, I'd pictured her dead. I'd kept thinking that whoever killed Marty Grice killed her too. I just couldn't figure out why. Now the uncertainty had crept in again. Something was off, but I couldn't figure out what it was.

16

Well, at least now I had a tiny mission in life. When I left Nelson, he was taking his temperature with a digital thermometer, confessing sheepishly a secret addiction to gadgets like that. I wished him a speedy recovery and hopped in my car, circling back around to Chapel.

The veterinary clinic is a small box of glass and cinderblock painted the color of window putty and tucked into the dead end formed when Highway 101 was cut through. I love that whole series of dead-end streets—relics of the town as it used to be, a refreshing departure from the pervading Spanish look. The small frame houses in that neighborhood are actually Victorian cottages built for the working class, with hand-turned porch rails, exotic trim, wooden shutters, and peaked roofs. They look like shabby antiques now, but it's still possible to imagine a day when they were newly constructed and covered with fresh paint, the full-grown trees no more than slender saplings planted in the midst of newly seeded lawns. The town then must have been dirt roads and carriages. I'm not above wishing more of it remained.

I parked in the lot behind the clinic and went in through the back door. I could hear dogs barking hoarsely somewhere in the rear; shrill cries for mercy, freedom, and relief. There were only two animals in the waiting room, both bored-looking cats who had formed themselves into bolster pillows. Their humans spoke to them in what was apparently cat-English, using high-pitched voices that made my own head hurt. Now and then when some dog set up a howl in the back, one or the other of the cats would appear to smile faintly.

There must have been two vets working because both cats got called at the same time and were carted off down the hall, leaving me alone with the receptionist behind the counter. She was in her late twenties, blue-eyed, pale, with an Alice-in-Wonderland blue ribbon across her straight blond hair. Her name tag read "Emily."

"May I help you?"

She spoke as though she'd never progressed beyond the age of six; a breathy, wispy tone, softly modulated, perhaps especially cultivated to soothe distressed beasts. Occasionally I run into women who talk like that and it's always puzzling, this perpetual girlhood in a world where the rest of us are struggling to grow up.

Dealing with her made me feel like a linebacker. "I wonder if you could give me some information."

"Well, I'll try," she whispered. Her voice was sweet and musical, her manner submissive.

I was going to show her the photostat of my P.I. license but I worried that it would seem brutal and coarse. I decided to hold off on that and whip it out if I had to turn the screws.

"Back in January, a woman brought a cat into the clinic for some kind of emergency treatment and I want to find out if she ever came back to pick it up."

"I can check our records if you like. Can you tell me the name, please?"

"Well, the woman's name was Elaine Boldt. The cat was Mingus. It would have been the night of January ninth."

Two patches of mild pink appeared on her cheeks and she licked her lips, staring at me fixedly. I wondered if she'd sold the cat to a vivisectionist.

"What happened?" I asked. "Do you know which one I'm talking about?"

"Well yes, I know which one. He was here for *weeks*," she said. Her speech had taken on a nasal cast, coming out through her nostrils now as though by ventriloquist. She wasn't exactly whining, but it was the tone of voice I've heard kids use in department stores when their moms accuse them of misbehavior and threaten to jerk their arms off. It was clear she was feeling defensive about something, but I wasn't sure quite what. She reached for a small tin box and walked her fingers through a file of index cards. She pulled out the record, snapping it onto the countertop self-righteously.

"She only paid three weeks' board and care and she never responded to any of our postcards or calls, so in

February the doctors said we'd have to make other arrangements because our space is so limited." She was really working herself into a snit here.

"Emily," I said patiently. "Is that your name, or somebody else's tag?"

"It's Emily."

"I really don't care where the cat is. I just need to know if the woman came back."

"Oh. No, she didn't."

"What happened to the cat? I'm just curious."

She stared at me for a moment, her chin coming up. She brushed her hair back across her shoulder with a flip of her hand. "I adopted him. He's really a fabulous cat and I just couldn't turn him over to the pound."

"That's fine. Hey, that's great. I've heard he was terrific and I'm glad you found a place for him. Enjoy. I will take your secret with me to the grave. If the woman shows up, though, would you let me know?" I put my card on the counter. She read it and nodded without another word.

"Thanks."

I went back to the office. I thought I better give Julia Ochsner a call and tell her I'd located the cat, thus saving her an unnecessary canvass of Boca kennels and vets. I left my car in the parking lot out back and came up the rear stairs. When I reached my office there was a man standing in the corridor, scribbling a message on a scrap of paper.

"Can I help you?"

"I don't know. Are you Kinsey Millhone?" His smile seemed superior and his attitude amused, as though he had a piece of information too precious to share.

"Yes."

"I'm Aubrey Danziger."

It took me a second to compute the name. "Beverly's husband?"

"Right," he said and then gave a little laugh in the back of his throat. So far, I didn't think either one of us had much cause for merriment. He was tall, maybe six foot two, with a smooth, thin face. He had very dark hair, lank, looking as if it would be silky to the touch, brown eyes, an arrogant mouth. He was wearing a pale gray three-piece suit. He looked like a riverboat gambler, a dandy, a "swell," if such persons exist in this day and age.

"What can I do for you?"

I put my key in the lock, opened the door, and went in. He followed, surveying the premises with the sort of look that told me he was pricing the furniture, calculating my over-head, estimating my quarterly taxes, and wondering why his wife hadn't hired a high-class outfit.

I sat down behind my desk and watched him while he took a seat and crossed his legs. Nice, sharp crease in the pants, nice narrow ankle, Italian leather pumps with a narrow polished toe. I caught sight of his snow-white shirt cuff, his initials—AND—in a pale blue mono-gram, hand-done no doubt. He was smiling at me faintly, watching me watch him. He took a flat cigarette case out of his inside jacket pocket and extracted a slim, black cigarette that he tamped on the case and then stuck in his mouth, flicking a lighter that shot out a jet of fire I thought might set his hair ablaze. He had elegant hands and his fingernails were beautifully manicured, with clear polish on each tip. I confess I was sure amazed at the sight, amazed by the scent of him that was wafting across the desk at me; probably one of those men's designer after-shaves called Rogue or Magnum. He studied the ember on his cigarette and then fixed me with a look. His eyes reminded me of hard clay, flat brown with no warmth and no energy.

I didn't offer him coffee. I pushed the ashtray toward him as I'd done with his wife. The smoke from his cigarette smelled like a smothered campfire and I knew it would linger long after he'd driven back to Los Angeles.

"Beverly got your letter," he said. "She was upset. I thought maybe I should drive up here and have a chat."

"Why didn't she come herself?" I said. "She can talk."

That amused him. "Beverly doesn't care for scenes. She asked me to handle it for her."

"I'm not crazy about scenes myself, but I don't see the problem here. She asked me to look for her sister. I'm doing that. She wanted to dictate the terms and I decided I should work for someone else."

"No, no, no. You misunderstood. She didn't want to terminate the relationship. She simply didn't want you to go to Missing Persons with it."

"But I disagreed with her. And I didn't think it was nice to take her money when I was ignoring her advice." I tried a noncommittal smile on him, swiveling slightly in my chair. "Was there something else?" I asked. I felt certain he was angling around for something. He didn't have to drive ninety miles for this.

He shifted in his chair, trying a friendlier tone. "I can tell we've gotten off on the wrong foot here," he said. "I'd like to know what you've found out about my sister-in-law. If I've pissed you off, I'd like to apologize. Oh. And you might be interested in this."

He took a folded paper from his jacket pocket and passed it across the desk to me. For a moment, I thought it was going to be an address or a telephone number, some scrap of information that might really help. It was a check for the $246.19 Beverly owed me. He made it seem like some kind of bribe and I didn't like that. I took the money anyway. I knew the difference whether he did or not.

"I sent Beverly a copy of my report two days ago. If you want to know what I've come up with, why not ask her?"

"I've read the report. I'd like to know what you've found out since then if you're willing to share that."

"Well, I'm not. I don't mean to sound surly about this, but any information I have belongs to my current employer and that's confidential. I'll tell you this much. I did go to the cops and they're circulating a description of her, but that's only been a couple of days and so far they haven't come up with anything. You want to answer a question for me?"

"Not really," he said, but he laughed. I was beginning to realize that his manner was probably born of discomfort, so I plowed ahead anyway.

"Beverly told me she hadn't seen her sister for three years, but a neighbor of Elaine's claims she was not only up here at Christmas, but the two had a knock-down-drag-out fight. Is that true?"

"Well, yeah, probably." His tone was softening and he seemed less aloof. He took a final drag of his cigarette and pinched the ember loose from the end. "To tell you the truth, I've been concerned that Beverly's somehow involved in this."

"How so?"

He'd stopped looking at me now. He rolled the tag end of his cigarette between his fingers until nothing was left but a small pile of tobacco shreds and a scrap of black paper. "She's got a drinking problem. She's had it for some time, though you'd probably never guess. She's one of those people who might not have a drink for six months, then . . . boom, she's off on a three-day drunk. Sometimes a binge lasts longer than that. I think that's what happened in December." He looked at me then and most of the pomposity had dropped away. This was a man in pain.

"Do you know what they quarreled about?"

"I have a fair idea."

"Was it you?" I asked.

He focused on me suddenly, with the first real life in his eyes. "What made you say that?"

"The neighbor said they probably quarreled about a man. You were the only one I knew about. You want to buy me lunch?"

We went to a cocktail lounge called Jay's just around the corner. It's very dark, with massive art deco booths in pale gray leather and black onyx tables that look like small free-form pools. The surface of them is so shiny you can almost see your reflection, like some kind of commercial for liquid diswashing detergent. The walls are padded with gray suede and the carpet underfoot is tricked out with matting so thick you feel as if you're walking on sand. The whole place comes close to a sensory-deprivation tank, dim and hushed, but the drinks are huge and the bartender puts together incredible hot pastrami sandwiches on rye. I can't afford the place myself, but it felt like the perfect setting for Aubrey Danziger. He looked like he could pay the tab.

"What sort of work do you do?" I asked when we were seated.

Before he could answer, the waitress appeared. I suggested two pastrami sandwiches and two martinis. That look of secret amusement returned to his face but he agreed with a careless shrug. I didn't think he was accustomed to women ordering for him, but there didn't seem to be any harmful side effects. I felt like this was my show and I wanted to work the lights. I knew we'd get blasted, but I thought it might take the high gloss off the man and humanize him some.

When the waitress left, he answered my question. "I don't work," he said, "I own things. I put together real-estate syndicates. We buy land and put up office buildings and shopping malls, sometimes condominiums." He paused, as though he could have said a lot more, but had decided that much would suffice. He took out his cigarette case again and held it out to me. I declined and he lit another slim black cigarette.

He tilted his head. "What'd I do that pissed you off? That happens to me all the time." The superior smile was back but this time I didn't take offense. Maybe that's just the way his face worked.

"You seem arrogant and you're way too slick," I said. "You keep smiling like you know something I don't."

"I've had a lot of money for a long time, so I feel slick. Actually, it amuses me to think about a girl detective. That's half the reason I drove up here."

"What's the other half?"

He hesitated, debating whether to say it. He took a long drag of his cigarette. "I don't trust Beverly's account of what went on. She's devious and she manipulates. I like to double-check."

"Are you talking about her transactions with me or hers with Elaine?"

"Oh, I know about her transactions with Elaine. She can't stand Elaine. She also can't leave her alone. Have you ever hated anybody that way?"

I smiled slightly. "Not recently. I guess I have in my day."

"It's like Bev has to know about Elaine and if she hears something good, it pisses her off. And if she hears something bad, she's satisfied, but it's never enough."

"What was she doing up here at Christmastime?"

The martinis arrived and Aubrey took a long sip of his before he answered. Mine was silky and cold with that whisper of vermouth that makes me shudder automatically. I always eat the olive early because it blends so nicely with the taste of gin.

He caught sight of the shiver. "I can leave the room if you want to be alone with that."

I laughed. "I can't help it. I never drink these things, but Jesus Lord, what a rush. I can already feel the hangover forming."

"Hell, it's Saturday. Take the day off. I didn't think I'd catch you in your office at all. I was going to leave you a note and then nose around seeing if I could find out something about Elaine myself."

"I take it you're as puzzled as everybody else about where she might be."

He shook his head slightly. "I think she's dead. I think Bev killed her."

That got my attention at any rate. "Why would she do that?"

Again, the long hesitation. He looked off across the room, checking the premises, doing some kind of mental arithmetic as though in placing a dollar value on his surroundings, he'd know where he stood. His eyes slid back to me and the smile hovered on his mouth. "She found out I'd had an affair with Elaine. It was my own damn fault. The IRS is auditing my tax returns from three years back and, like a fool, I asked Beverly to dig up some canceled checks and credit-card receipts. She figured out I'd been in Cozumel right at the same time Elaine went down there after Max died. I'd told her I was off on a business trip.

"Anyway, I got home from the office that day and she

flew at me in such a rage it's a wonder I got out alive. Of course, she'd been drinking. Any excuse to sock down the sauce. She took a pair of kitchen shears and stabbed me right in the neck. Caught me right here. Just above the collarbone. The only thing that saved me was my collar and tie and maybe the fact that I have my shirts done with heavy starch."

He laughed, shaking his head uncomfortably at the recollection. "When that didn't work, she got me in the arm. Fourteen stitches. I bled all over the place. When she drinks, it's like Jekyll and Hyde. When she doesn't drink, she's not too bad . . . bitchy and hard as nails, but she isn't nuts."

"How'd you get involved with Elaine? What was that about?"

"Oh hell, I don't know. It was stupid on my part. I guess I'd had the hots for her for years. She's a beautiful woman. She does tend to be self-involved and self-indulgent but that only made her harder to resist. Her husband had just died and she was a mess. What started out as brotherly concern turned into unbridled lust, like something off the back of a paperback novel. I've strayed before, but never like that. I don't shit in my own Post Toasties as the old saying goes. This time I blew it."

"How long did it last?"

"Until she disappeared. Bev isn't aware of that. I told her it was over after six weeks and she bought it because that's what she wanted to believe."

"And she found out about it this past Christmas?"

He nodded and then caught the waitress's attention, glancing over at me. "You ready for another one?"

"Sure."

He held up two fingers like a victory sign and the waitress moved over to the bar. "Yeah, she found out right about then. She tore into me and then jumped straight in the car and drove up here. I got a call through to Elaine to warn her, so we could at least get our stories straight, but I'm not really sure what was said between them. I didn't talk to her after that and I never saw her again."

"What'd she say when you told her?"

"Well, she wasn't crazy about the idea that Bev knew, but there wasn't anything she could do about it. She said she'd handle it."

The martinis arrived, along with the sandwiches, and we stopped talking for a while in order to eat. He was opening up a whole new possibility and I had a lot of questions to ask.

17

"What's your theory about what went on?" I asked when we'd finished lunch. "I mean, as nearly as I can tell, Elaine was in Santa Teresa until the night of January ninth. That was a Monday. I've tracked her from her apartment to the airport and I've got a witness who saw her get on the plane. I've got someone else who claims she arrived in Miami and drove up through Fort Lauderdale to Boca. Now, this person swears she was in Boca briefly and then took off again and was last heard from in Sarasota where she's supposedly staying with friends. I have a hard time believing that last bit, but it's what I've been told. When could Beverly have killed her and where?"

"Maybe she followed her to Florida. She was off on one of her benders just after New Year's. She was gone for ten days and came home a mess. I'd never seen her so bad. She wouldn't say a word about where she'd been or what had happened. I had a business deal I had to close in New York that week so I got her settled and then I took off. I was out of town until the following

Friday. She could have been anywhere while I was gone. Suppose she followed Elaine to Florida and killed her the first chance she had? She flies home afterward and who's the wiser?"

"I can't believe you're serious," I said. "Do you have any evidence? Do you have anything that links Beverly even superficially with Elaine's disappearance?"

He shook his head. "Look, I know I'm fishing here and I could be completely off base. I hope like hell I am. I probably shouldn't have said anything. . . ."

I could feel myself getting restless, trying to make sense of what he had said. "Why would Beverly have hired me if she'd killed Elaine?"

"Maybe she wanted to make it look good. The business about the cousin's estate was legitimate. The notice arrives in the mail and now what's she going to do? Suppose she knows Elaine is strolling along the bottom of the ocean in a pair of concrete shoes. She has to go through the motions, doesn't she? She can't ignore the situation because somebody's going to wonder why she doesn't show more concern. So she drives up here and hires you."

I looked at him skeptically. "Only then she panics when I say I'm going to the police."

"Right. And then she figures she better cover for that so she talks to me."

I finished my martini, thinking about what he'd said. It was very elaborate and I didn't like that. Still, I had to concede that it was possible. I made concentric circles on the tabletop with the bottom of my glass. I was thinking about the break-in at Tillie's place. "Where was she Wednesday night?"

He drew a blank. "I don't know. What do you mean?"

"I'm wondering where she was Wednesday night and early Thursday morning of this week. Was she with you?"

He frowned. "No. I flew to Atlanta Monday night and came back yesterday. What's the deal?"

I thought I should keep the details to myself for the time being. I shrugged. "There was an incident up here. Did you call her from Atlanta on either of those days?"

"I didn't call her at all. We used to do that when I was off on business trips. Talk back and forth long-distance. Now it's a relief to be away." He took a sip of his drink, watching me above the rim of the glass. "You don't believe any of this, do you?"

"It doesn't make any difference what I believe," I said. "I'm trying to find out what's true. So far it's all speculation."

He shook his head. "I know I don't have any concrete proof, but I felt like I had to tell someone. It's been bugging the shit out of me."

"I'll tell you what's bugging me," I said. "How can you live with someone you suspect of murder?"

He stared down at the table for a moment and the smile when it came was tainted with the old arrogance. I thought he was going to answer me, but the silence stretched and finally he simply lit another cigarette and signaled for the check.

I called Jonah in the middle of the afternoon. The encounter with Aubrey Danziger had depressed me, and the two martinis at lunch had left me with a nagging pain between the eyes. I needed air and sunshine and activity.

"You want to go up to the firing range and shoot?" I said when Jonah got on the line.

"Where are you?"

"I'm at the office, but I'm on my way home to pick up some ammo."

"Swing by and pick me up too," he said.

I smiled when I hung up the phone. Good.

The clouds hung above the mountains like puffs of white smoke left in the wake of a giant old-fashioned choo-choo train. We took the old road up through the pass, my VW making high-pitched complaints until I shifted from third gear to second and finally into first. The road twisted up through sage and mountain lilac. As we approached, the dark green of the distant vegetation separated into discreet shrubs clinging obstinately to the slopes. There were very few trees. Steep expanses of California buckwheat were visible on the right, interspersed with the bright little orange faces of monkey flower and the hot pink of prickly phlox. The poison oak was thriving, its lush growth almost overwhelming the silvery leaves of the mugwort which grew alongside it and is its antidote.

As we reached the summit, I glanced to my left. The elevation here was about twenty-five hundred feet and the ocean seemed to hover in the distance like a gray haze blending into the gray of the sky. The coastline stretched as far as the eye could see and the town of Santa Teresa looked as insubstantial as an aerial photo. From this perspective, the mountain ridge seemed to plunge into the Pacific, appearing again in four rugged peaks that formed the offshore islands. The sun up here was hot and the volatile oils, exuded by the underbrush, scented the still air with camphor. There were occasional manzanita trees along the slope, still stripped down to spare, misshapen black forms by the fire that had swept through two years back. Everything that grows up here longs to burn; seed coats broken only by intense heat, germinating then when the rains come again. It's not a cycle that concedes much to human intervention.

The narrow road to the firing range veered off to the left just at the mountain's crest, climbing at an angle through huge sandstone boulders that looked as light and fake as a movie set. I pulled into the dirt and gravel parking area and Jonah and I got out of the car, taking guns and ammo from the backseat. I don't think we'd exchanged six words the entire thirty-minute trip, but the silence was restful.

We paid our fees and tucked little wads of foam in our ears to muffle the sound. I had also brought along a headset, like earmuffs, for additional protection. My hearing had already sustained some damage that I was hoping wasn't going to be permanent. With the plugs in place, I could hear the air going in and out of my own nose, a phenomenon I didn't pay much attention to ordinarily. I like the quiet. At the core of it, I could hear my own heart, like someone thumping on a plaster wall two floors below.

We moved up to the range, roof overhead like a carport extending fifteen feet on either side of us. Only one man was shooting and he had an H&K .45 competition pistol that Jonah coveted the minute he laid eyes on it. The two of them talked about the adjustable trigger and adjustable sights while I inserted eight rounds of reloads into the magazine of my little gun. I inherited this no-brand semiautomatic from the very proper maiden aunt who raised me after my parents died. She'd taught me to knit and crochet when I was six, and when I was eight, she'd brought me up here and taught me to target-shoot, bracing my arms on a wooden ironing board that she kept in the trunk of her car. I had fallen in love with the smell of gunpowder when I first came to live with her. I'd sit out on her concrete porch steps with a strip of caps and a hammer, patiently banging away until each snapped out its load of perfume. The porch steps would be littered afterward with bits of red paper and gray spots of burned powder the size of the buckle holes in a belt. I guess she decided after two years of my incessant hammering that she might as well school me in the real thing.

Jonah had brought both his Colts and I fired a few rounds from each, but they felt like too much gun for me. The walnut grip on the Trooper handled like big hunk of petrified wood and the four-inch barrel made sighting a bitch. The gun bucked in my hand like that quick, automatic kick when a doctor taps on your knee, and each time the gun bucked a whiff of gunpowder blew back at me. I did slightly better with the Python, but it was still a distinct and familiar treat when I took up my .32 again, like holding hands with an old friend.

At five, we packed up our gear and headed over to the old stagecoach tavern, tucked into a shady hollow not far from the range. We had beer and bread and baked beans and talked about nothing in particular.

"How's your case going?" he asked me. "You turned up anything yet?"

I shook my head. "I've got some things I may want to talk to you about at some point, but not for now."

"You sound bummed out," he said.

I smiled. "I always do this to myself. I want quick results. If I don't get things wrapped up in two days, I get depressed. What about you? Are you okay?"

He shrugged. "I miss my kids. I used to spend Saturdays with them. It was nice you called. Gave me something to do besides mope."

"Yeah, you can watch *me* mope," I said.

He patted my hand on the table and squeezed it lightly. The gesture was brief and compassionate and I squeezed back.

I dropped him off at his place again at 7:30 or so and went home. I was tired of worrying about Elaine Boldt so I sat on the couch and cleaned my gun, taking in the smell of oil, finding it restful to dismantle and wipe and put it all back together again. After that, I stripped my clothes off and wrapped up in my quilt, reading a book about fingerprint mechanics until I fell asleep.

Monday morning, I stopped by Santa Teresa Travel on my way into the office and talked to an agent named

Lupe who looked like an interesting mix of Chicano and black, slim as a cat. She was in her twenties, with tawny skin and dark frizzy hair with a faint golden cast, cut close to the shape of her head. She wore small rectangular glasses and a smart navy blue pantsuit with a striped tie. I showed her the ticket carbon and told her what I was looking for. My guess was correct. Elaine had been a regular client of theirs for the past several years, though Lupe seemed puzzled by the carbon. She pulled the glasses down low on her nose and looked at me. Her eyes were a flat gold, like a lemur's, and it gave her face an exotic quality. Puffy mouth, small straight nose. She had fingernails that were long and curved and looked as tough as horn. Maybe she had been some kind of burrowing creature in another life. She pushed the glasses back into place again thoughtfully.

"Well, I don't know what to think," she said. "She always bought her tickets through us, but this one was purchased at the airport." She touched at one corner of the carbon, turning the ticket around so I could see the face of it. It reminded me of those teachers in grade school who somehow managed to read a picture book while holding it forward and to one side. "These numbers indicate that it was generated by the airline and paid for by credit card."

"What kind of credit card?"

"American Express. She usually uses that for travel, but I tell you what's odd. She'd made reservations for . . . wait a minute. Let me check." Lupe typed some numbers into her computer terminal, nails tap-dancing across the keys. The computer fired out line after line of green print-like tracers. She studied the screen.

"She was scheduled to fly out of LAX, first class, on February third, with a return 3 August and those tickets were paid for."

"I hear she left on the spur of the moment," I said. "If she set up the reservations over the weekend, she'd have had to go through the airlines, wouldn't she?"

"Sure, but she wouldn't just forget about the tickets she had. Hold on a sec and I'll see if she ever picked 'em up. She could have traded 'em in."

She got up and moved over to the file cabinet on the far wall, sorting through her files. She pulled out a packet and handed it to me. It was a set of tickets and an itinerary, tucked into a travel folder from the agency. Elaine's name was neatly typed across the front.

"That's a thousand dollars' worth of tickets," Lupe said. "You'd think she'd have called us and had 'em cashed in when she got to Boca."

I felt a chill. "I'm not sure she got there," I said. I sat for a full minute with the unused tickets in my hand. What was this? I reached into my purse and pulled out the original TWA folder Julia Ochsner had mailed to me. On the back flap, there were the four luggage tags sequentially numbered and still stapled firmly in place. Lupe was watching me.

I was thinking about my own quick flight to Miami, getting off the plane at 4:45 in the morning, passing the glass-fronted cases where abandoned suitcases were stacked.

"I want you to call Miami International for me," I said slowly. "Let's put in a claim for lost baggage and see if we come up with anything."

"You lost some bags?"

"Yeah, four of 'em. Red leather with gray fabric bindings. Hard-sided, graduated sizes, and my guess is that one is a hanging bag. These are the tags for them." I pushed the folder across the desk, and she wrote the numbers down.

I gave her my business card and she said she'd be in touch as soon as she heard anything.

"One more question," I said. "Was that flight she took nonstop?"

Lupe glanced at the carbon and shook her head. "That's the red-eye. She'd have had a layover and a change of planes in St. Louis."

"Thanks."

When I got to the office, the message light on my answering machine was blinking. I pressed the playback button.

It was my punker friend, Mike. "Hey, Kinsey? Oh shit, a machine. Well never mind. I'll call you back, okay? Oh. This is Mike and there's just something I want to talk to you about, but I have a class right now. Anyway, I'll call back later. Okay? Bye."

I made a note. The timer on the machine indicated that he'd called at 7:42 A.M. Maybe he'd try again at noon. I wished he'd left me a number.

I put in a call to Jonah and told him about Elaine's

stopover. "Could you circulate a description of her through the St. Louis police?"

"Sure. You think that's where she is?"

"I hope."

I intended to sit and chat with him, but I didn't have the chance. There was a quick knock and my office door flew open. Beverly Danziger stood on the threshold and she looked pissed off. I told Jonah I'd get back to him and hung up, turning my attention to Beverly.

18

"You goddamn bitch!" She slammed the door behind her, eyes flashing.

I'm not real fond of being addressed like that. I could feel the heat rise in my cheeks, my temper climbing automatically. I wondered if she was going to challenge me to hand-to-hand combat. I gave her a slow smile just to show her I wasn't impressed with the histrionics.

"What's the problem, Beverly?" I sounded like a smart aleck even to myself and I thought I better cast about for something to smite her with if she came flying across the desk at me. All I spotted was an unsharpened pencil and a Rolodex.

She put her hands on her hips. "What the fuck did you contact Aubrey for? How dare you! How fucking *dare* you!!"

"I didn't contact Aubrey. He got in touch with me."

"I hired you. *I* did. You had no right to talk to him and no right to discuss my business behind my own back! You know what I'm going to do? I'm going to sue you for this!"

I wasn't worried she'd sue me. I was worried she'd pull a pair of scissors out of her purse and cut me up like patches for a quilt.

By now, she was leaning over my desk, stabbing a pointed index finger into my face. Shout lines appeared to come out of her mouth as in a cartoon. She thrust her chin forward, cheeks pink, bubbles collecting in the corner of her mouth. I wanted to slap the shit out of her, but I didn't think it'd be smart. She was beginning to hyperventilate, chest heaving. And then her mouth began to tremble and the fiery blue eyes filled with tears. She sobbed once. She dropped her handbag and put both hands to her face like a little kid. Was this woman nuts or what?

"Sit down," I said. "Have a cigarette. What's going on?"

I glanced down at the ashtray. Aubrey's telltale pile of shredded tobacco and a scrap of black paper were still sitting in my ashtray. Discreetly, I removed it, tipping the contents into my trash. She sat down abruptly, her anger gone, some deep-seated grief having taken its place. I'm sorry to report myself unmoved. I can be a coldhearted little thing.

While she wept, I made coffee. My office door opened a crack and Vera peered in, making eye contact. She'd apparently heard the ruckus and wanted to make sure I was all right. I lifted my eyebrows in a quick facial shrug and she disappeared. Beverly fished out a Kleenex and pinched it across the bridge of her nose, pressing her eyes as though to extract the last few tears. Her porcelain complexion was now mottled and her glossy black hair had taken on a stringy look, like a fur muff left out in the rain.

"I'm sorry," she breathed, "I know I shouldn't have done that. He's making me crazy. He's driving me absolutely insane. He's such a son of a bitch. I just hate his *guts*!"

"Take it easy, Beverly. You want some coffee?"

She nodded. She got a compact out of her bag and checked her eye makeup, mopping up a run of mascara with Kleenex folded over her finger. Then she tucked the compact away and blew her nose without making a sound. It was just a sort of squeezing process. She opened her bag again and searched for her cigarettes and matches. Her hands were shaking, but the minute she got her cigarette lighted, all the tension seemed to leave her body. She inhaled deeply as though she were taking in ether before surgery. I wish cigarettes felt that good to me. Every time I've had a drag, my mouth has tasted like a cross between charred sticks and spoiled eggs. It's made my breath smell about that good too, I'm sure. My office was now looking like the fog had rolled in.

She began to shake her head hopelessly. "You have no idea what I've been through," she said.

"Look," I said, "just to set the record straight—"

"I know you didn't do anything. It's not your fault." Her eyes filled with tears briefly. "I should be used to it by now, I guess."

"Used to what?"

She began to fold the Kleenex in her lap. She recited

slowly, fighting for control, sentences punctuated with silences and little humming noises when the weeping closed off her throat. "He . . . um . . . goes around to people. And he tells them . . . um . . . that I drink and sometimes he claims I'm a nymphomaniac or he says I'm undergoing shock treatments. Whatever occurs to him. Whatever he thinks will do the most harm."

I wasn't sure what to do with this. He *had* told me she was an alcoholic. He'd told me she went off on three-day toots. He'd told me she attacked him with a pair of scissors and had possibly murdered her sister in revenge for an affair he was having with her. Now here she sat, sobbing her tiny heart out, claiming that he was the perpetrator of this weird pathological stuff. Which of them was I to believe? She composed herself, giving her nose the old silent squeeze. She looked at me, the whites of her eyes now tinted with pink.

"Didn't he tell you something like that?" she asked.

"I think he was just concerned about Elaine," I said, trying to hedge until I could decide what to do. "We really didn't discuss anything personal so don't worry about that. How did you find out he'd been up here?"

"Something came up in conversation," she said. "I don't even remember what. That's how he handles these things. He gives me these *clues*. He leaves the evidence around and waits for me to discover it. And if I don't stumble across it accidentally, he points me right to it and then sits back and pretends to be contrite and amazed."

I was just about to say, "Like his affair with Elaine,"

but it suddenly occurred to me that it might not even be true, or if true, that she might not actually know about it. "Like what, for example?" I said.

"He had an affair with Elaine. He was fucking around with my only sister. God, I can't believe he did that to me. I didn't doubt *she'd* do it. She was always jealous. She'd take anything she could. But *him*. I felt like such a fool. He was off balling her the minute Max died and I was such a dunce I didn't figure it out for years! It took me *years*."

She did one of those bubbling laughs, filled more with hysteria than mirth. "Poor Aubrey. He must have been at his wit's end trying to get me to pick up on that. He finally cooked up this absurd tale about the IRS auditing his taxes. I told him the accountant could take care of it, but he said Harvey wanted us to go through the canceled checks and credit-card receipts. So like a dodo I did it and there it was."

"Why don't you leave?" I asked. "I don't understand why you stay in a relationship like that." I always say the same thing. Every time I hear a tale like this. Drunkenness, beatings, infidelity, and verbal abuse. I just don't get it. Why do people put up with it? I had said it to Aubrey so I figured I might as well say it to her too. The marriage was a mess and regardless of where the truth lay, these two people were miserable. Was misery the point?

"Oh, I don't know. Part of it's the money, I guess." she said.

"Screw the money. This is a community-property state."

"That's what I mean," she said. "He'll walk away with half of everything I have and it just seems so unfair."

I looked at her blankly. "The money's yours?"

"Well of course it's mine," she said, and then her expression changed. "He told you it was his, didn't he?"

I shrugged uncomfortably. "More or less. He told me he put together real-estate syndicates."

She was startled for an instant and then she laughed.

She started to cough, patting her chest. She stubbed out her cigarette, pecking it in the bottom of the ashtray. Smoke was streaming out of her nostrils as though her brain had caught fire. She was shaking her head, smile fading. "Sorry, but that's a new one on me. I should have guessed. What else did he say?"

I held a hand up in protest. "Hey," I said. "Enough. I don't want to play this game. I don't know what your problems are and I don't care. . . ."

"You're right, you're right. God, we must seem like lunatics to you. I'm sorry you got sucked in. It's not your concern. It's mine. How much do I owe you for your time?" She was rooting through her handbag for her checkbook and her famous rosewood pen-and-pencil set.

I could feel my temper on the rise again.

"I don't want any money from you. Don't be absurd. Why don't you give me some straight answers for a change?"

She blinked at me, the china blue eyes glazing over like ice on a pond. "About what?"

"Elaine's neighbor claims you were up here at Christmas and the two of you had a big fight. You told me you hadn't seen her for years. Now which is it?"

She stalled, reaching for another cigarette so she'd have time to frame a reply.

I headed her off. "Come on, Beverly. Just tell me the truth. Were you up here or not?"

She took out a packet of matches and removed a match, scratching it repeatedly across the packet without effect. She tossed that one, a dud apparently, into the ashtray and took out a second match. This time, she managed to light her cigarette. "I did come up," she said carefully. She tapped the lighted cigarette on the lip of the ashtray as though to remove an ash when there was none yet.

I was going to scream if she did any more shit with that cigarette. "Did you quarrel with her or didn't you?"

She switched to her officious tone, mouth going all prim. "Kinsey, I had just found out about the affair. Of course we quarreled. That's exactly what Aubrey had in mind, I'm sure. What would you have done?"

"What difference does it make? I'm not married to him so who gives a damn what I'd have done! I want to know why you lied to me."

She stared at the desk, her face taking on a stubborn look.

I tried another tack. "Why'd you call me off? Why wouldn't you let me contact the police?"

She smoked for a moment and I thought at first she didn't intend to answer that question either. "I was worried he'd done something."

I stared a her.

She caught my look and leaned forward earnestly.

"He's crazy. He is a truly crazy man and I was worried that he'd . . . I don't know . . . I suppose I was worried he'd killed her."

"All the more reason to call the police. Isn't it?"

"You don't understand. I couldn't turn the police loose on this. That's why I hired you in the first place. When this whole business came up about the will, I didn't think anything of it. It was such a minor matter. I just assumed she'd signed the paper and sent it to the attorney. And then when I realized no one had heard from her, it occurred to me that something might be wrong. I don't even know what I thought it was."

"But when I mentioned she might be dead, the penny dropped, right?" I sounded bored. I sounded contemptuous too.

She shifted uncomfortably. "Before that. I guess I'd just never really put it in words until you said it and then I realized I better reassess the situation before I agreed to anything."

"What makes you think Aubrey's involved?"

"That day . . . when I drove up here and Elaine and I had words . . . she told me that the affair had been going on for years. She'd finally figured out that Aubrey was a psychopath and she was trying to break it off." She paused and the blue eyes came up to mine. "You don't understand about Aubrey yet. You don't know what he's like. You just don't *leave* him. You just don't break it off. I've threatened to do that myself. Don't think it hasn't occurred to me. But I'd never make it. I don't know what he'd do, but I'd never get away from him. Never.

He'd follow me to the ends of the earth and bring me back, only then he'd really make me pay."

"Bev, I've got to tell you I'm having trouble with this," I said.

"That's because you fell for it. He came waltzing up here and he laid a number on you. He conned you good and now you can't bear to admit you've been had. He's done it before. He does it to everyone. The man is certifiably insane. He was in Camarillo for years until Reagan became governor. Remember that? He cut the state budget and turned them all out in the streets. Aubrey Danziger came home at that point and my life has been hell ever since."

I picked up a pencil and tapped on the edge of the desk, then tossed it aside. "I'll tell you the truth. I want to find Elaine. That's all I want to do. I'm like a terrier pup. Somebody tells me to do something and it gets done. I'll worry the damn thing to death. I'm going to find out what happened to her and where she's been all these months. And you better hope it doesn't lead back to you."

She got up. She picked up her bag and leaned on my desk. "And you better hope it doesn't lead back to Aubrey, my dear!" she spat.

And then she was gone, leaving behind her the faint aura of whiskey that I'd just caught on her breath.

I hauled out my typewriter and wrote a detailed report for Julia, itemizing expenses for the last couple of days. I needed time to assimilate what Beverly had told me about Aubrey. It was like the paradox of the jungle tribes where one always lies and the other always tells the truth. How could one ever determine which was which? Aubrey had told me Beverly was Mr. Hyde when she drank. She had told me he was certifiably mad, but she'd apparently been drinking when she said so. I hadn't the faintest idea which of them was on the level and I wasn't sure how to find out. I didn't even know if it mattered. Was Elaine Boldt really dead? It had certainly crossed my mind more than once, but I hadn't imagined that Beverly or Aubrey might be at the heart of it. I'd been looking in the opposite direction, assuming somehow that Elaine's disappearance was linked to the murder of Marty Grice. Now I'd have to go back and take another look.

I went home at lunchtime and did a run. I knew I was just treading water at this point, but in some ways I had to wait it out. Something would break. Some piece of information would come to light. In the meantime, I was feeling tense and I needed to work that off. The run was a bad one and that put me in a foul mood. I picked up a stitch in my side at the end of the first mile. I thought I could shake it. I tried digging my fingers in, bending at the waist, thinking that if it was a muscle cramp it might ease. No deal. Then I tried expelling breath after breath, again bending from the waist. The pain was no worse, but it didn't go away either. Finally, I slowed to a walk until it subsided, but the minute I started to jog again, my side seized up, stopping me in my tracks. I'd reached the turnaround by then, but running seemed futile so I walked the entire mile and a half back to my place, cursing to myself. I hadn't even broken a sweat, and my frustration, instead of dissipating, had doubled.

I showered and dressed again. I didn't want to go back to the office, but I forced myself. I was going to have to start all over again, go back to the beginning and cast a new set of lines in the water to see if I could get a bite somewhere. I had just about used up my whole bag of tricks, but there had to be something else.

When I let myself into the office, I saw the message light blinking on my machine. I opened the French doors to let some air in and then punched playback.

"Hi, Kinsey. This is Lupe, over at Santa Teresa Travel. It looks like you hit the jackpot on that luggage trace. I put a call through to Baggage Claim at TWA and had the agent check it out. The four bags were sitting right there. He said he could put 'em on a plane this afternoon if you like. Could you call me back and let me know what you want to do?"

I snapped the machine off and shook both fists in the air, mouthing "All riiight!" to myself with a big grin. I put a call through to Jonah first and told him what was going on. I was jazzed. It was the first good news I'd had since I tracked down the cat. "What should I do, Jonah? Am I going to need some kind of court order to open those bags?"

"Screw that. Look, you have the claim tags, don't you?"

"Sure, I've got 'em right here."

"Then go down to Florida and pick up the bags."

"Why not just have them flown out?"

"Suppose she's *in* one," he said.

That certainly conjured up an image I didn't like. I could feel myself squirm. "Don't you think someone would have *noticed* by now? You know, an odor . . . something dripping out the side?"

"Hey, we found a body once had been in the trunk of a car for six months. Someone had shoved a high heel down some whore's throat and she ended up mummified. Don't ask me how or why, but she didn't decompose at all. She just dried up. She looked like a big leather doll."

"Maybe I'll get on a plane," I said.

By ten o'clock that night, I was back in the air again.

19

It was drizzling and the temperature was already in the seventies at 4:56 A.M. EST when we touched down. It was still dark outside, but the airport was filled with the flat light and artificial chill of a space station orbiting a hundred and ten miles out. Dawn travelers walked purposefully down deserted corridors while doors shushed open and shut automatically and the paging system seemed to drone on and on without hope of response. For all I knew, the whole operation was mechanical, running itself at that hour without any help from humankind.

The TWA baggage-service office didn't open until nine, so I had time to kill. I hadn't brought any luggage of my own, just a big canvas bag where I kept a toothbrush and all the odds and ends of ordinary life, including clean underpants. I never go anywhere without a toothbrush and clean underpants. I went into the women's room to freshen up. I washed my face and ran my wet fingers through my hair, noting how sallow my skin looked with the fluorescent lights overhead. There was a woman behind me, changing the diaper on one of those oversized babies who looks like a solemn adult with flushed cheeks. The child kept his eyes pinned on me gravely while his mother attended to him. Sometimes cats look at me that way, as though we're foreign agents sending silent signals to one another in an out of the way meeting place.

I paused at a stand and picked up a newspaper. There was a coffee shop open and I bought scrambled eggs, bacon, toast, and juice, taking my time about breakfast while I read a human-interest story about a man who'd left all his money to a mynah bird. I can't cope with the front section before seven A.M.

At quarter to nine, having walked the airport from end to end twice, I stationed myself near Baggage Claim with a portable cart I'd rented for a buck. I could see Elaine's bags, neatly lined up at on end of the locked glass-fronted cabinets. It looked as if someone had hauled them out from the bottom of the pile in readiness. Finally, a middle-aged man in a TWA uniform, with a big set of jangling keys, unlocked the small cubicle and started turning on lights. It looked like the opening curtain of a one-act play with a modest set.

I presented myself and the baggage-claim tags and then followed him out to the storage cabinets and waited while he extracted the suitcases and stacked them on the cart. I expected him to ask for identification, but apparently he didn't care who I was. Maybe abandoned bags are like litters of unwanted kittens. He was just grateful to have someone take them off his hands.

When the Penny-Car Rental desk opened, I rented a

compact car. I had given Julia a call the night before so she knew I was flying in. All I needed to do now was find the highway again and drive north. Once outside, I pushed the cart toward the slot where the rental car was parked. The drizzle settled on my skin like a layer of silk. The morning air was hot and close, smelling of rain and jet exhaust. I loaded the bags in the trunk of the car and headed toward Boca. It wasn't until I reached the condominium parking lot, unloading the suitcases one by one, that I realized all four were locked and I had no key. Well, how very cute. Maybe Julia would have a plan. I lugged them over to the elevator and went up to the third floor, hauling them to Julia's front door in two trips.

I knocked and waited a long interval while Julia thumped her way to the front door with her cane, calling encouragement.

"I'm coming. Don't give up. Six more feet to go and I'm bearing down hard."

On my side of the door, I smiled, peering over at Elaine's apartment. There was no sign of life. Even the welcome mat had been taken inside or thrown out, leaving a square of fine sand that had filtered through the bristles.

Julia's door opened. The dowager's hump sat between her shoulder blades like a weight, forcing her to bend with its burden. She seemed to be staring at my waist, tilting her head of dandelion fuzz to one side so she could peer up at me. Her skin seemed as sheer as rubber, pulled over her hands like surgical gloves. I could see veins and broken capillaries, her knuckles as knotted as rope. Age was making her transparent, crushing her from both ends like a can of soda pop.

"Well, Kinsey! I knew that was you. I've been awake since six this morning, looking forward to this. Come on in."

She hobbled to one side, making way for me. I set the four suitcases inside the door and closed it after me. She tapped one with her cane. "I recognize those."

"Unfortunately, they're locked."

Each of the four bags apparently had a combination lock, the numbers arranged on a dial embedded in the metal catch.

"We'll have to do some detective work," she said with satisfaction. "You want coffee first? How was your flight?"

"I'd love some," I said. "The flight wasn't bad."

Julia's apartment was crowded with antiques: a peculiar mix of Victorian pieces and Oriental furnishings. There was a huge carved cherry sideboard with a marble top, a black horsehair sofa, an intricate ivory screen, jade figures, a platform rocker, two cinnabar lamps, Persian rugs, a pier-glass mirror in a dark mahogany frame, a piano with a fringed shawl across the top, lace curtains, wall hangings of embroidered silk. A big portable television set with a twenty-five-inch screen loomed on the far side of the room surrounded by family photographs in heavy silver frames. The television set was turned off, its blank gray face oddly compelling in a room so filled with memorabilia. The only sound in the apartment was the steady ticking of a grandfather clock that sounded like someone tapping on Formica with a set of drumsticks.

I moved out to the kitchen, poured coffee for us both, and carried it back to the living room, the cups rattling slightly in the saucers like the tremor of a minor California earthquake. "Are these family antiques? Some of the pieces are beautiful."

Julia smiled, waggling her cane. "I'm the last person alive in my family so I've inherited all this by default. I was the youngest in a family of eleven children and my mother said I was fractious. She always swore I'd never get a thing, but I just kept my mouth shut and waited it out. Sure enough, she died, my father died. I had eight sisters and two brothers and they all died. Little by little, it all drifted down to me, though I hardly have a place to put anything at this point. Eventually you have to give it all away. You start with a ten-room house and finally you find yourself stranded in a nursing home with space for one night table and a candlestick. Not that I intend to let that happen to me."

"You've got a ways to go yet anyway from what I can see."

"Well, I hope so. I'm going to hold out as long as I can and then I'll lock and bar the door and do myself in, if nature doesn't take me first. I'm hoping I'll die in my bed one night. It's the bed I was born in and I think it'd be nice to end up there. Have you a large family?"

"No, just me. I was raised by an aunt, but she died ten years ago."

"Well then, we're in the same boat. Restful, isn't it."

"That's one way to put it," I said.

"I came from a family of shriekers and face slappers. They all threw things. Glasses, plates, tables, chairs, anything that came to hand. The air was always filled with flying missiles—objects rocketing from one end of the room to the other with howls on contact. This was mostly girls, you know, but all of us had deadly aim. I had a sister knock me out of my high chair once with a grapefruit thrown like a curve ball, oatmeal flying everywhere. Eulalie, her name was. Now that I look back on it, I see we were common as mud, but effective. We all got what we wanted in life and no one ever accused us of being helpless or fainthearted. Well now. Let's tackle those bags. If worse comes to worst, we can always hurl them off the balcony. I'm sure they'll open when they hit the pavement down below."

We approached the problem as though it were a code to be broken. Julia's theory, which proved to be correct, was that Elaine would have come up with a combination of numbers she already had in her life somewhere. Her street address, zip code, telephone number, social security, birthdate. Each of us chose one group of digits and started to work on separate bags. I hit it the third time around with the last four numbers on her social-security card. All four suitcases were coded with the same number, which simplified the task.

We opened them on the living-room floor. They were filled with exactly what one would expect: clothing, cosmetics, costume jewelry, shampoo, deodorant, slippers, bathing suit, but packed in a jumble the way they do in movies when the wife leaves the husband in the middle of a vicious snit. The hangers were still on the hanging clothes, garments folded over and bunched in, with the shoes tossed on top. It looked as if drawers had been turned upside down and emptied into the largest of the bags. Julia had hobbled over to the rocker and she sat there now, propping herself up with her cane as though she were a unwieldy plant. I sat down on the horsehair sofa, staring at the suitcases. I looked at Julia uneasily.

"I don't like this," I said. "From what I know of Elaine, she was almost compulsively neat. You should have seen the way she left her place . . . everything just so . . . clean, tidy, tucked in. Does she strike you as the type who'd pack this way?"

"Not unless she were in a fearful hurry," Julia said.

"Well actually, she might have been, but I still don't think she'd pack like this."

"What's on your mind? What do you think it means?"

I told her about the double set of plane tickets and the layover in St. Louis and any other facts I thought might pertain. It was nice to have someone to try ideas on. Julia was bright and she liked to pick at knots the same way I did.

"I'm not convinced she ever got here," I said. "We only have Pat Usher's word for it anyway and neither of us set much store by that. Maybe she got off the plane in St. Louis for some reason."

"Without her luggage? And you said she left her passport behind too, so what could she have done with herself?"

"Well, she did have that lynx coat," I said, "which she could have pawned or sold." I had one of those little nagging thoughts on the subject, but I couldn't bring it into focus for the moment.

Julia waved dismissively. "I don't believe she'd sell her coat, Kinsey. Why would she do that? She has lots of money. Stocks, bonds, mutual funds. She wouldn't need to pawn anything."

I chewed on that one. She was right, of course. "I keep wondering if she's dead. The luggage got here, but maybe she never made it. Maybe she's in a morgue somewhere with a tag on her toe."

"You think someone lured her off the plane and killed her?"

I wagged my head back and forth, not wholly convinced. "I don't know. It's possible. It's also possible she never made the trip at all."

"I thought you told me someone saw her get on the plane. The cab driver you talked about."

"That wasn't really a positive identification. I mean, a cab driver picks up a fare and the woman claims she's Elaine Boldt. He never saw her before in his life, so who knows? He just takes her word for it, like we all do. How do you know I'm Kinsey Millhone? Because I say I am. Someone might have posed as her just to establish a trail."

"What for?"

"Well now, *that* I don't know. We've got a couple of women who might have pulled it off. Her sister Beverly for one."

"And Pat Usher for another," Julia said.

"Pat did benefit from Elaine's being off the scene. She gets a rent-free condo in Boca for months."

"That's the first time I ever heard of anyone murdered for room and board," she said tartly.

I smiled. I knew we were floundering, but maybe we'd stumble onto something. I could have used a break at that point. "Did Pat ever leave that forwarding address she promised?"

Julia shook her head. "Charmaine says she left one, but it was humbug. She packed and took off the same day you were here and nobody's seen her since."

"Oh shit. I knew she'd do that."

"Well, it wasn't anything you could have prevented," she said charitably.

I leaned my head back against the sofa frame, playing mind games. "It could have been Beverly too, you know. Maybe Bev bumped her off in the ladies' room at the St. Louis airport."

"Or killed her in Santa Teresa and impersonated her from that point on. Maybe she was the one who packed the bags and took the plane."

"Try it the other way," I said. "Think about Pat. I mean, what if Pat Usher were a stranger to Elaine, just someone she met on the plane. Maybe they started talking and Pat realized—" I dropped that idea when I saw the expression on Julia's face. "It does sound pretty lame," I said.

"Oh, well—no harm done in speculating. Maybe Pat knew her in Santa Teresa and followed her from there."

I ran that around in my head. "Well, yeah. I guess it could be. Tillie says she heard from Elaine—at least, she assumed it was Elaine—by postcard until March, but I guess somebody could have faked that too."

I filled her in on my conversations with Aubrey and Beverly and right in the middle of it, my memory kicked in; one of those wonderful little mental jolts, like a quick electrical shock when a plug's gone bad. "Oh wait, I just remembered something. Elaine got a bill from some furrier here in Boca. What if we could track him down and find out if he's seen the coat? That might give us a lead."

"What furrier? We have quite a few."

"I'd have to check with Tillie. Can I make a call to California? If we can track down the coat, maybe we can get a line on her."

Julia wagged the cane toward the telephone. Within minutes, I'd gotten Tillie on the line and told her what I needed.

"Well, you know that bill got stolen along with the rest, but I just got another one. Hold on and I'll see what it says." She put the receiver down and went to fetch the mail.

She got back on the line. "She's being dunned. It's a second overdue notice from a place called Jacques— seventy-six dollars for storage and two hundred dollars for having the coat recut. Wonder why she'd do that? There's a little happy face drawn by hand: 'Thanks for your business'—followed by a sad face: 'Hope the delay in payment is just an oversight.' A few more bills have come in too. Let me see what those look like."

I could hear Tillie ripping open envelopes on her end of the line.

"Oops. Well, these are all overdue. It looks like she's run up a lot of charges. Let's see. Oh my. Visa, Master-

Card. The last date on these is about ten days ago, but I guess that was just the end of the billing period. They're asking her not to use her cards until she's paid the balances down."

"Does it indicate where she was when the purchases were made? Was she in Florida somewhere?"

"Yes, it looks like Boca Raton and Miami for the most part, but you can check them yourself when you get back. Now that I've had the locks changed, they should be safe."

"Thanks, Tillie. Can you give me the furrier's address?"

I made a note of it and got directions from Julia. I left her and went back down to the parking lot. The sky was an ominous gray and thunder rumbled in the distance like movers rolling a piano down a wooden ramp. It was hot and still, the light a harsh white, making the grass turn phosphorescent green. I was hoping I could take care of business before the downpour caught up with me.

Jacques was located in the middle of an elegant shopping plaza, shaded with latticework overhead and planted with delicate birches in big pale blue urns. Tiny Italian lights had been threaded through the branches, and in the prestorm gloom they twinkled like an early Christmas. The storefronts were done in a dove-gray granite and the pigeons strutting across the pavement looked as if they'd been placed there purely for their decorative effect. Even the sound they made was refined, a low, churring murmur that rode on the morning air like cash being riffled in a merchant's hands.

The window display at Jacques had been artfully done. A golden sable coat had been tossed carelessly across a dune of fine white sand against a sky-blue backdrop. Tufts of sea oats were growing on the crest of the sand and a hermit crab had crossed the surface, leaving a narrow track that looked like an embroidery stitch. It was like a little moment frozen in time: a woman—someone reckless and rich—had come down to the shore, had shrugged aside this luscious fur so that she could plunge naked into the sea—or perhaps she was making love to someone on the far side of the dune. Standing there, I could have sworn I saw the grasses bending in a nonexistent wind and I could almost smell the trail of perfume she'd left in her wake.

I pushed the door open and went in. If I'd had money and believed in wearing furry creatures on my back, I'd have laid down thousands in that place.

20

The interior was done in muted blues with a glittering chandelier dominating the high-ceilinged space. Chamber music echoed through the room as though there might be a string quartet sawing somewhere out of sight. Chippendale chairs were arranged in gracious conversational groupings and massive gilt-edged mirrors lined the walls. The only detail that spoiled an otherwise perfect eighteenth-century drawing-room was the little camera up in one corner monitoring my every move. I wasn't sure why. There wasn't a fur in sight and the furniture was probably nailed to the floor. I shoved my hands down in my back pockets just to show I knew how to behave myself. I caught sight of my reflection. There I stood in that rococo setting, in faded jeans and a tank top, looking like something deposited in error by a time machine. I flexed, wondering if I should start lifting weights again. The bicep made my right arm look like a snake that had recently eaten something very small, like a wad of socks.

"Yes?"

I turned around. The man who stood there looked as out of place as I did. He was huge, maybe three hundred pounds, wearing a caftan that made him look like a pop-open tent with a built-in aluminum frame. He was in his sixties with a face that needed to be taken up. His eyelids drooped and he had a sagging mouth and a big double chin. What was left of his hair had slipped down around his ears. I wasn't certain, but I thought he made a rude noise under his skirt.

"I'd like to talk to you about a past-due account," I said.

"I got a bookkeeper handles that. She's out."

"Someone left a twelve-thousand-dollar lynx coat here to be cleaned and recut. She never paid her bill."

"So?"

This guy didn't have to get by on good looks alone. He was gracious too.

"Is Jacques here?" I asked.

"That's who you're talking to. I'm Jack. Who are you?"

"Kinsey Millhone," I said. I took out a card and handed it to him. "I'm a private investigator from California."

"No fooling," he said. He stared at the card and then at me. He glanced around suspiciously like this might be a "Candid Camera" gag. "What do you want with me?"

"I'm looking for information about the woman who brought the coat in."

"You got a subpoena?"

"No."

"You got the money she owes?"

"No."

"Then what are you bothering me for? I don't have time for this. I got work to do."

"Mind if I talk to you while you do it?"

He stared at me. His breathing made that wheezing sound that fat people sometimes make. "Yeah, sure. Why not? Suit yourself."

I followed him into the big cluttered back room, taking in his scent. He smelled like something that spent the winter in a cave.

"How long have you been cutting fur?" I asked.

He turned and looked at me as if I were speaking in tongues.

"Since I was ten," he said finally. "My father cut fur and his father before him."

He indicated a stool and I sat, setting my big canvas handbag at my feet. There was a long worktable to my right, with a coarse brown-paper pattern laid out on it. The right front portion of a mink coat had been put together and he was apparently still working on it. The wall on the left was lined with hanging paper patterns and there were various quite ancient-looking sewing machines to my right. Every available surface was covered with pelts, scraps, unfinished coats, books, magazines, boxes, catalogues. Two dress forms stood side by side, like twins posing self-consciously for a photograph. The place reminded me of a shoe-repair shop, all leather smell and machinery and the feel of craftsmanship. He took up the coat and examined it closely, then reached for a cutting device with a nasty curved blade.

He glanced up at me. His eyes were the same shade of brown as the mink.

"So what do you want to know?"

"You remember the woman?"

"I know the coat. Naturally, I remember the woman who brought it in. Mrs. Boldt, right?"

"That's right. Can you tell me when you saw her last?"

He dropped his gaze back to the fur. He made a cut. He crossed to one of the machines, motioning me to follow. He sat down on a stool and began to sew. I could see now that what had looked at first like an old-fashioned Singer was actually a machine especially designed for the stitching of fur. He lined up the two cut pieces vertically, fur-side in, and caught them in the grip of two flat metal disks, like large silver dollars set rim to rim. The machine whipped the leather edges together with an overhand stitch while he deftly tucked the fur out of the way so it wouldn't get caught in the seam. The whole maneuver took about ten seconds. He spread the seam, smoothing it with his thumb on the backside. There were maybe sixty similar cuts in the leather, a quarter-inch apart. I wanted to ask him what he was doing, but I didn't want to distract him.

"She came in in March and said she wanted to sell the coat."

"How'd you know it was really hers?"

"Because I asked for some identification and the bill of sale." The irritable tone was back, but I ignored it.

"Did she say why she was selling it?"

"Said she was bored with it. She wanted mink, maybe blond, so I offered her credit against something in the store, but she said she wanted the cash, so I told her I'd see what I could do. I wasn't that anxious to pay cash for a used coat. Ordinarily, I don't deal in secondhand fur. There's no market for it here and it's a pain in the ass."

"I take it you made an exception for her."

"Well yeah, I did. The thing is, this lynx coat was in perfect condition and my wife's been after me to get her one for years. She's already got five coats, but when this one came in, I thought . . . what the hell? Make the old broad happy. What's it to me? Mrs. Boldt and I haggled and I finally got the coat for five thousand, which was a good deal for both of us, especially since I got the matching hat. I told her she'd have to pay to have the coat cleaned and recut."

"Why recut?"

"My wife is on the down side of five feet. She's four foot eleven, if you want her exact height, but don't ever tell her I told you that. She considers it some kind of birth defect. You ever noticed that? Short women get that way. From the time they're teenagers, they start wearing funny shoes, trying to look like tall people when they're not. Know what she finally did? Learned to roller skate. She said it was the only time she really felt like a real human being. Anyway, I thought I'd give her this lynx. Gorgeous. You know the coat?"

I shook my head. "I've never seen it."

"Hey, come on. You ought to take a look. I've got it right back here. I haven't cut it yet."

He moved toward the rear and I trotted obediently

behind. He opened the massive metal door to his vault. Cold air wafted out as though from a meat locker. There were fur coats hanging on both sides in double racks, sleeves almost touching, like hundreds of women lined up with their backs to us. He moved down the aisle checking coats as he went, wheezing from the effort. He really needed to lose some weight. His breathing sounded like someone sitting down on a leather couch and it couldn't connote good health.

He took a fur down off the top rack and we moved back out of the cold-storage room, the door shutting behind us with a clang. He held Elaine Boldt's coat up for me to inspect. The lynx was two shades—white and gray in a luscious blend, with the pelts arranged so that each panel ended in a tapering point at the hem. He must have guessed from the look on my face that I'd never seen a coat that expensive close up.

"Here. Try it on," he said.

I hesitated for a moment and then eased into the coat. I pulled it around me and looked at myself in the mirror. The coat hung almost to my shins, the shoulders protruding like protection pads for some strange new sport.

"I look like the Abominable Snowman," I said.

"You look great," he said. He looked from me to the image in the mirror. "So we take it in a little bit. Shorten the sleeves. Or maybe you'd look better in fox if this doesn't suit."

I laughed. "On my income, I think it's high-class to have a sweatshirt with a zipper up the front." I took the coat off and handed it to him, getting back to the subject. "Why'd you pay her for the coat before she paid you? Why not deduct your costs from the five grand and give her a check for the balance?"

"The bookkeeper wanted it the other way. Don't ask me why. Anyhow, it's not going to cost that much to clean the coat, and the alterations I'm doing myself, so what's it to me? I got a good deal. Adele probably bugged her for payment as a matter of course, but I can't get that upset over the whole thing."

While he returned the coat to cold storage, I went over to my bag and took out the Polaroid picture of Elaine and Marty that Tillie Ahlberg had given me.

When he came back out, I showed it to him. "Is this the woman you dealt with?"

He glanced at it briefly and gave it back.

"Nuh-un. I never saw either one of those women before in my life," he said.

"What did she look like?"

"How do I know? I only saw her once."

"Young, old? Short, tall? Fat, thin?"

"Yeah, about like that. She was middle-aged and she had blondish hair. And she wore a muumuu and chain-smoked. I wouldn't let her come back here because I don't like the smoke around my skins."

"What kind of identification did she have?"

"You know. The usual stuff. Driver's license. Check guarantee card. Credit cards. You gonna tell me the coat was stolen? Because I don't want to hear it."

"I don't think 'stolen' quite covers it," I said. "I suspect someone's been borrowing Elaine Boldt's identity. I'm just not sure where she is in the meantime. If I were you, I'd leave the coat intact until we figure out what's going on."

My last glimpse of him, he was pulling unhappily at the wattles on his neck and he didn't offer to accompany me to the door.

I went out into the oppressive Florida humidity. The cloud cover felt like a premature twilight and the first of several big raindrops had begun to splatter against the hot pavement. I scurried to my car, half-ducking as though I could avoid getting wet by shrinking myself to half my size. I thought about Jack's description of the woman who'd called herself Elaine Boldt. He'd seen the snapshot of Elaine and he'd sworn it wasn't her. It had to be Pat Usher as nearly as I could tell. I ran back through my encounter with her: her attitude of wary amusement, the questions about Elaine she'd fielded, the mixture of lies and truth she'd told. Had she simply stepped into someone else's shoes? She'd been staying in Elaine's condominium, but how had she acquired the lynx coat if not from Elaine? If she was the one running up charges on Elaine's credit cards, she had to be sure somehow that Elaine wouldn't catch her at it. It seemed to me she could only pull that off if she knew Elaine was dead, which had been my suspicion for days now anyway. There might be some other explanation, I supposed, but nothing that tied everything together so neatly.

The rain was coming down hard now, the windshield wipers on my rental car flapping back and forth like metronomes, doing little more than smearing the windshield with a thin film of grime. I found a phone booth and placed a credit-card call to Jonah at the Santa Teresa P.D. The connection was bad and we could barely hear each other over the static on the line, but I did manage to holler out what I needed, asking him if he'd expedite the request form I'd sent to the DMV in Tallahassee. A driver's license was the one thing Pat Usher would have had to come up with, since Elaine had none, but it wouldn't have been that hard to falsify. All she had to do was apply in Elaine Boldt's name, pass the test, and wait for the license to arrive in the mail. In some states, you could walk out of the Department of Motor Vehicles with license in hand within minutes of taking the test— at least for a renewal. I wasn't sure what the procedure was in Florida. Jonah said he'd put a call through to Tallahassee and get back to me. I expected to be in Santa Teresa again by the next day, so I said I'd call him when I got in.

In the meantime, I drove back to the condominium and had a brief chat with Roland Makowski, the building manager, who confirmed what I'd already heard through Julia. Pat Usher had departed, bag and baggage, the same day I'd spoken to her. She'd dutifully left a forwarding address—some motel down near the beach—but when Roland tried to get in touch, he'd found out it didn't exist. I asked him why he'd wanted to contact her. He said she'd taken a dump in the swimming pool as a parting gesture and then scrawled her name across the concrete in spray paint.

"She did what?" I asked.

"You heard right," he said. "She left a turd the size of a Polish sausage floating right in the pool. I had to have the whole thing drained and sanitized and I got people who still won't go in. That woman is demented and you know what pissed her off? I told her she couldn't hang her towels over the balcony rail! You should have seen her reaction. She was in such a rage her eyes rolled back in her head and she started to pant. She scared the hell out of me. She's *sick*."

I blinked at him. "She panted?"

"She was almost foaming at the mouth."

I thought about Tillie's night visitor. "I think we better take a look at Elaine's apartment," I said flatly.

The stench came at us like a wall the minute the door was opened. The destruction was systematic and complete. There was fecal matter smeared everywhere and the couch and chairs had been slashed with murderous intent. It was clear that she'd gone about it quietly. Unlike Tillie's apartment, no glass had been broken and no furniture overturned. What she'd done instead was to open all the canned goods and pour the contents on the carpeting. She'd ground in crackers and dried pasta, jams, spices, coffee, vinegar, soups, moldering fruit, adding contributions from her own intestinal tract. The whole sick stew had been sitting there for days and the Florida heat and humidity had cooked the mess to a boiling foment of fungus and rot. The packages of once frozen meat that she'd torn open and tossed into the thick of it were full of wiggling life of their own that I didn't care to inspect. Big flies buzzed around malevolently, their glittering fluorescent heads like beacons.

Roland was speechless at first and when I turned he had tears in his eyes. "Well, we're never going to get this cleaned up," he said.

"Don't do it yourselves," I said automatically. "Hire someone else. Maybe your insurance will cover it. In the meantime, you better call the cops."

He nodded and swallowed hard while he backed out the door so that I was left to search the apartment by myself. I had to be very careful where I put my feet and I made a little mental note never to chide Pat Usher for anything. As far as I was concerned, she could hang her towels anyplace she pleased.

21

With the cops on the way, I didn't have much time. I picked my way through the apartment, gingerly opening drawers with a hankie across my fingertips out of respect for latent prints. I did a superficial run-through and came up with nothing, which didn't surprise me. She'd stripped the place. All of the drawers and closets were empty. She hadn't left so much as a tube of toothpaste behind. By now, she could be anyplace, but I had a feeling I knew where she was. I suspected she'd used the last two flight coupons for a return trip to Santa Teresa.

I closed the place up again and went next door to tell Julia what was going on. It was two-thirty in the afternoon and I had a four o'clock plane to catch with almost an hour of driving just to get to the airport. The sky was miraculously clear again, the air smelling damp and sweet, sidewalks steaming. I loaded Elaine's suitcases back in the rental car and took off, promising to call Julia as soon as I learned anything new. This case was going to break for me. I could feel it in my bones. I'd been on it a week now and I had smoked Pat Usher out of hiding. I wasn't sure what she'd done to Elaine or why, but she was on the run now and I wasn't far behind. We were circling right back to Santa Teresa where the whole thing had begun.

When I reached the airport in Miami, I returned the rental car and picked up my seat assignment at the TWA counter, checking the four bags through to Santa Teresa. I got on the plane with six minutes to spare. I was beginning to feel a low-level anxiety, the sort of sensation you experience when you know you're having major surgery in a week. There was no immediate danger, but my mind kept leaping into the uncertain future with a churning dread. Pat Usher and I were on a collision course and I wasn't sure I could handle the impact.

With the three-hour time difference, I felt like I got back to California roughly one hour after I left Florida and my body had trouble dealing with that. I had to wait an hour at LAX to catch the short hop to Santa Teresa, but even so it was only seven in the evening when I got home, toting Elaine's bags with me like a packhorse. It was still light outside, but I was exhausted. I'd never eaten lunch and all I'd had on the plane were some square things wrapped in cellophane that I was almost too tired to pick open. It was one of those lurching flights with sudden inexplicable drops in altitude that make napping tough. Most of us were too worried about how they'd collect and identify all the body parts once we'd crashed and burned. Some woman behind me had two kids of the whining and screeching sort and she spent most of the flight having long ineffectual chats with them about their behavior. "Kyle, honey, 'member Mommy told you she didn't want you to bite Brett because that hurts Brett. Now, how would you like it if Mommy bit you?" I thought a quick chop in the ear would go a long way toward parent effectiveness training, but she never consulted me.

At any rate, when I got home, I headed straight for the couch and fell asleep, still in my clothes. Which is why it took me until morning to figure out that somebody had been in my apartment searching discreetly for God knows what. I got up at eight and did a run, came home, showered, and dressed. I sat down at my desk and started to unlock the top drawer. It's a standard-issue desk with a lock on the top drawer that controls the bank of drawers to the right. Somebody had apparently slipped a knife blade into the lock and jimmied it open. The realization that someone had been there made the nape of my neck feel like I'd just applied an ice pack.

I pushed back from the desk and got up, turning abruptly so that I could survey the room. I checked the front door, but there was no indication that anyone had tampered with the double-key dead bolt. It was possible that someone had made a duplicate of the key, though, and I'd have to have the lock replaced. I've never worried about security, and I don't run around doing tricky things to assume that my domain is inviolate—no talcum powder on the floor near the entranceway, no single strands of hair affixed across the window crack. I resented the fact I was going to have to deal with this break-in, surrendering a sense of safety I'd always taken for granted. I checked the windows, moving carefully around the perimeter of the room. Nothing. I went into the bathroom and examined the window there. Someone had used a glass cutter to make a small square opening just above the lock. Electrical tape had evidently been used to eliminate any sound of breaking glass. Where the strips of tape had been peeled off, I could still see remnants of adhesive. The aluminum screen was skewed in one corner. It had probably been popped out and then put back. The job had been cleverly done, set up in such a way that I might not have discovered it for weeks. The hole was large enough to allow someone to unlock the window, sliding it up to permit ingress and egress. There's a curtain at that window and with the panels in place, the small hole in the glass wasn't even visible.

I went back into the other room and did a thorough search. Nothing seemed to be missing. I could see that someone had eased sly fingers between my folded clothes in the chest of drawers, had deftly gone through the files, leaving everything much as it had been, but with faint disarrangements here and there. I hated it. I hated the cunning and the care with which it had all been done, the satisfaction somebody must have felt at pulling it off. And what was the point? For the life of me, I couldn't see that anything was gone. I didn't own anything of value and the files themselves were not worth much. Most of the ones I kept at home had been closed out anyway and my notes on Elaine Boldt were at the office. What else did I have that someone might want? What worried me too was the suspicion that this might be Pat Usher's handiwork. Somehow she seemed much more dangerous if, along with savagery, she was also capable of craftiness and stealth.

I called a locksmith and made an appointment to have her come out later in the day to change all the locks. I could replace the window glass myself. I did some quick measurements and then headed out to the street. Fortunately, no one had broken into my car, but I didn't like the idea that someone might try that too. I took my .32 out of the glove compartment and tucked it into the waistband of my jeans at the small of my back. I was going to have to lock it in my office file cabinet and leave it there for the time being. I was relatively certain that my office was secure. Since I'm on the second floor with a balcony right out in plain view, I didn't think anyone would risk a break-in from that vantage point. The building is kept locked at night and the door from the hallway is solid oak two inches thick with a double-key dead bolt that could only be breached if the lock itself were cored out with a power saw. Still, I was feeling apprehensive when I pulled into the parking lot behind the office and I ended up taking the back stairs two at a time. I didn't relax until I unlocked the office door and saw for myself that no one had been there.

I put the gun away and took out the file on Elaine Boldt. I typed up additional notes, bringing everything up to date. Inwardly, I was still fuming that someone had been in my apartment. I should have called the police and reported it, but I didn't want to stop for that. I tried to concentrate on the matter at hand. I had a lot of unanswered questions and I wasn't even sure which ones mattered at this point. Why, for instance, had Pat Usher closed up shop so abruptly in Boca after my first trip down there? I had to guess that once she knew I was looking for Elaine, she'd had to scuttle her plans. I was assuming, of course, that she'd headed to Santa Teresa and that it was she who'd broken into Tillie's apartment and stolen that stack of bills. But to what end? The bills had continued to arrive and if pertinent information might be gleaned from inspecting them, all we had to do was wait for the next batch.

Then I had Mike's account of what he saw on the night of his aunt's murder. I still wasn't sure how that fit in, if indeed it did. The fact remained that his estimate of the time of Marty Grice's death differed by thirty minutes from the time her husband and sister-in-law claimed they'd spoken to her. Were Leonard and Lily in cahoots?

There was still the minor matter of May Snyder next door who'd reported the sound of hammering at the Grices' house that night. Orris swore she was deaf and had it all confused with something else, but I wasn't quite willing to write her off like that.

When the phone rang, I jumped, snatching up the receiver automatically. It was Jonah. He didn't even bother to identify himself. All he said was, "I've got a response from the DMV in Tallahassee. You want to take a look?"

"I'll be right there," I said and hung up, heading out.

Jonah was waiting for me in the small reception area as I came into the police station and he walked me through the locked doors to the corridor leading back to Missing Persons.

"How'd you get the information so fast?" I asked. He held the gate open for me and I passed into the bullpen, where he had his desk.

He smiled faintly. "That's why cops are so much better at this business than private eyes," he said. "We've got access to information you can't even touch."

"Listen, *I* was the one who put in the original request! It's public record. I can't get it as fast as you can, but I was on the right track and you know it."

"Don't get so hot," he said. "I was just ragging you."

"Very cute. Lemme see it," I said, holding my hand out. He passed me a computer printout, a magnetic image of a driver's license issued to Elaine Boldt in January, with the Florida condominium address. I stared at the picture of the woman staring back at me and uttered a quick, involuntary "ah!" I knew the face. It was Pat Usher: same green eyes, same tawny hair. There were a few glaring differences. I'd seen her after an automobile accident, when her face was still a bit bruised and swollen. The resemblance was clear enough, though. Hot damn.

"I got her," I said. "Hey wow, I got her!"

"Got who?"

"I don't really know yet. She calls herself Pat Usher, but she probably made that up. I'll bet you money Elaine Boldt is dead. Pat had to know that or she never would have had the nerve to apply for a driver's license in Elaine Boldt's name. She's been living in Elaine's apartment ever since she disappeared. She's used her credit cards and probably helped herself to any bank accounts. Shit. Let's run a check on her through NCIC. Can we do that?" The National Crime Information Center might well turn up identification on Pat Usher in seconds.

"Computer's down. I just tried. I'm surprised you didn't ask me to do that before."

"Jonah, I didn't have the right data before. I had a name but no numerical identifier. Now I've got a birthdate. Can I have a copy of this?"

"That's yours," he said mildly. "I've got one for my files. What makes you think the birthdate is legitimate?"

"I'm just crossing my fingers on that. Even if she faked a name, it'd make sense for her to use her own birthdate. She might be forced to fabricate a lot of other stuff so why falsify this? She's smart. She wouldn't work harder than she had to."

I studied the printout, turning it toward the light. "Look at that. They marked the box that says 'corrective lenses.' Terrific. She has to wear glasses when she drives. It's great, isn't it? Look at all the information we have. Height, weight. God, she looks tired in this picture. And look how fat she is. Check the *bags* underneath her eyes. Oh boy, you should've heard her when I talked to her down there. So *smug*. . . ."

He'd perched himself up on the edge of the desk and he was smiling at me, apparently amused by my excitement. "Well, I'm glad I could help," he said. "I'm gonna be out of town for a couple of days so it's lucky that came through when it did."

For the first time, I really focused on his face. His

smile was slightly fixed and his posture had a self-conscious quality. "You're taking some time off?" I asked.

"Well yeah, something like that. Camilla's got a problem with one of the kids and I thought I better go straighten it out. It's no big deal, but you know how it is."

I looked at him, computing backward from what he'd said. Camilla had called and snapped her fingers. He was taking off like a shot. The kids, my foot. "What's going on?" I said.

He gestured casually and told me some long tale about bed-wetting and nightmares and visits to a child psychiatrist who'd recommended a session with the whole family. I said, uh-huh, uh-huh, not even tuning into which girl it was. I'd forgotten what their names were. Oh yeah, Courtney and something.

"I'll be back on Saturday and I'll give you a buzz. Maybe we can go back up and shoot some," he said and smiled again.

"Great. That'd be fun," I said, smiling back. I almost suggested that he bring a blowup of Camilla for a target, but I kept my mouth shut. I felt a tiny little moment of regret, which amazed me no end. I hadn't even gone to bed with this man . . . hadn't even *thought* of it. (Well, hardly.) But I'd forgotten what it's like with married men, how married they are even when the ex is somewhere else . . . *especially* when the ex is somewhere else. I didn't think she'd filed papers yet, which made the whole thing much simpler. He was running out of frozen dinners anyway, and by now she'd probably figured out how slim the choices were out there in Singlesland.

I suddenly felt myself growing self-conscious too. "Well. I better get on with this. Thanks a lot. You've been a big help."

"Hey, anytime," he said. "Spillman's gonna be on the desk while I'm gone if you need anything. I'll brief him so he knows the scoop, but I want you to take care of yourself." He pointed a finger at me as though it were a gun.

"Don't worry about it. I don't take chances if I don't have to," I said. "I hope things work out up north. I'll talk to you when you get back."

"Absolutely. Let's do that. Good luck."

"Same to you. Tell the kids I said hi."

That was dumb. I'd never met them and I couldn't think what the other one's name was in any event. Sarah?

I pushed through the gate.

"Hey, Kinsey?"

I looked back.

"Where's that hat of yours? I liked that. You should wear it all the time."

I smiled and waved and went on out. I didn't need advice on how to dress.

22

It was midmorning and I was suddenly starving to death. I left my car in front of the police station where it was parked and walked over to a little hole-in-the-wall called The Egg and I. I ordered my standard breakfast of bacon, scrambled eggs, toast, jelly, and orange juice, with coffee throughout. It's the only meal I'm consistently fond of as it contains every element I crave: caffeine, salt, sugar, cholesterol, and fat. How can one resist? In California, with all the health nuts around, the very act of eating such a meal is regarded as a suicide attempt.

I read the paper while I ate, catching up on local events. I had just gotten down to the second piece of rye toast when Pam Sharkey walked in with Daryl Hobbs, the manager at Lambeth and Creek. She caught sight of me and I waved. I didn't give it everything I had. It was a casual offhand wave to indicate that I was a good joe and wasn't going to lord it over her just because I bested her last time we met. Her expression faltered and she broke off eye contact, passing my table without a word. The snub was so pronounced that even Daryl seemed embarrassed. I was puzzled, but not cut to the quick, shrugging to myself philosophically. Maybe the aerospace engineer had turned out to be a jerk.

When I finished breakfast, I paid the check and retrieved my car, popping over to the office to drop off the data I'd picked up from Jonah. I was unlocking my door when Vera stepped out into the corridor from California Fidelity.

"Can I talk to you?" she said.

"Sure. Come on it." I pushed the office door open and she followed me in. "How are you?" I said, thinking this was a social call. She tucked a strand of auburn hair behind her ear, looking at me through the big pale blue-tinted lenses that made her eyes seem large and grave.

"Uh, listen. Just a word to the wise," she said uncomfortably. "All hell's broken loose over that Leonard Grice business."

I blinked at her. "Like what?"

"Pam Sharkey must have called him after you talked to her. I don't know what she said to him, but he's all up in arms. He'd hired an attorney who fired off a letter to CFI threatening to sue us within an inch of our lives. We're talking millions."

"For what?"

"They're claiming slander, defamation of character, breach of contract, harassment. Andy's livid. He says he had no idea you were involved. He says you weren't authorized by California Fidelity or anybody else to go out there and ask questions . . . blah, blah, blah. You know how Andy gets when he's on his high horse. He wants to see you the minute you come in."

"What *is* this? Leonard Grice hasn't even filed a claim!"

"Guess again. He submitted forms first thing Monday morning and he wants his money right now. The lawsuit was filed on top of that. Andy's over there processing papers as fast as he can and he's pissed. He's told Mac he thinks we should terminate the whole arrangement with you after the jeopardy you put us in. The rest of us think he's being a complete horse's ass, but I thought you should know what's going on."

"What's the total on the claim itself?"

"Twenty-five grand for the fire damage. That's the face value on the homeowner's policy and he has his losses itemized down to the penny. The life insurance isn't at issue. I think he's already collected some dinky little policy on her life—twenty-five hundred— and our records show he was paid that months ago. Kinsey, he's out for bear and you're it. Andy's looking for someone to point a finger at so Mac doesn't point a finger at him."

"Shit," I said. I couldn't think of anything else to say. The last thing in the world I needed right now was a dressing down by Andy Montycka, the CFI claims manager. Andy's in his forties, conservative and insecure, a man whose prime obsessions are biting his fingernails and not making waves.

"You want me to tell him you haven't come in?" she asked.

"Yeah, do that for me, if you would. Just let me check my phone messages and I'll disappear," I said. I unlocked the file and took out the folder on Elaine Boldt, looking back at Vera. "I'll tell you something, Vera. This is hot. Leonard Grice has had six months to file a claim, but he hasn't lifted a finger. Now, all of the sudden, he's putting pressure on the insurance company to pay off. I'd like to know what prompted him."

"Hey, I gotta scoot before they come looking for me," Vera said. "Just don't cross Andy's path today or you'll pay for it."

I thanked her for the warning and told her I'd be in touch. She eased out into the hallway again, closing the door behind her. Belatedly, I felt my cheeks flush and my heart begin to thump. I got sent down to the principal's office once in first grade for passing notes in class and I've never recovered from the horror of it. I was guilty as charged, but I'd never been in trouble in my life. There I was, a timid little child with skinny legs, so stricken with fear that I left the school and went home in tears. My aunt marched me right back and read everybody out while I sat on a little wooden chair in the hall and prayed for death. It's hard to keep passing myself off as a grown-up when a piece of me is still six years old and utterly at the mercy of authority.

A glance at my answering machine showed no messages. I locked up again and went down the front way so that I could avoid passing the glass double doors of California Fidelity. I got back in my car and drove over to Elaine's old condominium. I wanted to have a brief talk with Tillie and let her know what was happening. I was turning right on Via Madrina when I glanced in the rearview mirror and realized there was some guy on a motorcycle roaring right up my tailpipe. I eased over slightly to let him pass and glanced back again. He was beeping away at me frantically. What had I done, run over his dog? I pulled over to the curb and he pulled up behind me, turning his bike off and booting his kick-stand into place. He was wearing a shiny black jumpsuit, black gloves and boots, and a black helmet with a smoky face guard. I got out of my car and walked back toward him, watching him peel his helmet off as he approached. Oh hell, it was Mike. I should have guessed. The pink of his Mohawk seemed to be fading and I wondered whether he did his touch-ups with Rit dye, food color-ing, or cooked beets. He was irked.

"God, I been honking at you for blocks! How come you never called me back? I left a message on your ma-chine on Monday," he said.

"Sorry. I didn't realize it was you back there. I thought you said you were going to call *me*."

"Well, I tried to, but I kept getting your machine so I gave up. Where were you?"

"Out of town. I just got back last night. Why? What's happening?"

He pulled his motorcycle gloves off and tucked them in his helmet, which he cradled in the crook of his arm. "I think my Uncle Leonard has a girl friend. I just thought you might like to know."

"Oh really? How'd you find out about that?"

"I was moving that . . . uh . . . stash out of the shed at his old place and I saw him go into the building next door."

"The condo?"

"Well yeah, I guess that's what it is. That big apart-ment building."

"When was this?"

"Sunday night. That's why I called you so early Monday morning. At first, I wasn't sure it was him. I kind of *thought* it was his car pulling up out front but it was almost dark and I couldn't see that good. I figured he was coming over to the house for something and I was shovin' shit in my duffel bag like crazy. Man, I didn't know how I was going to explain what I was up to. Finally I was in such a panic, I whipped into the shed and pulled the door shut and watched through the crack. He ended up going over there instead."

"What makes you think he has a girl friend, though?"

"Because I saw him with her. I didn't have anything else to do, so I went across the street and hid behind a tree and waited until they came out. He was only in there five or ten minutes and then the lights went out, second floor left. Pretty soon they came out and shoved some stuff in the trunk and got in the car."

"Did you get a good look at her?"

"Not really. It was hard to see 'em from where I was and they were walking kind of fast. Then when they got in the car they were all over each other. He nearly jumped her bones right there in the front seat. It was kind of weird. I mean, you usually don't see people that age making out, you know what I mean? And anyway, I never thought about him like that. I figured he was just some old dried-out fart who couldn't even get it up. I didn't think he had it in him."

"Mike, the man is probably fifty-two years old. Would you knock that off! What did she look like? Had you ever seen her before?"

Mike held his hand up to his chin. "She came up to about here on him. I noticed that. She had her hair tied back with a scarf—like a babushka or whatever you call 'em. I don't think I'd seen her before. I mean, it wasn't like I thought, Oh yeah, there's old what's-her-face or anything like that. She was just some babe."

"Look, do me a favor. Go find a pencil and paper and write all this down while it's fresh in your mind. Make a note of the date and time and anything else you remember. You don't have to say what you were doing around here. You can always claim you came over to check on the house or something. Will you do that?"

"Okay, sure. What are you going to do?"

"I haven't made that part up yet," I said.

I got back in my car, and five minutes later I was being buzzed through from the lobby to Tillie's apartment.

She was waiting for me at the door and I followed her into the living room. She was wearing a pair of spectacles low on her nose and she peered at me over the rims. She took a seat in the rocker and picked up some needlework. It looked like a hunk of upholstery fabric printed with a scene of mountains and forest, deer grazing here and there, a stream gushing down through some rocks. She had wads of cotton and she was shoving them into the back of the cloth with a crochet hook. The deer were puffed out into three dimensions, surrounded by stitching, to produce a quilted effect.

"What *is* that?" I asked, sitting down. "Are you stuffing it?"

She smiled faintly. She'd finally let her new permanent wave have its way and her head was a nest of tight, frizzy curls the color of apricots. "That's right, I am. It's called trapunto. When I finish, I'll have it blocked and framed. I do it for the church bazaar in the fall. This is cotton I save out of the tops of pill bottles, so next time you open some Tylenol or cold caps, you keep the packing for me. Sit down. I haven't seen you for days. What have you been up to?"

I gave her a summary of events since Friday, which was when I had seen her last. I did some censoring. I told her how I'd found the cat, but deleted the stash of drugs Mike kept in the shed next door. I told her about Aubrey Danziger and my confrontation later with Beverly, the suitcases, the trip to Florida, the threatened lawsuit, and Mike's tale about Leonard Grice having a girl friend upstairs. That made her take her glasses off and click the stems against the frames.

"I don't believe it," she said flatly. "Mike must have been high."

"Well, of course he was high, Tillie, but a little grass isn't going to make him hallucinate."

"Then he's inventing it."

"I'm just telling you what he told me," I said.

"Well, who in the world could it be? I'd be willing to guarantee Leonard wasn't having an affair with any tenant of mine! And from his description, it would have been Elaine's apartment, and that's simply impossible."

"Oh come on, Tillie. Don't be naïve. It's the perfect setup. Why couldn't he have a woman over here?"

"Because there's no one in the building who fits that description."

"What about the woman in apartment 6? The one

you thought might be up early the day your place got broken into."

"She's seventy-five."

"But you have lots of other tenants."

"Young married couples. Kinsey, I have more single *men* who'd go for Leonard than I do single women."

"I'd buy that too. What about Elaine? Why couldn't it be her?"

Tillie shook her head stubbornly.

"What about yourself?"

Tillie laughed and patted herself on the chest. "Well, I'm flattered. I'd like to believe I'm still capable of hip-grinding out on the street, but he's not exactly my type. Besides, Mike knows me. He'd have recognized me even in the dark."

I conceded that one. I truly couldn't picture Tillie in a liplock with Leonard Grice. It just didn't parse.

"What *about* Elaine?" I persisted. "What if she and Leonard had a thing going and decided to eliminate his wife? She does the deed while he's off at his sister's place that night. She takes off for Florida a few days later and then lays low for the next six months, waiting for him to get his affairs in order so they can run away together into the sunset. Once they realize I'm on to something, they step up the pace so they can blow town."

Tillie stared at me for a long time. "Then who is Pat Usher?"

I shrugged again. "Maybe they enlisted her help and she's covering for them."

"But who broke in here and why? I thought you were convinced Pat Usher did that."

I could feel myself getting exasperated. "I don't have all the answers, Tillie! I'm just telling you it's possible that he had some little tootsie stashed over here. Maybe it *was* Pat."

She didn't say a word. She just put her glasses back on and started stuffing the mountain with cotton, making it bulge like Mount St. Helens before it blew.

"Can I have the key to the apartment upstairs?"

"Of course," she said. "I'll go too."

She put down her needlework and went over to the secretary, taking a set of keys out of the drawer. She handed me a bunch of bills while she was at it and I stuffed them in the back pocket of my jeans. It reminded me vaguely of something, but I couldn't think what.

She locked her apartment and we headed for the elevator.

"You haven't heard anyone walking around overhead?"

She looked back at me. "Not at all, but this place is well built and someone could be upstairs without my hearing them. You really believe he was keeping someone up there?"

"It does make sense," I said. "With Elaine off the scene, it's a perfect little love nest. Maybe Pat Usher found a way to get in. I'm sure she's somewhere here in town. If she had access to Elaine's place in Florida, why not this one too? By the way, were you here Sunday night?"

She shook her head. "I was at a church social and didn't get home until shortly after ten."

The elevator door opened at the second floor and Tillie moved down the corridor to the left, talking to me over her shoulder. She reached Elaine's front door and turned the key in the lock.

"I can't believe anyone's been here," she said as we went in.

She was wrong, of course. Wim Hoover, the tenant from number 10, was sprawled in the entryway with a bullet hole just behind his right ear. The air smelled of stale cigarette smoke and the fetid perfume wafting up from his souring flesh. He'd been dead for at least three days.

Tillie paled and went down to her place to call the police.

23

As is my usual habit, I did a quick tour of the place while Tillie called the cops. I had cautioned her to keep my name out of it because I didn't want to have to stop and take one of Lieutenant Dolan's famous pop quizzes. I was already in trouble with California Fidelity and I couldn't take on Dolan as well. The place smelled so foul that I didn't think Tillie would have any trouble explaining what had brought her up here to investigate.

I didn't have to be Sherlock Holmes to figure out that Pat Usher had been in residence. She'd made no attempt to disguise her presence. The gauzy float I'd seen her wear in Boca Raton was now tossed carelessly across Elaine's unmade bed. She'd apparently helped herself to whatever suited her—food, clothing, cosmetics. There were dirty dishes everywhere, ashtrays filled to the brim, trash spilling out of the brown paper bag with its neatly cuffed top. The crime-scene unit was going to have a ball with this place, but what interested me was the den. All the desk drawers had been opened, the contents scattered furiously, file folders ripped in half. It looked like Pat Usher's usual rage and impatience. I wondered what she'd been looking for and whether she'd found it. I didn't touch a thing. It had been maybe five minutes since Tillie went downstairs and I thought I better scram. I didn't want to be anywhere in the neighborhood when the black-and-whites came screaming into view.

I paused in the foyer and looked down at Wim. He was lying facedown, one hand tucked under his cheek as though he meant to nap. His flesh was swollen, the skin darkening, the bullet hole as tidy as the eyelet for a shoelace. The gun was probably a .22—not a lethal weapon as a rule, but let a slug ricochet around inside a human skull and it could turn brains into scrambled eggs in no time flat. Poor Wim. I wondered why she'd killed him. There wasn't any doubt in my mind it was Pat. Had she killed Marty Grice as well? The autopsy hadn't shown any gunshot wounds, only the repeated blows of an unidentified blunt instrument. What was the weapon, and where?

I went down on the elevator and left the building without talking to Tillie again. I unlocked my car and got in, suddenly aware of the crackle of paper in my jeans pocket. I pulled out the bunch of bills Tillie had given me and let out an involuntary "ooohh." It had just dawned on me what Pat Usher might have been looking for upstairs. Elaine's passport. I had come across it myself the second time I searched the place and I'd stuck it in the back pocket of my jeans. I couldn't remember taking it into the office, so it must be somewhere in my apartment. Had Pat broken in to look for it? If she'd found it, she was probably already on a plane headed into the great beyond. On the other hand, Leonard hadn't collected his insurance money yet, so maybe the two of them were still somewhere in town.

I started the car and pulled out, determined to clear the neighborhood before the cops showed up. I was thinking hard. Pat and Leonard must have eliminated Marty first, then disposed of Elaine Boldt, maybe because she'd guessed what was going on. In any event, it must have opened up a whole new possibility. They had now gained entrance to her properties and all of her bank accounts, helping themselves to her credit while Leonard waited the requisite six months for Marty's estate to clear. The payoff there probably wasn't large, but add it to Elaine Boldt's assets and the profits began to mount. Once Leonard had acquired sole possession of the property on Via Madrina, he could sell it off for a hundred and fifteen thousand. The lot was probably worth more with the house gone anyway. In the meantime, all he had to do was pose as the grief-stricken spouse, feigning disinterest in the proceeds. Not only did he garner sympathy, but he deflected attention from his true motivation, which was monetary from the get-go. The scheme might have gone off without a hitch except that Beverly Danziger showed up, needing a routine signature on a minor document. Pat's claim about Elaine being off in Sarasota with friends simply wouldn't bear up under close scrutiny because Elaine's whereabouts couldn't really be accounted for. But how was I going to prove any of this? I was speculating like crazy, probably making a few wrong guesses here and

there, but even if I had it right on the nose, I'd have to
come up with some kind of concrete evidence to take to
the police.

In the meantime, Leonard had effectively blocked my
path, putting me in check at least where the insurance
company was concerned. I didn't dare go back and question *him* again and I knew I'd better be careful about
any inquiries I made in the world at large. Any line I
pursued was going to be interpreted as slander, harassment, or defamation from his point of view. What had I
gotten myself into? Leonard Grice and Pat Usher
would have to stonewall my investigation or the whole
operation would come tumbling down around their
ears.

I stopped off at the hardware store to pick up a pane
of glass and then went back to my place. I had to find
Elaine's passport. I checked the trash bags, behind
couch cushions, under furniture, and all the other
niches where I tend to tuck odds and ends. I didn't remember filing it and it hadn't occurred to me to hide it.
I knew I hadn't thrown it out, which meant it had to be
here somewhere. I kept standing there, doing a 360 degree turn, surveying every corner of the room—desk
top, bookcase, coffee table, the small counter that separates the kitchenette.

I went out to the car and looked in the glove compartment, map pocket, down behind the seat, sun visor,
briefcase, jacket pocket—shit. I went back into my
apartment and started all over again. Where had I put
the damn thing? It *might* be at the office. I decided to
try there after CFI had closed up and Andy Montycka

had gone home. God, what did he know anyway? I was beginning to unravel the knots and I only hoped I could finish before he got nervous and paid off the claim.

I checked my watch. It was a little after one and I had the locksmith coming at four. I sat down at my desk and hauled out my file on Elaine Boldt. Maybe there was something I'd overlooked. I baited my hook and started to cast about randomly. I felt like I'd been through my notes a hundred times and I couldn't believe anything new would surface. I went back and read every report I had. I tacked all my index cards to the bulletin board, first in order, then haphazardly just to see if any contradictions would appear. I reread all the material Jonah had photocopied from the homicide files and I studied glossy eight-by-tens of the murder scene until I knew every detail by heart. How had Marty been killed? A "blunt instrument" could mean just about anything.

A lot of things were bothering me—minor questions buzzing around at the back of my brain like a swarm of gnats. I had begun to believe that if Elaine was dead, she'd been killed fairly early on. I had no proof yet but I suspected that Pat Usher had masqueraded as Elaine and had staged that whole bogus departure for Florida as a sleight of hand, laying a false trail to create the illusion that Elaine was alive and well and on her way out of town when, in fact, she was already dead. But if she'd been killed in Santa Teresa, where was the body? Disposing of a corpse is no mean feat. Fling one in the ocean and it swells up and floats right back. Toss it in the bushes and a jogger will stumble across it by six A.M. What else do you do with one? You bury it. Maybe the body was concealed in the Grices' basement. I remembered the floor down the—cracked concrete and hard-packed dirt—and I thought, now that might explain why Leonard had never had the salvage crew come in. When I'd first searched the Grices' house I'd just been grateful for my good luck, but even at the time it had seemed almost too good to be true. Maybe Leonard didn't want the demolition experts knocking around down there.

Pat Usher bothered me too. Jonah hadn't had a chance to run a check on her through the National Crime Information Center because the computer had been down. By now he'd left for Idaho, but maybe I could have Spillman run the name for me to see what he could come up with. I didn't think Pat Usher was her real name, but it might show up as an alias—*if* she had a criminal record, which was uncertain at this point. I took out a legal pad and made myself a note. Maybe with some judicious backtracking, I could figure out who she was and how she'd gotten involved with Leonard Grice.

I sorted through the new stack of Elaine's bills that Tillie had given me, tossing out the few pieces of junk mail. I came across an appointment reminder from a dentist in the neighborhood and tossed that aside. Elaine Boldt didn't drive and I knew she patronized businesses within walking distance of her condominium. I remembered in the first batch of bills I'd seen, there was a bill from the same dentist. John Pickett, D.D.S., Inc. Where else had I run into him? I leafed back through the material from the homicide file, running my eye down each page. Ah. No wonder the name rang a bell. He was the dentist who supplied the full mouth X rays used to identify Marty Grice. There was a knock at the door and I looked up, startled. It was already four o'clock.

I glanced out through the little fish-eye peephole and opened the door. The locksmith was young, maybe twenty-two. She flashed me a smile that featured nice white teeth.

"Oh hi," she said, "I'm Becky. Is this the right place? I tried up front and the old guy said I probably wanted you."

"Yes, that's right," I said, "come on in."

She was taller than I and very thin, with long bare arms and blue jeans that hung on her narrow hips. She had a carpenter's belt slung around her waist, a hammer hanging down like a gun in a holster. Her fair hair was cut short with a boyish cowlick across the front. Freckles, blue eyes, pale lashes, no makeup, all the gawkiness of an adolescent. She had an athlete's no-nonsense good looks and she smelled of Ivory soap.

I moved toward the bathroom. "The window's in here. I want some kind of heavy-duty hardware installed that can't be breached."

Her eyes lit up when she saw the cut in the glass. "Gee, not bad. Slick job, huh. You want to put new locks on the other windows or just this?"

"I want new locks on everything including my desk. Can you rekey the dead bolt?"

"Sure. I can do anything you want. If you got glass, I'll reglaze the window for you too. I love doing things like that."

I left her to install the heavy-duty hardware. Belatedly, I snatched up several articles of dirty clothing strewn about my living room. There's nothing like an outsider's idle glance to make you conscious of your own environment. I chucked two beach towels, a sweatshirt, and a dark cotton sundress on top of some other stuff in the washing machine. I tend to use my washer as a dirty-clothes hamper anyway since I'm pinched for space. I tossed in a cup of detergent. I cranked the dial around to permanent press, just to keep the cycle short, and I was on the verge of popping the door shut again when I spotted Elaine's passport poking up out of the back pocket of a pair of blue jeans. I think I must have hooted my surprise because Becky stuck her head out of the bathroom door.

"Did you call me?"

"No, that's all right. I just found something I'd been looking for."

"Oh. Okay. Good for you." She went back to work. I put the passport at the back of my bottom desk drawer and locked it. Thank God I have the passport, I thought. Thank God it had turned up. It was like a talisman, a good omen. Cheered, I decided I might as well type up my notes, so I hauled out my little portable typewriter and set it up. I could hear Becky thumping around with the window, and after a few minutes, she stuck her head out of the bathroom again.

"Hey, Kinsey? This thing is all gimmicked up. You want me to fix it?"

"Sure, why not?" I said. "If you get the window to work right, I've got some other things you can take care of too."

"Hey, great," she said and disappeared again.

I could hear a big wrenching noise as she pried the window frame away. It was worrisome. All that pep and enthusiasm. I thought I heard something crack.

"Don't worry about the noise," she called out. "I saw my dad do this once and it's a snap."

After a moment, she passed through the room, tip-toeing elaborately, finger to her lips. "Sorry to disturb your work. I have to go out to the truck and get some line. You go right ahead," she murmured. She was speaking in a hoarse whisper as though it would be less intrusive if she used a softer tone.

I rolled my eyes heavenward and went on typing. Three minutes later, she came back to the front door and tapped. I had to get up to let her in. She apologized again briefly and went back into the bathroom where she settled in. I did a cover letter for Julia and caught up with my accounting. Becky was in the other room going bang-bang-bang with her trusty hammer.

After a few minutes, she appeared again. "All done. Want to come try it?"

"Just a minute," I said. I finished typing the envelope and got up, moving into the bathroom. I wondered if this was what it felt like to have a little kid around the house. Noise, interruptions, the constant bid for attention. Even the average mother amazes me. God, what fortitude.

"Look at this," she said happily. She raised the window. Before, it had been like lifting a fifty-pound weight. It would stick midway and then shriek, flying up unexpectedly, glass nearly cracking as it whacked into the frame. To lower the window, I practically had to hang by my hands, humping it down inch by inch. Most of the time I just left it shut. Now it slid up without a hitch.

She stepped back so I could try it. I reached over and lowered it, apparently unprepared for the improvement because the window dropped so fast, it made the window weights thump against the studs in the wall.

Becky laughed. "I told you it worked."

I was staring from her to the window frame. Two ideas had popped into my head simultaneously. I was thinking about Dr. Pickett and the dental X rays and about May Snyder's claim that she heard someone going bang-bang-bang the night Marty died.

"I have to go someplace," I said. "Are you nearly done?"

She laughed again; that uneasy, false merriment that burbles out when you think you're dealing with someone who's come unhinged. "Well, no. I thought you said you had other things you wanted me to do."

"Tomorrow. Or maybe the next day," I said. I was moving her toward the door, reaching for my handbag.

Becky allowed herself to be pushed along.

"Did I say something?" she asked.

"We'll talk about it tomorrow," I said. "I really appreciate your help."

I drove back to Elaine Boldt's neighborhood and circled the block, looking for Dr. Pickett's office on Arbol. I'd seen it before; one of those one-story clapboard cottages once so prevalent in the neighborhood. Most of them had been converted into branch offices for real-estate companies and antiques stores that looked like someone's tiny, crowded living space with a sign hung out front.

Dr. Pickett had paved over some flowerbeds to create a little parking lot. There was only one car out back: a 1972 Buick with a vanity plate that read: FALS TTH. I pulled in beside it and locked my car, moving around the front and up to the porch. The sign on the door said PLEASE WALK IN, so I did.

The interior felt distinctly like my old grade school: varnished wood floors and the smell of vegetable soup. I could hear someone clattering around out in the kitchen. There was a radio on out there, tuned to a country-music station. A scarred wooden desk was angled across the entry hall with a little bell and a sign that said PLEASE RING FOR SERVICE. I tapped on the bell.

To my right was a waiting room with Danish-modern plastic couches and low tables done in wood laminate. The magazines were lined up precisely, but I suspected the subscriptions had run out. I spotted an issue of *Life* with "Starlet Janice Rule" on the front. A partition had been put up between the reception area and Dr. Pickett's examining room. Through the open door, I caught sight of an old-fashioned dental chair with a black plastic seat and a white porcelain spitting sink. The instrument tray was round and apparently swiveled on a metal arm. The surface was protected with white paper, like a placemat, and the instruments were lined up on it like something out of a dental museum. I was certainly thrilled that I didn't need my teeth cleaned right then.

To my left, along the wall, were some battered wooden

file cabinets. Unattended. I could hear the devil call out to me. Dutifully, I rang the bell again, the country music wailed right on. I knew the tune and the lyrics routinely broke my heart.

There were little brass frames on the front of each file cabinet into which hand-lettered white cards had been slipped. A–C read the first. D–F read the next. You can't lock those old files, you know. Well, sometimes you can, but not these. I was going to have to go through such a long song and dance too, I thought. And I might be on the wrong track, which would just waste everybody's time including my own. I only hesitated because the courts are real fussy about the integrity of evidence. You're not supposed to run around stealing information that you later hope to offer up as "Prosecution's Exhibits A & B." The cops are supposed to acquire all that stuff, tag it, initial it, and keep meticulous records about who's had access to it and where it's been. Chain of evidence, it's called. I mean, I read all this stuff and I know.

I called "Yoo-Hoo!" and waited, wondering if "yoo-hoo," like "mama" and "dada," was one of those phrases that crop up in most languages. If nobody responded in the next ten seconds, I was going to cheat.

24

Mrs. Dr. Pickett appeared. At least, I assumed it was she. She was stout, with a big round face, rimless glasses, and a soft pug nose. The dress she wore was a navy blue nylon jersey with a print of tiny white arrows flying off in all directions. Her hair was pulled up to the top of her head and secured with a rubber band, curls cascading as though from a little fountain. She had on a wide white apron with a bib front and she smoothed the lap of the fabric down self-consciously.

"Well now, I thought I heard someone out here, but I don't believe I know your name," she said. Her voice was honeyed, tinted with faint southern overtones.

I had one split second in which to decide whether to tell the truth. I held my hand out and gave her my name. "I'm a private detective," I said.

"Is that right?" she said, wide-eyed. "What in the world can I do for you?"

"Well, I'm not sure yet." I said. "Are you Mrs. Pickett?"

"Yes, I am," she said. "I hope you're not investigatin'

John." Her voice rode up and down musically, infused with drama.

I shook my head. "I'm looking into the death of a woman who lived here in the neighborhood. . . ."

"And I bet you're talkin' about Marty Grice."

"That's right," I said.

"Aw, and wadn't that the awfullest thing? I can't tell you how upset I was when I heard about that. Nice woman like her to meet up with such a fate. But now idn't that just the way."

"Terrible," I said.

"And you know what? They never did catch whoever did it."

"She was a patient of Dr. Pickett's, wasn't she?"

"She sure was. And a sweeter person you couldn't hope to meet. You know, she used to stop in here all the time. She'd set right there and we'd have us a chat. When my arthritis was actin' up, she'd help out with the phones and what not. I never saw John so upset as when we had to go out there and identify the remains. I don't believe he slept for a week."

"Was he the one who took the dental X rays during the autopsy?"

"The pathologist did that. John hand-carried the X rays he'd done in the office and they compared 'em right on the spot. There wasn't any doubt, of course. It was just a formality, is what they told us. He'd taken those X rays not six weeks before she died. I felt so sorry for that husband of hers I just thought I'd choke. We went over to the funeral too, you know, and I made the awfullest fool of myself that ever was. Cried like a baby and John did too. Oh, but now he's the one you'll want to talk to, I'm sure. This is his day off, but he should be home soon. He's out runnin' some errands. You can wait if you like or come back later on."

"You can probably help me as well as he could," I said.

"Well, I'll do what I can," she said dubiously. "I'm no expert, but I've assisted him all our married life. He's often said I could probably fill a tooth as well as he could, but now I don't like that Novocain. I won't fool with needles. It makes my hands turn to ice and I get all goose-bumpy on my arms." She rubbed her arms, giving a mock shiver to illustrate how upsetting it was. "Anyway, you go on and ask what you want. I don't mean to interrupt."

"I understand Dr. Pickett had a patient named Elaine Boldt," I said. "Could you check your records and tell me when she came in last?"

"The name sounds familiar, but I can't say I know her offhand. She wouldn't be anyone regular, I will say that, because I'd know her if she'd been here more than once." She leaned closer to me. "I don't suppose you're allowed to tell me how this applies," she said in a confidential tone.

"No, I'm not," I said, "but they were friends. Mrs. Boldt lived right next door to Mrs. Grice."

Mrs. Pickett nodded slightly, giving her eyebrows a lift as though she got the drift and wouldn't repeat a word of it. She went over to the file cabinets and pulled open the top drawer. I was right next to her. I wondered if she'd mind my looking over her shoulder, but she didn't seem to object. The drawer was packed so tightly she could barely squeeze her fingers in. She started reciting the names on the tags.

"Let's see. Bassage, Berlin, Bewley, Bevis . . . Uh oh, looka here now. That's out of place," she said. She switched the two files around and started where she'd left off. "Birch, Blackmar, Blount. I have Boles. Is that the name you gave?"

"No, Boldt," I said. "B-o-l-d-t. I know you billed her once and I just saw a reminder for a six-month checkup."

"I believe you're right. I wrote that recall card myself and I remember now. Via Madrina, wadn't it?" She looked back into the file drawer, checking a few folders forward and a few folders back. "I bet you for some reason he's got that on his desk," she said. 'You come on in here and we'll take a look."

I followed her down a short hallway and into a small office on the left that had probably once been a powder room. Dr. Pickett's desk was stacked with files and his wife put her hands on her hips as though she'd never laid eyes on such a sight.

"Oh my stars. Now if that's not a mess." She began to check through the nearest pile.

"Why would he have it on his desk?" I asked.

"We might have had a request for dental records is all I can think of," she said. "Sometimes patients transfer out of state."

"You want me to help?"

"I sure do, hon. This might take all day at this rate."

I pitched in, riffling through the stack nearest me, then rechecking the pile she'd done to make sure she hadn't overlooked anything. There was no Elaine Boldt.

"I got one more place," she said. She held a finger up and marched us back to the front desk where she opened the top desk drawer and reached for a small gray metal file box. "This is the recall file. If she got a notice, she'd be in this box. I don't guess she gave any hint when she might have been in."

"Nope," I said. "I'd guess December, though, if she just got a six-months' notice."

Mrs. Pickett gave me an appreciative glance. "Good point. I guess that's why you're a detective instead of me. All right, let's see what December looks like." She sorted through about fifteen cards. Already, I was worried about Dr. Pickett's annual income if he saw fewer patients than one a day.

"Light month," I remarked, watching her.

"He's semiretired," she said, absorbed in her hunt. "He still takes care of these old people in the neighborhood, but he tries to limit his practice. He's got varicose veins worse than me and his doctor doesn't want him on his feet all day. We get out and walk every chance we get. Keeps the circulation up. Here it is." She held an index card up, handing it to me with a mixture of triumph and relief. They might be near retirement age, but the office was still well run.

I studied the card. All it had on it was Elaine Boldt's name and address and the date she'd been in. December 28. Was I on the right track? I turned the notion over in my mind.

"Marty Grice would have come in first," I said, "and then recommended Dr. Pickett to Elaine."

"That's not hard to verify," Mrs. Pickett said. "See?

On the back of the card, I have that line says 'referred by' and here's Mrs. Grice's name sure enough. Actually, we do that so if folks skip out on their bill, we have some way to trace back."

"Could I see Marty's chart?" I asked.

"Well, I don't see why not."

She went back to the file cabinet and pulled a slim folder out of the drawer marked G–I and passed it to me. Marty's name was neatly typed across the tag on the top. I opened the file. There were three sheets inside. The first was a medical questionnaire, asking for information about medications, known allergies, and past illnesses. Marty had completed the form and signed it, automatically authorizing "all necessary dental services." The second was a dental history inquiring about root canals, bleeding gums, occasional bad breath, and grinding or clenching of teeth. The third sheet contained information about treatment actually rendered, with a line drawing of the top and bottom rows of teeth laid out like a Mercator projection, current fillings marked in ballpoint pen. Marty's name was neatly typed on the top line. Below were Dr. Pickett's brief hand-written notes. A routine visit. She'd had her teeth cleaned. There were apparently no dental caries. X rays had been done and she was scheduled to return in June. I stared at it for a long time, running the whole sequence of events through my head. Everything seemed to be in order except for the date: December 28. I moved over to the window and held the chart to the light. I could feel a chill smile forming because somehow I'd known it would come down like that. I just hadn't believed I would actually find the proof. Yet here it was. Someone had neatly whited out the name originally typed in and typed Marty's name right over it. I ran my finger across the top line, feeling for the name typed underneath as though it were done in Braille. Elaine Boldt's name was visible as a faint imprint under the name Marty Grice. The last few pieces were falling into place. I was certain hers were the charred remains recovered from the Grices' house that night. I closed my eyes. It suddenly seemed very strange. I'd been tracking Elaine for ten days without realizing I'd already seen her in a photograph in the homicide file, burned beyond recognition. Marty Grice was alive and I suspected that she and Pat Usher were one and the same. There were details to nail down yet, but I had a very good idea how the murder had been set up.

"Are you feelin' all right?"

"I'm fine," I said briefly.

"Did you want to talk to John?"

"Not right now, but at some point, yes. You've been a big help, Mrs. Pickett. Thanks."

"Well, I don't know what I did, but you're certainly welcome."

I shook her hand, dimly aware of the mystified gaze that followed me as I left. I got in my car and sat there, trying to figure out what to do next. Jesus, how had they assured that the stomach contents would match? That must have been a slick one. The autopsy report indicated the blood type was O-positive, the most common type, so that was easy enough. Marty and Elaine were close in height. It wasn't as though the murder victim was completely unknown. Everyone assumed it was Marty, and the dental X rays had simply been used to confirm her identity. There was no reason to imagine that the dead woman was anyone else. Leonard and his sister had talked to her on the phone at nine and Lily claimed Marty had hung up to go answer the door. The call to the police station was a little flourish someone thought up for the effect. Mike was right about the time. At 8:30 that night, there *was* a woman's body wrapped up in a rug. It just wasn't his aunt. Elaine must have been bludgeoned to death sometime earlier, with enough of her jaw and teeth left intact to make identification possible. So many things were suddenly falling into place. Wim Hoover must have recognized Marty going in or out of Elaine's apartment. Marty or Leonard apparently got to him before he got to a phone.

I started the car and pulled out of the lot, turning left. I headed over to the police station and parked out front in a fifteen-minute green zone across the street. Once inside the station, I stopped at the counter on the left. Beyond the counter, there was a doorway leading back into the squad room.

Some cop in plainclothes I'd never laid eyes on spotted me standing there as he passed the door. He paused.

"You need some help?"

"I'm looking for Lieutenant Dolan."

"Let me check. I was just back there and I didn't see him."

He disappeared. I waited, glancing over my shoulder into Identification and Records. The black clerk was the only one there and she was typing away like crazy. I kept going back over it in my mind. It was so clear now how it all fit. Marty Grice had gone to Florida and lived in Elaine's apartment. It wasn't hard to figure out what she'd done. Lost some weight. Had her hair restyled and dyed. No one down there knew her from Adam so it wasn't as if she had to hide. She probably just got herself spiffied up once she had Elaine's bucks to do it with. I thought back to my encounter with her: the bruised, puffy face, the tape across her nose. She hadn't been in any automobile accident. She'd had cosmetic surgery— a new face to go along with her new identity. She'd told me herself that she was "retired" and didn't expect to work another day in her life. She and Leonard had fallen on hard times and there sat Elaine Boldt with money to burn and a tendency to indulge herself. How Marty must have seethed at the sight. Murder had been an equalizing force, with grand larceny providing a pension fund after the fact. Now all she had to do was wait until Leonard freed up and the two were set. It was Dolan's case. If the murder weapon turned up, I thought he'd have enough evidence to act on. For now, at least I could tell him what was happening. I didn't think it was smart to keep it to myself.

The plainclothesman returned. "He's gone for the day. Is there something I can help you with?"

"Gone?" I said I bit back my customary expletive but inside my head, I was saying, "Shit!"

"I'll be in touch first thing in the morning."

"Sure. You want to leave him a note?"

I took one of my cards out and gave it to him. "Just tell him I'll stop by and fill him in."

"Will do," he said.

I went back to my car and took off. I had a theory about where the murder weapon was, but I wanted to talk to Lily Howe first. If she'd figured out what was going on, she'd be in danger. I glanced down at my watch. It was 6:15. I spotted a pay phone at a gas station and pulled in. My heart had begun to thud with dread. I didn't want Mike in jeopardy. If he realized his aunt was alive, he'd be in trouble too. Hell, we all were. My hands were trembling as I paged through the telephone book, feverishly scanning for the other Grice listings. I found a Horace Grice on Anaconda, which looked like a good bet, and then had to scramble around in the bottom of my handbag for twenty cents. I dialed, holding my breath while the phone rang once, twice, four times, six. I let twelve rings go by and then I put the receiver back. I ripped the page out of the phone book and shoved it into my bag, hoping I'd have an opportunity to call again.

I got back in my car and headed out to Lily Howe's place. Where were Leonard and Marty at this point? Could they have skipped or was it possible they were still together somewhere in town—at Lily Howe's perhaps? I missed Carolina Avenue and had to circle back, peering at house numbers as I passed. I spotted the Howes' residence and slowed, much to the annoyance of the people in the car behind me. I drove on by and did a turnaround in a driveway six doors down. As I pulled in to the curb to park, my heart gave a lurch. Leonard and his lady friend had just pulled into Lily's drive.

I slouched down in my seat abruptly, banging one knee on the dashboard. Oh jeez, that hurt! I eased up slightly, peering over the edge of the steering wheel. They apparently hadn't paid any attention to me because they were both getting out of the car, moving toward Lily's front door with nary a backward glance. They knocked and she opened the door for them without any exclamation of surprise, horror, shock, or dismay. I wondered how long she'd known that Marty was alive. Had she been in league with them from the beginning? I watched the house uneasily. As long as Leonard was there, I was reasonably certain that Lily was safe, but I didn't think Marty would be at all inclined to leave Lily Howe alive when they went off. I was going to have to do a little hovering over Lily Howe, playing guardian angel to her whether she knew it or not.

25

I sat there while an incredibly painful, probably permanent bruise formed on my knee, trying to figure out what I should do next. I didn't want to leave the scene now that I had the enemy in range. There wasn't a public phone within miles, and who was I going to call anyway? I thought about getting out of the car and creeping up to the house, but I've never had very good results with that sort of thing. There are never windows open where you want them to be. On the few occasions when I've managed to eavesdrop, the subject matter has always been irrelevant. People just don't sit around verbalizing the pertinent details of recent crimes. Peer over a windowsill and chances are you're going to watch the villains play Crazy Eights. I've never seen anyone dismember the body or divvy up the bank heist. I decided to stay in my car and wait.

There's nothing as conspicuous as someone sitting alone in a parked car in a residential neighborhood. With any luck, some worried homeowner would spot me and call the cops and then I could have a nice chat

with someone in uniform. Mentally, I organized a condensed version of the murder plot so I could tell it succinctly when the time came. The house was quiet. An
hour and forty-five minutes passed and the gathering
darkness gradually reduced visibility to mush. Lights in
houses all up and down the street came on, including
Lily Howe's. Somebody sprayed the neighborhood with
barbecue cologne. I was hungry and I wanted to take a
leak and I couldn't decide if I should risk squatting
down behind someone's bush. I don't feel I suffer from
penis envy, but in moments like this, I do yearn for the
anatomical advantages.

At 9:23, Lily's front door opened and Leonard and
Marty came out. I leaned forward, squinting. There
weren't any lingering farewells. The two of them got in
the car, slammed the doors, and backed out of the drive.
I waited until their car had disappeared and then approached the house. The porch light had gone off. I
knocked. There was as moment of silence and then I
heard the chain slide into place. Lily had read all the
manuals on rape prevention. Good for her.

"Who is it?" came the muffled voice from inside.

I reduced my voice to a whisper. "It's me. I forgot my
handbag."

The burglar chain slid back and Lily opened the door
a crack. I pushed forward so fast, the door almost broke
her nose. There was a clunk and she cried out, but by
then I'd closed the door behind me again.

"We have to talk," I said.

She had a hand to her face and tears had risen in her
eyes, not because of any damage I'd done, but because

she was upset to begin with. "She said she'd kill me if I said anything."

"She's going to kill you anyway, you twit. What do you think—she's going to walk off and leave you around to spill the beans? Did she tell you what she did to Wim Hoover? She put a bullet right behind his ear. You're dog meat. You don't stand a chance."

Lily paled. A sob broke the surface like a bubble of air from the bottom of a pond, and then she seemed to collect herself. She closed her eyes and shook her head, like a prisoner faced with the rack. She didn't care what I did to her, she was not going to talk.

"God damn it! Tell me what's going on!"

Her expression hardened and I got a sudden glimpse of what she must have been like as a kid. Leonard's sister knew how to deal with bullies like me. She became stubborn, passive, a defensive stance she'd apparently perfected over the years as a way of warding off attack. She simply withdrew, pulling in on herself like a mollusk. She must have been threatened routinely as a child with everything from tetanus shots if she didn't wash her hands every time she peed, to police arrest if she didn't look both ways before she crossed the street. Instead of learning the rules, she'd learned to disappear.

To my amazement, she crossed to one of the turquoise chairs and sat down without another word. She picked up the remote control and flicked the television on, moving through six channels until she found a sitcom she liked. She was going to tune me out. I went over to the chair and hunkered beside her, talking earnestly while she kept her face to the screen. She watched intently as a buxom platinum blonde in a tank top proceeded to put together a birthday cake.

"Mrs. Howe, I'm not sure you understand what's going on here. Your sister-in-law has killed two people and no one seems to be aware of it but us."

Flour puffed up in a big cloud, obscuring the blonde's baby face. Befuddled, she'd apparently used baking powder *and* yeast, causing the dry flour to explode. The laugh track was cranked up to "hilarious." Oh that gal! Wasn't she a screech! Lily smiled faintly, reminded perhaps of baking disasters of her own.

I touched her arm. "We're running out of time, Lil, because know what? I think Marty Grice is going to double back and kill us too. She'll have to."

No response. Maybe what I said had no more reality for her than this bimbo with the birthday cake. She was cracking eggs now, getting splatted in the face with yolks. Simple laws of nature were being violated here and she was the butt of the joke. In walked the husband. His mouth fell open at the mess she'd made. New paroxysms of laughter erupted. I wondered if anything in the real world had ever struck me with such force.

I said, "Where did they go just now? Are they leaving town?"

Lily laughed aloud. The blonde had turned the mixing bowl upside down on her husband's head. She showed *him*. A few bars of the show's dizzy theme song played and the station cut away to the commercial. I reached over and pressed the volume button, extinguishing the sound. In silence, a dog skidded across the linoleum with a can of chopped liver in pursuit.

"Hey," I said, "Leonard's in trouble. Are you going to help him or not?"

She glanced over at me, and I saw her lips move. I leaned closer.

"Excuse me. What?"

The strain was showing in her face and her eyes seemed unfocused. She watched me with all the concentration of a drunk, dependent and out of control. "Leonard never hurt anyone," she said. "He had no idea what she was doing 'til it was too late."

I thought about Mike's report of Leonard's passion for his wife. I didn't see him as an innocent victim in all of this, but I kept my big mouth shut. "As long as he knows anything, he's in danger. If you'll tell me where they're going, I can get him out of it."

She spoke in a whisper. "Just to Los Angeles 'til the new passport for Marty comes through, and then they're flying to South America." Her eyes filled with tears. "I might never see him again," she said. "And we were always so close. I can't turn him in. I can't betray him, don't you see?"

"You're trying to do what's best for him, Lily. He'll understand."

"It's been awful. It's been a nightmare. When you showed up, I thought he'd die of fright. He nearly had a heart attack and that's when she came back. She thinks you took Elaine's passport and she's furious at the delay. He's afraid of her. He's always been frightened by the fits she throws. . . ."

"Of course he has. I'm afraid of her myself. She's nuts. Do they have the bags in the car with them?"

She was breaking down now, caving in. The notion of Leonard's desertion caused too much pain and the image of packed suitcases cracked her heart. It was all too much. What difference did any of it make now that he was leaving her?

"They've gone off to pack," she said. Her voice came out in a gasp and her nose had started to run. "That's were they went. The motel out by the pass and then the house. They fought about it, but she wouldn't leave it behind, because it was evidence."

"Leave what?"

"The . . . uh . . . you know . . ."

"The murder weapon?"

Lily nodded and nodded gain. I didn't think she could stop. It was as if the cords in her neck had come loose and her head was destined to wag indefinitely. She looked like one of those bobble-head dogs people have perched up in the back windows of their cars.

"Lily, listen to me. I want you to call the police. Go to a neighbor's house and stay there until somebody comes. Do you understand? Come on. Do you need anything? A sweater, a handbag?" I wanted to scream at her to hurry, but I didn't dare.

She was looking at me with washed-out, worried blue eyes, her gaze as trusting as a dog's. I got her to her feet and flipped the TV off, and then bundled her out the front. I scanned the street, but there was no one in sight. I couldn't believe Leonard would let Marty hurt her, but we all knew who was in charge. In some ways I felt as if I was wasting time, but I had to make sure Lily Howe was safe. We went up to the first house that showed a light, a cedar-shingle place two doors down.

I rang the bell. Some man opened the door and I pushed her forward, explaining that there was trouble and she needed some help. I urged Lily to call the cops and then I left. I wasn't sure if she'd do it or not.

I got in my car and squealed out, burning rubber as I skidded around the corner two blocks down. I drove tensely, sliding through stop signs, bypassing traffic any way I could. I had to get to the house before they did. I got stuck at a light and used the time to paw through my glove compartment, looking for the flashlight. I pulled it out and checked the batteries. They seemed fine. The signal changed to green and I took off again.

Belatedly, I realized my gun was still locked in the file cabinet at the office. I nearly slammed the brakes on and went back for it, but I didn't have time. If they went to the motel first, packed, checked out, and loaded the car up, I might have time to get to the murder weapon before they did. If they beat me to the punch, I was going to head straight for Tillie's and call the police. I had no intention of taking on Marty Grice all by myself.

I could feel a big rush of adrenaline and my neurons fired up, completing a circuit with a joyous leap. An answer to an old question popped into my head and I suddenly knew how they'd maneuvered the stomach contents. Marty had stolen Elaine's kitchen trash. It wasn't any more complicated than that. The brown grocery bag Mike had seen in the hall was Elaine Boldt's garbage, containing the empty tuna can and the soup can that comprised her supper that night. Marty had had hours to set it up and I could visualize the scenario as though I had powers of clairvoyance. Leonard went out to dinner with Lily and Marty gave Elaine a call, inviting her over on some casual pretext. Elaine stopped by and at some point was bashed in the face until dead. Marty took the keys and went over to Elaine's as soon as it was dark. She retrieved the kitchen garbage and took it back to her house, leaving it in the hall for a minute while she went down to the basement for the kerosene. That's when Mike had appeared, opening the front door and closing it again when he realized that something was desperately wrong. Marty finished dousing the place with kerosene and sat back to wait for Leonard's pre-arranged call at nine, reporting by phone what Elaine had eaten so he could later mention it to the police. A tuna sandwich and tomato soup. Maybe Marty stuck the leftovers on her own refrigerator shelf so it would all tally up and look legitimate. Marty set the fire and then slipped over to Elaine's where she holed up in comfort until her flight to Florida the following Monday night. My guess was that she'd dyed her hair before she left and I suspected that the fine clump of gray-brown hair I'd seen in Elaine's bathroom wastebasket during my initial search was, in fact, additional evidence that Marty Grice had been there.

I reached the Grices' house and pulled up across the street, taking a moment to study the house and yard. In the darkness, the fire damage was hidden, but the place still exuded that aura of ruin and abandonment. There was no sign of the car out front. No lights anywhere in the house. No pedestrians on the street.

I left the keys in the ignition and got out of the car, leaving the door ajar. I wanted to be able to ease back in and take off without a lot of fumbling around, if it came to that. I opened the trunk and took out the tools I thought I'd need. As soon as I determined that nobody was coming, I crossed the street and cut through the Grices' side yard.

I moved quietly along the walk, surveying windows as I passed. Most of the windows at the front of the house had been broken out by the fire and boarded back up again, but there were two near the back of the house that were still intact. I chose one and jimmied it open. It was pitch-black, and the neighborhood was quiet except for crickets chirring in the grass. I knew I should give myself an escape route, but I couldn't take the chance. If the two of them showed up, they'd spot any open windows or doors. I'd just have to work fast and hope my guess about the murder weapon was correct. I didn't have time for mistakes.

I climbed into the kitchen and pulled the window shut. The floor crackled with broken glass as I passed through. My flashlight streaked across blackened door-frames, smoke-tinged walls, into a hallway dense with shadow. I held my breath, listening. The silence was flat, one-dimensional. The electricity was turned off and I missed the soft hum of machinery. No refrigerator, no furnace, no wall clock, no water heater ticking from the other room. Some vague phrase about the silence of the tomb came to mind, but I pushed it away.

I moved forward, startled as a shard of glass popped underfoot. Was someone moving around upstairs? I swung the light across the ceiling, half expecting footsteps to appear up there like visible dents. The imagination has primitive, cartoonlike qualities, as any child can testify. I moved again. There was some illumination farther on, a pale light spilling in from the house next door. I paused at the window that looked directly into the living room across the way. Mr. Snyder was watching a television show, images flickering silently. The only other window on this side of the house was a small one just off the kitchen near the rear. I had a theory now about the banging May Snyder heard that night and I was about to test it out. I glanced toward the room where she slept, but it was already dark. I wondered if that's what old age is about—sleeping longer and longer hours until one day you simply don't bother to wake.

I ran my fingers along the window frame, shining the light across the fire-warped paint, a shriveled and puckered white, like dead skin. I could see where the wood had been damaged before. I could see where it had been secured with nails again: bang-bang-bang. I propped the flashlight on the window sill. It took me a few minutes to get the flashlight angled properly so I could see what I was doing and still have both hands free to work. I edged the narrow curve of the crowbar into the window frame and pried it loose with a crack so deafening it made my heart skip. I believed Elaine had been killed with a sash weight that had been tucked back in the window frame and nailed into place. The notion had come to me in one of those flashes of insight when I heard the weights in my own bathroom window thump dully against the studs.

It was nice. It had a certain domestic tidiness about it that Marty must have liked. If the house had burned down entirely that night, then who would ever have figured it out? The bulldozers would have mowed down what was left of the house, rubble loaded into high-siders, hauled off to the dump. Even now, even as it was, who was going to know? In a way, she was foolish to come back for it. Why not just leave it where it was? She was being pushed into a panic, probably anxious to tie up loose ends so that she could feel safe wherever she went. They might catch her, but what could they prove? The murder weapon probably had her prints all over it. Maybe it still bore strands of Elaine's hair or fragments of broken teeth and bones, microscopic particles of flesh. I wondered what she planned to do with the grisly thing. Bury it somewhere perhaps . . . toss it off the end of a pier. I jammed a big screwdriver into the tight crack between the framing and the strip of wood that held it in place. Window parts must have names, I thought, but I didn't know what they were. I was just imitating Becky's carpentry. The result was the same. I had the frame dismantled, exposing both sets of weights, the cord connecting them, and the pulleys that regulated the raising and lowering of the sash. I hauled both sets into view, four weights all together, careful not to touch anything. Shit, prints weren't going to show up on these things. The metal was covered with a thin film of saw-dust and grime. Moisture in the wall had generated so much rust that any latent prints had probably been obliterated now. It wasn't going to help that six months had passed. Flecks of dried blood would still show up on a microscopic exam, but I wasn't sure what else. I shone the flashlight along the sash. At the tip were two glinting blond hairs caught in a knot of dark brown. I could feel my lips purse with distaste.

I eased a small plastic Baggie over the tip and secured it with tape. I advanced the blade in the utility knife I'd brought with me and slashed through the cords, clanging the weights together inadvertently as I lowered them into a big plastic bag. Lieutenant Dolan and his trusty crime-scene crew would have fits if they saw me manhandling evidence this way, but I didn't have any choice. I tossed the utility knife in the plastic bag along with the rest of my tools, plastic rustling with my every move—which is why I didn't hear Leonard and Marty until they had already reached the back steps.

26

The key rattled in the lock and my head whipped up. Fear shot through me like a jolt of electricity and my heart started thudding so hard it made my whole neck pulse. My single advantage was that I knew about them before they knew about me. I snatched up the flashlight, tucking the plastic-wrapped packet of weights under my arm. I was already on the move, assessing my options with a brain that felt slow and cold, as though plunged in an icy surf. My temptation was to head up to the second floor, but I scotched the impulse. There was no cover up there and no access to the roof.

I eased to my left, toward the kitchen, my hearing opened to the full. I could pick up low conversational tones out there. They were probably trying to get their bearings just shining a flashlight here and there. If Marty hadn't been in the house since the night of the fire, she might be reacting to the damage, momentarily repelled as I had been by the charring, decay, and ruin. They hadn't figured it out yet, but soon they would. The minute they saw that window frame, they'd start looking for me.

The basement door was ajar, a vertical black slot against the gloom of the hallway. I allowed myself one flicker of light from the flashlight and slipped through the crack, descending as quickly as I could without making noise. I knew the slanted basement doors leading out to the side yard were padlocked shut, but at least I'd find someplace to hide down there. I hoped.

Down I went, pausing at the bottom of the stairs so that I could orient myself. Above me, I heard the snap and crunch of footsteps. It was pitch-bloody-black where I was. It felt like the darkness was lying on the surface of my eyes, a thick, black mask that no light could penetrate. I had to risk the flashlight again. Even after so short a time, I felt myself recoil from the glare, turning my head abruptly to shield my eyes. I blinked, willing my eyes to adapt. Oh God, how was I going to get out of this?

I did a quick search, raking the beam in a 360-degree arc. I had to hide the sash weights and there wasn't much time. They might catch me, but I didn't want them to get their hands on the murder weapon, which is exactly what they'd come to fetch. I crossed to the furnace which stood massive and dead, looking somehow as ominous as a tank down there. I eased the door open and shoved the weights in, jamming the packet down between the outer wall and the housing for the gas jets. The hinge gave a harsh shriek as I pushed the door shut. I froze, glancing up automatically, as though I might make a visual assessment of how far the sound had carried.

Silence overhead. They had to be in the hall by now, had to have seen the damage I'd left. Now they were listening for me as I listened for them. In the dark of an old house like this, sound can be as deceptive as the voice of a ventriloquist.

Frantically, I scanned for someplace to hide. Every nook and cranny I spotted was too small or too shallow to do me any good. Overhead, a floorboard creaked. It wasn't going to take them long. There were two of them. They'd split up. One would go upstairs and one would come down.

I cut left, tiptoeing across the basement to the short concrete stairwell that led to the outside world. I crouched and crept upward, squeezing into the narrow space at the top. My hunched back was right up against the wood doors, my legs drawn up under me. With the electricity shut down in the house, they'd be forced to search by flashlight and maybe they'd miss me. I hoped I'd be hard to spot wedged up here, but I couldn't be sure. In the meantime, the only thing that separated me from freedom was that slanted expanse of wood at my back. I could smell the damp night air through the cracks. The sweet scent of the jasmine near the house blended unpleasantly with the musk of soot and old paint. My heart was pounding in my chest, anxiety flying through me with such force that my lungs hurt. I held the flashlight like a club and stilled my breathing to some infinitesimal sibilance.

I became aware of a hard knot pressing into my thigh. Car keys. I shifted my weight, extending my right leg with care, reluctant to allow so much as a whisper of tennis shoe on gritty concrete step. I placed the flashlight ever so carefully on the stair below me and inched the keys out, holding onto the bunch to prevent their jingling together. Attached to my key ring was a small ornamental metal disk, maybe the size of a fifty-cent piece with no rim, the closest thing to a tool I had access to at this point. I thought with longing of the utility knife, the crowbar, and hammer wrapped in plastic and wedged down in the furnace along with the weights. I ran my left hand up along the wood just above my head, feeling for the hinge. It was shaped like an airplane wing, maybe six inches long, and flat. The screws protruded unevenly, some loosened with age, some gone.

I tried using the edge of the disk like a screwdriver, but the heads of the screws had been painted over and the groove was too shallow now to afford any leverage. I hunched, pushing up. I sensed a little give. Hands shaking with hope, I sorted through the keys, picking out the VW key, which was longer than the rest. I eased it between the hinge and the wood and applied a slight pressure. The hinge yielded a bit. If I could work a little slack into the hinge, maybe the door could be forced up and wrenched free. I pried at it, pressing my lips tight to keep from wheezing with the effort.

I paused. All I could hear was my own breathing, labored now as I struggled to loosen the hinge. The wood was pine, old and rotting and soft. I shifted my weight again, trying to give myself more room to work. The basement door creaked.

I heard the soft scratch of a shoe on the basement stair.

And then I heard the panting and I knew who it was. Slowly I turned my head to the right. I could see the dim yellow glow from a flashlight, one of those big jobs the size of a lunchbox, throwing out a wide square beam of light. The batteries were weak, washing back only pale illumination. Even so, I recognized the woman I'd met in Florida. Pat Usher . . . Marty Grice. She wasn't looking good. The tawny hair seemed lifeless and her eyes were in deep shadow, cheekbones exaggerated by the angle of the light. She swung the beam to the far wall. I held my breath, wondering if there was any chance whatever she'd bypass my hiding place. She moved out of my line of sight for a moment. I didn't dare move. The tension made my bones ache. I could feel my legs start to shake, that uncontrollable trembling made up of stress and muscle cramp and the need to move. It was the drive toward flight turned inward, my body locked in place with no hope of relief. The flashlight beam made a slow turn in my direction, illuminating item by item everything in its path. She was going to pick me up any second and I did the only thing I could. I launched myself upward like a surfacing whale, pushing the locked doors with such force that they nearly sprung apart. I simply didn't have enough purchase and she was too quick. I strained, shoving upward again.

She must have crossed the room like a shot. My upward motion had taken me almost into an upright position, the doors bulging outward with a cracking sound. My feet were snatched out from under me and I went down, cracking my head on the concrete step. Her flashlight had careened off to one side, its fading beam aimed ineffectually now at the wall, the light as pointless as a television picture after sign-off. In the thick dark of the basement, there was just enough illumination to work to my disadvantage.

I scrambled sideways, pushing to my feet again. She flew at me, nearly climbing my frame, her arms locked around my head. I staggered backward, thrown off-balance by the sudden weight. I tried to heave her sideways, skinning her off by bashing with her into the stairs. She was on me like an octopus—tentacles, suckers, and ravaging mouth. I was going down. I tried driving into her with my elbow, but there was no way to connect with enough force to do her any harm. I got one hand up, grabbing her by the hair, tucking forward abruptly so that her own weight carried her to the concrete with a soft grunt.

I caught a quick impression of weaponry, warned by a whistling sound, but not soon enough to duck. I heard a sickening crack on impact. She'd come up with what looked like an ax handle, wielded with such force that I felt no pain at all at first. It was like that interval between lightning and thunder, and I wondered if there was some way to gauge the intensity of pain by how many seconds it took to register on the uncomprehending brain. The ax handle came whistling up at me again, and this time I got a hand up, protecting my face, taking the blow on my forearm. I didn't even associate the cracking sound with the pain that shuddered up my frame. My mouth came open, but no sound emerged. She drove down at me again, her eyes bright, her mouth pulled back in something that would pass for a smile among lunatics. I hunched, taking the blow on the shoulder this time. The pain was like heat licking up my side. My fingers closed around the handrail. I hung on to the stairs for dear life. A bright cloud was reducing my vision to a pinpoint, and I knew once the aperture closed I was dead. I sucked air in, shaking my head, noting with relief that the dark flooded back.

I pulled my right fist back. With a low cry, I pushed off, driving forward with everything I had. I connected, and the blow rang all the way back down my arm. I felt the pain arc from my battered knuckles to her face, and she made a low sound I liked. She staggered back and I launched myself at her, getting a headlock on her that closed her throat. I swung her sideways, keeping her off-balance, moving backward at the same time so she couldn't get her feet under her. She was being hanged by the force of her own weight. I braced myself then and concentrated on narrowing the V of my arm where her neck was caught. I heard a loud pop, and for a moment, I thought I'd broken her neck. She sagged to the floor. I released my hold to keep from being pulled down on top of her. I looked down at her blankly and then looked up. Leonard was standing there with a .22 that was now aimed at me.

Marty was wheezing. "You shot me, you fool." Her voice was hoarse.

Leonard's gaze shifted to her with dumb amazement.

I stepped back. The slug had caught her in the side; not a fatal wound but one that had taught her a little respect. She was on her knees, clutching at herself. She hurt and she made little mews of outrage and pain.

I was winded, still heaving for air, but I felt the strange exhilaration of victory. I had almost killed her. I'd been seconds away from converting her live body to a quite corpselike state. Leonard couldn't shoot straight, so he'd felled her himself, thus spoiling the fun, but the battle had been mine. I wanted to laugh, until I caught the look on his face.

The craziness that had consumed me for the last few minutes drained away, and I realized my troubles were starting all over again. I was dead on my feet. Somehow, I'd taken a blow right across the mouth and I was tasting blood. I felt gingerly to see if a tooth was broken, but everything seemed to be intact. It was a dumb time to worry about the possibility of a cap, but that's what I did.

I was trying to pay attention, but it was very hard. I had this weird desire to grovel around on the floor with Marty, the two of us snuffling like wounded animals looking for a way to crawl off and hide. I would have to go after Leonard soon. Already too much time had passed, and I knew I was losing ground.

He was staring at me without expression. I didn't know how to read him anyway.

"Come on, Leonard. Let's pack it in."

He said nothing. I tried to keep my tone conversational, as if I spent part of every day talking guys out of shooting me dead.

"I'm tired and it's late. Let's go home. She needs help."

Wrong move. Marty seemed to rouse herself, focusing on him. She didn't represent any kind of threat at this point, but he was teetering on the brink, maybe testing, as I had, the odd new sensation that death-dealing brought.

"Shoot the bitch," she gasped at him. "Shoot!"

I used every last ounce of strength I had, pulling myself together. He fired at me as I moved forward, but by then I was carried along by my own momentum. I yelled, "*No!*" and kicked him in the kneecap so hard I heard it crack. He dropped, warbling with pain like some kind of weird songbird. The gun skittered off across the floor. I thought Marty would try for it, but she only stared, making no move at all as I bent to retrieve it. I released the cylinder and popped it out. There were four more live rounds in the chamber. I snapped it back and made sure the safety was off, turning so that I could keep them both in my line of fire. Leonard was sitting up now, rocking back and forth. He looked at me with momentary venom.

I extended the gun, aiming at his face. "I'll kill your ass if you move, Leonard. I've had a lot of practice of late and I'll drill you right between the eyes."

Marty started to cry. It was an odd sound, like an infant with colic. Leonard leaned over and put his arm around her protectively.

In that moment, I wished there was someone to comfort me. My left arm was hanging like a piece of wood with a loose connecting pin. I glanced down and saw blood spreading out across my sleeve from a rip the size of a pea. The sucker *shot* me, I thought with astonishment. I steadied the gun in my good hand and started yelling for help. It was May Snyder who finally heard me and called the cops.

Epilogue

I've been in the hospital now for two days with my left arm in a cast. There's an orthopedist coming in this afternoon to assess the X rays and figure out what kind of rehabilitation I'll need once I get out of here. I've talked to Julia Ochsner by phone and she's invited me to recuperate at her place down in Florida. She promises sunshine and rest, but I suspect she sees it as a chance to set me up as a fourth for bridge. My final bill came to $1,987.35 but she says she won't pay me until I arrive on her doorstep. You gotta watch out for little old ladies— they're tough—which is more than I can say for myself. I hurt just about every place there is. I look in the mirror and I see someone else's face: puffy mouth, bruised cheeks, the bridge of my nose looking flat. I'm feeling some other kind of pain as well and I don't know quite what that's made of. I'm closing the file, but the story's not over yet. We'll have to wait and see what the courts do now, and I've learned to be cautious about that. In the meantime, I stare out the window at the palms and wonder how many times I'll dance with death before the orchestra packs it in for the night.

—Respectfully submitted,
Kinsey Millhone